The baby had to come first.

Both men started to move. She saw one of them grab the carrier seat with the baby, and the other took some keys from his pocket.

Holden got them moving, too. Fast. Off the porch, and he headed straight for the car. The moment they reached it, he maneuvered her to the far side away from the house, and they ducked down.

He pulled out a knife from his pocket and jammed it into the front tire and went to the rear to do the same. That would slow them down, but it wouldn't stop them. Those men were in a hurry to get out of there, and they'd drive on the rims if they had to.

The men raced out the door of the house, making a beeline for the car. They were just yards away when Nicky heard a sound she didn't want to hear.

Footsteps.

Behind Holden and her.

Holden pivoted, aiming his gun, but it was already too late.

HOLDEN

BY
DELORES FOSSEN

First Published in Great Britain 2017
By Mills & Boon, an imprint of HarperCollins*Publishers*
1 London Bridge Street, London, SE1 9GF

© 2017 Delores Fossen

ISBN: 978-0-263-92866-2

46-0317

Our policy is to use papers that are natural, renewable and recyclable products and made from wood grown in sustainable forests. The logging and manufacturing processes conform to the legal environmental regulations of the country of origin.

Printed and bound in Spain
by CPI, Barcelona

Delores Fossen, a *USA TODAY* bestselling author, has sold over fifty novels with millions of copies of her books in print worldwide. She's received a Booksellers' Best Award and an RT Reviewers' Choice Best Book Award. She was also a finalist for a prestigious RITA® Award. Contact her at www.deloresfossen.com.

Chapter One

Something wasn't right.

US Marshal Holden Ryland didn't have to rely on his lawman's instincts to know that. The Craftsman-style house was pitch-dark except for a single dim light in the front room. The home owner, Nicky Hart, hated the dark, and whenever she was home, every light was usually blazing.

So, either she'd skipped out on their little chat, or... Holden decided to go with the skipping-out theory because at the moment it was the lesser of two evils. After all, there was a reason why they needed to talk.

A bad one.

Holden slid his hand over the gun in his holster and got out of his truck. He'd barely made it a few steps when her white cat came darting out from beneath the porch. It headed right toward him, coiling around his leg and meowing.

Another sign that something was wrong.

Nicky didn't let the cat outside—ever.

So, was Nicky inside? And if so, had something happened to her? Holden cursed himself for not having done a silent approach. That way, he could have parked up the street, slipped around to the side of the house and looked in the windows. It might have alerted her neighbors, but that was better than dealing with some of the bad scenarios going through his head. Still, he hadn't taken that precaution because he hadn't figured he would run in to any kind of immediate trouble.

Well, no trouble other than an argument with Nicky.

When he'd called Nicky an hour earlier and told her that he was on his way to their hometown of Silver Creek to talk to her, she hadn't said a word about anything being wrong. In fact, she sounded as if she'd been expecting his call. But then, she'd sent a text just a few minutes later, saying she wouldn't be available after all.

Right.

Holden wasn't about to believe that lie. She was dodging him. And not doing a very good job of it, either, because her garage door was up, and he could see her car. That meant she was probably inside and that there was a good explanation for no lights on and the cat being outside. He hoped there was a good explanation anyway.

He kept watch around him, kept watch of the house, too, and made his way to the porch. However, before Holden could even ring the bell, the front door flew open, and he braced himself for what he might see.

But it was only Nicky.

He looked at her, from head to toe. She was wearing jeans and an old concert T-shirt, and had her auburn hair pulled back in a sloppy ponytail. No visible injuries or signs of distress. She was scowling at him, but over the past year or so, that was the norm whenever she laid eyes on him.

"Didn't you get my text?" she asked.

"Got it. Ignored it. Because we need to talk." Holden moved to go around her and inside, but she stepped in front of him, blocking his path.

"It's not a good time." She paused. "I'm expecting some-one."

All right. That gave him a new theory. Maybe Nicky had a hot date who was on the way over. That might explain the lack of lights if she was aiming for something romantic.

A thought that bothered him a lot more than it should have.

Nicky was an attractive woman. Bullheaded and reck-less, too. And she was married to her job as an investi-gative reporter. That said, she was still human and she probably did have a man in her life.

It still didn't mean Holden was going to skip that talk with her. He wouldn't.

Because he needed her to know that she was on the verge of being arrested.

He owed her that much. Barely. After the stunt she'd pulled last year, though, some members of his family might believe he owed her nothing. Still, here he was. He didn't play Mr. Nice Guy very often, and he hoped he didn't re-gret it this time.

"Tomorrow, you'll get a visit from an FBI agent," he told her.

Nicky didn't even blink. "I don't have time for this." And she would have shut the door in his face, if Holden hadn't blocked it with his foot. The edge of the door smacked against his cowboy boot.

"Make time," he snarled.

She blew out a quick breath. "Look, I know you're still in love with me," she said, "but you have to leave."

Holden tightened the grip on his gun. Yeah, something was definitely wrong. Because there was no way in hell he was in love with Nicky, and she knew it, too.

She shook her head, just a little, and glanced at the hold

that he had on his gun. Was she telling him not to draw? Or was that head shake about something else?

Holden intended to find out.

But it was best not to confront this head-on. Because the living room behind her was dark, he couldn't tell if there was someone waiting in the shadows. Someone armed and ready to kill her. Or maybe she'd discovered her house was bugged and she didn't want to say anything incriminating.

Holden hoped it was the second option.

"I'll be back tomorrow," Holden lied. "And we *will* talk then."

Leaving was a risk—anything he did at this point could be. But Holden hoped if there was someone inside that it was a good sign that the person had let Nicky answer the door. The person didn't want her dead.

Not yet anyway.

In her quest to get info on a story she was working on, she could have gotten herself mixed up with some very dangerous people, and that involvement might be coming back to bite her. To bite him, too, since Holden had to see what was going on. This was well past being a nice guy.

This had just become the job.

He drove his truck up a block, parked and fired off a quick text to his cousin Landon, who was now a deputy in Silver Creek. Holden didn't request backup but told Landon that if he didn't hear from him in fifteen minutes, to send some help—fast.

With that done, Holden hurried to Nicky's house. Not going through the front yard but rather through the back. The houses in the small neighborhood didn't have fences, but there were plenty of mature trees that he ducked behind and used for cover. The darkness helped, too, and for once he was glad Nicky didn't have all the lights blazing.

Holden knew the layout of her house. He'd even spent

the night there a couple of times, and he knew the best way to approach this wasn't through the back porch. Instead, he drew his gun and went to the French doors off her bedroom.

Unlocked.

He silently cursed. Since Nicky was afraid of the dark, you'd think she would be equally concerned with locking up, but Holden knew she could be lax about that.

He eased open the door, slipped into her bedroom and stood there. Listening. He didn't hear anything at first, only someone moving around in the living room where he'd last seen Nicky.

"You'd better be sure he doesn't come back," someone said. A man. And Holden didn't recognize his voice.

In case this was a lover she was meeting, Holden waited for more. He didn't have to wait very long.

"If that marshal does come back, I'll kill him," the man growled.

Hell. So, probably not a lover unless it was some jealous nut-job. Holden sent a second text to Landon requesting that backup, and he made his way to the bedroom door and then into the hall.

The house was old and had creaky floors in spots. He prayed he didn't step on one of those because he wanted to get the drop on whoever it was that had just threatened to kill him.

"The marshal won't be back," Nicky assured the man. "Not until tomorrow anyway."

"He said the FBI was coming. Your doing?" her visitor demanded.

"Hardly. The FBI will be looking for the same thing you want. Something I don't have."

Holden didn't know specifically what she was talking about, but it might have something to do with her latest project. A state senator who'd been missing over two weeks. Nicky had been investigating his disappearance and had cut some corners. Ones that could land her in jail.

Of course, at the moment that seemed to be the least of her worries.

"You have those files all right," the man argued. "Now, where are they? And don't try to hold any of them back. I want every file you stole from Conceptions Clinic."

Everything inside Holden went still.

Conceptions Clinic?

It was the name of the fertility clinic that Holden knew well, and just hearing it brought back some painful memories. Of his brother Emmett and his brother's wife, Annie. Annie had been Nicky's sister, and now both Emmett and Annie were dead. Annie had died in a car accident, but that hadn't been the cause of Emmett's death.

No. He'd been murdered only months after Annie's death. His killer was dead, but that didn't soften the blow for Holden. Emmett wasn't coming back from the grave just because the Rylands had managed to get justice for him.

Before their deaths, Emmett and Annie made multiple trips to Conceptions Fertility Clinic in San Antonio with the hopes of finally getting the baby they so desperately wanted. But that hadn't happened. Because they'd both died before the process could be completed.

So, why would Nicky steal files from the place now?

"You're either going to give those files to me now, or I'll start putting bullets in you," the man warned her. "I won't kill you, yet, but I'll make you wish you were dead."

Every word of that threat put Holden on higher and higher alert, and he had to move fast.

Still trying to keep quiet, Holden hurried to the end of the hall and peered into the living room. Nicky was still by the front door, and there was a man between Holden and her. And yeah, the guy had a gun pointed right at her.

Nicky didn't say a word, but her eyes widened just a fraction when she saw Holden, and the man must have noticed even her slight reaction. He pivoted, taking aim at Holden.

The thug fired.

Not a loud blast. He was using a silencer on his gun.

Holden jumped out of the way just in time, and the bullet tore through a chunk of the wall.

"Get down," Holden shouted to Nicky, but she was already doing just that.

She scrambled behind the sofa. It wouldn't give her much cover, but Holden was counting on this moron shooting at him instead of her.

And that's just what he did.

The gunman ducked down beside a chair and fired another shot at Holden. Then, another. The shots wouldn't be loud enough to get the attention of the neighbors, which was a good thing. Holden didn't want bystanders hurrying over to Nicky's house to check on this.

Whatever *this* was.

"You want him to die?" the man barked. "Because that's what'll happen if you don't tell him to get the hell out of here."

Holden wasn't going anywhere. He dropped lower to the ground, leaned out and fired a shot at the guy. However, before Holden could even tell if he'd hit him, all hell broke loose.

There was the sound of something metal clanking onto the floor, and a few seconds later, tear gas began to spew through the room. The effects were instant. Holden's gray eyes burned like fire, and he started to cough. He could hear Nicky having a coughing fit, too.

But not the man.

Maybe he'd brought a gas mask or something because Holden heard him take off running, and saw him bolt out the back door.

Even though he was coughing too hard to catch his breath, Holden hurried after the guy, but he'd only made it a few steps when Nicky called out to him.

"Let him go. We have to leave now." Covering her mouth with her hand, she staggered her way to him, caught him by the wrist and led him toward the side entrance to the garage.

"Landon will be here soon," he choked out.

"We don't have time to wait around for him. Please, we need to go."

Holden didn't fight her as they'd gone into the garage because he welcomed the fresh air. Also welcomed getting into her car since he didn't want to be standing out in the open with that gunman still out there. But he did clamp his hand over hers when she tried to drive away.

"What the hell's going on?" he demanded. "Who was that man and what files did you steal?"

Nicky shook her head, fighting to get his grip off her, but Holden held on.

"The people at Conceptions Clinic did some very bad things. There are babies in danger," Nicky said, her breath shivering. "And one of them is *our* nephew."

Chapter Two

Nicky knew that Holden had plenty of questions, but she couldn't wait any longer. That gunman who'd broken into her house was no doubt on the way to the person who hired him.

And that person might move the baby before she could get to him.

"We have to get out of here fast," she reminded him.

Even though Nicky was still coughing, she threw the car into Reverse and gunned the engine despite the fact that Holden still had his hand gripped around hers.

Nicky didn't look at him. Partly because she was trying to maneuver her car out of the garage. Hard to do that, though, with him holding on. He finally let go.

"Start talking," Holden insisted. He, too, was still coughing and rubbing his eyes. "I want answers, and I want them now."

Easier said than done. There were a lot of pieces to this puzzle, some that could get her arrested, but the only one that mattered right now was the baby. Nicky had failed her sister in so many ways, but she couldn't fail this time.

"Who was that man?" Holden added when she didn't say anything.

"A hired thug. I don't know his name, but I'm sure he's already told his boss what happened."

And what had happened was that things had just fallen apart. Nicky had thought she had more time, hours at least, to come up with a plan. But time had just run out.

She couldn't help herself. The tears came, and she tried to fight them back. The tears wouldn't save Annie's baby. Right now, she had to focus and get to the hotel as soon as possible.

"Where are we going?" Holden demanded, and he took out his phone and texted someone.

Probably one of his cousins or brothers. They were all lawmen, and under different circumstances, they might be able to help. But in this case, they could make things much, much worse.

"The Victorian bed-and-breakfast about ten miles from here."

"The place out in the middle of nowhere?" he asked.

She nodded. "I'm pretty sure that's where they're holding the baby."

Holden cursed and sent another text. "There'd better be a damn good explanation as to why you're *pretty sure* about that. And there'd also better be an equally good explanation as to why you told me Emmett and Annie had a baby."

It was hard to think with everything racing through her mind, with her heart racing, too, but she tried. Sometime in the next five minutes she needed to convince Holden that he had to help her.

"This all started when I was investigating the missing senator, Lee Minton," she said. "I found out he and his wife had gone to Conceptions Fertility Clinic around the same time as Emmett and Annie. So, I went to Conceptions, too, not expecting to find much, but they stonewalled me. That made me push even harder to find out what they were hiding."

He mumbled, "Right." Probably a dig at the fact that she usually pushed too hard. Sometimes, with deadly consequences.

"And what they were hiding was a baby? Emmett and Annie's baby?" There was a boatload of skepticism in his voice.

Once, she'd been plenty skeptical, too. If she hadn't been, if she'd jumped on this earlier, they might not be racing to save a child.

"Yes, their baby," Nicky affirmed. "And don't ask why they did all of this because I don't know. Not yet anyway. But I think it might somehow be connected to the senator's disappearance." But she could be a long way from figuring how exactly.

"Senator Minton?" he asked, though he probably wasn't asking for clarification but was rather puzzled as to how Minton would play into this. The answer was maybe he didn't, but the senator had been missing for two weeks now, and it was while looking for him that she'd stumbled on to Conceptions.

"Yes, Senator Lee Minton," she confirmed.

"How are you sure of any of this?" Holden snapped.

Oh, he was not going to like this. "I hacked into the clinic's computer and copied some files," she added. "Hacked into the senator's computer, too, and then I put a listening device in Conceptions Clinic."

Now, Holden's cursing got a whole lot worse. For good reason. Because she'd just rattled off enough crimes to put her in jail. But she'd had an even better reason to do this.

To save Annie's son.

"That's what the thug was talking about," Holden snarled. "Where are the files and what's in them?"

Nicky decided to skip the *where* part and move to the

what. Just in case the thug had managed to turn the tables on her and bug her car.

"The ones I copied from Conceptions were marked 'the Genesis Project,'" she explained. "No names were connected with them, just case numbers, and when I looked at one, I figured out from the dates that the case number was Annie and Emmett's."

She'd tell him about the other info in them later. For now, Nicky focused on taking the road to the B and B.

"I don't know who did it, but someone stole Annie and Emmett's embryo and implanted it into a surrogate. And last week, the surrogate gave birth to a boy." Nicky turned off her car's headlights as she approached the B and B, and she pulled off the road, parking behind some trees.

Holden shook his head, stayed quiet a moment. "Could be it was a mix-up. Or maybe the embryo was donated to another couple who used a surrogate?"

Mercy, she wanted to latch onto that and believe it. "Then, why did that man just threaten me?"

"I don't know. Maybe you stole more than one set of files or pissed off more than just these people. Or it could have something to do with why the FBI wants to arrest you."

Even if it was true, it was still too big of a risk to let them move the baby. Of course, Holden might not believe there was a baby. He soon would, though.

"Who's inside that place?" he asked.

"Probably more men like the one who came to my house tonight." Hired guns to protect very precious cargo until they could get her father to pay up. "Look, I don't have time to explain all of this, but if they move the baby, we might never find him."

She didn't voice her greatest fear, that the goons inside might try to harm him so there'd be no proof of what they'd done.

"What if there really is a baby inside?" he went on. "How would we even know if it's Emmett and Annie's?"

She motioned toward her hair. "According to what I heard from the eavesdropping device, he's a ginger." *Not exactly rare but at least it was something like Annie and me.* Besides, she thought she might recognize her own sister's child.

"You have backup on the way?" she asked.

Holden nodded. "It's Landon. I told him to do a silent approach." He tipped his head to the house. "If the guy who was at your house had already contacted them, they could shoot us on sight."

"No. They want me alive so I can tell them where the files are. That's why he didn't kill me right away when he barged his way into my house." Not exactly a reminder to steady her nerves. Of course, her nerves hadn't been steady in a long, long time.

Nicky eased open the door, but Holden stopped her.

"I'm not letting you go in there," he insisted.

"They want me alive," Nicky repeated. "They'll want you dead. If anyone should go in there, it's me. But I need you...well, if something goes wrong, I need you to get the baby out."

Holden took hold of her again, and this time he didn't let go. "You're *not* going in there. Wait here. And so help me, if you disobey that order, I'll arrest you myself."

But he'd no sooner said that when someone opened the back door of the house. The place had a wraparound porch, and while the front was well lit, the back wasn't. Probably on purpose. Because Nicky saw something she didn't want to see.

Two men. A woman. And the woman had something bundled in her arms.

They didn't linger on the porch. They hurried, practically running down the porch steps.

Nicky's heart went to her knees. "They're getting away. Go after them. We have to stop them."

If Holden was listening to her, he didn't respond. He just kept watching, kept his grip on her until he finally pulled back his hand so he could send a text.

"I don't think she's holding a baby," Holden said. "I think it's a decoy."

Nicky tried to fight through the panic so she could see why he'd said that. Maybe because the bundle was huge. No way to miss that. And it wasn't anywhere near cool enough for the baby to need multiple blankets. It was September, and the temps were still close to ninety.

Plus, there was something else that was off. The woman was as tall and bulky as the two men who'd hurried *her* out of the house.

Mercy.

This was some kind of trap.

"They probably suspect we're here and will be expecting us to follow them," Holden said without taking his attention off them.

The trio got into an SUV parked behind the inn. Almost immediately, she saw the headlights of the SUV come on.

"Landon will follow them instead, and he'll have two other deputies do a quiet approach here," Holden added. "Come on. Get out of the car. Stay low and move fast. I'm going to see who's inside the house. I can't leave you here or they might try to kidnap you."

Nicky tried not to let that statement rob her of what breath she'd managed to gather. Because this was a risk. And not just the possible kidnapping. Nicky had to consider that this could be a ruse of a different kind. One where the baby was actually inside that SUV and these thugs wanted to lure Holden and her to the house.

Well, if so, it was going to work.

Of course, it was just as possible that at this very moment someone was escaping with the baby on the other side of the house. Everything inside Nicky was screaming for her to hurry.

"Do you have a gun?" he asked.

She shook her head, and he gave her one of those looks. The one that made her feel like an idiot. "I don't keep a gun in my vehicle. And besides I didn't plan on shooting anyone tonight, especially with the baby around."

"Then, what was your plan, to ask them pretty please to hand over the child?" Holden snapped.

"No. I was going to sneak in and take him. I'm pretty good at sneaking in places," she added in a mumble.

No way could he argue with that, but Nicky wished she'd had time to come up with a better plan. Too bad that thug had shown up at her house and thrown things into chaos.

"Just do everything I tell you," Holden warned her. *"Everything."*

With his gun drawn, Holden threaded them through the trees, but he stopped at the edge of the yard. There were plenty of windows, but she couldn't get a glimpse of anyone inside. However, there was another car in the small parking area on the side of the house.

She glanced back at the road and the SUV, but the trees were in the way, and Nicky couldn't tell if it actually stopped. She prayed that if the baby was indeed inside the vehicle, Landon would be able to follow them and find out where they were taking the child.

Holden led them onto the porch, and even though the

door was partly open, they didn't go inside. Instead, he went to a window and peered around the edge. He snapped back so fast that she knew there had to be someone in the room. Someone who had caused his muscles to go iron-stiff.

"Two men," Holden whispered. "Both armed. There's a baby carrier on the table."

Even though she figured Holden didn't want her to move, Nicky had to see for herself.

Nicky took in everything in one quick glance. The two men, one bald and the other wearing a black baseball-type hat.

And the ginger-haired baby asleep in the carrier.

Mercy. She'd tried to steel herself for whatever they might face, but it sickened her to think of a baby being around hired guns.

"If you create a distraction," she said, trying to make as little sound as possible, "I can sneak in."

Holden gave her a look again, to let her know that wasn't going to happen. But she didn't want to stand around there and wait. If these goons heard the other deputies, they might start a gunfight, and the baby would be caught in the middle.

Even though the window was closed, she had no trouble hearing a phone ring inside. She also had no trouble hearing one of the men answer it. Not with a greeting, either.

He simply said, "What now?"

Too bad he hadn't put it on speaker because Nicky would have liked to know who she was dealing with. But nothing. For several snail-crawling moments. She had no idea what the caller was telling him, but it caused the man's forehead to bunch up.

"All right," the man finally said. "We'll move the kid now. See you in a few." He ended the call and turned to the bald guy. "That reporter's car was just up the road. She wasn't in it, but they're sending someone to torch it and the house just in case."

Considering all the other things going on, that was small potatoes. Still, it sickened her to think of these snakes destroying her home. And it would all be for nothing. Because the files weren't even there.

"You know she didn't just leave," the other man said. "She's out there somewhere."

The first one nodded and slapped off the lights. "If she really knows what's going on, she won't shoot around the kid, and she'll make sure the marshal doesn't, either."

The thug was right about not wanting to start a gunfight, but he was wrong about her knowing what was going on. She still didn't understand why someone would do this.

"You don't shoot around the kid, either," the hat-wearing guy warned his partner. "But if you get a clean shot of the marshal, take it. Do the same to any of the locals who might show up to poke around here. Nobody who sees or could see anything gets away from here to rat us out."

Nicky's chest was already so tight that she couldn't breathe, and that didn't help. She hated that she'd involved Holden in this, and she didn't want him or anyone hurt. But the baby had to come first.

Both men started to move. Even though there wasn't much light in the room now, she saw one of them grab the carrier seat with the baby, and the other took some keys from his pocket.

Holden got them moving, too. They were quickly off the porch and headed straight for the car. The moment they reached it, he maneuvered her to the far side, away from the house, and they ducked down.

He pulled out a knife from his pocket and jammed it into the front tire and went to the rear to do the same. That would slow them down, but it wouldn't stop them. Those men were in a hurry to get out of there, and they'd drive on the rims if they had to.

The men raced out the door of the house, making a bee-line for the car. They were just yards away when Nicky heard a sound she didn't want to hear.

Footsteps.

Behind Holden and her.

Holden pivoted, aiming his gun, but it was already too late.

Chapter Three

The man seemed to come out of nowhere.

Before Holden could do anything to stop him, the guy grabbed Nicky by her hair, hauled her back against his chest and jammed a gun to her head.

Damn.

This was not how Holden wanted things to play out.

He hoped there would be time to curse himself later for this botched rescue attempt. He should have waited until he had better measures in place. But maybe he could still figure out a way to fix this before it was too late for Nicky, him and, especially, the baby.

Holden scrambled to the front end of the car so he could take cover. That didn't do a darn thing to help Nicky, but he wouldn't be able to help her at all unless he stayed alive. Of course, another thug could gun him down, but right now using the car was the only option he had.

Nicky didn't stay put, either. Despite having a gun to her head, she rammed her elbow into the guy's stomach. The guy called her a couple of bad names and staggered back a step, but then latched onto her even harder.

"Try that again and I'll bash you upside the head with this gun," the thug growled.

Even though it was a clear enough warning, Nicky must have realized that he truly didn't intend to kill her. Holden could see her face tighten, could practically feel her gearing up for a fight.

"No," Holden warned her. "Don't."

And much to his surprise, Nicky listened. She also looked at Holden as if expecting him to tell her what to do next. He would.

When he figured out what the next step was.

For now, though, he didn't want her in a wrestling match with a goon who was twice her size. Just because the guy had no plans to shoot her, it didn't mean the gun wouldn't accidentally go off, and Holden couldn't risk a misfired bullet. Not just for Nicky's sake, but for the baby's.

"Can I punch her?" the thug asked his comrades approaching him.

"Not yet," the guy carrying the baby answered. "I don't want her bleeding in the car. Too hard to clean up."

His voice was ice-cold. As was his expression. He was the one wearing a baseball cap and was also the one who'd talked about torching Nicky's house and car. Holden figured he was the boss.

Well, the boss of these three anyway.

They were likely working for the person who'd been on the other end of that phone conversation. If Holden could just get the guy's phone, he might learn who that was. First, though, he had to get them out of this alive.

All three of the men were dressed in black—that was probably the reason Holden hadn't seen the third one sneaking up on them. They were all also heavily armed and wearing masks.

"Any sign of the locals?" the boss asked.

"No. But we got somebody watching the road. If they try to get here, we'll see 'em."

Holden hoped not. He hadn't made that last text sound like a life-and-death matter, but his cousin would come prepared for trouble. Which was exactly what Holden and Nicky were facing right now.

"The marshal flattened two tires," the one holding Nicky said. "What do you want me to do about that?"

"Nothing." The boss, again. He adjusted the baby carrier in his hand so he could read a text he got. "Someone's already on the way to pick us up. They should be here any second now."

Hell. More hired guns. Just what Holden didn't need.

Holden knew he had to do something fast, but he still wasn't sure what that would be. Maybe he'd get a chance when the other car arrived. The men would no doubt look in the direction of the vehicle when it approached, and Holden could use that distraction.

Maybe.

But Landon also had to be nearby, too, and Holden had told him to do a quiet approach. Maybe his cousin would be in place before the thugs' backup arrived.

The one holding Nicky made eye contact with Holden before glancing at his partners. "You want me to go ahead and shoot the marshal?"

"No shots around the kid, remember," the boss insisted. "This is our million-dollar baby, and we can't risk it."

Even in the darkness, Holden could see Nicky's eyes widen slightly. A million bucks. That was a lot of money to pay for a baby. So, maybe this wasn't just some black-market deal.

But if it wasn't that, then what the hell was it?

Holden glanced on the other side of the car at the two men approaching, and thanks to the angle of the lights coming out of the house windows, he saw the baby then.

And he felt as if someone had slugged him.

He'd thought when he saw the kid that it would take some hard proof before he would believe the baby was

Emmett and Annie's. It hadn't taken more than a glimpse. The kid was theirs, all right. The proof was all over the baby's face and that hair. However, Holden pushed aside his thoughts and concentrated on the situation directly in front of him.

"You obviously have a buyer for the baby," Nicky said. "Well, I'll match whatever offer you have. I can have the money to you within an hour."

That was probably a lie. Nicky came from money, but it would take more than an hour to gather up that much cash even if Holden was contributing. Which he would. No way did he want his nephew sold like property, and neither would anyone in his family.

He wasn't sure paying a ransom to the thugs would actually get them the baby, though. No. These men would just probably take the cash and the baby while going through with the plan to kill him. They wouldn't want to leave a marshal alive.

The boss huffed. "Save your breath, sweetheart," he said to Nicky. "I'm not gonna listen to a thing you try to tempt me with. Making a deal like that with you would get me killed the hard way."

Later, Holden would want to know what the guy meant by that, but for now he had to focus on the mess that was unfolding right in front of him. He heard the car engine. Saw the headlights, too.

And he knew this wasn't his cousin because Landon would be doing a quiet approach. In fact, Landon could already be there, but he wouldn't have let these snakes know about it.

The thugs weren't alarmed to see the black four-door pull into the parking lot and drive straight toward them.

"She goes with us," the boss said, tipping his head to Nicky. "She's got to hand over those files before we *fin-*

ish things with her. We might be able to use her father as added pressure."

That got Holden's attention. Nicky's, too. "What does my father have to do with this?" she asked.

Holden wanted to know the same thing, and he got an even worse feeling about this. Not that he needed anything else to put him on full alert.

The thug didn't answer her question, but Holden—and apparently Nicky—had no trouble filling in the blanks.

"You're planning to get that million dollars from my father," she snapped.

Bingo. Her father, Oscar, was stinking rich and would indeed pay a very high price to get his own grandson back. But there was no way a monster like Oscar Hart should raise a child. Oscar was barely a step above these thugs.

Again, the boss didn't answer. Instead, he turned to the bald guy. "As soon as we're in the car and out of firing range, go ahead and kill the marshal and torch the place."

So, this was it. Holden had to make his move.

He volleyed glances between the men and the car, but the thugs weren't looking at the car as he'd hoped. They still had their attention on Holden. That meant he'd have to wait a few more seconds until they were moving Nicky and the baby inside.

"There's no reason for you to kill the marshal," Nicky said. "In fact, if you hurt him, I'll never give you those files."

All three men stared at her. "Really?" the boss challenged. "And why would you care what happens to him? You two aren't exactly on friendly terms. Not anymore."

It shouldn't have surprised Holden that this goon knew about Nicky and him. The rumor mill was in full swing in Silver Creek, and there probably wasn't a person over the age of ten who hadn't heard about the short affair he'd had with Nicky.

Very short. As in twice.

Too bad Holden thought about those two times with her more than he did all his other relationships. Much to his disgust. He chalked up his time with her as a hard lesson learned. She was the daughter of a criminal and always would be.

"In fact," the boss went on, looking at Nicky, "the marshal might be wondering right about now if he can even trust you. He might be thinking you knew exactly what was going on before you ever convinced him to come here."

She shook her head, as if defending herself, and then she looked at Holden. "I'm not lying. Not this time. I didn't know my father was involved."

Maybe not. But she'd lied before, about her father's involvement in another crime, and that was the reason their so-called relationship had been so short. She'd put Holden in danger. His brother Drury, too.

A lot like now, in fact.

There'd been no baby involved then, but Drury certainly had been, and her lies had nearly gotten Holden's brother killed.

Holden had to tamp down the anger he still felt just thinking about that. But Nicky no doubt saw, or maybe even felt, that anger.

The car stopped only a few yards from the men, but when the doors didn't open, the bald guy went closer and reached for the handle.

Reaching, however, was as far as he got.

Because the door flew open, fast, knocking right into the bald guy and sending him flying back. Landon barreled out of the car, his gun aimed right at the boss. But the boss only lifted the baby carrier in front of him like a shield.

There was a special place in hell for a coward like that.

Holden didn't especially need another reason to want this guy dead, but that did it. He ran toward the boss, going at him low so that he could tackle the guy. It was a risk because the baby could still be hurt, but anything he did at this point was a risk he had to take.

Nicky yelled something he didn't catch, and from the corner of his eye, Holden saw her elbow the guy in the gut again. Maybe he wouldn't shoot her, but Holden couldn't do anything about that now. He grabbed hold of the boss's legs, knocking him off balance, and the two of them went to the ground.

So did the carrier.

It didn't fall, thank God. Even now, the boss was making sure his investment didn't get hurt, and Holden was thankful for it.

Holden didn't show the guy any such carefulness, though. He couldn't shoot him, not with the baby so close, but he could punch him, and that's what he did.

Landon scooped up the carrier and put it on the backseat. "We need to get out of here now," he warned Holden and Nicky. "We managed to steal their car, but there are at least four gunmen on the road. All of them heavily armed. They'll be on the way here by now."

Yeah, they would be, because they'd no doubt heard Nicky's shout and all the commotion.

Holden punched the boss again, the guy's head flopping back, and he raced to Nicky. He had to give it to her. For someone so outmatched, she was fighting like a wildcat, scratching and clawing the guy.

When the guy saw Holden approaching, though, he

took aim at him. Holden had faced down killers before and knew without a doubt this guy would pull the trigger.

So, Holden fired first.

Nicky was about six inches shorter than her attacker, and that was just enough to give Holden a clean shot. He put a bullet in the guy's head. Before the kidnapper even dropped to the ground, Holden grabbed Nicky and ran with her to the car.

He stuffed her into the backseat next to the carrier and followed in right behind her. Holden saw his cousin Gage behind the wheel, and Landon jumped into the passenger seat.

"Hold on," Gage warned them a split second before he gunned the engine.

But Gage had barely gotten started when the shot crashed into the front windshield. Holden pushed Nicky lower onto the seat even though she was already headed in that direction, and she covered the baby with her own body. Holden covered both of them with his.

Gage sped away with the bullets still coming right at them.

Chapter Four

Nicky had so many emotions going through her. Especially fear. She had found the baby, and he was safe.

But things might not stay that way.

More shots slammed into the rear window of the car, but the glass was reinforced, and the bullets didn't make it through. Thank God. Since this was supposed to be the kidnappers' getaway car, they'd probably made sure it could withstand an attack from the cops, but Gage and Landon had turned the tables on them and had obviously managed to somehow steal the car.

"They're dropping back," Holden said. He lifted his head even more, no doubt so he could have a better look. "They're turning around to leave."

Nicky's first instinct was to say "good!" She didn't want these monsters anywhere near the baby, but there was a huge downside to that. If they got away, she wouldn't get answers she needed as to why the kidnapping had happened in the first place.

And worse, they could regroup and come after the baby again.

A million dollars was a lot of incentive to try to kidnap the newborn and to eliminate anyone who got in their way. Plus, as long as those men were out there, they would want to get to her, too. To get their hands on those files.

From the front seat, Landon made a call, but because Nicky's heartbeat was crashing in her ears, she could only hear bits and pieces of the conversation. But she did hear him give someone their location with a request that other deputies go in pursuit of the kidnappers. He also asked that someone secure the inn. Nicky doubted the kidnappers had left any kind of evidence there, but it was a start in case the deputies didn't manage to catch the men.

"How did you get this car?" Holden asked.

"Makeshift roadblock," Gage answered, still keeping watch around them. "We parked an unmarked car sideways in the road. I hadn't planned on someone else coming in, though. I just wanted to stop someone from going out. But when the car approached, and Landon and I spotted two guys armed to the hilt, we waited until they got out of the vehicle, sneaked up on them and clubbed them."

Smart thinking. If they'd shot at the men, the others would have heard it and probably wouldn't have gotten close enough to the car for Gage and Landon to help Holden and her escape.

"The men are tied up and cuffed in a ditch," Landon added. "So even if the rest of them get away, we'll have those two. Grayson and one of the other deputies are on the way now to get them, and they'll bring them to the sheriff's office for questioning."

Nicky finally felt some relief. "Thank you. For everything."

No one acknowledged what she'd said. Maybe because they considered this part of the job. Also maybe because they didn't want to waste their breath speaking to her. She wasn't exactly on friendly terms with the Rylands even though her sister, Annie, had been married to one of them. But that connection didn't outweigh what Nicky had done.

It never would.

In their eyes, Nicky would always be the one who nearly got one of their own killed. And that was unforgivable.

"There were other men in those woods," Holden reminded them.

Landon made a sound of agreement, and there went what relief Nicky had felt. Because those men could make it to their tied-up comrades in the ditch and free them before Grayson and the others could get to them.

"We didn't want to get into a gunfight with those men patrolling the woods," Gage explained. "Because we didn't want anyone in the inn alerted. And we didn't want to risk shots hitting any of you."

Nicky whispered a thanks for that, too.

Holden had another look behind them, around them as well, and he must have been satisfied that the men weren't following them because he eased off of her. In the same motion, he looked down at the baby. Not that he could see much in the dark car, but she figured Holden had a lot of thoughts going through his head right now. She certainly did.

First things first, though—she had to make sure the baby was okay. He was squirming a little so Nicky checked to make sure he hadn't been hurt. He didn't appear to be harmed, and his diaper was even dry. He also smelled of baby formula so maybe that meant the kidnappers had taken good care of him.

That was something at least.

But there was no telling what the little guy had been through. And that broke her heart. He'd come much too close to danger tonight. Much too close to being taken away from Nicky forever, and the threat still wasn't even over.

"Is that really Emmett and Annie's baby?" Landon suddenly asked.

"Yes," Nicky said. "I have proof from some computer files and then recordings from the clinic." Of course, that got Gage's and Landon's attention so she added, "You can't use the recordings or files to make an arrest, but one of the files identifies the baby as Emmett and Annie's son."

Landon stared back at her, and Gage even looked at her in the rearview mirror. Since they were clearly still skeptical, she huffed and tried to make this a quick explanation. Her voice was shaky. Heck, *she* was shaky, and with the adrenaline pumping through her, it was hard to think.

"I stole the information, all right," she snapped. "But if I hadn't done that and if I hadn't put a listening device in Conceptions Clinic, I wouldn't have even known the baby existed, much less found out where they were holding him."

And she wasn't going to apologize for that—especially since the info had turned out to be true and they had the baby.

"I'll want those files," Holden insisted. "The recordings and anything else you have. I don't suppose in all your snooping you also got proof of who's behind this?"

"Behind what exactly?" Gage queried.

This was probably going to be as hard for him to hear as it had been for her. Mainly because Nicky hadn't believed that anyone could do something like this.

"Someone connected to Conceptions Fertility Clinic— I don't know who, yet—used Annie and Emmett's stored embryos to make this baby. And not just him," Nicky added. "There are others. Not necessarily Annie and Emmett's child, though. In fact, I don't think it is, but there are two other newborns out there somewhere."

That got the responses she expected. A stunned look from Landon. A sound of surprise from Gage. A glare from Holden.

"Where are the other babies?" Gage asked.

"I don't know." That was the truth. "It was pure luck that I overheard them talking about Annie and Emmett's baby, and there were no other names mentioned."

"This could be connected to the missing senator, Lee Minton," Holden added after a long pause. *"Could be,"* he stressed. "But it could also be connected to Nicky's father, Oscar."

That caused both Holden and Gage to curse again, and Nicky didn't have to ask why. Her father wasn't any better liked by the Rylands than she was, and worse…he was dirty. He'd never been arrested for his shady business dealings, but that was only because he hadn't gotten caught.

Gage looked at her again in the mirror. "Oscar wanted a grandchild?"

Nicky had to nod. "Specifically, he wanted a grandson to carry on his so-called legacy."

"A daughter wouldn't do?" Landon snapped.

"My father and I are, well, estranged," she admitted. "And he wasn't exactly thrilled with Annie when she married Emmett."

"Probably because he didn't like the idea of having a federal agent for a son-in-law," Holden mumbled.

She had to add another nod to that as well. It was true. Her father hated Emmett, resented Annie for marrying him, and that's why this didn't make sense.

"It's true that my father wants an heir," Nicky continued, "but this seems…extreme considering that he hated Emmett."

"Your father does extreme things all the time," Holden reminded her. "Plenty of them illegal. Plus, if you two really are *estranged*, maybe he figured this was his only chance at having an heir from his own gene pool." Then, he shook his head. "But if he did do this, something must have gone wrong because those kidnappers said this was the million-dollar baby."

Nicky thought about that for a second. "I need to talk to my father."

"It can wait," Holden insisted. "We're almost at the sheriff's office."

She glanced out the window and saw that they were only a mile or so away, and maybe because they were so close, Landon and Holden started making preparations. Landon called the hospital and asked that a doctor come to the sheriff's office. To check out the baby, no doubt. If something was indeed wrong, though, the child would have to go to the hospital. Still might have to do that since he was obviously still a newborn.

Holden made a call, too. To his cousin Josh, who was also a Silver Creek deputy. Holden asked Josh to arrange to have some baby supplies brought in. He also asked Josh to have a CSI process the car they were driving and especially check it for a tracking device.

That got Nicky's heartbeat revving up again because she realized the kidnappers could know exactly where they'd gone. Of course, there weren't too many other places they could have taken the baby, considering that an army of kidnappers were out there.

"Are your legs steady enough to run inside while holding the baby?" Holden asked her.

Nicky nodded, prayed that was true. She wasn't anywhere near steady enough, but there was no way she'd drop the baby.

Her nephew.

He wasn't just a baby. He was her own flesh and blood.

The first time she'd heard about him on those recordings from the fertility clinic, the news had hit her like a lightning bolt. The blow didn't feel any less now that she had him in her arms.

This was Annie's son. The baby her sister had so desperately wanted that she'd gone through months and months of fertility treatments, some of them dangerous to her health. It broke Nicky's heart to know that her sister wasn't here to see the baby she'd sacrificed so much to have.

But maybe someone else had sacrificed, too.

Nicky didn't have time to bring up her concern because Gage pulled to a stop in front of the sheriff's office. Even though she'd assured Holden that she was steady enough, he still took hold of her arm as they hurried into the building.

The moment they were inside, Gage took the car to the parking lot, getting it away from the sheriff's office. Maybe because he was concerned there was something more than a tracking device in it. After all, the men had said they were going to torch her house and car so they could have been carrying some kind of accelerants.

Holden didn't stay by the door. He hurried her through the squad room and into one of the interview rooms. It wasn't especially comfortable, what with the metal table and chairs, but Nicky breathed a little easier because there weren't any windows in the room. That would make it harder for the kidnappers to come after the baby again.

Nicky sank down onto one of the chairs, but Josh and Holden stayed in the hall. They had a whispered conversation before Holden joined her, and she could tell from his expression that he was about to deliver bad news. And he did.

"The men that Gage and Landon tied up in the ditch got away," Holden said. "In fact, there are no signs of any of the kidnappers."

Nicky tried not to let that send her into a panic. Hard

to do, though, and she gently pulled the baby even closer to her.

"They'll come after him again," she whispered.

"They'll try." Holden came closer, looking down at the baby. Unlike in the car, the overhead light was on, and Nicky figured he saw exactly what she was seeing.

The resemblance.

Annie's hair. But the baby's face was all Emmett.

"I've seen baby pictures of Emmett," Holden said. "That's his son."

Yes. Nicky had no doubts about that, but knowing it was just the start. They still didn't have a lot of answers.

"Obviously Conceptions Fertility Clinic was onto you," Holden continued a moment later. "That's why they sent that thug to your house. Where are the files and recordings?"

Nicky hesitated only because she'd been so terrified of the kidnappers finding them. It was the only thing she had to bargain with them in case she hadn't been able to find the baby. But now that she had her nephew—*their* nephew, she mentally corrected—there was no reason to keep them hidden.

Well, except for the sickening dread of what Holden and the others might find when they reviewed them.

She adjusted the baby's position in her arms so she could take the notepad and pen from the table and write down the storage cloud and her password. "I don't know what all the files mean," Nicky explained. "Some are just numbers and code, and I wasn't able to connect them to any names in the Conceptions database."

A muscle flickered in Holden's jaw when he took the notepad with the info. "You should have come to me or the cops the moment you found out what was going on."

"There was no time—"

"So help me," he interrupted, "you better not have with-held this because you wanted to do a story on it."

It felt as if he'd slapped her, and Nicky flinched.

More of Holden's jaw muscles flickered. "Sorry, but you don't have a good track record when it comes to this sort of thing."

No. She didn't. She'd often put the story ahead of a lot of things, including other people's safety. "I learned my lesson with your brother."

And it wasn't something she would forget anytime soon. She'd almost gotten Drury killed by withholding some evidence too long. Nicky had been working with a CPA who was helping her gather information on a crime family.

A crime family who'd done business with her father.

But the research had taken much longer than Nicky had expected. By the time she had given it to Drury, the crime family had been alerted, probably her father had, too, and Drury essentially walked into a trap. He'd nearly been killed by people he possibly could have arrested hours earlier if Nicky hadn't been digging for more.

It wouldn't do any good to tell Holden that she'd been searching for more evidence to put Drury's attackers away for life. It wouldn't do any good to tell him she was sorry. Or that she hadn't lied or withheld anything to protect her father. Sometimes, she felt as if she was drowning in the water under that particular bridge.

Holden stepped out into the hall to make a call. To his other brother, Lucas, she realized. A Texas Ranger. Holden gave him a quick update, including the cloud-storage info, and asked him to see what he could find. He then went back into the squad room for several moments.

"I wouldn't have put the baby in danger," Nicky said when Holden came back into the room. She brushed a kiss on the baby's forehead. "I'd just figured out where he was when that thug showed up at my house. And then you showed up."

With everything else going on, Nicky had forgotten about the reason Holden had come. To warn her that she was on the verge of being arrested. "Is the FBI really involved in this?" she asked.

He nodded. "Senator Minton's family hired a team of PIs to help find him. I didn't know what they found, but I got word that the FBI was looking at you as a person of interest."

Oh, mercy. She didn't need this now. "They think I had something to do with his disappearance?"

"I'm not sure. They're keeping what they have close to the vest, but now that I know what went on, I can probably stop them from taking you into custody."

"I can't go with them." She got to her feet so she could look him straight in the eyes. "Whoever hired those kidnappers had plenty of money. No doubt resources, too, to pull off a scheme like the one at Conceptions. He or she could also have a dirty cop or two on the payroll."

Holden didn't argue with that. Something that didn't help steady her nerves one bit. Even though she'd been the one to point out that particular possible danger, she'd hoped that Holden could have assured her that it wasn't likely. No way could he do that, though.

"There's one more thing," she said. "The surrogate." Nicky had to take a deep breath before she continued. "There are no surrogate names in the files, but I saw something, well, disturbing in our nephew's folder."

That got Holden's attention. He stared at her, waiting for her to continue.

"There were two notes entered on the day the surrogate delivered him. One was the location where the baby was being taken. The other was…contract terminated."

Even though it'd been hours since Nicky had first seen those two words, it still gave her a jolt. "Do you think they killed her?"

Holden opened his mouth, closed it and then scrubbed his hand over his face. "Yeah."

There it was again, another jolt. Of course, Nicky had already considered it, especially after what'd gone on at the inn, but she'd held out hope. Hope that was quickly fading because the surrogate would have been a loose end. No way would the person behind this want her around so she could tell anyone about the baby she'd delivered.

Holden took out his phone again and fired off a text. "Since Grayson and the deputies are tied up here," he told Nicky, "I'll have someone in the marshals' office check and see if there have been any reports of a dead or missing woman who recently gave birth."

Nicky nodded, and even though she dreaded hearing that a woman could be dead, a woman who'd given birth to their precious nephew, they had to find out the truth. And not just about the surrogate, either.

"How will we handle the investigation into Conceptions?" she asked.

"There is no *we* in this. You aren't handling anything," he snapped, but he quickly reined in his temper.

"How are you handling it, then?" Nicky amended.

He took a deep breath first. "The other lawmen and I will have to go at it head-on. After everything that just happened, they know we're onto them so there's no need to back off. Gage is already contacting San Antonio PD and the FBI."

That meant soon Conceptions Clinic would be swarming with cops and agents. Maybe there'd be something to find, including those other babies that were out there somewhere.

She heard the footsteps in the hall, and Nicky's heart went into overdrive again, her body preparing for another threat. But it was only Landon.

"We have visitors," Landon said, not sounding too pleased about that. "The doctor's here to check the baby." Then, his attention went to Nicky. "And your father just arrived."

Nicky's stomach went to her knees. No. Not this. Not now. She was still reeling from the attack, but she also knew she had to confront him, to try to get those answers they so desperately needed.

"Why is he here?" Nicky asked. "Why did he come?" She knew it wasn't because he was worried about her, and there hadn't been time for too many people to have heard news about the attack.

Landon's gaze dropped to the baby, but he didn't have to verbally answer. That's because Nicky heard her father's voice booming through the squad room.

"Nicky, I know you're here," her father shouted. "I want you to bring me my grandson *now*!"

Chapter Five

Holden wasn't sure whose profanity was worse—his or Nicky's. She obviously wasn't looking forward to this visit any more than Holden was, and he wished he could delay it until they had more information. But he couldn't.

Because Oscar might be the very one to provide that information.

"Wait here with Nicky and the baby," Holden told Landon, and he gave Nicky a warning glance to stay put before he headed to the squad room to confront her father.

Holden passed Dr. Michelson along the way. The doc was a fixture in Silver Creek and had been taking care of the Rylands and the other townsfolk for nearly three decades, so he was someone Holden definitely trusted.

"Try to keep the baby quiet," Holden whispered to the doctor. "I don't want Oscar to know he's here. And close the door when you go into the interview room."

Dr. Michelson cast an uneasy glance over his shoulder, nodded and went into the interview room.

Holden instantly spotted Oscar when he entered the squad room. Nicky's father was still by the reception desk, and Gage was frisking him. Good. Holden doubted Oscar would come in with guns blazing. He was more the sort to hire blazing guns, but judging from the intense look on his face, anything could happen.

It'd been a while since Holden had seen the man, but Oscar hadn't changed. He was still wearing one of those pricey suits he favored. Still looked formidable despite being in his late sixties. That had something to do with his size. He was well over six feet tall and still had the body of a linebacker, which he no doubt kept toned from spending hours with a personal trainer.

"Where's Nicky?" Oscar demanded the moment he saw Holden. "And where's my grandson?"

"Your grandson?" Holden countered. Best not to show his hand until he knew exactly what hand Oscar was holding, and Holden didn't figure Oscar would just give it up.

Oscar's eyes narrowed. "Don't play innocent with me. I know they're here. Why else would the doctor be here?"

"He came for one of the deputies," Holden lied. "What makes you think Nicky is here?"

That didn't help those narrowed eyes, but Holden figured his own eyes were doing some narrowing, too. That's because Oscar had to have some kind of insider information about the attack. And the baby. He'd gotten here way too fast.

"Start talking," Holden demanded. "Don't leave out the good stuff, either, even if it incriminates you in the assorted felonies that went down tonight."

Oscar glanced around as if he expected someone to defend him. That wasn't going to happen in an office of Ryland lawmen, and the man must have figured that out right away.

"I didn't have any part in this," Oscar snarled.

"And yet you're here," Holden snarled right back. "Explain that. *Now*."

Oscar continued to glare at him, and the glare went on for so long that Holden was ready to arrest Oscar just to let him know how serious he was about getting that explanation.

Oscar finally shook his head. "I'm not sure exactly what's going on."

Welcome to the club. "Then tell me all about the stuff you do know."

"Just tell me first if the baby is safe," Oscar ventured.

But Holden wasn't in a bargaining mood. "I'm not discussing anything else with you until I know what role you had in orchestrating this."

"I had nothing to do with it," Oscar practically shouted, and it took him a few moments to regain his composure. "This morning a package was delivered to my office. No postmark, and the courier who delivered it was gone before I knew what was in it."

"And what was that?" Holden demanded when Oscar paused.

"Photos. Some DNA results." Oscar stopped, swallowed hard. "Those bastards had my grandson."

There was plenty of concern in the man's voice, but that concern could be there because Oscar had put this sick plan into motion and then it had backfired on him.

"I want that package," Holden declared. "Call one of your lackeys and have them bring it here right now."

Oscar looked as if he might disobey that order, but he finally sent off a text. "How did Nicky know they had the baby?" Oscar asked. "Did they send her a ransom notice, too?"

"No, I found out on my own," she answered.

Holden glared at her. He didn't want her confronting her father. Not yet anyway. But at least she hadn't brought the baby out with her to do that. That meant she'd handed off the baby to Landon or the doctor before she'd come out of the interview room. Later, Holden would want to know why Landon hadn't stopped her. Then again, that was an answer he already knew. Nicky was darn pigheaded, and Landon had likely just given up on trying to hold her back.

"Where's the baby?" Oscar repeated, this time to Nicky. "Was he hurt in the attack?"

Holden latched onto that question. "What do you know about the attack?"

Oscar suddenly got very quiet. He wasn't a stupid man, but he obviously hadn't thought this visit through. Which meant he was driven by emotion. Or what substituted for emotion when it came to a man like him.

"After I got a ransom demand," Oscar finally continued, "I had my men start looking for the baby. A million dollars is a lot of money, and I wanted to make sure I actually got my grandson in exchange for the cash."

Holden groaned. "And it didn't occur to you to call the cops so they could handle this?" Like father, like daughter.

"The note in the package said if I went to the cops, my grandson would disappear forever, that I'd never find him."

"Of course they'd say that. It's what kidnappers tell their marks nearly every time." And now that he'd given out that lecture, Holden continued. "How did you find out about the attack?"

"The ransom drop-off was to be here in Silver Creek. I was supposed to meet them fifteen minutes ago at the entrance to the park. I was there, had the money and my men in place in case something went wrong. And it apparently did."

"You bet it did." Holden motioned for him to keep going.

"I got a phone call that said there'd been a change of plans, that if I wanted my grandson and daughter to stay alive, then I'd still pay the million dollars or else they'd be attacked again. I figured you or your lawmen cousins had brought Nicky and the baby here." Oscar looked at Nicky then. "You have the baby. The kidnapper said you did, and I want him. He's my grandson."

"He's my nephew," she added.

"Mine as well," Holden said. He went to Nicky, to stand by her side.

Holden had never thought of Nicky as an ally, but in this matter, they appeared to be on the same side. Neither of them wanted Oscar to get his hands on that baby.

Oscar didn't miss the side-by-side stance that Nicky and Holden had taken. "Are you sleeping with Holden again?" Oscar asked Nicky. "Is that why he's helping you?"

Holden tapped his badge. "*That's* why I'm helping her. And as for the sleeping-with-me part, that's none of your business. In fact, you're not allowed any more questions until you answer this one, and trust me, a wrong answer will get you jail time. Are you the one who stole Annie and Emmett's embryos and had them planted in a surrogate?"

"No!" Oscar didn't hesitate, either, and if he was lying, he was doing a convincing job of it. "Something like that never crossed my mind."

"Really? Because I figured just about anything down and dirty had crossed your mind at one time or another."

That got Oscar's eyes to turn to slits again. "This isn't about me. It's about my grandson. I was willing to pay a million dollars to get him. If I'd put together this plan, I certainly wouldn't have kidnapped him."

"Not intentionally anyway," Nicky said. "But maybe the plan backfired. That happens sometimes when you hire criminals to carry out criminal activities."

Oscar cursed her, and it wasn't a mild profanity, either. Clearly, there was no love lost between father and daughter.

It was also clear that Oscar did indeed want his grandson. But that didn't make him innocent in all of this.

"How soon before that package arrives?" Holden asked him.

Oscar shook his head, as if gathering his thoughts. "As soon as my assistant can retrieve it from my San Antonio office and drive it here. Maybe an hour or two."

Holden glanced back at Gage, and even though he didn't say anything to him, Gage made a phone call and asked for SAPD to escort Oscar's assistant to Silver Creek. There were two reasons for that. First, to make sure the guy actually did what he was supposed to do, and second, to keep him safe if those kidnappers decided to stop him along the way. Holden doubted the kidnappers or their boss had left anything incriminating in or on that package, but the thugs might be in the midst of tying up all possible loose ends.

Which brought Holden to his next concern. Well, a concern only because he was a lawman.

"You got a bodyguard?" Holden asked Oscar.

"Of course. He's waiting for me in the car." He tipped his head to the black limo parked just outside.

"Keep him with you. Heck, hire a couple more because if you're truly innocent, those kidnappers could come after you. Since they didn't get the million for the baby, they might make you a target instead. Or maybe they'll just put a bullet in your head because they think you know too much about their operation."

Judging from Oscar's glare, he didn't like that reminder. Or maybe he just didn't like it that Holden could be right. Oscar wasn't going to like this next part, either.

"You can leave now," Holden told him, and yes, it was another order. He wanted to get the man out of there before the baby made a sound to confirm to Oscar that the child was indeed there at the sheriff's office.

"I can't leave," Oscar argued. "Not until I see my grandson and know that he's safe."

"That's two different things," Holden argued right back. "Seeing him could put him in danger because I'd have to take you to him, and those kidnappers could follow us."

It surprised Holden when Oscar seemed to accept his answer, but he didn't accept it for long. "Soon, then. *Very* soon. I'll hire as many bodyguards as it takes, but I will see him. And if you try to keep him from me, I'll get a court order."

"Good luck with that. It won't be easy to convince a judge that you have a newborn grandson when your daughter's been dead for months now. And I wouldn't count on the FBI just handing you their records of the investigation."

Oscar turned his sharp gaze on Nicky. "You know more about this than you're saying."

"That's the pot calling the kettle black," Holden said, stepping in front of her. He didn't want Nicky to start blurting out what she did and didn't know because this could be a fishing expedition on Oscar's part.

And if Nicky knew too much, or even if Oscar thought she knew too much, it could spur another attack.

"This is your last warning," Holden told Oscar. "Leave now, or I'll arrest you for obstruction of justice."

If looks could have killed, Oscar would have just sent Holden to the hereafter. "Charges like that won't stick."

"Maybe not, but at least it'll get you out of my face and behind bars for a while." That wasn't a bluff, and Oscar must have figured that out because after he belted out some more profanity, he turned and finally left.

One down, one to go. Well, one immediate to go anyway. He had a mile-long list of things to do, but it started with Nicky.

"You shouldn't have let your father know you were here," Holden told her.

"I think he already knew."

"Then you shouldn't have confirmed it," Holden amended. "Let's not give the bad guys anything else they could possibly use."

She glanced out the front windows, where her father was getting in his limo. "You really think he's behind this?"

"I'm not taking him off my suspect list." Of course, right now the only name Holden had on that list was Oscar. Oscar had means, motive and opportunity. But then again so would anyone else with a sick mind and a desire to make a boatload of money.

Since Nicky was still staring at her father's car, Holden got her moving back toward the interview room, in part because he didn't want her in front of the windows and also because he wanted to see how the baby was doing.

Soon, very soon, he'd have to deal with some major feelings stirring inside him. He'd loved Emmett, and now this baby was like having a piece of his brother. That wasn't exactly a feeling to dwell on right now, though, because it could cause him to lose focus.

Ditto for Nicky.

For whatever reason, he was still attracted to her. At least his body was anyway. But even thinking about her that way was yet another distraction that Holden didn't need.

When they got to the interview room, the doctor appeared to be finishing up his exam. Landon was holding the baby, and the doctor was putting away his stethoscope.

"He's fine," Dr. Michelson said. "Not a scratch or a bruise on him." He volleyed glances between Nicky and Holden. "Can either of you tell me what's going on?"

Since he trusted the doctor, Holden went with the simplified version. "The baby is Emmett and Annie's. We believe someone used the embryos that they'd stored at Conceptions Clinic."

Hearing the simplified version aloud gave Holden a not-so-simple jolt. Nicky had already said there were other babies, and she'd said those babies weren't Emmett and Annie's. But how did she know that?

He turned his gaze to Nicky. "Was there anything, no matter how small, in the files or the conversations you recorded to hint that one of the other babies could be our niece or nephew as well?"

She shook her head. "From what I could tell, Emmett and Annie only had two embryos stored, and both were implanted into the surrogate. But she only had one baby."

Now it was Holden who shook his head. "Why would they implant both of them?"

"That's not unusual," the doctor explained. "They often do that with in vitro to ensure the success of getting one baby. Sometimes, even with multiple embryos, the procedure fails."

It certainly had failed once with Annie and Emmett, but it'd obviously worked with the surrogate. Holden was still caught between being furious about this whole surrogacy situation and being thrilled to still have some living part of Emmett. One thing was for sure, he loved this kid—and there was no way he was going to lose him or that part of Emmett.

"I took a DNA sample with a cheek swab," the doctor volunteered. "You want me to run it?"

Holden nodded. He didn't have any doubts that the baby was Emmett's, but he might need DNA proof in case this turned into a custody battle.

"I can tell you something about the baby," the doctor

went on. "He appears to have been delivered via C-section. That's an educated guess, mind you, but his head is perfectly shaped. You don't usually see that with a vaginal birth. Plus, his birth weight seems to be a little low, maybe an indication that he was delivered before his due date."

So, they were looking for a surrogate who'd had a C-section. Possibly a dead surrogate.

The doctor motioned toward a bag on the table as he headed toward the door. "There are diapers and bottles with premade formula. All you have to do is warm it up," he added and left.

Since Holden had more cousins than most day-care centers had employees, he figured there was someone at the Silver Creek Ranch who could tell him how to warm formula. Of course, that led him to his next question.

Where the heck was he taking Nicky and the baby?

Just thinking about it required a deep breath. "Stay in here," Holden told Nicky. She took the baby from Landon. "I'll get to work on a place for us to stay for the night."

"Us?" she asked.

Holden gave her a flat look in case she thought he was going to let her out of his sight. He wasn't. "Us," he confirmed.

Landon mumbled something about having a lot of work to do. Which he probably did. But Holden also thought his quick exit had something to do with the sudden, thick tension in the room.

"We're joined at the hip until this is resolved," Holden added to Nicky.

The corner of her mouth lifted. Not quite a smile but close to one, and it vanished as quickly as it came. "I was just thinking that you're probably not very happy about that."

"I'm not, but it should tell you just how serious I am about keeping him safe."

Him.

It was yet another reminder that they needed to work on a name, but in the grand scheme of things, it would have to wait.

"Stay here," he repeated. "I'll see if I can get an update on those kidnappers. Plus, the CSIs should be out at the inn by now."

Holden wasn't holding out hope that either would produce good results, but before he could even make it to one of the desks in the squad room, Gage was making his way toward them.

Hell.

Gage was the one Ryland who could usually put a positive spin on things, but even he was scowling.

"What now?" Holden asked.

Nicky must have heard his rough tone because she stepped into the doorway.

Gage glanced down at the paper he was holding. Paper that Holden recognized, since it was the info about the storage cloud and the password that Nicky had given him.

"It appears that about an hour ago someone erased all the files in the storage cloud," Gage said. "Everything in it is gone."

Chapter Six

Gone.

Nicky had no trouble hearing what Gage had just said, but the trouble was getting it to sink in.

"That can't be right," she insisted. She handed the baby to Holden, and she would have bolted to the squad room to find a computer to use, but both Gage and Landon stopped her.

"Your father could be watching the sheriff's office," Holden reminded her. "Or those kidnappers could be. Best not to make it easy for them to see you."

"But I need a computer," Nicky persisted.

"Wait here. I'll bring you one," Gage said, and he headed back to the squad room.

The moments crawled by. Unlike the thoughts in her head. Those thoughts were going at lightning speed. The files had to be there. They just had to be. Gage had likely just accessed the wrong account or something, and she could clear this up with a quick search.

She hoped.

Gage finally returned, and Nicky immediately took the laptop from him, sat at the table and pulled up the online storage. She put in her password. Waited.

And it felt as if her heart had actually stopped beating.

Because Gage had been right. It was empty. No files. Nothing.

Both Landon and Holden cursed, but Nicky ignored them. She logged out and logged in again, hoping it was just a glitch. It wasn't. The files weren't there even after she rebooted a fourth time.

"How could someone have done this?" Holden asked.

She was about to say she didn't know, but then Nicky remembered something critical. "Paul Barksfield. Quick, I need a phone."

Landon handed her his cell. "Who's Paul Barksfield?"

Nicky had purposely memorized his number just in case something happened to her own phone, and she pressed in the number. "He's a PI who does some work for me from time to time. I told him if something happened to me that he should make sure the files get to the cops."

"He had the password?" Holden asked, and this time his voice was loaded with suspicion.

"Yes, but I can trust Paul."

She was certain of it. But Nicky didn't like that shiver that went down her spine when the call went straight to voice mail. She left a message for Paul to call her immediately and then tried the number once more. Again, he didn't answer.

"You're sure you can trust him?" Holden asked, and Gage must have had the same question because he used the laptop to start a search.

On Paul.

"Paul's done PI work for me for nearly five years. He wouldn't have just deleted the files." She paused. "Unless he heard about the attack and thought the kidnapper might have gotten the password from me."

Of course, there were ways they could have done that— torture, drugs or some kind of coercion that would involve a threat to the baby. None were good scenarios, and Paul would have known that.

"The files could still be safe," she said, and Nicky prayed that was true. Because by now, there was probably nothing left at Conceptions Clinic that would help them unravel all of this.

"Could the kidnappers have known you gave any info to Paul?" Holden asked. The baby started to fuss a little, and he looked down at him as if he didn't have a clue what to do. Maybe he didn't, but when he started to rock the baby, he hushed.

She nearly said no, but Nicky had no idea if that was true. As she'd already pointed out, Paul had worked for her a long time, and it was possible the kidnappers had made the connection.

Judging from his expression, Landon must have thought so, too, and he took his phone back. "I'll call and have someone check on him."

Oh, mercy. That meant something could be wrong. Or more than wrong. The kidnappers could have killed him.

"Don't borrow trouble," Holden said as if he knew exactly what she was thinking. Probably because she had a panicked look on her face.

The panic continued to rise as Nicky considered who else those thugs might go after. Because of her job and her constantly being on the go, she didn't exactly have a lot of friends, and in this case that could turn out to be a good thing. Just in case, though, she needed to contact the various newspapers that often bought her stories to warn them of the possible trouble.

"We'll find Paul and get the files," Holden said. "In the meantime, we need to get the baby to a safe place. Not here," he quickly added. "Because your father already knows you're here, and he might send his own hired thugs to try to take the baby."

That gave Nicky another slam of adrenaline that she didn't need.

"We could take them to the Silver Creek Ranch," Landon suggested.

But Nicky was already shaking her head before he even finished. "Too risky. Many of your cousins live there, and they have children."

Gage made a sound of agreement. "There are also dozens of ranch hands who could help protect you."

She still shook her head and looked at Holden. "I don't want to put another Ryland in harm's way."

"Admirable," Holden said, and there wasn't as much sarcasm in his voice as there could have been. "But whichever way we go with this, the Rylands are involved."

That meant the danger was automatic. Because they were lawmen. But that didn't mean she couldn't do something to stop them from becoming targets. Well, most of them anyway. Like her, Holden was already a target since he wasn't going to stop protecting their nephew.

"Maybe you can go to Kayla's place?" Gage suggested.

"Kayla?" Nicky asked.

"Dade's wife," Holden explained.

Dade was Gage's brother and a fellow Silver Creek deputy, but Nicky didn't know his wife.

"Kayla's, well, very rich," Gage went on, "and she has a ranch with a huge house and a lot of acreage about a half hour from here. For a while a group used it as a place for trouble teens, but it's empty now."

"The kidnappers might suspect we'd go there," Nicky pointed out.

"The Rylands own a lot of houses," Gage said, "and this one is in Kayla's maiden name. It's got a high-end security system as well as a wrought-iron fence surrounding the place. Either Landon or I could stay with you until we can come up with a real safe house."

Holden made a sound of agreement. "The house isn't far," he told her, "but it'll take us a while to get there."

Yes, because they'd have to drive around to make sure they weren't followed. It was a necessary precaution but would only add to the already long night. Not that Nicky figured she'd get any rest once they arrived at the house, but being there might be better than this limbo of waiting around for something else bad to happen.

"I'll pull a cruiser up in front of the building," Gage said.

Landon added, "And I'll get the reserve deputies that we'll need for backup. Two of them live in town so they can get here right away."

Nicky still wasn't certain of this, but then she wasn't certain of anything right now. Well, nothing except that something had to be done to protect the baby.

Holden handed her the newborn and took one of the premade formula bottles from the bag. "I'll warm this so we can feed him on the drive."

He followed his cousins, and it didn't take long, less than fifteen minutes, before Holden returned to the interview room. He scooped up the rest of the baby supplies and motioned for her to follow him. He didn't waste any time getting her into the cruiser that was just a couple of inches from the front door. Holden got in the backseat with her, and Landon was behind the wheel.

It was a good thing Holden had thought of warming up the formula because the baby started to fuss the moment Landon pulled away from the sheriff's office. Nicky had zero experience feeding a baby, but thankfully the infant took the nipple the moment she touched it to his mouth.

"The reserve deputies are behind us in an unmarked

car," Landon said, glancing back at the dark blue sedan that was following them.

With the reserves, that meant there were four lawmen to protect the baby. Nicky prayed that was enough.

"Tell me everything you remember about those files you copied from the clinic and the recordings," Holden demanded.

Nicky had been expecting that demand, and Holden probably would have made it sooner if they hadn't had to deal with the aftermath of the attack. Now, though, they were dealing with the possibility that the files were lost, and if that had indeed happened, what Nicky could recall might be the only information they would have.

Not exactly a comforting thought.

"As I said, Conceptions called it the Genesis Project, and there were three files. The files didn't have names, only case numbers, but they had notes including the dates of the in vitro procedures, whether or not it was a success and then the delivery date. Except the only delivery date was for our nephew."

"Why did you hack into the Genesis Project file in the first place?" Holden asked.

"Senator Minton. I went to Conceptions, hoping to find some clues as to his disappearance, and they stonewalled me. That's when I hacked into their system and started poking around. That led me to the Genesis Project, and that in turn led me to Emmett and Annie's file."

Even now it caused her stomach to tighten into a hard knot. The last thing she'd expected to find in those files was that she had a nephew.

Holden glanced around, keeping watch just as Landon was. "Does Senator Minton have a child out there somewhere?" Holden added.

She had to shake her head. "I don't know. The notes

in his file ended with the surrogate getting the in vitro procedure. It didn't say if it was successful or not. And I couldn't match his regular file at Conceptions with one of the numbers in the Genesis Project. I could only assume it was him because the dates of his wife's harvested embryos matched the ones used with the surrogate."

He took a moment, clearly processing what she'd said, and then Nicky voiced the theory that she was sure was already forming in his head. "If Senator Minton does have a child out there, and they tried to get ransom money from him, he could have refused. Or something could have gone wrong. The person behind this could have murdered him."

Holden didn't hesitate with his sound of agreement. "Or Minton could be on the run like you. Either way, Minton will need to be investigated. His wife, too."

"Beatrice," Nicky began. "I looked into her background when I was searching for her husband. She has a reputation of being a gold digger. It's his second marriage," she added. "Beatrice is the trophy wife."

"How does wife number one feel about that?"

"Her name is Dorothy, and she seems to have been glad to be rid of Minton because of all the cheating he did when they were married. The police have ruled her out as a suspect and so have I. Minton and she had been divorced for six years. No kids. Along with having a new man in her life, she's financially independent."

"Unlike Beatrice?"

"Unlike Beatrice," she confirmed. "From what I can tell, the reason Beatrice was so driven to have a child was so that she could make sure to hang on to her rich husband."

"A husband who's now missing." Holden scrubbed his hand over his face. "As soon as I can arrange it, I'll interview Beatrice."

"Good luck with that. Beatrice refused to see me."

"She'll see me because if I have to, I'll get a warrant for her arrest," Holden insisted. "Once the FBI has the info in those files, Beatrice will become a person of interest not only in her husband's disappearance, but also the Genesis Project itself."

That was true, and maybe under interrogation Beatrice would reveal something to help them with this investigation. But then Nicky had to shake her head.

"Even if Beatrice had something to do with her husband's disappearance, it doesn't explain why she would have been involved with the Genesis Project. After all, she and her husband had already gone through the process to have a baby. She was getting what she wanted."

"Maybe she wanted more. As in more money. Think about it. The person behind this was going to get a million at least from your father and probably more money from us because I doubt they had plans to hand the baby over to Oscar tonight."

True. The kidnappers could have demanded a lot more from Nicky and Holden, and unless they had found another way around it, they would have paid the ransom.

"You said there was a third file in the Genesis Project," Holden went on. "And you have no idea who that is?"

"No. I couldn't find a case that matched the reference number in the files, and it didn't have the info about the harvest date for the embryo. That could mean the clients didn't go to Conceptions, that perhaps the kidnappers got the embryo from some other facility."

Nicky figured whoever the clients were, they must have money. Like her father, the Rylands and Senator Minton.

Holden mumbled some profanity. "I hope this isn't just the tip of the iceberg. I hope there aren't more projects like this under a different name."

Mercy, she hadn't considered that, but she should have. Anyone who would create babies only to ransom them to their loved ones had a sick enough mind to do just about anything.

"As soon as we get to Kayla's house, I'll write down everything I can remember from those files," Nicky said. Holden might be able to see something else she'd missed.

And while that was important, critical even, so was taking care of the baby.

"We'll have to stop my father from getting that court order," she said. Not exactly a news flash to Holden, but it helped her to say everything out loud. "Question Beatrice, too. I have a list of employees and former employees at Conceptions so we'll need to go over that as well."

"That's already in the works. Gage will be working on that along with anything we learn from the package that the kidnappers sent to your father."

She certainly hadn't forgotten about that or the kidnapper's car being processed, but with everything else on her mind, she'd pushed it to the back burner. The baby was on the front burner now. And not just his safety, either.

"You heated the formula," Nicky reminded Holden. "Does that mean you know how to take care of a baby?"

"Not even close," Holden mumbled.

From the front seat, Landon groaned. "I guess that means I'll be giving some instruction on diapering. Burping lessons, too. One of you will be taking the two a.m. feeding, though."

Gladly. "I want to take care of him, but I don't want to mess things up," she answered.

"Oh, he'll take care of the messing part," Landon joked. "By the way, are we going to keep calling the baby *he* or *him*? Or do you plan to give him a name?"

Nicky looked at Holden, and he shrugged. "For now

we could call him Carter since that was Emmett's middle name," Holden suggested.

Both Nicky and Landon voiced their agreement, and then she looked at that precious face again. Yes, Carter suited him just fine.

With that off of her list, Nicky moved on to something else she remembered. "In the grand scheme of things," she said, "this might be minor, but I'll need to call my neighbor and ask her to take care of my cat."

Holden took out his phone and sent a text to someone. Probably Gage. Nicky was about to thank him for that, but before she could say anything, Holden's phone buzzed, and she saw Gage's name on the screen. With everything going on, he could be calling about a dozen different things, but her first thought, and fear, was that someone was following them.

Holden didn't put the call on speaker, perhaps so he could try to hide the news from her if it was indeed bad. And it was. She could tell from the way the muscles in his shoulders and arms went stiff.

"How?" Holden asked, and whatever answer Gage gave him caused Holden to mumble more profanity. "Call me back as soon as you know something."

He ended the call and put his phone away before Holden turned to her. "SAPD found Paul."

At first, she wanted to jump for joy. They'd found him, and he could explain what'd happened to those files. But that wasn't a jumping-for-joy look on Holden's face.

"Is Paul all right?" Nicky asked hesitantly, though she wasn't sure how she was able to speak. Her throat suddenly got very tight.

"No." And it took Holden a moment to continue. "The cops found Paul when they went out to his house." Another pause. "Someone shot him."

Chapter Seven

Holden read the latest text from Gage and groaned. Paul Barksfield was alive—barely. That was the good news. The bad news was that the man hadn't regained consciousness while he'd been at the hospital.

And the doctors weren't optimistic about him waking up anytime soon, either.

That meant Paul couldn't tell them who'd shot him and left him for dead. Nor could he tell them what'd happened to those files that Nicky had put in online storage. In case Paul was never able to give them that info, Holden had already moved on to the next step.

He was going through the personnel files from Conceptions.

And he was also going through the copies that Gage had sent him of the contents of the package Oscar had received from the kidnappers. The personal files had too much information. The package contents, too little. On top of which, Holden hadn't gotten much sleep and was now running on caffeine.

No wonder Landon hadn't volunteered to take the nighttime feedings.

Carter had woken up every hour, causing either Holden or Nicky to scramble to the kitchen to warm up his formula, only to have the baby take a couple of sips and then fall asleep. Around 4:00 a.m., Nicky had offered to do it on her own so that Holden could get some rest. In the massive house, that wouldn't have been a problem since it had nine bedrooms, but Holden had stayed there in the room with Nicky and Carter.

He owed his brother that much.

If their situations had been reversed, Emmett would have done the same thing for him. That would have included sleeping with the enemy. Or rather staying in the room with her.

It'd been over a year now since he'd had sex with Nicky. Holden didn't like to label them as lovers because of what'd happened afterward. Lovers made the whole thing seem too intimate. Besides, it'd been lust, that's all.

Still was.

And Holden got a full dose of that lust when Nicky came into the kitchen, where he was working. She had Carter in her arms, and the baby was fussing again. Clearly he was ready for a bottle that he wasn't going to finish, but Holden got to his feet to warm it up anyway.

"Thanks," Nicky said, sinking down onto one of the chairs at the table.

When Holden had left the bedroom about an hour earlier, both Nicky and Carter had been asleep, and he'd hoped they would stay that way for a couple of hours. No such luck, though.

Nicky yawned and after mumbling an apology, she helped herself to Holden's coffee, his cue to fix another cup. Despite the yawn, her mussed hair and the fatigue in her eyes, Holden still saw something he didn't want to see.

A damn attractive woman.

Even with no sleep or a hairbrush, Nicky was beautiful. Always had been. And that beauty had only fueled the lust when they'd first hooked up.

Was fueling it now.

Holden cursed the thought and shoved it aside. He came back to the table with both the bottle and a fresh cup of coffee. Apparently, it was exactly what both of them wanted because Carter took the bottle right off, and Nicky had some of the coffee.

"Any updates on Paul?" she asked. Her voice was tentative, as if she might not want to hear the answer.

She didn't.

But Holden gave it to her anyway. "He's still critical, still not responsive."

Nicky showed no signs of surprise about that. Probably she knew he would have come and told her if there'd been a significant change. But that lack of surprise was accompanied by some sadness and frustration.

"I'm responsible for this," she said. "Once again, I nearly got a man killed."

Holden didn't want to address what had gone on with Drury. Actually, he didn't want to address any of it, but then he saw Nicky blinking back tears.

Hell.

He hated the hole that it punched inside him at seeing her grief. Holden didn't consider himself a warm and fuzzy person, but he wasn't a jerk, either. Not most days anyway. He put his hand on her arm. Hoped that it would give her some reassurance. But no. More tear blinking.

"Paul's a PI," he offered. "He knew the risks of his job before he ever agreed to work for you."

She nodded but her body language indicated she didn't buy that at all, that she still felt this was her fault. That got him out of his chair, and because he knew it would get her mind on something else, Holden leaned down and brushed a kiss on her forehead. It probably qualified as warm and fuzzy, and it was sincere, but it caused her to give him a funny look.

That look.

Yeah, mixed with those tears was the slam of heat she'd just gotten from what should have been a chaste kiss. Apparently, nothing could be chaste between them.

Nicky avoided eye contact by staring at the baby, who had already gone back to sleep. Heck. He needed to talk to his cousins and find out how to fix this.

"Where's Landon?" she asked, looking everywhere but at him.

"Working in one of the offices. There are three in the house."

"It's a big house," Nicky agreed. She tipped her head to the stuff he had laid out on the table. "You're working, too. What is all of this?"

"Grayson emailed me copies of what was in the package the kidnappers sent to your father."

That got her attention. She shifted the baby in her arms and leaned in for a closer look.

"There's not much," Holden explained. "DNA results which may or may not belong to Carter. We won't know if it's a match for a while." And even then it wouldn't tell them much since they already knew the kidnappers had had the baby. It wasn't much of a stretch to accept they'd also done a DNA test on him.

Nicky picked up a picture of Carter. It had probably been taken only a couple of hours after he'd been born, and other than his carrier seat and the gown he was wearing, there was nothing else in the picture. That almost certainly had been by design. No way would those kidnappers have sent a photo to Oscar if it could have identified them in any way.

She put the picture aside and went to the page of typed

instructions on how to deliver the ransom money. It was all to have been done as a cash drop in the park, so there wasn't even a bank account number to try and trace.

The final item she saw was a photo of a lock of Carter's hair. It was a stupid response because it was just hair, but it was a powerful reminder that if these thugs had managed to cut his hair, they could have done anything with the baby. Once Holden got his hands on them, those snakes were going to pay for this.

"Anything on the kidnappers?" she asked.

He shook his head. Holden would have considered that good news since that meant there hadn't been another attack, but in this case, out of sight was not out of mind. They were out there, and they would try to come at them again.

That's why Holden had used every security measure available at the house. Not just the internal alarms that were armed for every window and door, but also the ones for the perimeter. If the kidnappers tried to get onto the grounds, then the security system would alert them.

"And the kidnappers' car?" Nicky added. "Did the CSIs find anything?"

"Nothing useable. The car was registered to a dummy company, and it could take years to dig through all the layers to find out who owns it. By then, the company and its owner will be long gone, I'm sure."

In fact, the person was likely already gone or else had set up the account with an alias. Or even a front person.

Since Holden didn't want to keep harping on all the bad news, he turned his laptop in her direction. "I got the personnel files for Conceptions Clinic, and it's not as big of an operation as I thought it would be. A clinic manager, a medical records guy who did their computer entries, three nurses, a lab tech and two doctors. I also have the files of anyone who worked there in the past year."

Nicky put the bottle aside and scrolled through the records.

"Grayson and the others will check out each person who worked there," Holden explained. "The marshals will help with that. So will I, of course."

But Nicky didn't seem to be listening to him. She tapped one of the names on the screen.

"Amanda Monroe," Nicky said. She looked up at Holden. "I talked to her."

"When?"

"When I first started looking into Conceptions. No one at the clinic would speak to me so I asked around and found out that Amanda had once been the manager there. And she was fired."

Holden pulled up the rest of her file. Nothing about being fired in there, but then it wasn't a complete record of her employment at Conceptions. It only covered about a year. "Did she say why she was fired?"

"Amanda claimed it's because she had asked too many questions. She didn't get into specifics, though. When I pressed for details, she said she'd have to meet face-to-face, and she'd call me back to set that up. She never did, and after I found out about Carter, I didn't follow through on getting in touch with her."

Holden would do something about that. He sent a text to Grayson asking him to have someone question Amanda. The woman might have been fired because she'd learned about the illegal operation going on there.

Holden heard footsteps, and even though he knew nothing had triggered the alarm, he still put his hand over the gun in his holster. However, it was only Landon. At first Holden thought he was just there to refill his coffee—something he'd been doing ever since Holden had gone into the kitchen—but Landon had his phone in his hand instead of his cup.

"We might have gotten a break," Landon announced. "The CSIs at the inn found the body of the guy Holden shot. But they also found some blood. Not in the inn itself or by the body, but outside in that same area where we hit one of the kidnappers with the car door."

Holden hadn't noticed the guy bleeding, but the door had slammed into him hard. Or maybe one of the other men had been hurt. That was pretty much the best option here since Holden didn't want that blood to belong to one of the other babies who could have been born and then taken for ransom.

"The CSIs will try to match the DNA of the blood they found and the DNA from the body to someone in the system," Landon went on. "I'm guessing those men had records. Hope so anyway. Then we can get IDs on them."

Yes, and once they had a name, they could start looking for connections to their suspects. Of course, right now the only suspects they had were Oscar and Beatrice Minton. Still, this blood was a lot more than they'd had before, and Holden would take what he could get.

"What about the safe house?" Landon asked. "Anything on that yet?"

"It'll be ready soon. I didn't want to go through normal channels since I wasn't sure who or what we were dealing with, so I'm having a friend make the arrangements."

In an ideal world, he would have wanted those kidnappers caught and behind bars before he moved Nicky and Carter again, but Holden figured it was going to be a while before anything was ideal for any of them.

Landon went closer to Nicky and glanced down at the baby. Then he glanced at Nicky and Holden. "Makes you wonder why people say 'sleeping like a baby,' huh?" The corner of his mouth lifted. "Because babies aren't especially good sleepers." Landon's half smile quickly faded, though. "So, what will happen to him after we catch the dirtbags who brought him into this world?"

Good question, but Holden didn't have a good answer. Apparently neither did Nicky.

"My father won't back down on getting custody," she said. "But neither will I. Holden and his brothers probably won't, either."

"We won't," Holden assured her, and that meant Carter was going to be at the center of a fierce custody battle.

"Did Emmett or Annie have a will that might cover this sort of thing?" Landon asked.

Both Nicky and Holden shook their heads. Not only was there no will, Holden hadn't even had discussions with Emmett as to who would raise his future children if something happened to Annie and him. Of course, Annie and Emmett had been young, only in their early thirties, and there's no way his brother could have known that he'd have a son who would be born an orphan.

Landon made his way to the coffeepot and poured himself a fresh cup. Hesitated. "I know this is an out-there idea, but once we catch these kidnappers, you two should probably consider getting married."

Nicky choked on her own breath, and the sound caused Carter to wake up and start squirming. Holden didn't exactly choke, but he was certain Landon had lost his mind.

Landon turned back around to face them before he continued. "Oscar has a lot of money, and he probably owns a judge or two."

"He does," Nicky agreed.

Landon lifted his shoulder then, as if the rest was obvious. And it was. Oscar wouldn't back down on getting custody of his grandson, and one of the ways to possibly

stop him would be for Holden to present a united front—
with Nicky. Yeah, a marriage of convenience might work,
but there had to be another way.

Judging from Nicky's expression, she was on the same
page.

Holden's phone buzzed, and even though it was in his
pocket, the sound still caused Carter to start fussing again.
Nicky went over to rock him, but she didn't leave the room.
Probably because she'd seen Grayson's name on his phone
screen and knew this could be an update about the investigation.

Or bad news.

"Is everything okay?" Holden asked Grayson when he
answered.

Grayson's slight pause let Holden know that this wasn't
going to be just a simple update.

"The hospital just called," Grayson answered. "Paul's
dead."

Holden couldn't help it. He groaned, and Nicky must
have heard what Grayson had just said because more tears
sprang to her eyes. Landon must have heard it, too, because he set his coffee aside and took the baby from her.
Probably because she didn't look too steady.

"There's more," Grayson continued. "Paul didn't die
from the gunshot wound. We're still trying to work out
what happened, but someone murdered him in his hospital bed."

Chapter Eight

Nicky had hoped this nightmare would end soon, but apparently it was just getting started.

Oh, God.

Paul was dead.

"He was murdered?" Landon asked the moment Holden relayed what Grayson had told him. "How?"

"Grayson's still trying to figure that out, but it appears someone injected him with something."

Nicky's breath was so thin that it took her a moment to gather enough to speak. "Wasn't there a guard or a deputy outside Paul's hospital room?"

Holden nodded. "But he was in ICU so there were a lot of doctors and nurses coming and going."

Landon cursed. "And one of those who came and went might not have been a real doctor or nurse."

Another nod from Holden. "Grayson's getting the footage from the security cameras."

Nicky heard the doubt in Holden's voice. Saw it in his eyes, too. Because someone who could have waltzed right into ICU and murdered a man probably could have tampered with the security cameras. Or worn a disguise. Heck, even if they saw his or her face, the killer was no doubt just another hired gun who they wouldn't necessarily be able to link to the person who'd hired him.

Holden shifted his gaze to her. "With Paul dead, that means you're the only person who can confirm those files ever existed."

She heard something else in his voice now. Concern. And Nicky was certain she knew why.

"The kidnappers will come after me again," she said.

Neither man denied it. But that did bring her to something she wasn't sure she wanted to consider, but she had to—for the baby's sake.

"Maybe it's a good idea to put some distance between Carter and me." Mercy, it hurt just to say those words. She'd just found him and hadn't had nearly enough time with him. "I don't want him hurt if those men manage to get to me again."

Landon made a sound of agreement. Holden didn't.

"I doubt the kidnappers are just going to give up on taking the baby. They have a million-dollar incentive to get their hands on him again." Holden shook his head. "But it might be wise to keep Carter and you apart just so we can spread the kidnappers thin."

"They could just hire more kidnappers," Landon pointed out.

True, but Nicky was counting on that taking a while, and this way she could maybe buy Carter some time until they could catch the person responsible. Because now that person was also a killer.

Paul's killer.

Nicky squeezed her eyes shut a moment and started to pace. Holden had told her that because Paul was a PI, danger had been part of the job, but he wouldn't have been on this particular job if not for her. That ate away at her like acid. He'd died because of those files.

"Don't go off half-cocked over this," Holden warned

her. "I know you want to avenge Paul's death, but we have to be smart."

Normally, she would have been offended by a warning like that. She didn't go off half-cocked. Not since the incident with Drury.

"I have to do something," she said. And apparently that something caused her to get moving. She walked out of the kitchen, not heading anywhere in particular, but Nicky just had to move.

So did Holden.

Because he caught up with her in the massive foyer by the equally massive staircase, and he stepped in front of her.

"We'll catch the person responsible for this," he said, as if it was gospel.

Nicky knew that wasn't necessarily true, but she wanted to hang on to the hope. *Had* to hang on to it.

Holden gave a heavy sigh, reached out and pulled her into his arms. She could tell from the stiffness of his muscles that this was probably the last thing he wanted to do, and she hated that he felt the need to comfort her.

Hated even more that she needed the comforting, but it was good to be in Holden's arms again. He might have thought the same thing—*might have*—because his muscles relaxed a little, and she felt a tension of a different kind.

That blasted attraction.

There wasn't time for it, and even if there had been, it wasn't something Holden wanted. Because he would never be able to trust her. Remembering that had Nicky stepping back.

At least that was the plan.

But Holden tightened his grip on her. "Swear to me that you won't do anything dangerous," he whispered.

It was another warning, one that she expected, but that

wasn't a warning tone. The attraction again, and Nicky got a full dose of that heat when she pulled back enough for their eyes to meet.

Their gazes held.

For a long time.

And during that long time, his breath hit against her mouth. Almost a kiss. With the way he was looking at her, she thought she might get a real kiss. One they'd both regret, of course, but with the need stirring in her, Nicky thought the regret might be worth it.

Holden apparently didn't, though.

He eased away from her. Oh, no. She felt a lecture coming on, but before he could tell her why a kiss or anything else wasn't going to happen, his phone buzzed again.

Another call from Grayson.

Since this could be news about Paul's murder, Nicky automatically moved closer to Holden so she could hear, but maybe he'd had enough of their closeness because he put the call on speaker.

"I have a woman on the other line," Grayson said. "Her name is Amanda Monroe, and she said she needs to speak to Nicky. Do you know who she is?"

"I do," Nicky answered. "She's the former manager at Conceptions."

"Did she say why she wanted to talk to Nicky?" Holden asked.

"No, but she says it's important. Is your phone secure?"

"It is," Holden assured him.

"Then I'll give her your number. I probably shouldn't have to remind you to record the conversation."

"No reminder needed." Holden hit the end-call button, and they waited.

Of course, time seemed to grind to a halt, and it didn't help that Nicky's imagination started to run wild. Was it a coincidence that Amanda was calling so soon after Paul's murder? Maybe. But Amanda had said she would get back to her, and maybe it had taken her this long to do it.

Even though Nicky had been anticipating the call, she still got a jolt when the buzzing sound of Holden's phone cut through the silence. He answered it and also hit a button to record the conversation.

"Nicky?" Amanda immediately said.

"I'm here. What's wrong?" She could hear the panic in the woman's voice.

"Thank God you remember me. I wasn't sure if you would."

"I remember you," Nicky confirmed. "You said you would get back in touch with me, and you didn't."

"I couldn't," Amanda explained. The woman made a hoarse sob. "I'm in so much trouble, and I need your help."

"What's wrong?" Nicky repeated at the same time that Holden said, "Is this something you should be reporting to the police?"

"Yes, I should," she said, answering Holden's question. Another sob. "But I'm not sure who I can trust because someone's trying to kill me."

Mercy. Not this. There had already been too many attacks. Especially on people who might have answers about what had gone on at Conceptions. And as the former office manager, Amanda definitely might have those answers.

"Where are you?" Holden asked the woman.

"On the way to the Silver Creek sheriff's office. I'll be there in about an hour. Can I trust you? Can I trust Nicky?"

"Yes," Holden answered. "But can we trust you?"

"Yes," Amanda responded without hesitation. "I'm not the one who tried to kill you."

There was enough emotion dripping from her voice,

but Nicky knew that emotion could be faked. "Then who is trying to kill us?"

"I don't know." Another sob and then Amanda repeated those three words. "But I have some information that might help. Information that I'll only give to Nicky."

Holden rolled his eyes. "Why only her? If this is a police matter, you should be giving it to the cops."

"Because I know she's trying to make sense of all of this. That's why she called me to try to figure out what was going on at Conceptions. I want to make sense of it, too. And I want to make sure the baby is safe."

Everything inside Nicky went still. "The baby?"

"The newborn baby boy," Amanda confirmed. "I was the surrogate who gave birth to your nephew."

"AMANDA COULD BE LYING," Holden reminded Nicky again.

Nicky nodded, obviously understanding that, but that wasn't going to stop her from seeing the woman. Holden had known that from the moment he ended the call, and that's why he'd gotten started on making security arrangements.

Not exactly easy.

Not exactly foolproof, either.

Yes, Holden wanted answers as badly as Nicky, but he also didn't want this to be an opportunity for the kidnappers to come after the baby, or for the killer to come after Nicky. That's why two of his cousins, Josh and Mason, had come to the house to help guard the baby. Landon would be staying behind with them, too, and Gage and Dade would be following Nicky and Holden to the sheriff's office.

This would tie up a lot of manpower—five deputies—so Holden only hoped Amanda would give them some information that was worth the trip.

"Too bad Amanda didn't just tell us everything over

the phone," Holden grumbled as he pulled away from the house. It wasn't the first time he'd grumbled or thought that, and it wouldn't be the last.

And it wasn't as if Holden hadn't tried to have the woman fess up. He had. But Amanda had been just as adamant about having a face-to-face meeting with Nicky. Holden hoped that wasn't because Amanda was trying to lure them into the middle of another attack.

"When you first spoke to Amanda, did she mention anything about being a surrogate?" Holden asked.

Nicky quickly shook her head, and like Holden, she kept watch all around them. It was something they'd have to do on the entire trip to the sheriff's office. On the return trip as well, since someone could try to follow them back to Kayla's ranch.

Nicky made a sound to indicate she was giving his question some thought. "But if she's telling the truth about being a surrogate, that means she delivered Carter only a week ago. We might be able to tell from looking at her if she recently gave birth, especially since the doctor thought Carter had had a C-section birth."

True, but to confirm something like that meant Amanda would have to submit to a physical exam. Since Amanda didn't seem in a trusting mode, that might not happen.

Plus, there was something else bugging Holden.

"If Amanda really was a surrogate, then why would Conceptions Clinic have fired her? Why would they want to risk pissing off someone who was carrying a million-dollar baby?"

Nicky obviously processed that as well. "Maybe she wasn't actually fired. Maybe that was a front so she could take maternity leave."

And if so, that could mean Amanda might still be working for Conceptions and the person who'd orchestrated all of this. That would also mean just seeing her could be dangerous.

"If this does turn out to be a trap," Holden said, "there's a gun in the glove compartment. That doesn't mean I want to return fire," he quickly added. "But I want you to be able to protect yourself."

That caused some of the color to drain from her face. Nicky had no doubt already considered some of the bad things that could happen, but it was another thing to hear it spelled out.

Holden's phone rang, and he saw Grayson's name on the screen again. Hell. He hoped this wasn't more bad news. He put the call on speaker so that he could keep his hands free.

"No sign of Amanda yet," Grayson said. "But I just got a visitor. Beatrice Minton. She wasn't supposed to be here until later, but she said that didn't work with her schedule."

At least she'd shown up. "Has she volunteered anything?"

"Only that she's not happy that the Silver Creek lawmen seem to have a vendetta against her."

"What?" Nicky and Holden said in unison.

"Yeah. She actually used the word *vendetta* and said the interview I scheduled with her is akin to police harassment. She's a piece of work all right and seems a lot more concerned about this interview than about her missing husband."

"I want to ask her about that," Holden insisted. He wanted to ask Beatrice a lot of things including, if she knew anything about what had happened at Conceptions.

"I'll try to keep Beatrice here as long as I can so you'll get a chance to see her, but she's got her lawyer with her and I'm sure he'll advise her not to stay too long," Grayson continued. "How far out are you now?"

"About five miles from town. No one was on the road when I left the house, and I haven't spotted another vehicle."

But just saying that must have tempted fate because that's when Holden saw an SUV just ahead. Not only wasn't it moving, but it also appeared to be in a ditch.

"I'll have to call you back," he said to Grayson, and ended the call.

Holden took his gun from his holster. "It's just a precaution," he told Nicky when he heard her suck in her breath. "The person could be drunk and just have run off the road."

However, with their luck Holden figured it was just as likely to be an SUV filled with kidnappers who would start shooting at them. He prayed this trip didn't turn out to be a fatal mistake.

He slowed his car to a crawl, and behind him Gage and Dade did the same. Once Holden was closer to the SUV, he could see that the passenger window was down and that someone was inside. Not a gunman.

But a woman.

And she was slumped over the steering wheel.

Holden motioned for Nicky to get down, but as she was sinking lower into the seat, she also had a look in the SUV. "That's Amanda."

He couldn't see much of her face, only the woman's brunette hair. "You're sure?"

Nicky nodded, and she touched her fingers to her mouth. "Is she dead?"

Maybe. But Holden sure as hell hoped not. There'd already been one murder. And that was more than enough. Especially if it involved a woman who could have helped them.

"Stay in the car," he told Nicky. "And call Gage and tell him what's going on."

"What *is* going on?" she asked.

"I'm going to check and see if Amanda's alive." It probably wasn't the wisest move, but if the woman was hurt, he needed to get an ambulance out here fast.

Holden waited until Nicky had finished her call with Gage before he stepped out of the car. Gage and Dade did the same, both of them drawing their weapons.

"Keep watch," Holden warned them. "This could be a setup to get to you." Of course, they likely already knew that since their gazes were firing all around them, and they were primed for an ambush.

Holden took aim at the SUV and started toward it. Slow, easy steps while he tried to listen for any sound of movement coming from inside the vehicle. He didn't hear movement, but he did hear a sound.

A moan.

Amanda lifted her head and looked at him. "Help me," she said after another moan. That's when he saw the blood on her cheek.

Holden still didn't go charging toward her. He took his time, though it was hard when she kept repeating that "help me." When he made it to the SUV, he lifted his gun, taking aim in case someone was in the back waiting to attack. But there was no one.

Amanda was alone.

And in pain.

"Call the ambulance," Holden told Gage.

Holden opened the passenger's side door and had a better look at the woman. Other than the blood on her face, there were no other visible injuries. He also didn't see any weapons, but that didn't mean there weren't any in the SUV.

"I'm Marshal Holden Ryland," he said. "And you're Amanda?"

She gave a weak nod. "Help me, please."

"Help is on the way. Tell me what happened to you."

It took her a moment and several deep breaths. "Someone ran me off the road." More of those deep breaths. "I'm not sure who it was. The car came out of nowhere."

There was a side road a few yards back, but there was no one on it now. No visible signs of damage to her SUV, either, and there was something else about this that didn't look right.

"Why didn't your air bag deploy?" Holden asked.

She lifted her head again, staring at the steering wheel as if trying to figure that out. "I don't know. Maybe it's not working."

Or maybe someone had tampered with it.

Of course, Holden had another theory about what had gone on here. Amanda had to know she was a suspect so maybe all of this had been orchestrated to throw suspicion off her.

"How long before the ambulance gets here?" she muttered.

"Not long. While you're waiting, can you answer some questions?"

She shook her head. "I didn't see who did this to me."

Yeah, he got that. "I meant questions about the baby, about Conceptions."

That caused her to pull back her shoulders, and she suddenly looked a lot more alert than she had been. "I can't talk about that yet."

"Why not?" And she'd better have a damn good reason for it.

Tears sprang to her eyes, but like the moaning and the accident, Holden wasn't sure they were genuine, either. If he was wrong about all of this, then he would owe her a huge apology, but she wasn't getting that from him now.

"I did some things, and I don't want to go to jail," she said, her voice cracking. "I need...whatever it's called."

"Immunity?" Holden asked.

"Yes. I didn't know what was going on there. I swear, I didn't know until it was too late, but I was too scared to report it. Too scared that someone would silence me for good."

Maybe. Again, he was going to withhold judgment on her innocence. "What was going on there?" he persisted.

"The babies," Amanda said after a long pause. "It was all about getting the money for the babies."

They'd already figured out that part. He needed more. "Who set all of this up?"

Amanda didn't say anything for a long time. "If I tell you, you'll have to arrest her so she doesn't come after me."

"Her?" Holden asked.

Amanda groaned, maybe from pain and maybe because she just didn't want to say it aloud. "The woman who's behind this. Her name is Beatrice Minton."

Chapter Nine

Beatrice.

It wasn't exactly a surprise that Amanda had claimed the senator's wife was behind the things going on at Conceptions Clinic. After all, Beatrice was on Nicky and Landon's suspect list, too.

But so was Amanda.

Holden had explained the reasons why he thought Amanda's accident looked staged. No damage to her vehicle. No skid marks on the asphalt. No serious injuries. However, there were injuries—a cut to Amanda's chin and some bruises—but Nicky was hoping the doctor would be able to tell them a whole lot more once he examined the woman.

Especially be able to tell them if Amanda had indeed had a C-section recently.

"You know the drill," Holden said when they pulled up in front of the Silver Creek sheriff's office.

Nicky did. She moved out of the car as soon as she opened the door, and Holden was right behind her. Behind him, Dade came in. He'd followed them to the sheriff's office, but Gage had gone in the ambulance with Amanda.

Along with the dispatcher, there were two other deputies in the squad room. Josh and Kara Duggan. Nicky didn't know Kara that well, but she'd heard the woman had worked for San Antonio PD before coming to Silver Creek.

Dade immediately went to his desk to get to work, but she and Holden went in search of Grayson. They found him in his office. Alone.

"Did Beatrice leave?" Holden asked.

"No. I wouldn't let her, not after you told me what Amanda said. I'm just letting her and her lawyer cool their heels in an interview room." Grayson paused. "I was also hoping you'd have more for me before I go in there. For instance, some proof that Beatrice really is guilty of something other than being a pain in the neck."

Holden had to shake his head. "No proof, and yes, I did press Amanda all the way up to the time the ambulance arrived, and she insisted that she couldn't say more until I could promise her that she wouldn't be charged with anything."

Grayson huffed and leaned back in his chair. "It'd be nice to know what exactly she did wrong." His attention wandered to the room across the hall where Beatrice was. "But maybe Beatrice will be willing to spill something if I tell her she'd just been accused of some assorted felonies."

Nicky doubted Beatrice would say anything incriminating, not with her lawyer there to stop her, but Grayson was right. If he managed to shake her up a little, then Beatrice might tell them the pieces that Amanda was withholding.

Grayson stood, ready to go into the interview room, but then he stopped and looked at Nicky. "I'm guessing you'd like to be in there when I'm questioning Beatrice, but I need to keep this official. That means as a marshal, Holden can be in there, but you'll have to watch from the observation room. There's a two-way mirror so you'll be able to see and hear everything."

He was right. Nicky did want to be in there to face the

woman who might be responsible for this nightmare, but she also didn't want to do anything that would compromise an arrest if they did manage to get enough to put Beatrice behind bars.

Grayson led her to the observation room, and Nicky immediately went to the mirror. Beatrice was there all right—pacing with her arms folded over her chest. A man in a suit was seated at the table.

Beatrice looked exactly like the photos that Nicky had seen of her. Blond hair that tumbled onto her shoulders, the curls and waves looking as if they'd each been perfectly placed. Tasteful makeup that was as flawless as the rest of her. Ditto for her clothes. In the photos with her husband, Beatrice often wore blue, probably to match her eyes, and today was no different.

When the door opened and Holden and Grayson walked in, Beatrice whirled around to face them. Or rather to glare at them.

"I've been waiting a long time," she snarled. "Need I remind you that I'm doing you a favor by coming in here to answer your idiotic questions? I guess you were too busy eating doughnuts and drinking coffee to get in here and finish this so I can go home."

Nicky could see why Grayson had called the woman a pain in the neck.

"No doughnuts or coffee," Grayson said. "Holden was waiting for an ambulance to take a woman to the hospital."

"Was it Nicky Hart?" Beatrice asked without hesitation. However, she didn't wait for an answer. "She's been hounding me for a story about my husband, and I'm fed up with her, too."

Holden took a step closer to the woman, looked her straight in the eye. "Why would you think Nicky needed an ambulance?"

Beatrice shrugged as if the answer was obvious. "She does all those articles about criminals, crimes and such. I figure there's someone out there who might want to silence her."

A chill went through Nicky. Because it was true. Someone did want to silence her for good. Was that someone Beatrice? If so, Beatrice wasn't doing much to cover up her guilt. Maybe because there was no guilt for her to cover up.

"It wasn't Nicky who was hurt," Holden continued a moment later. "It was Amanda Monroe."

That got a reaction from Beatrice. Her eyes widened. "The office manager from Conceptions Fertility Clinic?"

"That's the one," Grayson said. "What do you know about her?"

Beatrice actually seemed surprised by the question, as if it was the last thing she'd expected they would want to know. So maybe this wasn't Beatrice's attempt to cover her involvement after all.

"I don't actually know her," Beatrice answered. "The only time I met her was when she was still working at the clinic. She did the initial paperwork when Lee and I went in to start the process for my egg harvesting." She paused. "How was she hurt? *Why* was she hurt?"

Holden went even closer, violating the woman's personal space. "You tell me. Amanda said you're the one behind her attack."

Beatrice dropped back a step, and she volleyed some stunned glances between Grayson and Holden. "Amanda said…?" But she stopped and made a sound of outrage. "I had nothing to do with anything that happened to her." She jammed her thumb against her chest. "I'm the victim here."

Her lawyer practically jumped to his feet and reached out for her, but Beatrice slapped his hand away. "I'm the victim," she repeated. "And I won't be treated like a criminal when I've done nothing wrong."

She no longer had that pain-in-the-neck tone or glare. Beatrice sank down onto one of the chairs and buried her face in her hands for a moment.

"We need to talk before you say anything else," her lawyer insisted.

"She needs to talk now," Holden argued. "Someone ran Amanda off the road, and Nicky was nearly killed. I want answers about that."

Beatrice shook her head. "I don't know if what happened to me is even connected to them."

Grayson went closer to the woman, too. "Then tell us what did happen, and we'll figure out if it's connected or not."

"Mrs. Minton," the lawyer said, his voice a warning for her to stay quiet.

But it was a warning she ignored. "Lee and I went to Conceptions Fertility Clinic about a year and a half ago. I desperately wanted a baby and had been unable to get pregnant. I went through all the egg harvestings, all the procedures, but I still wasn't able to conceive. Lee said we had to stop trying…that it was putting too much strain on our marriage."

"Was it?" Holden asked, and Nicky was thankful he had because she wanted to hear the answer, too.

Beatrice shrugged. Then her eyes narrowed a little after she paused. "This stays here in this room, and you'd better not breathe a word of it to anyone else." Despite the fact that neither Holden nor Grayson agreed to that, she continued. "Lee was having an affair, and that was putting far more strain on our marriage than my trying to have our baby, his heir."

She spat out the last two words like venom. Clearly, Beatrice was not a happy wife.

"Who was he having an affair with?" Grayson asked.

"The latest one is some bimbo ex-beauty queen. Sharon Bachman."

Nicky knew the name and had heard the rumors linking Sharon to the senator. But then, several other names had come up, too. Apparently, Lee had a roving eye. Of course, Beatrice had known that when she married him because he'd cheated on his first wife with Beatrice.

"Do you think Sharon had anything to do with your husband's disappearance?" Holden continued.

"Maybe," Beatrice readily admitted. "The two could have run off together. I suspect he'll turn up when he realizes what a mess he's made of things. Well, I'm not taking him back this time. I won't be treated like dirt again."

The woman certainly had a lot of anger, but if what she was saying was all true, then Nicky could understand that anger. Well, except for the fact that Beatrice had made her own bed by cheating with a cheater.

"There's more," Beatrice said a moment later. The lawyer tried to stop her again, but Beatrice gave him a stern look of her own. "I have to tell someone, and it might as well be them."

"What do you have to tell us?" Holden prompted when Nicky didn't continue.

She took a few more moments, some deep breaths as well. "A couple of days after my husband went missing, I got a call. The voice sounded mechanical, like it was a computer speaking. Anyway, he said that Lee and I had a son. One that'd been born using a surrogate, and that if I wanted the baby, I was going to have to pay a million dollars to get him."

Oh, mercy.

That put the knot back in Nicky's stomach. That was the same thing that'd happened to her father. Of course, it didn't mean Beatrice was telling the truth, but there were tears in the woman's eyes now.

"I told the caller that I didn't believe him," Beatrice went on. "And he said he had proof. DNA proof. He claimed that they'd implanted my embryo into a surrogate, and that she'd given birth to our child."

"And you believed that?" Grayson asked.

"Not at first, but then I got this package with photos of the baby, and I knew that was my son." Her voice was trembling now. So was Beatrice. Or at least she was pretending to tremble. "They said if I went to the cops that I wouldn't see the baby so I went to Lee's financial manager and begged him for the money. My name's not on Lee's accounts so I couldn't just take it. He finally gave it to me, and I arranged to pay the ransom."

Holden cursed. "That was risky and stupid. You could have been killed. That's why people take matters like this to the cops."

"I know that now." A hoarse sob tore from her throat. "I dropped off the money in a park just like the kidnapper asked, but they demanded more. A half a million more." She looked at Holden, and while she was blinking hard, as if trying to stave off tears, there weren't any actual tears in her eyes.

"Did you pay it?" Holden asked.

She nodded. "Again, I had to beg Lee's financial manager, and he told me that it was all I was going to get, not a penny more. He went with me that time to pay the ransom." Beatrice paused. "And we got the baby."

Nicky didn't know who looked more surprised by that—Grayson, Holden or her.

"Where's the baby now?" Holden demanded.

"At one of Lee's estates. I hired three bodyguards to stay with him so I could come here, but that's why I'm so anxious to get back to him. I'm afraid someone will try to take him."

That could happen despite the fact the kidnappers had gotten a million and a half out of the deal. They could want more. In fact, that could have been their plan all along, to continue to get as much as possible from the birth parents.

However, hearing all of this reminded Nicky of something she'd read when she had been researching the senator, and while Grayson probably wasn't going to like the interruption, Nicky went to the interview room and tapped on the door.

Holden was the one to open it, and yes, she'd been right about Grayson not liking this. He shot her a scowl, but maybe the scowl would ease up when he heard what she had to say.

"Beatrice signed a prenup agreement," Nicky whispered to Holden. But obviously she didn't whisper it softly enough because Beatrice got to her feet again.

"So?" Beatrice challenged.

Nicky hadn't intended on spelling this out herself, but now everyone had their eyes on her. "So, if your husband divorces you or even if he dies, you won't get any of his money or properties."

Nicky had been guessing about the dying part, but judging from the way Beatrice's chin came up, she'd been right about that.

"What are you implying?" Beatrice snapped.

Since Nicky had already opened this particular box, she emptied the rest of the contents. "That maybe you arranged for the surrogate to have the baby. Then you set up the kidnapping so that you could milk money from your husband's accounts."

The flash of temper went through Beatrice's eyes, and she moved as if to launch herself at Nicky. The lawyer intervened, stepping between them, but he had to take hold of Beatrice's shoulders to stop her.

"If you repeat that to anyone, I'll sue you for everything you have," Beatrice warned her.

"Are you saying you didn't arrange for your own son's birth and then *kidnapping*?" Holden asked. Unlike Beatrice, his voice was calm. So was he, and that seemed to agitate Beatrice even more.

"I'm not saying anything else to any of you." Beatrice snatched up her purse. "This interview is over."

"Think again," Grayson said. "You just admitted to a participation in a crime."

"A crime where I was the victim!" Beatrice fired back.

"A crime where your son was the victim," Holden amended. "You didn't report that crime to the police, and by doing that you concealed critical information in a federal investigation."

Grayson nodded. "You're not going anywhere until we get a full written statement about what happened," he added. "Even then you might not be leaving anytime soon. The faster you cooperate, the faster you might get out of here. *Might*."

The lawyer didn't argue with that, which meant he knew his client had just dug herself a massive legal hole. But it wouldn't necessarily lead to Beatrice's arrest because if the woman was telling the truth about all of this, she'd done what any normal person would have done to get her baby.

"I'll take her statement," Grayson said to Holden. "Why don't Nicky and you head on out?"

"Remember what I said about suing you," Beatrice snarled when Nicky and Holden turned to leave. "I will if you say a word about this to anyone."

It wasn't even worth her breath for Nicky to respond. Nor did she have time. That's because the moment they were in the hall, Holden's phone buzzed, and she saw Gage's name on the screen.

"How's Amanda?" Holden asked. He put the call on speaker, but he didn't do that until after they were out of earshot of Beatrice.

"I'm not sure. Amanda's lawyer showed up, and he won't let us talk to her. The doctor wanted to keep her overnight for observation, but after she found out a man had been murdered here earlier, she insisted on being transferred to a hospital in San Antonio."

Nicky couldn't blame the woman for not wanting to stay there, but it could also be part of some ploy to make her look innocent. Because if Amanda was indeed the one behind this, then she would have been responsible for that murder.

"I'll go with her to make sure she doesn't try to run or do something stupid," Gage continued. "How'd it go with Beatrice?"

"She claims that kidnappers had her son. A son born under the same circumstances as Carter."

"Claims?" Gage repeated, unable to hide the skepticism in his voice.

"Yeah. Grayson's with her now, and I'm hoping he can sort out the truth. Maybe you can do the same thing with Amanda when her lawyer lets you talk to her."

"Funny thing about that—the lawyer's not going to let that happen. But Amanda did hint that she'd be willing to talk to Nicky and you. Any chance you two can get to the hospital before she's moved?"

Holden groaned, and Nicky knew that was the last place he wanted her. However, it was the one place where they might learn whatever role Amanda played in all of this.

"We can go there now," Nicky said.

It took Holden a moment before he agreed. He ended the call, his attention immediately going to Kara, probably because his two cousins were on the phone.

"I need backup while I go to the hospital with Nicky," Holden told her.

Kara nodded, called out to the others that she was leaving, but Holden had them wait inside until he went to the parking lot and drove a cruiser directly in front of the door. The moment they were in the cruiser, he didn't waste any time driving away.

"You think Beatrice was telling the truth about anything?" Holden asked her.

"Yes, about the affair. About taking the money from her husband's account, too. But remember, there was nothing in the files about a surrogate being successfully implanted with the Minton's baby." Nicky paused. "That doesn't mean it didn't happen, though."

"And it doesn't mean that Beatrice wasn't the one behind it," Holden added. "This way, she could get the money, an heir to the Minton fortune, and she wouldn't have to ruin her figure to do it."

Yes, Beatrice seemed vain enough for that to have been a consideration.

"We need to find out what happened to her husband," Nicky said, thinking out loud. Of course, plenty of people had been searching for the senator for over two weeks now, and there was still no sign of him.

Maybe for a reason.

"You believe that Beatrice could have murdered him?" Nicky asked.

"I do." Since Holden didn't hesitate, it meant his mind was already going in that direction. "Beatrice could have killed him because of the affairs, but then hidden his body until she had the money she could get from his estate."

True, but Nicky had to shake her head. "With a Minton heir, she'd get the entire estate anyway."

"Yeah, but it would likely have conditions attached. Minton probably has a will where he named a trustee to control any heir's accounts. That could mean Beatrice wouldn't have been able to touch the money for herself."

Nicky had to agree with that, and it meant they had some more digging to do. This was where she could help since she'd already established contact with a lot of the senator's family and friends. If there was dirt to dish on Beatrice, one of them might do it.

Holden pulled into the parking lot, slowly, and looked around. "I'll pull up to the door again," he instructed. "You two get out and stay in the waiting room while I park."

He turned in the lane to do just that when Nicky felt the jolt. It was as if someone had shot out one of the tires, but she certainly hadn't heard a gunshot. But it didn't take long, only a couple of seconds, before she heard something.

A blast.

And it ripped through the cruiser.

HOLDEN HADN'T SEEN what had caused the blast, but he'd certainly heard it.

It was deafening. He felt it, too, because the blast lifted the front end of the cruiser off the ground and then slammed it back down again.

Nicky, Kara and Holden were all wearing their seat belts, thank God, but that didn't stop them from being slung around like rag dolls.

Holden's shoulder slammed into the steering wheel, and the pain stabbed through him. So hard that he thought he saw stars. But he fought through that and checked on Nicky and Kara in the backseat. Both women looked dazed, but they didn't seem to have any injuries.

But that might not last.

Holden got a glimpse of something he darn sure didn't want to see. It was one of those ski-mask-wearing thugs like the one who had attacked them the day before. The guy was armed, and he was crouched down behind a car. He didn't stay crouched for long, however. He started running toward the cruiser.

"On your left," Holden warned Kara.

The deputy was moving slowly, but she'd already drawn her gun. She pivoted in that direction now, and Holden was about to do the same when something else caught his eye. Something that sent his heart into overdrive.

A second gunman.

This one was coming at them from the other side.

"Stay down," Holden warned Nicky, but that was only a temporary measure.

Holden hit the locks on the doors just as the first shot blasted into the window next to Kara. The glass was bullet-resistant, but that didn't mean bullets wouldn't eventually get through. And the gunman was trying to make that happen sooner rather than later. He started firing nonstop at the window.

And he wasn't doing that alone.

The other guy started shooting at Holden's window.

Holden tried to get the cruiser moving, but the explosion had disabled the engine in addition to putting a big crater in the concrete in front of them. He threw the cruiser into Reverse and tried again.

Nothing.

"I'm calling for backup," Kara said, taking out her phone.

Good. But even though the sheriff's office was just

up the street, Grayson might not be able to get there fast enough.

"Gage is inside the hospital," Holden reminded Kara, and the deputy immediately called him.

"He's on the way out," Kara said a moment later, though it was hard to hear what she was saying. Both gunmen were continuing to rip apart the glass in the windows.

"If they get through, you stop the one on your side," Holden told the deputy. "Don't let him get to Nicky."

Because he would kill her.

This wasn't a kidnapping attempt. These men wanted her dead. Or at least their boss did, and he or she had paid them to commit murder.

"I need a gun," Nicky insisted.

Holden got her one out of the glove compartment, though he hated the idea of her having to shoot to protect herself. He and Kara were in law enforcement so it was different for them. This was their job. But as a reporter, Nicky hadn't signed on for a gunfight in the middle of a parking lot.

In the distance Holden heard sirens. A welcome sound, but he saw something else that would help, too.

Gage.

His cousin was skulking around some cars, coming toward them. Holden only hoped the gunmen didn't see him first because unlike the thugs, Gage wasn't wearing body armor.

Holden had to do something to make sure Gage didn't get shot while trying to help them. He lowered his window, just enough to stick out the barrel of his gun, and he took aim at the gunman. Well, he took aim as best he could considering he had no room to maneuver. He also had to be careful. He couldn't just fire off a random shot because it might hit an innocent bystander. He waited until he had the best shot he thought he might get.

And Holden fired.

His shot hit the guy in the chest. Of course, the Kevlar was protecting him from a kill shot, but he staggered back and stopped firing.

Holden knew it wouldn't last, knew he only had a couple of seconds at most before the gunman regained his balance. Holden adjusted his aim. Fired again.

This time Holden didn't shoot him in the chest. But rather in the head.

The guy went down like a rock.

Holden pivoted to try to do the same to the second man, but Gage was already in position. The thug probably didn't even see Gage since his focus was on his shots, which were eating their way through the window. And he succeeded.

The bullet came crashing through the cruiser.

Holden yelled for Nicky and Kara to get down. They did, but he couldn't tell if either were hit. That's because the shooter left cover to come in for the kill.

Big mistake.

Gage left cover, too.

The thug saw him at the last moment, and he pivoted in that direction. But Gage got off the shot he needed. No shot to the chest. This one went into the guy's head, and like his comrade, he fell to the ground.

Holden felt a split second of relief. But it didn't last. That's because he looked in the backseat to check on Kara and Nicky.

And that's when he saw the blood.

Chapter Ten

"It's just a cut," Nicky said.

She wasn't sure how many more times she'd have to remind Holden of that before it sank in. Or got that troubled expression off his face. He had the look of a man who'd just made a huge mistake.

And he might indeed see it that way.

Nicky saw it differently. They were all alive, and the only injury had happened when the gunman's bullet had sliced across Nicky's arm. It'd stung like fire then. Still did. However, she didn't want Holden to see any signs of her pain because he was already beating himself up enough about this.

"All done," the nurse told them when she finished the stitches and placed a bandage over it. "The doctor's writing a script for some pain meds—"

"No need," Nicky interrupted. She didn't want them—not just for Holden's sake, but also because she didn't want a fuzzy mind. There were too many things about this investigation they still had to work out.

The nurse glanced between Holden and her as if waiting for Nicky to change her mind about those meds. "Okay, then I'll get your paperwork so you can leave."

"Could you make it fast?" Nicky asked. "I have some things I want to check on."

The nurse shrugged, mumbled that she would see what she could do and walked out, leaving Holden and her alone in the treatment room. Nicky immediately got up and would have started out, too, but Holden stepped in front of her.

"You were just shot," he snarled.

"No, I was just grazed. I'm fine, and I want to talk to Amanda before she leaves."

Holden didn't budge. He just stared at her. Then, he reached out, put his fingertips on the bandage and used his thumb to measure the distance between the graze and her heart.

"Three inches," he said, "and that bullet could have killed you."

"Yes, but it didn't."

He looked down at the space and must have realized that his thumb was not only over her heart, but was also on her breast. She expected him to jerk back his hand, and he did move it, but Holden did it slowly. In the same motion, he lowered his head.

And he kissed her.

Nicky wasn't sure who was more surprised by the kiss, but the sound she made got trapped between their mouths. This wasn't some little peck of comfort, either. Holden kissed the right way, and he eased his arm around her, inching her closer to him.

He was careful with her arm. Careful with her. Treating her as if she was fragile glass that might shatter in his hands. She wasn't sure how he could manage to deepen the kiss with such a soft touch, but he did it. When he finally pulled away from her, Nicky wasn't just breathless. She was plenty aroused.

Hardly the right time for it since they were in the ER.

"I'm sorry about you getting shot," Holden said. "I'm not sorry about the kiss, though."

Yes, he was, because he groaned right after the words had left his mouth.

"It's okay," Nicky assured him. "It doesn't have to mean anything."

That was a lie. It did mean something, and it broke down barriers that she needed in place to protect her heart. Obviously, all the danger had made her a little crazy because she was already thinking about what it would be like to land in bed with Holden again.

Oh, yes, she was definitely a little crazy.

And maybe it'd done the same thing to Holden.

As if to prove that it didn't have to mean anything—or to disprove it—he pulled her back to him. In the same motion, his mouth came to hers for another kiss. This meant something all right. It was deeper than the other one, and there wasn't a hint of sympathy in it.

It was pure heat.

It didn't stay just a kiss, either. Holden pulled her closer and closer to him until they were body-to-body. Pressed together in all the right places. Or rather the wrong places, since it fired up that heat even more.

Being in his arms brought back all the old memories. Of the time when they'd been lovers. Hard to forget something that amazing, but they were clearly making new memories, too. Ones that Holden might not want to be making with her.

That didn't stop him, though.

He staggered back, taking her with him, and he landed against the wall. She landed against him. Her breasts against his chest. Against his hand, too. That's because Holden slipped his hand between them and cupped her breast while he took those clever kisses to her neck.

She melted and forgot all about the gunshot. The pain. Heck, she forgot how to breathe.

Nicky figured at any second he would come to his senses and stop this. He didn't. The kiss raged on until she felt it in every part of her body. Until she was the one who was grappling to pull him closer.

Until she was thinking that sex was a possibility.

It wasn't.

Nicky repeated that to herself several times, but it didn't sink in until Holden finally pulled back, and she could see the apology in his eyes. An apology that was about to make it to his mouth.

"Don't say you're sorry," she told him.

He stared at her. A long time. "We don't need this right now. Agreed?"

She nodded. Easy to agree to that considering they'd just been attacked. "Will it help if we agree?" she asked.

"Not at all," he drawled. "Still, I have to try."

Nicky had to nod at that, too. They did have to try, but she figured they both knew they were failing big-time. They'd just made out in a hospital ER so there wasn't much chance of resisting each other if they ever got some time alone. Thankfully, that probably wouldn't happen anytime soon. Then, when this was over, she could stand back and assess whatever the heck she was going to do about these wildfire feelings she had for Holden.

"You're sure you're up to seeing Amanda?" Holden asked.

Good. They were moving on to something they should be doing. Even though her body disagreed with that.

"Of course I want to see her." That was possibly a lie, too. She wasn't up to seeing anyone right now except Holden and Carter, but Amanda might tell Nicky things that she wouldn't tell the cops.

Holden stared at her as if trying to decide whether to call her on that lie or not. He didn't. "This way," he finally said, and he started with her down the hall.

Nicky spotted two uniformed guards, one at each end, and she figured there were other guards and deputies posted around the building. The explosion had happened just yards from the entrance, and security was going to be tight.

"Nothing on the dead guys yet. They had no IDs on them," Holden said. "I got an update while you were getting a shot to numb your arm for the stitches."

Yes, she'd heard him just on the other side of the curtain, but Nicky hadn't been able to make out much of the conversation.

"Their prints should be in the system, though," he added a moment later. "So, once Grayson has those, we'll probably get a match."

Good. That was the first step in figuring out who hired them.

But Holden wasn't acting as if that was good news.

"Is something wrong?" Nicky finally asked.

"Your father found out about the attack. And he knew you'd been hurt. He called Grayson before you were even examined."

"How did he find out?" However, Nicky waved off the question. Waved and then flinched when she felt the pain in her arm. Obviously, the numbing meds were already wearing off.

Holden noticed the flinch all right, she thought. He cursed. And the muscles in his jaw got very tight again. Best to get his focus back on the investigation rather than her injury.

"What did my father say to Grayson?" she asked.

That tightened his muscles even more. "Oscar says he'll

use this to get custody of the baby, that it's not safe for Carter to be around you because someone's trying to kill you."

Nicky wished she could argue with that, but it was true. Still, that didn't mean her father should have the child.

"Grayson's going to call Oscar and tell him to back off, that the baby is in protective custody," Holden added. "*My* protective custody."

She doubted that would get her father to back down even a little, but it was better than nothing. Plus, it was good to know they had Grayson on their side.

"The safe house is ready," Holden added. "I got a call about that, too."

Again, Holden didn't make it sound as if that was good. Probably because they still had to get Carter there, and with the threat seemingly all around them, that might not be easy to do.

"But we got some bad news on the blood that the CSIs found at the inn," Holden explained a moment later. "No match."

Nicky shook her head. "That doesn't make sense. Those men who attacked us almost certainly had records." She froze. "Oh, God. You don't think it could have belonged to a baby?"

"No," he said immediately. "There's no evidence that there was another baby in that place. It probably just means we wounded the one gunman who wasn't in the system."

Yeah, the odds were against that. Well, maybe. Maybe whoever was behind this hadn't hired the usual thugs to do thug work.

They continued to another hall, where Nicky saw yet another guard. This one was outside one of the hospital room doors, and as they got closer, she spotted Gage just inside the room. With Amanda and a tall lanky man. Her lawyer, no doubt.

"The doctor decided to release her," Gage volunteered. "She won't be transferred to another hospital after all."

Amanda was dressed not in a gown but in regular clothes, and she was sitting on the edge of the bed. "As soon as the paperwork is done, I'm leaving. I would have already left, but if I do, the doctor said my insurance wouldn't cover any of this."

So, Nicky apparently wasn't the only one caught in the red-tape maze today.

"Gage said you'd been shot," Amanda continued.

"Grazed," Nicky explained. "It's nothing, really."

Amanda shook her head. "It is something. It means someone tried to kill you just like they tried to kill me."

Nicky hadn't made up her mind yet if that last part was true or not. She went closer to the woman.

"Will you tell me how you became a surrogate for my nephew?" Nicky asked.

Silence.

"Amanda already knows she's a person of interest in this case," Gage said.

"I'm innocent," she snapped. "I became a surrogate because I needed the money. I didn't know until afterward what was going on."

"And when exactly did you learn what was going on?" Holden asked. He, too, went closer.

More silence.

It caused both Holden and Gage to huff.

Since Nicky wasn't sure how much time there'd be before that paperwork was done, she asked the one question she desperately wanted Amanda to answer. "Who set all of this up?"

Amanda's exhaled breath was long and weary. "I don't

know. But I can tell you who it wasn't. It wasn't me. If I'd just gotten all that ransom money, do you think I'd be worried about insurance paperwork?"

She would if she wanted to add to the facade of being an innocent woman.

"Then guess who's behind it," Holden persisted.

"Beatrice," Amanda readily answered. "But I've already told you that." She paused, looked at Nicky. "And your father, of course."

Nicky felt her heart thud. Not because Amanda had mentioned her father, but because the woman had added that *of course.*

"Why my father?" Nicky asked.

Amanda made a sound as if the answer was obvious. "When I was still the manager there, he came to Conceptions several times. He made a pest of himself by demanding to know what procedures we were doing on his daughter. I told him I couldn't give out that kind of information. The man was obsessed with having a grandchild."

Yes, he was, and it obviously didn't seem to matter that he'd resented Annie for marrying Emmett. Or maybe Oscar had simply decided that he didn't care about his feelings for his daughter as long as he got that heir he wanted.

"Annie died ten months ago," Nicky reminded Holden, "and the in vitro would have been done on the surrogate— on Amanda—just a month later. Maybe less."

He nodded. "You think your father was so racked with grief that he did this and then covered it up with the ransom demand."

"It's possible."

"But I wasn't the only surrogate," Amanda blurted out. Her hand flew over her mouth, and it was obvious she hadn't intended to spill that.

Even though Nicky knew there'd been others, at least

two of them since she had seen the files, what Amanda said gave her a very uneasy feeling.

"Emmett and Annie don't have another baby out there, do they?" Nicky asked.

Amanda frantically shook her head. "I've already said too much."

No, she hadn't said what Nicky needed to hear. One of those three in vitro procedures was still unaccounted for.

"Please," Nicky said to the woman. "I just need to know if I have another niece or nephew because he or she could be in grave danger."

More head shaking from Amanda. "I can't help you."

"Can't or won't?" Holden snapped.

"Can't," Amanda answered. "I honestly don't know anything about a third baby. Heck, I don't know much about my own delivery. They put me to sleep during the C-section, and when I woke up, the baby was already gone. They took him without even letting me see him."

"That's all my client intends to say," the lawyer said. "And you'll have to leave now. You're agitating her."

"A baby's life could be at stake," Nicky insisted.

But Amanda just lowered her head. No eye contact. Nothing.

"Sheriff Ryland will expect you to bring your client in for questioning," Holden told the lawyer. "Or for her to surrender for an arrest."

"I'll be at the sheriff's office in the morning," Amanda said, her voice a raw whisper. "Just make sure you have enough cops there to protect me. Because a baby isn't the only one at risk. We all are."

For once they could agree on something, and as much as Nicky wanted to be at Amanda's interrogation, she was betting that Holden wasn't going to let her out of the house.

"Let's go," Holden told Nicky, and he put his hand on her back to get her moving.

"By some miracle you don't remember anything else about that third file, do you?" he asked once they were in the hall and away from Amanda's room.

"No, and that's why I need to find out what happened to those files." That gave Nicky another wave of grief and guilt over Paul's murder.

"Is there any place where Paul could have stored them so he knew you'd find them?" Holden asked.

Nicky gave that some thought. "We worked together many times so I guess he could have put the info in some of his old case files."

That prompted Holden to take out his phone and make a call. Not to Grayson this time. But to Drury. Holden didn't put the call on speaker, but judging from what she could hear of the conversation, Drury was going to get started on that process.

"Paul probably had a lot of case files," she reminded Holden when he finished the call. "He'd been a PI for over twenty years."

A search would be a needle in a haystack. Still, it wasn't as if they had a lot of leads at the moment. And the search was now more pressing than it had been. The file had said that both of Annie's embryos had been implanted into a surrogate, but maybe there had been two surrogates and not just one.

It turned Nicky's stomach to think of another baby being out there—any baby—but this third child might also be Emmett an Annie's.

With that thought eating away at her, she and Holden made their way back to the ER, where Nicky hoped her release paperwork would be waiting for her. If not, she was going to ask Holden if they could leave anyway. She figured she wouldn't get him to agree to that.

Until she saw who was waiting for them in the treatment room where she'd gotten her stitches. Not the doctor or the nurse.

But rather Beatrice.

Holden automatically stepped in front of Nicky, and he put his hand over his gun. Beatrice's eyes widened for a second, but then the glare came.

"Really?" the woman snapped. "You think I'd come here to attack you?"

Holden tipped his head toward the parking lot. "Considering what happened out there, I'm not taking any chances."

Beatrice added a huff to her glare. "I'm here to help you, and this is the thanks I get."

"What kind of help?" Holden asked, and his tone was one of a lawman questioning a hostile suspect. Beatrice qualified as both.

"First, I need your assurances that you won't bother me or my son any further."

"No deal." Holden didn't hesitate, either. "You're a suspect in not only what happened at Conceptions Clinic, but also your husband's disappearance."

"And I've already told you I'm innocent of both," she snapped. Beatrice shifted her attention to Nicky. "I understand Amanda is hospitalized here."

Nicky only lifted her shoulder and didn't intend to verify that. She wasn't sure what Beatrice would do with the info.

However, Holden had something to say. "Where's your lawyer?"

"In the car waiting for me. Why?"

"I just wanted to make sure he wasn't sneaking around

trying to find Amanda and putting together another attack. Nicky and I have had our fill of bullets being fired at us."

"Fine, be that way. Believe what you will," Beatrice continued, her voice a snarl now. "But I know Amanda's here, and I know the things she's been saying about me. She's the reason you suspect that I might have done those horrible things. Well, I have proof that I didn't."

"I'd be very interested in that proof," Holden assured her.

Even after making the claim of having something to clear her name, Beatrice looked as if she was still debating what to do. She finally reached in her purse, a move that had Holden drawing his gun.

"I don't carry a weapon," Beatrice spat out.

Holden didn't holster his gun. He kept it aimed at her until they saw what Beatrice took from her purse. It was a flash drive. She didn't hand it to them, though. She just lifted it for them to see.

"What is that?" Nicky finally asked.

"Proof. It's the surveillance footage of me paying the ransom to get my son."

Of all the things that Nicky had been expecting the woman to say, that wasn't one of them. Judging from the way he pulled back his shoulders, Holden was surprised, too. Or maybe he was just skeptical.

"How did you get footage like that?" Holden demanded.

"After things went wrong with the first kidnapping demand, I hired a PI, and he did surveillance not only of the park before the ransom drop, but also during and afterward."

Now it was Nicky who was skeptical. "The kidnappers didn't notice they were being recorded?"

"No." But then Beatrice paused. "Or they didn't seem to notice."

That was the key word here, *seem*. Whoever was paying those kidnappers had set up a complex operation with a lot of security in place. It seemed strange that they wouldn't check for someone filming them. Of course, if the kidnappers were wearing ski masks, maybe they didn't care since they couldn't be identified.

Nicky shook her head. "Why didn't you give this to the cops?"

"Because those monsters who brought me the baby said for me to stay quiet or they'd kill me and take the child." Her breath was rapid now, and she looked away. "But now that so many people know what went on at Conceptions Clinic, I'm worried my son and I are in danger whether I talk or not."

Holden took a moment, no doubt to process that comment, since that's what Nicky was doing. "How would a surveillance tape of a ransom drop prove you're innocent?" Holden asked.

Beatrice took Nicky's hand and put the flash drive in her palm. "Just watch it, and you'll see who's really responsible for all of this."

Chapter Eleven

Holden put the flash drive in his laptop and watched as the info popped onto the screen. There was only one file, and it was indeed a video. However, that didn't mean Beatrice was right about Nicky and him seeing the person who was responsible for the Genesis Project and the kidnappings.

"The images could be doctored," Holden reminded Nicky, though he doubted she needed such a reminder.

After all, Beatrice was still a suspect and whatever was on the footage could be there simply to clear her name. Holden seriously doubted that the woman would have given them anything to incriminate herself. Just the opposite.

Nicky nodded, her attention already nailed to the screen, but Holden didn't miss that her forehead was bunched up. "Are you in pain?" he asked.

"No." But Nicky must have realized she said it too quickly because she flexed her eyebrows. "Just a little."

Translation—she was hurting *bad*. It didn't matter that the bullet had only grazed her—she had five stitches, and the area around those stitches was no doubt throbbing.

Even though the footage was already loading, he hit the pause button, and went to the bathroom off the master suite. While he was there, Holden checked on the baby and Landon—both were napping so he didn't disturb them. He went back into the kitchen with a bottle of over-the-counter painkillers and got her a glass of water.

It was a testament to how much Nicky truly was hurting because she didn't argue with him about taking the meds. While he was at it, he sent a text to Gage so he could contact the doctor to write Nicky that prescription for pain meds that she'd turned down earlier.

"I'm okay, really," she said after she took the pills and set both the bottle and the water on the kitchen table.

Holden went closer. In fact, he got right in her face, and he stared at her.

"All right, I'll be okay once the painkillers kick in," she admitted.

Holden sighed, eased her onto one of the chairs and, because he thought they both could use it, he leaned down and kissed her.

"You keep doing that," she whispered against his mouth.

"Yeah. Want me to stop?"

The corner of her mouth lifted. "Only because we should be reviewing the video."

Holden certainly hadn't forgotten about it, but he silently cursed the distraction. And it wasn't even Nicky's fault. It was his own. His body had the notion that Nicky was his for the taking.

And she wasn't.

He sank down beside her and got the footage moving. As he'd expected, the quality sucked. It was nighttime, and the PI had obviously shot from a distance. Probably an attempt to stop the kidnappers from seeing him. The problem was Holden couldn't see the kidnappers. Or Beatrice, for that matter.

"You recognize that part of the park?" Nicky asked.

Holden nodded. "It's a trail that coils around the creek."

Not exactly on the beaten path, which was why the kidnappers had likely chosen it.

He fast-forwarded it until he saw the headlights come into view. Since the vehicle was a limo, Holden figured this was Beatrice. It was. The woman stepped out several moments later, and she had her lawyer right by her side.

She was also wearing a Kevlar vest.

Hardly her usual attire, but Holden was a little surprised that she would have remembered to wear body armor. Most parents of kidnapped children were in a panicked state by this point, and their own safety was usually the last of their concerns.

What Beatrice was missing was the money. Neither she nor her lawyer was carrying a bag, and that probably meant the ransom was inside the vehicle.

Thanks to some moonlight, Holden could see Beatrice look around. He could also see the moment she stepped even farther behind her lawyer. That's because a second vehicle approached. An SUV, and it pulled close enough that the front bumper butted against the front bumper of the limo. From that angle, Holden couldn't see a license plate, but even if he could have, the plates probably would have been bogus.

Two men barreled out of the SUV. Both of them were wearing ski masks, just as Holden had figured they would be. They were also armed, and the sight of those armed thugs sent Beatrice scurrying back into her limo.

"No audio," Nicky mumbled when they watched as one of the thugs appeared to shout something.

That was too bad, but Holden figured he'd ordered Beatrice out of the car because the woman came out, finally, and she clutched on to her lawyer. It was the lawyer and the shouting thug who did all the talking, and it was only a few seconds before the lawyer leaned into the limo and came out with two huge bags.

No doubt the ransom.

With Beatrice still cowering by the limo, the lawyer came forward, and he put the bags of money on the ground for the kidnapper to inspect. The guy riffled through both, and then motioned to someone in the SUV. It didn't take long for another kidnapper to get out.

And he was holding a baby.

The exchange happened fast. The kidnapper with the baby took him to the lawyer, practically thrusting the infant into his arms. In the same motion, the other kidnappers grabbed the bags with the money.

Beatrice and the lawyer didn't waste any time getting the heck out of there. The moment the lawyer was behind the wheel, he took off.

The SUV didn't.

Holden was about to say that there'd been nothing on that footage that had proven Beatrice was innocent. She could have been faking the fear. Faking everything if those kidnappers were actually working for her.

But then Holden saw something.

When the kidnappers opened the back passenger door, the moonlight hit just right for him to see the person sitting there. And judging from Nicky's gasp, she had no trouble seeing it, either.

Because it was her father.

She staggered to her feet, catching onto the chair for support. Since she still didn't look too steady, Holden looped his arm around her, mindful of her injury. Also mindful that this had knocked the breath out of her.

"I knew he was dirty," she said, "but this?"

Yeah, Holden was right there with her. It was sick enough to create a project to produce your own heir, but here Oscar had done it to Senator Minton and milked him for a million dollars.

Well, maybe.

Holden shook his head. "Why would your father have risked going to the ransom drop?" The question was for himself more than Nicky, and he was trying to piece this together. "I mean, there are three hired guns so why would he have gone knowing that something could have gone wrong?"

"You think he was set up?" Nicky asked.

His initial reaction was to say "heck, no," but that's because it was hard to think of Oscar as anything but a criminal. However, Oscar wasn't stupid, and this was a stupid thing to do.

Unless…

"Maybe Oscar didn't trust his hired guns." But there was a problem with that theory, too. "How much do you think your father's estate is worth?"

"Millions. And I haven't heard of him losing a large sum with investments and such. In fact, if anything, he's only added to his fortune with his shady business deals."

Holden gave that some more thought, knowing that the thinking would have to end fast and that he would have to call Grayson to tell him about this. Of course, these were the same questions Grayson would need to ask as well.

"Is there a personal connection between your father and Lee Minton?" Holden added.

"Nothing obvious. I checked for that when I first learned about the Genesis Project. The only thing they had in common was the embryos stored at Conceptions Clinic."

If Oscar didn't have a grudge against Minton and since he didn't appear to need the money, maybe Oscar had orchestrated this for a different reason. To throw suspicion off himself. After all, he could claim he'd been forced to pay a million dollars as well to get his grandson.

There was only one way to find out for sure.

He took out his phone and called Oscar. Part of Holden didn't expect the man to answer, but he did on the first ring.

"I want my grandson," Oscar snarled before Holden could even say anything. Obviously, he'd seen Holden's name on the caller ID.

"I want a lot of things," Holden countered. "Like the truth. Is there something you want to tell me?"

Considering that Holden hadn't given the man much of a clue as to what he was looking for, it didn't surprise him that Oscar hesitated. But the hesitation went on for several long moments.

"The only thing that matters now is getting my grandson," Oscar finally said. "I heard about the other attack, and I don't want him in the middle of that. The court order is in the works, and I'll have custody of him by tomorrow."

Probably not.

"If you're telling the truth about wanting your grandson out of danger, maybe you can just stop the attacks," Holden suggested.

Another hesitation. "If you've got something to say to me, then just come out and say it."

Holden considered it a moment and thought about just waiting until he had Oscar in front of him. But the sooner he could get this information, the better. Then he could bring in Oscar not just to interrogate him, but also to arrest him. Since there was no bail for a murder charge, it would get Oscar off the streets and perhaps put an end to the danger.

"Well?" Oscar taunted. "Cat got your tongue?"

"No. I thought you'd like to know that Beatrice had a

PI film her ransom drop with the kidnappers," Holden finally said.

Silence. For a very long time. "I think I should call my lawyer now."

"I think you should, too. You should call your lawyer and show up with him at the sheriff's office in one hour."

That wouldn't give Holden much time to set up the interview and go over the charges with Grayson, but it also wouldn't give Oscar much time to go after Nicky again.

"Be there," Holden ordered. "Because if you're not, I will send someone to arrest you."

With that, Holden hung up and immediately called Grayson. While he was explaining things, he emailed Grayson a copy of the surveillance footage. Grayson agreed that both Oscar and Beatrice needed to be brought in for another round of questioning, and Holden wanted to be there for that.

"What about Nicky?" Grayson asked. "Are you going to leave her at the house when you come here?"

Nicky was obviously close enough to hear that question because she started shaking her head. Even though Holden didn't like this, he was actually going to agree with her.

"I think we need to keep the baby separate from Nicky," Holden explained. "Starting now. I'll bring her with me to the sheriff's office, and Landon and the reserve deputies can go ahead and take the baby to the safe house."

Grayson made a sound of agreement. "I'll get Kara out there now to drive in with you. The reserve deputies, too, to go with Landon."

Holden figured Kara might not be too happy about that considering she'd been attacked earlier because of them. And Grayson likely didn't want her out on a call so soon afterward. But what with everything going on, Grayson's deputies were probably all tied up. That would continue because Landon and the reserve deputies would have to stay at the safe house indefinitely with Carter. Although *indefinitely* might not be that long.

"This is the right thing to do," Nicky said as if trying to convince herself.

She turned, making her way to the master suite with Holden following right behind her. Yeah, it was the right thing to do, but he didn't feel good about this. In a way it felt as if he was abandoning his brother's son. Of course, this was temporary, and if the interviews with Beatrice and Oscar went well, then Carter might not have to stay in the safe house for long.

And then what?

The question wasn't out of the blue exactly. Holden had been thinking about what the next step would be. A step that would no doubt include a custody battle unless they could put Oscar behind bars. Even then, he and Nicky might square off since both could make a case for a claim to the baby.

Nicky seemed unaware of the emotional battle that was going on inside Holden. That was probably because she was having her own battle, and by the time they made it to the bedroom, she was blinking back tears.

"I know Carter hasn't been in our lives for long," she said, "but in a way, it feels as if he's always been here."

Holden felt the same way, and it crushed his heart to say goodbye.

Landon sat up when they walked in, and he glanced at both of them. "Time for me to take him to the safe house?" Landon asked.

Holden nodded, not trusting his voice. There was a lump in his throat.

Nicky went to the bassinet ahead of Holden, and she leaned down and kissed Carter on the cheek. The baby stirred but went right back to sleep. Holden waited a moment before he, too, gave the baby a kiss.

Nicky got busy packing up the baby's things, probably to give herself something to do. Holden decided to try that ploy as well, and he headed back toward the kitchen to warm up a bottle. However, he didn't get far into the process when his phone buzzed, and he saw Grayson's name on the screen.

Hell. He hoped nothing else had gone wrong.

"Please tell me there's not a problem," Holden said when he answered.

But Grayson didn't jump to respond to that. "As soon as Kara arrives, I need you here at the sheriff's office."

Holden groaned. Yeah, there was a problem all right. "Why? What happened?"

"A detective from San Antonio PD just called. They've been going through Paul's business records, and they think they found something. They're emailing it to me now."

Holden went still. "What did they find?"

"Information about the Genesis Project." Grayson paused. "Get here as fast as you can."

Chapter Twelve

For Nicky it seemed to take an eternity for Holden, Kara and her to make the drive to the sheriff's office. However, saying goodbye to Carter had gone by as fast as a blink of an eye. Maybe he wouldn't have to be in that safe house for long.

Because there could be something in Paul's files to put an end to this.

Grayson hadn't gotten into the details over the phone, mainly because he was waiting for the emails to arrive from SAPD, but when she and Holden finally arrived and hurried back to his office, Grayson had those emailed documents printed out and spread on top of his desk.

"What did they find?" Nicky couldn't ask the question fast enough.

"This." Grayson moved one of the papers for her to have a look.

It was Paul's handwritten notes for a case where she'd hired him to interview some witnesses to an old unsolved murder. Since that murder had happened on the other side of the state, Nicky wasn't sure how it connected to what was going on now.

She shook her head. "This was the last case Paul worked for me before Conceptions." But she stopped the head shaking when she saw the note at the bottom. Paul had added the address for a website.

Grayson turned his laptop for her to see. "The site was for online storage, and I used your password from the other site to access it."

Nicky went closer, and she saw the files that she'd copied from Conceptions. "Why would Paul have moved them?" she asked.

Grayson lifted his shoulder. "Maybe because he knew the other site had been compromised or had the chance of being compromised. He probably knew that eventually you'd see the note and realize what it was."

Holden went closer, too. "Are all the files there?"

Nicky scrolled through and nodded, then she froze. Yes, all her files were there, but there was also another file that Paul had created. There were lots of notes and what appeared to be test results, but like the other files she'd copied from Conceptions, this one didn't have names, only a file number. She looked up at Grayson to see if he knew about it.

He did.

Grayson cleared his throat. "According to Paul, there's a third baby."

Mercy. Of course, she'd known all along this was possible, but there was something in Grayson's expression that warned her there was more to this than just a third baby.

Holden must have picked up on it, too, because he stepped in front of her and almost frantically scrolled through what Paul had left them. Specifically, it was another file that he'd apparently gotten from Conceptions.

Paul had written, "The computer geek I hired managed to recover this from the clinic's files before it was erased for good." And he'd written that note on the same day he'd been murdered.

That explained why he hadn't told her what he'd found.

But what exactly had he found?

Holden kept scrolling, and when Nicky saw Paul's other notes, her breath vanished.

"The other baby is Emmett and Annie's," Holden said. "And it's a girl."

The blood rushed to Nicky's head, and before the panic could hit her, she kept searching for information in Paul's notes. And there was more.

"Payment requested," she said, reading the note.

But that was it. Paul hadn't written anything else, and Nicky's gaze snapped to Grayson's for answers. Answers that he clearly didn't have because he shook his head.

"Your father is in the interview room just across the hall," Grayson said. "Beatrice should be here any minute, and I'll get Amanda back in here as well."

Nicky tried to make sense of this, but like everything else in this case, she couldn't make sense because of the slam of emotion. There was a baby out there. Somewhere. Her niece. And someone had apparently requested payment for her.

But what did that mean?

Did it mean she'd been sold on the black market? And if so, who'd bought her?

"You think Amanda might have delivered twins?" Grayson asked.

"That's one of the things I intend to find out," Holden insisted. He looked at Nicky. "I would tell you to let Grayson and me handle this, but I'm figuring you'll want to talk to your father."

"I do," she insisted, and Nicky stormed toward the interview room.

Grayson was right behind her. Holden, too, and they were both mumbling some profanity. Maybe because more had just been added to this nightmare, but it might also be because they were worried she was going to compromise the investigation. And she prayed she didn't, but she needed answers now.

She threw open the interview room door, and her father and his lawyer immediately got to their feet. Her father didn't sling one of his usual barbs at her. Perhaps because he saw the raw emotion on her face. The anger as well.

"Start talking," she demanded.

She expected him to stonewall her or hide behind his lawyer, and to stop him from doing that, Nicky charged toward him. She didn't push him against the wall—something she desperately wanted to do—but she did go toe-to-toe with him.

"Why were you in that kidnapper's SUV, and where is Annie and Emmett's daughter?"

Her father had opened his mouth, maybe to answer some part of that, but he went silent. His eyes widened, and he shook his head.

"A daughter?" he asked, his voice mostly breath and almost no sound.

He certainly acted surprised, but Nicky wasn't ready to buy in to that surprise just yet. "Yes. Now, tell me where she is."

Her father shook his head again and looked at Holden as if he expected him to make some sense of this.

"If the file is right, someone paid for her," Holden explained. "Maybe a ransom, maybe just payment from the person who arranged for her to be born. And I'm thinking that person is you."

"No," Oscar said. He stepped around Nicky and went to one of the chairs. He tilted back his head, sucked in some long breaths. "The only baby I knew about is their son."

Nicky went to the table so she could look him in the

eyes. "But you were in the kidnappers' SUV. We have proof."

"So-called proof that you got from Beatrice," the lawyer said.

Oscar motioned for him to get quiet, something that surprised Nicky. But then maybe her father had done that because it would make him look innocent.

"I was in the SUV because the kidnappers took me at gunpoint," her father said. "They made me go to that ransom drop and told me if anything went wrong that they'd set me up to take the blame for it."

Nicky went through each word, hoping she could see a flaw in what he was saying, but she had to admit that it could be true. *Could be.*

"There's really another baby?" Oscar asked.

Holden stepped forward to answer. "According to some information we just learned, yes. Now, where is she?"

Her father gave a weary sigh, followed by a groan. "I told you that I don't know, and those men never once mentioned another child. If they had, I would have arranged to pay a ransom for her, too."

"You're sure?" Nicky snapped. "Or maybe because she was a girl, you decided one male heir was enough."

Oscar shifted his gaze to her. "I would have paid the ransom," he repeated, and it was the most convincing thing he'd said since this whole ordeal had started.

"Are you sure the kidnappers didn't mention anything about another baby?" Grayson asked.

"Positive. Trust me, I would have remembered something like that. They kept me blindfolded and put headphones on me until we got to the ransom drop. I didn't see or hear anything that would help me identify who they were or if they had another baby."

"How did the kidnappers get to you?" Holden pressed.

Oscar gave another weary sigh. "I wasn't being careful enough. After I got that package and knew I had a grandson, I hurried out of my San Antonio office to go to the bank. They grabbed me in the parking lot."

Holden jumped right on that. "Were there security cameras in the parking lot?"

Oscar scrubbed his hand over his face. "No. They malfunctioned or something."

Nicky was betting it was the *or something*. The kidnappers had probably disabled it before they even took her father. That didn't mean he was innocent, though, because they could have done that on his orders so that no one could analyze it to disprove it was an actual kidnapping.

But even if Oscar had set up all of that, it didn't mean he knew of the newborn baby girl.

"I have a theory," Nicky said to him. "You wanted an heir so after Annie died, you paid someone at Conceptions Clinic, maybe Amanda, to carry Annie and Emmett's child. But someone decided a good way to make some money would be to have a second child, another million-dollar baby. Except this time, you'd actually have to pay the million to get her."

"Your theory is wrong," her father spat out, and it earned her one of his harshest glares. "If that had happened, why hasn't someone contacted me by now? There have been no other ransom demands."

"Yes, there has been," someone said.

Beatrice.

She was in the hall, and it appeared that Josh had been escorting her to an interview room. Clearly, she'd heard at least part of their conversation, and she got everyone's attention.

"What do you mean?" Holden snapped.

"I mean I just got a call on the way over here, just min-

utes ago, and the kidnappers said there was another child.
A newborn girl. And that if I wanted her, I'd need to pay
another ransom."

"That doesn't make sense," Nicky said. "Why would the
kidnappers contact you? Did they say the child was yours?"

Beatrice flinched. "I, uh, just assumed that she was, that
the kidnappers had implanted one of my embryos into another surrogate. I have six of them stored at Conceptions."

And maybe they had used one of Beatrice's for this
child. Maybe the baby didn't belong to Emmett and Annie
after all.

But then why had Paul thought it was theirs?

There was also the problem with the payment requested.
Paul would have copied that file days ago. So, did that
mean the kidnappers had requested payment from someone else? Like her father. And that he'd refused? Or had
the file been wrong altogether?

Nicky looked at Holden to see what his take was on this,
but he only shook his head. "Come on. Grayson needs to
finish this interview with your father."

Yes, and maybe Oscar would say something that would
shed some light on what the heck was going on. In the
meantime, though, Nicky wanted to get to work on finding the third baby. That started with Beatrice.

Holden and Nicky went into the hall with the woman,
and they followed Josh and Beatrice into the other interview room.

"I recorded the call," Beatrice volunteered, handing
Holden her phone. "I don't usually do that, but after what
happened with my son, I do. I've also hired several more
bodyguards for him." She shuddered. "God, I'm so scared
someone's going to try to take him again."

Nicky knew how she felt. Or at least how the woman

was pretending to feel. Beatrice wasn't off the suspect list just yet.

Holden hit the play button on the call, and it didn't take long before Nicky heard the voices. First, Beatrice answering, and then the man's voice. It was muffled as if he was trying to disguise it.

"Mrs. Minton, guess what I'm holding right now?" The caller didn't wait for her to answer. "A cute little newborn girl. She looks just like her twin brother. If you want her, it'll cost you another million. Get the money by tonight, and I'll be back in touch with you."

That was it. The man hadn't given Beatrice a chance to say anything.

"I'm not sure I can get the money," Beatrice said. There were tears in her eyes now. "I mean, I had to beg for the last ransom." She looked up at Holden. "But you think this might not even be my child?"

"We're just not sure. It's possible the kidnappers will try to get additional ransoms from both Oscar and you."

Mercy, that would be a huge haul of cash. And the problem? They just might succeed, especially if they managed to get their hands on Carter and the Minton boy again.

"So, what do I do?" Beatrice asked.

Nicky didn't have the answer, and even Holden hesitated. "We'll monitor your phone and will tell you what to say when the kidnapper calls back."

Beatrice didn't look very comforted about that. "Should I demand DNA proof like what they gave me with my son?"

"Don't make any demands. In fact, don't say anything to them until we instruct you." Holden turned to Josh after Beatrice nodded and then walked out into the hall.

"Wait," Josh told the woman. "I'll stay with you."

Beatrice moved away from the door, but judging from the sound of her footsteps, she didn't go far.

"You've got experience with this sort of thing from your FBI days?" Holden asked.

Josh nodded. "I'll find a place to set up the drop. You think you'll be able to tell if the baby is Emmett's if you have a photo of her?"

"Maybe. The kidnapper did say she looked like her brother. He could have been lying."

True. In fact, all of this could be a lie. There might not even be another baby, and the person who'd put this plan together could have added that fake file so he or she could get more money.

"I feel like I'm on an emotional roller coaster," Nicky said.

But before she even got out the words, Holden was already putting his arm around her. He eased her to him and brushed a kiss on her forehead. Josh would have been blind not to notice, and he did notice all right. She saw just the flash of disdain in his eyes.

Disdain because of what'd happened to Drury, no doubt.

Since that was something Nicky could never escape with the Rylands, she backed away. Or she would have if Holden hadn't kept his arm around her.

"You're not the only one on that roller coaster," Holden assured her, and he kept her there in his arms. "It might be a little while before I can take you back to the house," he added. "Everyone's tied up at the moment."

They were, and what with everything they'd just learned, the being tied up might last for a while.

"I'd like to go through Paul's files some more," Nicky said. "The files I got from Conceptions, too. There could be something in them I missed."

And even if there wasn't, she had to do something.

Anything. The nerves were raw and right at the surface, and if she didn't get busy, she might break down and cry again. That wouldn't help Carter, this possible baby or anyone else.

She and Holden went back to Grayson's office, but they'd barely made it inside when Holden's phone buzzed. With all the bad news they'd gotten, Nicky's muscles tensed. Then, they did more than tense when it hit her that something could have gone wrong with getting the baby to the safe house.

Her gaze flew to Holden's phone screen, but it wasn't Landon's name there. However, it was a name she recognized.

Amanda.

Holden answered right away, no doubt ready to start firing off questions to the woman about the third baby, but Amanda spoke before he could say a word.

"You have to help me," Amanda insisted. She sounded out of breath. Sounded as if she was also crying. "Please. You have to get here right away."

"Where are you and what's wrong?" Holden asked.

"I was at the inn just up the street, and my lawyer went out to get something. Oh, God." Amanda was definitely crying. Sobbing, actually. "Please, come. Someone broke in to my room. I climbed out the window and ran, but he's chasing me."

Holden cursed. "Who broke in? The kidnappers?"

"No." Another sob. "I only got a glimpse of his face, but I'm pretty sure it's Senator Lee Minton."

Chapter Thirteen

Holden wasn't sure he was doing the right thing, but either way he went with this could be dangerous for Nicky.

Amanda could have lied to get Nicky and him out into the open again. But the lie could have merely been to get some of the cops out of the building so it'd be easier for the kidnappers to have another go at killing them. There'd been attacks at the Silver Creek sheriff's office before, and he wouldn't have put it past Amanda—or whoever was behind this—to try to orchestrate another one.

Holden already had his gun drawn and ready, but he had no idea if Amanda was even coming their way. Josh and Kara had responded immediately, heading to the inn to see if they could spot Amanda. Spot the person who was chasing her, too.

If that person existed, that is.

"Just stay back," Holden reminded Nicky when he saw her peering out the doorway of Grayson's office.

She nodded. "You really believe Minton broke in to Amanda's room?" Nicky asked.

"I don't know."

But Beatrice must have heard Nicky mention her husband's name because she came running out of the interview room.

"You found Lee?" she asked.

"Don't get your hopes up," Holden told her. "It might not be the senator at all." Or in Beatrice's case, maybe it was a hopeful situation because she might not want her husband to be found.

"What's going on?" Beatrice demanded, and she started to charge forward, but Nicky caught onto her arm, not only holding back the woman, but also filling her in on what they knew.

Which wasn't much.

"As soon as the deputies find Amanda, she'll be able to tell us what happened," Holden added to Beatrice when Nicky had finished. Whether or not Amanda would be telling them the truth was a different matter.

"Amanda had a C-section a little over a week ago," Nicky added. "She probably won't be able to get far."

Yeah, that was the good and bad news. The woman probably wasn't going to be able to run for long, if at all, but that meant if this was a real attack, Amanda could already be dead.

Holden decided to keep that to himself.

Beatrice took out her phone and frantically pressed in some numbers. "I'm trying to call Lee. I've been trying ever since he went missing, but his phone was turned off and the card was taken out so it couldn't be traced. But maybe his phone is working now."

It was a serious long shot, but Holden preferred Beatrice to be doing something other than pestering him. If possible, something that would also get her away from Nicky. Beatrice wouldn't have made it through the metal detector to get into the building if she'd been carrying a weapon, but that didn't mean she couldn't signal some thugs to attack.

"Go back in the interview room," Holden ordered the woman.

But Beatrice didn't move. She seemed frozen. "Lee?"

she said when someone apparently answered her call. "Oh, God. It is really you?"

Holden hoped like the devil that this wasn't some kind of trick, but since the senator's body had never been found and there'd been no signs of foul play, it was indeed possible that he was still alive. But how had Minton gotten mixed up in all of this?

"Lee wants to talk to you," Beatrice said. She walked toward Holden, her hand shaking while she held out the phone.

"Put it on speaker," Holden instructed, and he stayed near the door. Keeping watch. "Nicky, get Grayson."

Nicky nodded and hurried across the hall to do that, and it only took a couple of seconds for Grayson to tell her father and his lawyer to stay put and then come out. Only a couple of seconds for Holden to hear the caller, too.

"Marshal Ryland?" the caller asked.

It was a man all right, but Holden had no idea if this was really Minton or not. Though Beatrice seemed to believe it was her husband.

"Where are you?" And that was just Holden's starter question. He had a boatload of others.

"In Silver Creek." Like Amanda, this guy sounded out of breath. "It's not safe here. Someone's trying to kill me."

"Who?" Holden snapped.

"I'm not sure. The person who hired someone to kidnap me. That's also the same person who's responsible for these babies being born."

Holden jumped right on that. "You know about the babies?"

"Yes." The caller paused. "I have one of them. A girl."

Holden certainly hadn't seen that coming. But maybe he should have. Because if Beatrice had put this plan together, then the caller could be one of her hired guns. And this could be another attempt to get some ransom money or to draw them into the open.

"Start talking," Holden demanded. "Tell me why you have the baby and what you want."

"I only want her safe. I want to be safe, too."

"Then bring her here to the sheriff's office." Holden didn't figure the man would take him up on that.

And he didn't.

"I can't," the caller insisted. "Too risky."

"It was risky to break in to Amanda's hotel room, too," Holden growled.

"I was looking for something, anything I could find out about Conceptions Clinic, but I left as soon as I saw the car. The car with the baby. I took her, and now they're after us."

No way could Holden not react to that. The fear came, and it was bone-deep. That could be his niece out there, and he had to fight the kick of adrenaline to stop himself from going out there to look for her.

"Bring the baby here right now," Holden demanded.

But he was talking to himself because the man was no longer on the line.

"Lee?" Beatrice shouted, snatching back her phone so she could call him.

Holden ignored her for the moment and fired off a text to Josh, to warn him that there might be a baby nearby. And he waited.

Nicky was clearly having trouble tamping down her fears, too. Her gaze was firing all around as if she were looking for whatever she could do to keep the baby safe.

"It could have all been a lie," Holden reminded her. A reminder for himself, too.

However, Beatrice must have thought it was all real because she kept trying to get in touch with the caller again.

"What did he say to you before you brought me the phone?" Holden asked her.

Beatrice shook her head, and it took her a moment to answer. "Only that he was in danger and that he needed to talk to Marshal Holden Ryland."

So, the man had asked for him specifically. If it was indeed Minton, then that meant he knew a lot about this investigation. Was that why someone was after him? Had he figured out too much?

"He didn't ask about our son," Beatrice said under her breath, and then she started to cry.

"Go back to the interview room," Holden told her again. "But leave your phone in case the man calls back."

"That man is my husband," she insisted. And she kept on insisting. Kept on crying, too.

Holden was about to repeat his order for her to move, but then he heard something he didn't want to hear. The door to the other interview room opened.

"What the hell is going on out here?" Oscar asked.

"My patience is at zero right now," Holden warned him. "Either you and your lawyer stay in the interview room with the door closed, or I'll put you both in a holding cell. Move!" Holden added when Oscar just stood there.

Oscar finally turned and went back into the room, but he'd barely gotten the door closed when there was another sound.

A gunshot.

The shot cracked through the air, and it was close. Too close.

That got Beatrice running away from the windows and to the interview room. What she didn't do was leave him her phone, and Holden didn't have time to remedy that now.

Because there was another shot.

Grayson hurried to the front of the building with

Holden, and they both looked out. No sign of who'd fired those shots. Holden also kept an eye on Nicky and cursed when he saw that both her father and Beatrice were now at the back of the squad room, only a couple of feet from Nicky. Grayson didn't miss it, either.

"Go to Nicky," Grayson told him. "If I see the shooter, I'll let you know."

Holden debated what to do for a second. He didn't want to leave Grayson up front without backup, but he reminded himself that Nicky was the target here. Holden went to her, grabbing Beatrice's phone along the way. He maneuvered Nicky into the empty interview room, and he stood in the doorway.

"What can I do to help?" Nicky asked. She looked surprisingly strong for a woman who was so close to gunfire—yet again.

Holden passed Beatrice's phone to Nicky. "Try calling Minton again." It definitely wasn't just busywork, either, because if that man had been telling the truth, then he had the baby.

There was another shot. Then another. Both of them closer than the other shots had been. He hoped the deputies weren't in the middle of gunfire. The baby, too. If there was a baby.

"Minton or whoever that was isn't answering," Nicky informed him.

He was about to tell her to keep trying, but Holden's own phone buzzed. Since he didn't want to take his attention off Grayson and the front door, he handed his phone back to Nicky.

"It's Amanda," she said, and put the call on speaker.

"Who's shooting?" Amanda whispered.

"I was hoping you would know."

"No, I can't see any gunmen, but the shots sound close. Holden, I'm so scared."

"Where are you?" Holden asked.

"In the alley about three or four buildings from the sheriff's office. I'm hiding on the side of the Dumpster behind what looks to be a hardware store."

"Stay put. I can send a deputy to get you."

"No!" Amanda insisted. "I don't trust the deputies. I'm not even sure I can trust you."

"Then why even call me?" Holden cursed. "I'm trying to stop you from being killed."

At least he was if she was innocent, and since he didn't know if she was innocent or not, Holden wanted her alive so he could question her.

"I don't know what to do," Amanda sobbed. "I don't want to die. Oh, God. They're here. The gunmen are here."

Holden didn't get a chance to say anything to her because Amanda was no longer on the line. And worse, there was a series of shots. Six of them, and from the sound of it, they were being fired from different weapons.

"Amanda's in the back of the hardware store," Holden told Grayson.

This time it was Grayson who cursed. And Holden knew why. If the deputies were in a fight for their lives, a call or text might be a fatal distraction. Still, they had to do something if only to let the deputies know Amanda's location.

"Let Josh know about Amanda," Grayson finally said, but before Holden could even have Nicky start the text, Grayson's phone rang. "Hold off on that text. It's Josh."

Well, at least if Josh was calling that meant he was alive, but that didn't mean he or someone else hadn't been hurt.

As Nicky had done, Grayson put the call on speaker

and placed his phone on the reception desk behind him. No doubt to free up his hands in case he had to return fire.

"I'm coming in," Josh immediately said. "And I'm not alone. Grayson, I found the baby."

EVEN THOUGH NICKY was several rooms away, she had no trouble hearing what Josh had just said.

There was a baby, and he had it.

That got Holden moving toward the front with Grayson, and both of them stood, shoulder-to-shoulder, their guns ready. At least there wasn't any gunfire at the moment, but time seemed to have stopped. Unlike the thoughts flying through her head. Those were speeding through her mind, and even though Nicky knew the worst could have happened, she prayed for the best.

For Josh and the baby's safety. For Kara's, too.

Although Holden warned her to stay back, Nicky still peered out from the doorway of the interview room, and she was able to see when Grayson and Holden stepped back. Making the way for Josh.

And he finally came in.

Josh had the baby clutched to his chest, but Nicky couldn't see much of the infant because she was wrapped in a blanket. Josh didn't stay near the door. He headed up the hall where Nicky was waiting.

"Where's Kara?" Grayson asked.

"Still looking for Minton and Amanda," Josh answered. "Kara and I got separated when the gunmen started shooting at us. Here, take her," he added, handing Nicky the baby. "I'll go back out and find Kara."

"I'll go," Grayson insisted, and he headed out.

Holden stayed near the front, probably to make sure those gunmen didn't show up, but he was volleying glances between Josh, the baby and her.

Nicky eased back the blanket, and the first thing she saw was the ginger hair. Identical to Carter's. And Annie's.

"This is Annie and Emmett's daughter," she told Holden when she managed to gather enough breath to speak. Of course, it would have to be verified with DNA, but Nicky was certain of it.

Certain, too, that the love she felt for the baby was instant. So was the fear. Because now they had to keep her safe. Soon, she'd need to deal with the shock she was feeling, too. She'd had to deal with a lot of things, including what was happening between Holden and her. But for now, she just held her niece and said a prayer of thanks.

However, Nicky wasn't very thankful when her father came rushing out of the interview room. She wanted to kick herself for blurting out that this was her niece because obviously her father had heard it.

Oscar didn't say anything. He just came closer, his attention fixed on the baby.

"Don't you dare mention a word about custody and court orders," Nicky warned him. "Because I've had more than enough of you and your threats."

She expected him to glare at her or toss out one of his stinging remarks, but the shock must have taken over because he groaned and leaned against the wall.

"Is the baby okay?" Holden asked.

"She appears to be." The baby was squirming and fussing a little, but she didn't have any visible injuries, thank God. Along with the DNA test, though, she'd need to be checked by a doctor.

"How'd you get her?" Oscar asked Josh as Nicky continued to examine the baby.

"Luck," Josh answered. "When I was making my way through the alley to the hardware store, I saw her lying on the ground."

That sickened Nicky. Infuriated her, too. Because someone had been so careless with something so precious.

"I want to hold her," Oscar said.

Nicky shook her head. "Not until I'm sure you're innocent, and right now, I'm not sure of that at all."

Now she got the glare, and while it didn't please her, it didn't please Josh, either. "Come with me," Josh told her father. "You, too. Because I'm not any more convinced of your innocence than Nicky is."

"Where do you think you're taking us?" Oscar snapped.

"To a holding cell. It's for your own safety. For ours, too, and please resist so I can handcuff you and charge you with some assorted crimes like interfering with an officer and impeding an investigation."

Oscar gave Josh a glare for that sarcasm. "This isn't over," her father warned her, but neither he nor his lawyer resisted when Josh led them out of the hall and to the other side of the building, where there were holding cells.

Nicky felt some relief at having Oscar away from the baby, but she knew he wouldn't stay away. It wouldn't be long at all before he got out of that cell and then came for this little girl as he'd been trying to do with Carter.

Josh was only gone a couple of minutes. Probably because he hadn't wanted to leave Nicky and the baby so close to yet another of their suspects—Beatrice.

"Tell me who did this," Nicky said to Josh. "Who put the baby there in that alley?"

Josh shook his head. "I don't know. When I found her, there was no one around. I didn't even get a good look at the gunmen."

The shooters were almost certainly from the same team of thugs who'd been tormenting them from the start, but that didn't explain why they would have left the baby like that. Or maybe they hadn't. Maybe Minton truly had managed to take her from them.

But then where was Minton?

"Let me trade places with Holden," Josh suggested. "And he can see his niece." He gave the baby another glance. "She looks like her mother."

She did. From all the photos Nicky had seen of Annie when she was a baby, this little girl was practically a genetic copy.

As soon as Josh was at the front door, Holden hurried back to her, and he gave the baby the same once-over that Nicky had. "I'll find out who did this. I promise."

She didn't doubt it. Didn't doubt the raw emotion he was feeling, either, because Nicky was experiencing the same thing. The problem was, they didn't have a lot of options for putting a stop to the dangerous situation they were in unless they found Amanda and Minton. There wasn't much she could do about Amanda now, but Minton was a different story.

Nicky tipped her head to the interview room and handed Holden back the phone he'd taken earlier from Beatrice. "Maybe Beatrice knows of another way we can try to reach her husband."

Holden didn't look any more optimistic about that than she was, but he went into the room anyway. Beatrice was right there when he opened the door, and she'd clearly heard everything.

Considering all that had gone on, Nicky figured there'd be tears. Or at least some more concern than the woman had shown earlier. Or rather pretended to show.

"I've tried every way to contact my husband, and other than that call where I reached him earlier, I didn't talk to him," Beatrice insisted. "Obviously, he didn't want to get in touch with me before now, or he would have. And when he called, he didn't even want to speak to me. He wanted to talk to him." She flung her fingers in Holden's direction.

Still no tears, but Nicky heard the anger, and while she didn't want to speculate if it was real or not, Nicky could certainly understand why the wife of a missing man would feel that way. Unless Beatrice had had some part in her husband's disappearance, she might have thought he was dead.

This proved otherwise.

And it could also give Beatrice a complication she didn't want. If Minton had been dead, then their son would have likely inherited his estate, and that would have given Beatrice access to more money. That wouldn't happen, though, with Minton alive. Plus, now Beatrice couldn't play the part of the grieving widow.

"Lee's probably been with her this whole time," Beatrice snarled.

Her. As in Minton's mistress. Sharon Bachman. During interviews with the police, Sharon had admitted to the affair but had claimed she had no idea where Minton was.

"Call *her*," Holden insisted.

Nicky wasn't sure Beatrice would do that, but if the woman had refused, Nicky could have managed to contact Sharon. But having Beatrice do it would save time because Nicky was betting that Beatrice knew the woman's number.

She did.

Beatrice had the number in her recent calls, and she pressed it. When Holden prompted Beatrice to put it on speaker, she did. Though judging from the way her mouth tightened, she wasn't looking forward to any part of this call.

"Have you heard from Lee?" Sharon asked the moment she answered, and Nicky heard something in the woman's voice that she hadn't heard in Beatrice's—genuine concern.

Beatrice didn't answer, and she looked at Holden as if waiting for him to tell her what to say. However, he didn't tell her. He took the phone from her.

"Sharon, I'm Marshal Holden Ryland, and a man claiming to be Senator Minton called me about twenty minutes ago. Has Minton been in touch with you?"

"No. He called you? Is he okay? Where is he?" Her words rushed out, filled with sobs, relief and more worry.

"I'm not positive it was actually Minton—"

"It was Lee," Beatrice interrupted, and she went closer to the phone. "Sharon, if you know where Lee is, for God's sake, tell us."

"I don't know, but he's alive, right? Did he say what had happened to him?"

"You'd know that better than we would," Beatrice growled. "Because I suspect he's been with you since you're his flavor of the month. What, did you two have a lovers' spat and he left when he realized what a bimbo you really are?"

"No! Of course not. I swear, I haven't spoken to him or seen him since he went missing."

Beatrice made a sound to indicate she wasn't buying that. "Is Lee pretending to be in danger because he's trying to save face?"

"What are you talking about?" Sharon asked, and Nicky wanted to know the same thing.

"I think you convinced Lee to run off with you, and then when he figured out what he was giving up by being with you—his career and his reputation—he broke things off and pretended that he'd been kidnapped or something. But now he's been taken for real."

"Oh, God." Sharon gave another sob. "You know for certain that Lee's really been kidnapped?"

Nicky and Holden exchanged glances, and she could tell from the look in Holden's eyes that he didn't believe they were going to get anything from Sharon. The woman didn't seem to have a clue what'd happened to Minton.

"If Minton contacts you, tell him to call me," Holden instructed Sharon.

"I will, and please do the same for me. I have to know if he's all right."

Holden assured her that he would, and he ended the call. Perfect timing because Beatrice appeared to be gearing up to sling another round of insults.

"Am I free to go?" Beatrice asked.

"Aren't you even going to look at the baby to see if she might be yours?" Holden asked.

Beatrice's mouth tightened. "I heard Nicky say it was Emmett and Annie's baby."

"Yeah, but you haven't taken our word for anything else," Holden said. "Why would you on something as important as this?"

"I don't like your tone," Beatrice snapped. "I don't know anything more about these babies than you do." However, she did spare the baby a glance. "And I agree that she is Emmett and Annie's. She doesn't look anything like me, my son or Lee."

"And yet the kidnappers contacted you for ransom money," Holden persisted.

"Because they were trying to scam me."

"But the scam would be on your husband, not you, since the money is his."

If Beatrice's eyes narrowed any further, she wouldn't have been able to see. "I'm leaving."

"Gunmen and kidnappers are still out there," Nicky reminded her.

"I'd rather be with them than stay another minute here with you," Beatrice snarled, and she headed for the door.

"Should I stop her?" Josh asked Holden.

Holden shook his head. "Let her go," he answered, but then stopped when they saw the man who was coming in through the front of the building.

Not one of their suspects or one of the gunmen, but it was someone who put Nicky's heart right back in her throat.

Drury.

She hadn't seen him since the attack that could have killed him. The attack she was partly responsible for, but Drury, like some of the other Rylands, might think she was entirely to blame.

Nicky certainly felt that way now.

He was the same height as Holden and had a similar build. Of course, both were good-looking. All the Ryland men were. But unlike Holden, Drury had a dangerous edge to him, and he always seemed to scowl. At least he did whenever he was around her. But then, she had earned each and every one of his scowls and much more.

"Can I help?" Drury asked Holden. He didn't come closer, though his attention landed on the baby.

"This isn't Annie and Emmett's son," Holden explained. "It's their daughter. They had twins."

Drury didn't react to that, but he spared Nicky a glance while he walked toward them. He nodded once he saw the newborn girl. "Yeah" was all he said for several long moments. "I'm on the team that's going through the files at Conceptions Clinic, but we haven't found anything useful."

Nicky hadn't known he was part of that investigation, but it didn't surprise her since Drury was an FBI agent. A good one, too, and she was thankful he was part of the team. Drury wouldn't give up until he'd exhausted every possible bit of information.

"I was about to take Nicky and the baby out of here," Holden volunteered.

Maybe it was the way Holden said her name, but it caused Drury to look at her again. Holden's tone hadn't exactly been a loving one, but it didn't have its usual venom, either.

"Are you two back together?" Drury asked. A muscle flickered in his jaw, though she wasn't sure how any muscles could stir there because his expression was rock-hard.

"No," Nicky answered at the same moment Holden said, "It's complicated."

Drury shifted his attention back to his brother. "It always is." He gave Holden a pat on the arm, and using just his index finger, Drury eased back the blanket to have a better look at the baby. "I don't want the past to get in the way of making sure the baby's all right. Her twin brother, too."

"Thanks for that," Holden answered, and Nicky silently added her own thanks. It wasn't exactly a truce, but she would take it.

"You need an escort to wherever you're going?" Drury asked.

Holden nodded. "Can you follow us and make sure we're not ambushed along the way?"

"Of course." Drury turned back toward the door, but he'd hardly made it a step when the sound of Holden's phone stopped them.

Nicky glanced at the screen and saw Grayson's name there.

"Any sign of Amanda or Minton?" Holden asked the moment he answered.

"No. I'm at the Dumpster where Amanda said she was. She's not here, but we found something." Grayson cursed. "Blood."

Chapter Fourteen

Holden looked down at his niece as he held her. At that precious little face. And he felt the same emotions that he'd felt when he held Carter. He loved her, would do whatever it took to protect her, but he also knew she was in danger.

Nicky, too.

Holden's phone dinged, and he saw the text message from Drury on the screen. His brother had made it back to San Antonio and was at Conceptions Clinic—where Holden hoped like the devil there was still something to find that would help put an end to the danger.

"Everything okay?" Nicky asked.

He nodded. Everything was okay with Drury anyway. They hadn't managed to catch the kidnappers, and that meant the threat was still there, and it left Holden with no choice but to send the baby to the safe house as well. Especially now that they might not have Amanda to give them answers.

Because Amanda might be dead.

There hadn't been a large amount of blood found by the Dumpster, but it was enough to cause concern. He was also concerned that it had been hours since the latest attack, and no one had heard from her. Ditto for Minton. With no other new information in the investigation, Holden was worried they were stalled.

Well, no other new info than the baby.

The newborn girl was definitely news. Amanda hadn't said anything about delivering twins, but Holden remembered her mentioning something at the hospital about being put to sleep during the C-section. If that was true, then it was possible she hadn't even known.

"Wouldn't a woman have realized she was carrying twins?" Holden looked up at Nicky with that question. She was in the process of warming up another bottle of formula—something they'd both mastered, what with the practice they'd gotten with Carter and now his sister.

She shrugged. "You'd think so, but maybe the person responsible didn't allow Amanda to see the ultrasounds. Besides, even if Amanda did suspect it, she might have been too afraid to say anything."

Yeah, because if Amanda had started asking a lot of questions, it would have put her in danger. If she'd realized something was wrong with the whole surrogate plan, then she might have decided just to stay quiet.

But Holden shook his head. "She's still a suspect, though."

"I agree," Nicky said without hesitation. "She could have put the blood there to throw suspicion off her. And of our three suspects, she was still in the best position at Conceptions to have orchestrated all of this."

True. Except for the part about Amanda being fired, but then she could have arranged for that as well, just so it would look as if she was no longer connected to Conceptions.

"What about Minton?" she asked. "You think either Sharon or he have anything to do with what's going on?"

It was something Holden had already considered. And dismissed. "The last thing Sharon probably wants is for Beatrice and Minton to have a child."

"I agree, and there are some problems with Beatrice's theory of Sharon and Minton running off. If that'd happened and Minton had indeed changed his mind, he could have just shown up at a police station with a story about being kidnapped. I doubt he would have involved himself in the mess at Conceptions."

No, but it made Holden go back to one of the questions he couldn't answer. How had Minton gotten his hands on Emmett and Annie's baby? If he got a chance to talk to the man again, that was something Holden definitely wanted to know.

Nicky returned with the bottle and handed it to him. Unlike Carter, the little girl latched on and kept drinking. Not for just a couple of sips, either.

"Bittersweet, isn't it?" Nicky asked when she saw him staring at the little girl.

Yeah, it was. "Annie and Emmett wanted a baby so much, and now they have two. Twins. And they aren't even here to see them." That caused a pain so deep within Holden that it felt as if the pain had seeped into his bones.

Now, the pain would be even deeper because after just meeting her, Holden was going to have to say goodbye. And soon. Josh and another deputy were already on their way to pick up the baby and drive her to the safe house with Carter, Landon and the others. It was the right thing to do, their only option really, but that didn't make it any easier.

"What will happen to them?" Nicky asked. She touched her fingertips to the baby's toes, which were peeking out from the bottom of her pink gown.

Holden knew she wasn't just talking about the immediate future. "I think we've neutralized Oscar for now what with him being on the surveillance footage at the ransom drop."

"Yes." Nicky paused, repeated that. "But I'm sure he was furious at being placed in a holding cell."

Holden was certain of it, but Nicky and he hadn't waited around to find out. As soon as Grayson and the other deputies had returned to the sheriff's office, Holden and Kara had brought Nicky and the baby back to Kayla's house.

"My father will keep trying to get custody," Nicky continued after Holden had finished feeding the baby and had put her against his shoulder to attempt a burp. "That's why I think we should make our own petition to get at least temporary guardianship of them. A joint petition," she added. "We could share custody."

Their gazes connected. "Under the same roof?" he asked.

But it wasn't just a simple question of logistics. The memory of their kiss in the ER was still fresh. Heck, it'd be fresh months from now because he'd probably still be feeling it.

Nicky felt it, too.

The corner of her mouth lifted. "Would it matter if we were under separate roofs?"

Not in the least. The heat would still be there, but this was the exact opposite of out of sight, out of mind. Being next to each other would lead to things Holden wasn't sure he, or his family, could accept.

He didn't answer. Didn't have time because he heard Kara open the front door. It didn't take long for Holden to hear voices, too. Josh and Mason. Several moments later, his cousins came into the kitchen.

"How's she doing?" Josh asked, going straight to the baby.

"Good. Thanks again for finding her," Holden answered, and he refused to think of what would have happened to her if Josh hadn't been in the right place at the right time.

"A girl," Mason remarked, moving closer as well. Since this was Mason, he didn't seem to have an opinion if that was a good thing, but as Nicky had done earlier, he touched the baby's toes.

"Don't get all sentimental on us," Josh joked.

"Not sentimental," Mason growled. Of course, every time he spoke, it sounded like a growl. "Girls are just easier to diaper than boys. Does she have a name yet?"

That started some surprised looks, and Mason huffed. "You should come up with something soon before she gets a nickname like Scarlett or Strawberry."

Yeah, Holden definitely didn't want the kid getting stuck with that.

"We could call her Kate," Nicky suggested. "It was Annie's middle name, after our grandmother."

That caused Josh and Mason to nod in approval. Holden approved, too, and it worked since Carter was Emmett's middle name. But for some reason, with the baby having a name, it made all of this even harder. Because it was yet another reminder that this baby—Kate Ryland—was part of the family. Part of him, too.

Holden hadn't needed to think of how high the stakes were, but that did it.

Josh took the baby, holding her so that Holden and Nicky could get a goodbye kiss. "We'll call you as soon as we've made it to the safe house," Josh assured them.

Nicky and Holden thanked him, and after Mason scooped up the diaper bag with the baby supplies, they all went to the door. Mainly because Mason didn't waste any time getting out of the house, there was no long goodbye. Which was probably a good thing. However, Nicky and Holden stood in the door and watched until they drove away.

With Kate.

It felt as if someone had put a fist around his heart and was squeezing pretty damn hard.

"I need a drink," Holden grumbled. Heck, he needed six of them, but would settle for just one so he could keep a clear head.

He reset the security system, and Kara headed back to the office, where she'd been monitoring the cameras and sensors positioned around the property. Holden would relieve her soon, but for now he went in search of that much-needed drink. He found one in the bar in the family room, and he made a mental note to thank Kayla for stocking the good stuff.

Holden poured himself a glass of whiskey and lifted the bottle to offer Nicky one as well, but she shook her head. That's when he saw that she was blinking back tears.

Hell.

He should have known this was going to send her crashing. It wasn't just the baby, either, but Nicky had to be dealing with the aftermath of being shot. The aftermath, too, of knowing this nightmare was far from being over.

Holden downed the drink and went to her, ready to pull her into his arms. It would be a mistake, of course. They were under the same roof. Semi-alone. And no one was currently shooting at them.

A perfect storm.

But he could try to keep it at just a comforting hug.

Nicky didn't play by the rules, though, and it was obvious she'd need much more than just a hug from him. The moment he reached for her, she reached for him. And she was the one who started the kiss.

NICKY HADN'T KNOWN exactly what she was going to do when Holden had started toward her, but she heard him say something under his breath.

A perfect storm.

Yes, that's exactly what this was.

But it was a storm that she had no intention of stopping. She didn't care about the consequences. Not at the moment anyway. She would later, but there were plenty of other things she would have to deal with later.

"Your arm," Holden said like a warning.

That wouldn't stop her, either. The only thing that would put an end to this was Holden telling her that it wasn't going to happen. But he wasn't saying anything like that. In fact, he'd stopped talking and was kissing her.

Exactly what Nicky wanted him to do.

He tasted of whiskey, but there was also Holden's own familiar taste beneath that. She hadn't needed that taste to start the fire simmering inside her. The fire was always there whenever she was around Holden. But it only added to the moment, and this was a moment she intended to savor.

Because she might not have Holden like this again.

Yes, later she'd have to deal with a lot of things, including the fact that they might never be able to get past their old wounds and do something more than just have sex with each other. For now, though, this was enough.

Holden made the most of that *enough.* He deepened the kiss, and he slipped his arm around her waist, bringing her closer to him. He was gentle. Too gentle. A reminder that he was thinking about the stitches on her arm. Part of Nicky appreciated that, but she needed more from him now.

She dropped her hand to his chest, opening the buttons, and slid her fingers over his chest. She got just the reaction she wanted. He made a sound of pleasure, and the kiss kicked up a notch. So did her heartbeat.

So did the heat.

He turned her, putting her back against the bar, anchoring her in place. Nicky immediately felt the pressure of his body on hers, and it settled her for a moment. Just long enough to allow her to savor the feeling, but it wasn't long before it only made her want more.

Holden gave her more.

He pushed up her top, lowered his head and kissed the tops of her breasts. Then, he pushed down the cups of her bra and took her into his mouth.

Now, it was Nicky's turn to make a sound of pleasure, and her legs would have buckled if Holden hadn't kept her in place against the bar. She made even more of those sounds when he added some touching to those kisses. She wanted to think he knew just the right spot to make her burn because they'd been together before, but the truth was, he'd known all the right spots their first time.

And he repeated that now and upped the ante by going lower and kissing her stomach.

Nicky was wearing loose jeans that she'd borrowed from Kayla's closet, and Holden unzipped them. He didn't stop kissing, either, and it became very clear what he had in mind. Some foreplay that she was sure would set the fire inside her blazing. But there was a problem.

"Kara could come in," she said breathlessly.

Holden still didn't stop, but he did curse. And he shoved down her jeans just enough to deliver one melting kiss to the exact place she wanted his lips to touch.

If Kara came in now, she'd certainly get an eyeful, and Holden must have accepted that because he scooped her up in his arms. She didn't know where he was taking her, didn't care because he continued to kiss her with every step.

They didn't go far. To one of the guest rooms just a few rooms away. Holden shut the door and locked it before he carried her to the bed. He didn't join her, though, and Nicky reached for him, to pull him down to her. But she stopped.

Because he stripped off his shirt.

And she lost her breath in the process.

He was perfect, just as she remembered him. His body was chiseled—not from working out in a gym but from working on the ranch. Toned and tanned. Yes, perfect.

It got even better.

He unzipped his jeans, and the rest of his clothes came off.

Nicky was well aware she was staring. Couldn't stop herself. Mercy, how could she feel this way just by looking at him? She didn't have time to figure that out, though, because he finally got on the bed with her.

"Let's do something about getting you naked, too," he drawled.

She would have gladly helped him with that if he hadn't made her senseless with another of those scalding kisses. But thankfully Holden had no trouble peeling off her top and bra. Had no trouble kissing her breasts again and driving her crazy.

He started the trail of kisses again, retracing his steps to her stomach. Her zipper was already undone so he shimmied the jeans off her, removing her panties with them.

And now she got that kiss she'd been wanting.

Nicky could have sworn the earth tipped on its axis. Maybe it did. Holden was certainly working some magic, and Nicky knew this would end much too soon if it continued.

She latched onto him, dragging him back up toward her, but he seemed to have his own notion about that as well. He dug through his jeans and located a condom in his wallet.

Something that made her groan.

Here she'd gotten so caught up that she hadn't remembered that they needed to use protection. At least one of them was thinking straight.

When Holden returned to the bed, he maneuvered them to the headboard and adjusted their positions until they were in a sitting position with her on his lap.

"Your arm," he said.

Nicky still hadn't managed the thinking-straight part so it took her a moment to realize this way there wouldn't be any pressure on her stitches. Yes, Holden was definitely thinking a lot straighter than she was.

So she did something about that.

She reached between their bodies, helped him with the condom and then took him inside her. Deep and quick. While she kissed him. After a few strokes, she thought maybe she'd managed to cloud his mind as well.

There was a problem with that, though. This was still all going to end too soon, and there was nothing she could do to stop that. The need was too great. The fire, too hot.

Holden must have realized that because he caught her hips and began controlling the rhythm, bringing her toward the only thing Nicky wanted now.

For him to take her over the edge. For him to ease the fire and the storm that was raging out of control.

And that's what he did.

Holden pushed into her and sent her flying. The climax slammed through her. Nicky couldn't speak. Couldn't breathe. But she could feel. And what she felt was Holden falling over the edge with her.

HOLDEN GAVE HIMSELF a couple of seconds to catch his breath. Then another couple of seconds to come to his senses, and he checked to make sure Nicky wasn't in pain, or that her stitches weren't torn.

She was clearly okay.

Nicky's face was right against his, and she was so relaxed that the muscles in her body had gone slack. There
was no indication whatsoever that she was hurting. Not
from her injury anyway. But when she lifted her head,
and her gaze met his, Holden did see something he wasn't
sure he liked.

"Don't regret this," she whispered.

Too late. He already did.

Not because it wasn't mind-blowing sex. It had been.
But because he was in bed with someone in his protective
custody, and he'd just completely lost focus. Definitely
not something that would help them. Plus, there was another complication. One that he didn't especially want to
consider, but it came to the forefront of his mind anyway.

Maybe this had been more than just mind-blowing sex.

"You are regretting it," she said. Nicky huffed and
moved off him.

That was Holden's cue to move, too, and he eased off
the bed and went into the bathroom. Despite the realiza-
tion that this had just complicated the heck out of things,
Holden was already thinking about being with her again.

Soon.

And with that on his mind, he came back into the bedroom and saw that Nicky and he were not on the same
page when it came to sex. She was already out of the bed
and getting dressed.

"Are *you* regretting what happened?" he asked. And he
hated that it felt like a punch to the gut that she might be.

She didn't look at him when she pulled on her jeans.
"Not the way you're thinking." She put on her shoes and
would have headed for the door if Holden hadn't stepped
in front of her to stop her.

Holden tried to figure out what was going on in her

head but couldn't tell. She seemed angry or something, and he glanced at her arm again to make sure that wasn't the problem.

"I'm not in pain," she insisted. "I just want to get back to work. I have Paul's files to go through."

Since she obviously wasn't in the mood to talk about what just happened, Holden leaned in and kissed her. Judging from the slight sound of surprise she made, Nicky definitely hadn't been expecting that. Heck, he hadn't been expecting it, either, but whenever he was around Nicky, he always seemed to be flying by the seat of his pants.

Holden kissed her until that sound of surprise turned to one of pleasure, and she sort of melted into his arms. Considering he was still naked and that his body was revved up into overdrive, it felt better than good.

And that was the problem.

Holden understood why she was in flight mode, or at least why she'd been just seconds earlier.

"I'm scared, too," he admitted, and he wasn't talking about the danger now.

She nodded. "I just don't want my heart crushed again."

Again?

He nearly asked if he'd been the one to cause a heart crushing, but Holden knew that he had been. They hadn't exactly been in a relationship before, but it had certainly been the start of one, and it had all come crashing down when Drury had nearly been killed.

She looked down between them. At his naked body. "You're very tempting," she said, causing him to smile.

He looked at her mouth. "Tempting," Holden repeated.

Nicky smiled, too, and that moment washed away some of the regret, some of the doubts about that possible heart crushing. But it didn't last. That's because his phone buzzed. Holden fished it from his jeans pocket, and they both saw whose name popped up on the screen.

Kara.

Considering the deputy was just up the hall, or at least that's where she was supposed to be, this probably wasn't good news.

"Holden, are you in there?" Kara asked the moment he answered and put the call on speaker.

"I'm here." That sent him scrambling for his clothes.

"You need to come right away and take a look at the computer that monitors the security," she said. "We have an intruder on the grounds."

Chapter Fifteen

Nicky's heart jumped to her throat, and just like that, the heat between she and Holden was gone. Oh, God. Had the kidnappers found them?

"I'll be right there," Holden assured Kara, and he hurriedly dressed.

Nicky made sure her clothes were fixed, too, and then followed him up the hall. Kara was in an office. Not an ordinary office, though. There were no windows in the room, and it was jammed with equipment. Six monitors, all with split screens to show every angle of the grounds. But it was dark outside, and it took Nicky a moment to look at each one.

Nicky finally saw the man near one of the fences.

There wasn't much of a moon, but the camera was rigged like night-vision goggles. Without that, he would have just blended into the darkness, which was probably what he'd intended. But with the night vision, he looked a little like a ghost.

"Are there security lights out there?" Nicky asked.

Holden shook his head. "But there are plenty if he gets closer to the house. Those are motion-activated."

Good. So, if anyone tried to get near the place to start shooting, they should trigger the lights. The alarm, too.

"He doesn't appear to be armed," Kara said, "but then he's staying in the shadows so it's hard to tell."

In this case the shadows were from a cluster of towering pecan trees and the night itself, and while the man might not have been armed, he was definitely hiding between the trees.

"Try to zoom in on his face," Holden instructed.

This particular one didn't have on a ski mask, but there were too many shadows for them to clearly see his face. Which was probably also part of his plan. After all, if he'd trespassed onto private property, then he was probably up to no good.

Nicky glanced at the other monitors but didn't see anyone else. Thank goodness. That didn't mean they weren't in danger, but at least they weren't facing down an entire army of kidnappers. Not yet anyway. It could be this guy was sent to scope things out, maybe even to test the security system.

But how had he found them?

"Has Kayla had trouble in the past with people trespassing?" Nicky asked because she had to consider that this person may not even be connected to the attacks.

Kara shook her head. "None that I know of. Everyone in the area knows she has a state-of-the-art security system."

So, the man was likely there because of them. Not exactly a thought to help settle her nerves.

Nicky had her attention so focused on the monitor that she gasped when the sound shot through the room. Not the threat that her body had anticipated. But rather Holden's phone buzzed.

"Minton," he said, looking at the screen. Holden put this call on speaker, too.

"Can you see me?" Minton asked.

At that moment the man leaned out from the tree, and

Nicky got a better look at his face. Yes, it was Senator Minton all right, but he quickly ducked behind the tree.

Holden didn't jump to answer, probably because he didn't want to confirm that they were indeed on the property and watching.

"I put a tracking device on your car," Minton added. "That's how I knew where you were."

"A tracking device?" Holden challenged. "How did you manage to get one of those when you were on the run?"

"It was in the baby's blanket. When I realized what it was, I left the baby in the alley and sneaked into the parking lot. I knew which car was yours because I saw you drive up in it."

Holden cursed, and Nicky hated that he would blame himself for this, but there'd been a lot of craziness going on in Silver Creek, and they hadn't exactly been focusing on the car. She prayed that didn't turn out to be a fatal mistake.

"You left a baby in the alley," Holden snarled. "Tell me why the hell you would do that, especially considering there was gunfire."

"I didn't want to take her out into the open, and I knew those kidnappers weren't going to do anything to harm her."

"And how did you know that?" Nicky blurted out. She couldn't help herself. The anger hit her hard, and she wanted to throttle this fool for doing that to a baby. "They could have hurt her or worse."

"No," Minton argued. "I heard them call her their two-million-dollar baby, and I knew they wouldn't risk hurting her. They were shooting at the deputies."

"And at you?" Holden challenged.

"No," the man repeated. "Those men were never after me." He paused. "Is the baby all right? And my son—is he okay?"

"The baby girl is fine. I'm not sure about your son, though. I haven't seen him." Holden's voice was filled with just as much anger as Nicky's. "Now, tell me how you got the newborn girl?"

"Some men had her in a car just up the street from the sheriff's office. I was hiding, watching them, because I thought maybe they were the same men who'd kidnapped me. But they weren't."

The anger was still there, but Nicky felt something else—surprise.

"You're sure?" she asked.

"Positive. My kidnappers have held me for two weeks, and even though they wore masks, I know how they moved, and the sounds of their voices. The ones who had the baby wore ski masks, too, and they were on their phones a lot. Whoever they were talking to told them to put a tracking device on your car. They left the baby alone, I took her. That's when I saw that she had a tracking device in her blanket."

Mercy. Nicky looked at Holden, and he shook his head, maybe telling her not to borrow trouble. But Nicky was already thinking the worst.

Had those kidnappers put a tracking device on Nicky's car, too?

She frantically searched the screens and didn't see anyone, but there were a lot of barns, two guesthouses and several other outbuildings. Maybe those kidnappers had managed to get past security and were already on the grounds.

"I'm glad the baby's safe," Minton continued several moments later, "but that's not why I'm calling. I need your help, and I'm not sure I can trust anyone else."

"And why would you trust me?" Holden snapped.

"Because of Nicky. She's been trying to find me."

"So has half the state," Holden quickly pointed out.

"Maybe, but I heard one of the kidnappers talking to a cop once. Or maybe the guy was an ex-cop. I could tell he had some kind of law enforcement background from the slang he used."

"Or maybe he just watched a lot of crime shows." Holden kept his attention on Minton. The man hadn't moved an inch. "How did you get away from the kidnappers?"

"I offered one of them money. Lots of it. Not to the one who was talking with the cop, but the other one. He helped me escape, but something went wrong. Other kidnappers came after us. They killed him and tried to kill me. That's why I need your help. I want you to assure me that my son and I will be protected."

Holden stayed quiet a moment. "Who hired those kidnappers who took you, and are they connected to what happened at Conceptions?"

"Conceptions," Minton repeated like a profanity. "Yes, they're connected. Or at least I think they are. My kidnappers knew about my son, but they didn't take credit for what went on. In fact, the one who didn't end up helping me said it was a scam he wished he'd thought of."

A scam. Nicky hadn't needed anything else to anger her, but that did it. "Who's behind this *scam*?" she demanded.

"My wife. At least maybe she is. Or maybe she only had part in kidnapping me."

Holden jumped right on it. "Why would you say that?"

"Because my kidnappers never demanded a ransom. They just held me captive, and I had a lot of time to think about why they would do that. I think it was to give Beatrice some time to rob me blind."

That was one of Nicky's theories, too, but that didn't mean she was dismissing Beatrice's involvement at Conceptions. The baby—the Minton heir—was the perfect way to hang on to some of her husband's money.

"If you think your wife is guilty," Holden went on, "then why did you break in to Amanda's room at the hotel?"

"I was looking for something, anything to tie her to the Conceptions babies. She was a businesswoman, and I thought it was suspicious that she would become a surrogate. Especially a surrogate for a shady operation like the one going on at Conceptions." Minton huffed. "Will you help me now?"

Nicky saw the debate in Holden's eyes. Yes, he could call the sheriff's office, but he could be leading them into an ambush if those kidnappers were nearby. The goons could have put Minton up to this and could be hidden nearby with a gun pointed at him.

"Go back over the fence and toward the road," Holden finally said, "and I'll have some of my cousins come and get you."

"That's not safe," Minton argued. "I need to stay hidden or else they'll find me."

Holden didn't have time to respond though because there was a sound. A series of soft beeps. It took Nicky a moment to pick through all the screens and see what had caused those beeps.

A dark blue SUV.

It was coming up the road directly toward the house, and the closer it got to the house, the more security lights flared on.

"Are you expecting anyone?" Kara asked.

"No," Holden answered.

And he drew his gun.

FROM THE MOMENT Holden had seen Minton on the monitor, he'd known this was going to be trouble. He just hadn't expected trouble to come so soon.

"Should I call the sheriff?" Kara asked.

Holden knew that Grayson and the others were neck-deep in this investigation, and this could still turn out to be nothing. But Holden figured that was wishful thinking on his part. Best to go ahead and alert Grayson, especially since it would take backup a while to get there.

"Call him," Holden answered, "but tell him about Minton. Minton might have tampered with the sensors on the back fence."

Or else Minton could have been forced to tamper with them. Holden still wasn't convinced that the senator was alone, and the kidnappers could have put him up to this. There were still questions to which they didn't have an answer, though.

Who was controlling the kidnappers?

"What can I do to help?" Nicky asked as Kara made the call to Grayson.

His first instinct was to tell her to hide, and he still might do that, but for now Holden opened the storage cabinet and took out a gun that Landon had told him would be there. In fact, there wasn't just one gun but three. Holden only hoped he didn't need them and that what he was doing was overkill.

"Keep watching the monitors," he told Kara. "I'm going to the front of the house to see if I can get a better look at our visitors. There's an intercom by the front door so you can talk to me through that." It would free up his hands if he didn't have to hold his phone.

"Should I go with you?" Nicky asked.

"Not a chance. Wait here." But he had to add something else. Something she wouldn't want to hear. "If anything goes wrong, I need you to stay in here and get down, understand?" he asked.

Holden waited until she nodded before he brushed a kiss on her mouth and hurried to the foyer. There were stained glass windows on each side of the door, and he looked out just as the SUV was coming to a stop in the circular drive.

There were no other vehicles visible on the grounds because Holden had parked in the garage. There were some lights on in the house but none that their visitors would be able to see from the front.

Holden waited. Watching for any movement inside the SUV, but it was hard to tell who or how many were inside because of the heavily tinted windows.

He pressed the intercom button. "Kara, can you zoom in on the SUV?" And he immediately heard the clicks on the computer keyboard Kara was using.

"I've zoomed in as much as I can, but the windows are too dark."

"Try getting a different angle from one of the other cameras," he instructed. "Nicky, you keep an eye on Minton."

Holden moved away from the intercom but left it on so he'd still be able to hear Nicky and Kara. He, too, tried a different angle. He went to the window in the living room and peered around the edge. The security lights hit the windshield just right so that Holden could see the silhouette of someone inside.

Or rather two silhouettes.

A driver and someone in the front passenger seat.

That didn't mean, however, that there were only two of them because if these were the hired thugs, there could be more in the backseat.

"Minton's on the move," Nicky blurted out.

Hell. Holden didn't need this now. "Is he coming toward the house?"

"Not at the moment. He's skirting along the fence line, though. There's a barn about an eighth of a mile from where he is, and he could be trying to get to it." Nicky paused. "He looks scared, and he keeps glancing over his shoulder."

Holden didn't like the sound of that at all. Of course, there wasn't much he liked about any of this. The only silver lining was that the babies were tucked away at the safe house.

He hoped.

The knot in his stomach tightened, and even though he knew this wouldn't help steady Nicky, it needed to be done.

"Don't take your eyes off Minton," Holden told her. "But call Landon and make sure everything's okay."

He had no trouble hearing Nicky suck in a hard breath. Practically a gasp. Something he totally understood. It cut him to the core that their attackers might have found a way to get to Landon and the babies, too.

The moments crawled by. Not his heartbeat, though. It was racing now and so was his breath. Still, all Holden could do was wait and listen as Nicky called Landon and filled him in on what was happening.

"They're all okay," Nicky finally said. "Landon says to keep him posted."

Holden would, if he could. "Where's Minton right now?"

"Still skulking toward the barn. Still looking around as if someone's going to jump out at him. He's getting close enough to the barn, though, that he'll trigger the security lights. If someone really is tracking him, that'll make it much easier for them."

Yeah, but there wasn't much Holden could do about that now. If and when Minton made it closer to the house, he'd deal with it then. But since the barn doors were wide-open, Minton would be able to run inside even if the lights gave away his location.

"Uh, Holden?" Kara said. "We have a problem. All the monitors just went blank. All I'm getting is static."

It felt as if someone had grabbed hold of his throat. No. This couldn't be happening.

"Try to reboot the system," Holden instructed.

More seconds crawled by.

"It's not working," Kara said. "Somebody's jammed the whole system."

Yeah, definitely wasn't what he wanted to hear. But then something else got Holden's attention. He saw the passenger door of the SUV open.

Then he saw the gun.

Except it wasn't a gun. It was some kind of launcher, and whoever was holding it had it aimed directly at the house.

Chapter Sixteen

Nicky kept watch at the door of the office as Kara tried once again to reboot the security system. She didn't want to think the worst—that someone had tampered with it and was ready to attack—but it was hard not to think just that what with everything that'd gone on.

"I believe someone's using a jamming device," Kara said. "I'm going to call the security company and see if they can access the cameras a different way."

Kara was taking out her phone when they heard the footsteps. Someone was running toward them.

"Get down!" Holden shouted.

Nicky didn't have time to even move before she heard the sound of shattering glass. Then, an even louder sound.

A blast.

It seemed to shake the entire house, and it caused the fear to slam into her. *Holden.* God, had he been hurt?

She leaned out into the hall and saw him running toward them. Not hurt, thank goodness, but Nicky wasn't sure it would stay that way.

Because there was a second explosion.

"They're using grenades," Holden said when he reached them. "We're going to have to move."

He didn't wait for Nicky to do that. Holden hooked his arm around her waist, and with Kara right behind them, they hurried toward the back of the house. Not a second too soon, either.

The third blast was even louder than the others, and Nicky heard the sound of walls and maybe even the roof collapsing. Their attackers were literally trying to bring down the house with them inside it.

"Stay away from the windows," Holden reminded them when they reached the kitchen.

Hard to do that, though, since there were three large windows that faced the backyard. That's probably why Holden led them into the massive pantry.

The lights weren't on, and Holden kept it that way. No doubt so that those thugs wouldn't be able to pinpoint their exact location. However, whoever was shooting those grenades had to know that they would try to escape, and that they'd likely do that through the back so they could get as far away as possible from the explosions—and their attackers.

The fourth blast was even louder than the others, and with this one, Nicky smelled something that caused her heart to slam against her ribs.

Smoke.

Holden cursed, and Nicky knew why. It would take more grenades to destroy the house, and it was such a big place that they could probably find a safe area to hide until backup arrived. But if there was smoke, there was also likely fire, and that meant they'd have to get out.

"Stay here," Holden instructed, and he hurried to the exact place he'd told them to avoid.

The windows.

He looked out the side of the one nearest to them, but he also kept watch behind him, too. That's when Nicky knew she had to do something to help. She didn't know if it was possible for their attackers to get to them through the front of the house, but it was too big of a chance to take. She stepped out just enough so she could better keep watch. Kara did the same.

"I don't see Minton," Holden said after looking out the back.

That didn't mean he wasn't there. Nicky doubted the senator would have kept running toward the front of the house once he heard the explosion. Of course, he could be anywhere now that the sensors were off. It was the same for their attackers. They could already be in the back, waiting for them.

That gave her a new slam of adrenaline that she didn't need.

The smoke kept coming at them. Thick, dark and suffocating. They definitely wouldn't be able to stay here much longer.

Holden looked back, meeting Nicky's gaze, and she could see the apology in his expression. He was silently saying he was sorry for letting things get to this point. Of course, he would put all of this on his shoulders and would see it as a failure on his part. It wasn't. Whoever wanted her dead just wasn't stopping, and now Kara and Holden had gotten caught in the cross fire.

"This way," Holden ordered.

He didn't lead them out the back door, though. Instead, he went to the side of the house, but the smoke was even thicker and they all started to cough. They definitely couldn't stay here much longer or they'd die.

They went to the one room that Nicky hadn't expected them to go—the sunroom. It was literally all glass except for the roof and door frame. And maybe that's why Holden had chosen it. Because their attacker probably wouldn't think they would try to escape this way.

"Once we're outside stay low and move fast," Holden added. "We'll need to get to the barn."

That was all he said before they started running. Holden unlocked the door, threw it open and they hurried out into the night. It was terrifying to be out in the open, but at least the smoke wasn't as bad here so she could breathe.

Nicky tried to keep her gun ready as they ran toward the barn. If this had been normal circumstances, it wouldn't have been that far—only about twenty yards—but it felt as if it was miles.

Other than some shrubs and a few scattered trees, there wasn't much they could use for cover, but when they reached one of the large oaks, Holden pulled them behind it and glanced around. Probably trying to make sure someone wasn't already waiting for them at the barn.

Nicky cursed because she couldn't see much of anything, but it tapped into one of her phobias. Mercy, she hated the darkness and, in this case, everything that it could conceal. She prayed their attackers hadn't had time yet to make it to this part of the grounds.

"Let's go," Holden said.

They started running again, but instead of making a beeline toward the barn, Holden continued to use the trees for cover. They darted behind another oak. Then another. Until the barn was only about ten yards away.

Now that they were closer, Nicky tried to pick through the darkness to see if Minton or the attackers were there. She didn't see anything, but Holden must have thought their chances were better in the barn than behind the tree because he motioned for them to get moving again. They did. But they'd barely made it a step.

When someone fired a shot at them.

FROM THE MOMENT he'd seen the SUV pull up in front of the house, Holden had figured it would come down to this.

To an attack.

Later he would curse himself for not being able to prevent it. But for now, he had to protect Nicky before these goons could kill her.

Holden pulled her to the ground and hoped that he hadn't hurt her arm in the process. It wasn't a serious injury, but just bumping it could cause a lot of pain. Enough that she wouldn't be able to think straight, and right now he needed all three of them thinking straight.

Shooting straight as well.

"Keep watch that way," Holden told Kara when she landed on the ground next to them. He tipped his head toward the barn. He didn't want anyone sneaking up on them from behind and ambushing them.

"Nicky, you keep an eye on the right side of the house," Holden added. "But stay down."

She gave a shaky nod. Actually, she was shaking all over, but that didn't stop her from lifting her gun and aiming it at the right side of the house.

There was another shot.

It smacked into the tree in the spot where Holden had just been standing. Whoever had fired was obviously in good position to see them.

But where?

He cursed the darkness and looked around but couldn't pinpoint the location of the shooter.

Holden's phone dinged, and because he didn't want to lose focus, he took it from his pocket and handed it to Nicky.

"It's from Grayson," she said when she read the text message. "He's still about fifteen minutes out."

Fifteen minutes was an eternity when they were under attack like this. "Text him back and tell him about the gunfire. And the fire in Kayla's house. I want him to approach with sirens blaring."

That might not do much to deter their attackers, but at least the thugs would know that backup had arrived and that maybe they were outgunned.

Holden still didn't have a clue how many they were up against.

There could be an entire army of hired guns out there now. With the commotion of the grenade blasts, the fire and their escape, a dozen more vehicles could have pulled in front of the house by now.

There was another shot, and this time Holden got a glimpse of the shooter. He was at the left rear side of the house, but the moment he fired, he ducked back behind cover. Holden took aim, waiting for the idiot to lean out again so that he'd have a decent shot.

"I just saw someone near the barn," Kara whispered.

"Minton?"

"Hard to tell, but I think the person might have gone inside. Either that, or he's on the ground just outside the barn."

Not good. Because Holden didn't have many options here, and the barn was the nearest building.

The tree wasn't big enough to give them good cover, especially if someone launched another grenade at them. Of course, they could fire a grenade into there, too, but to do that, they'd have to come out into the open.

Like the shooter on the left of the house.

He finally leaned out again, and Holden didn't waste a second. He took aim and fired. Two shots. They slammed into the guy's chest, and he went down. Probably not dead, though. He was almost certainly wearing body armor, but the shots were enough to knock him off his feet.

"Let's move," Holden told them.

They hurried from the cover of the tree, staying as low as they could. With each step Holden prayed that there wouldn't be any more shots fired at him, but he knew it was only a matter of time before the gunman's partners realized he was down, and they would no doubt pick up where he left off.

Holden didn't see Minton or anyone else near the barn. It didn't mean someone wasn't there, though. That's why he darted inside just ahead of Nicky and Kara. He and Kara both brought up their guns, their gazes slashing from one side of the barn to the other.

"Stay close to me," Holden whispered to Nicky.

It was dark inside, too dark to see much of anything, and Holden didn't like that the back doors were wide-open as well. That had probably been intentional since there was nothing stored in the barn, but with both doors open, their attackers could trap them.

"Keep watch out back," Holden told Kara, and he moved to the side of the front door so he could look for more gunmen.

Nothing.

Well, nothing except for the fact that Kayla's house was now in flames. Kayla had done them a huge favor by letting them stay there, and now her house would be destroyed. Even if the fire department made it there in time, they wouldn't be able to get onto the grounds until it was secure.

It was far from being secure, and Holden got proof of that when he saw another gunman. This guy was on the opposite side of the house from his fallen comrade. He didn't lean out but rather fired, still using the house for cover.

But he didn't fire into the barn.

The shot went to the pasture area just on the side of it.

It didn't stay just a single shot, either. The guy fired another one. Then another. However, even over the thick gunfire, Holden heard something else he certainly hadn't expected to hear.

"Help me!" someone called out.

Beatrice.

What the hell was she doing here?

"Help me!" Beatrice screamed again, and with that scream still echoing in Holden's head, he heard the movement at the back of the barn. And a moment later, Beatrice came running.

Chapter Seventeen

Nicky pivoted, taking aim at Beatrice. Kara did as well. But Holden stayed put, volleying glances over his shoulder while he kept watch at the front.

"Put up your hands," Kara immediately ordered the woman.

Beatrice stopped in her tracks when she saw the two guns pointed at her, and she shook her head. "Someone's trying to kill me," Beatrice insisted.

"Yeah, and it'll be me who does that if you don't put up your hands," Holden assured her.

"I'm the victim here," Beatrice said through a heavy sob. "Someone kidnapped me and forced me to come to—" she glanced around "—wherever this place is."

Nicky wasn't ready to believe that just yet. Maybe not ever. Because after all, Beatrice was one of their suspects, and she could have come running in there to ambush them.

Except Beatrice wasn't armed.

And her hands were tied behind her back.

Other than the plastic cuffs around her wrists, she was wearing one of her usual blue skirts and tops. Heels, too, even though one of them was broken. Her hair was a tangled mess, and there was either a bruise or some dirt on her face.

Beatrice certainly looked as if she might have been

kidnapped, but Nicky still wasn't buying it. She could have had someone put those plastic cuffs on her to make it seem as if she'd been kidnapped. And the only reason she would have had for doing that was to get close enough to kill them.

Apparently Kara wasn't buying it, either. She went to the woman and frisked her. "Sit there," Kara ordered.

The deputy used the barrel of her gun to motion toward one of the handful of bales of hay that was in the barn. It was the nearest one to the door.

Outside, some more shots came, and these slammed into the barn. Holden had to move to the side and he motioned for Nicky and Kara to do the same.

"Quit treating me like a criminal," Beatrice snarled despite the deafening gunfire. "I didn't have anything to do with this."

"Yeah, right," Holden mumbled. "Don't let her out of your sight," he added to Nicky and Kara.

Nicky had no intention of doing that, but she also kept watch at the back doors. She wanted to shut them, but that would put her in the possible line of fire if there were indeed kidnappers or gunmen out there.

More shots came, and Holden leaned out just long enough to fire some shots of his own. Maybe that would keep the gunmen at bay until Grayson and the others could arrive.

"Who *kidnapped* you?" Nicky asked Beatrice, and she didn't bother to sound as if she believed the woman.

It took Beatrice a moment to finish the sob she was in the middle of so she could answer. "Some men wearing ski masks. They looked like the same ones who had the baby."

Oh, God. The baby. That tightened Nicky's chest. "Is your son here, too?"

Beatrice shook her head, kept on crying. "No. He was

at the house with the nanny and his bodyguards. I was on my way to Lee's office when the men ran me off the road and took me at gunpoint."

"What do they want with you?" Holden snapped. "And why would they just let you go so you could come running into the barn where we just happen to be?"

Holden had Nicky beat in the skepticism department.

"They didn't *let* me go," Beatrice insisted. "I escaped. I was in the SUV when they started shooting those grenade things at the house. When two of them got out, I managed to get the door opened. I got out and started running. I ended up here. Didn't you see that man shooting at me?"

Beatrice looked at Holden when she asked that question, and Nicky glanced at him, too. He nodded. A surprise. Nicky had heard the shots, but she'd thought the gunman was shooting at Holden.

"The man could have been shooting into the ground or over your head," Holden added. "That doesn't prove you're innocent."

No, but it did lead Nicky to her next question. "How many men brought you here?"

"Three," Beatrice answered without hesitation.

If the woman was telling the truth, then that meant there were only two of them left since Holden had shot one of them. But maybe that wounded one was still capable of doing some damage.

There were more shots, but Nicky also heard something else. A welcome sound this time.

Sirens.

Grayson was close now, and it wouldn't be long before he was on the grounds. Nicky had no idea how close he could get to the house, but she hoped he and the deputies would be able to put a stop to this.

A permanent stop.

That meant capturing at least one of the gunmen alive so he could tell them who'd hired him. Nicky had to believe that could happen because there was no way Holden, she and the twins could continue to live like this.

"Get down!" Holden called out to them. He charged toward Nicky, pulling her to the ground just as the explosion tore through the barn.

Holden and she both fell, and even though she knew it wasn't intentional, his arm hit hers, and the pain shot through her. Nicky had to fight for breath, and her eyes watered.

But that was the least of their problems.

Their attackers had obviously launched another grenade their way, and it had taken off a good portion of the front of the barn. They didn't just have the open doors to worry about, there was a hole large enough to drive an SUV through. And maybe that's what they had in mind because Nicky also heard the sound of an engine.

Beatrice was screaming now, perhaps because the impact had sent her to the floor, too, but Nicky couldn't tell if it was Beatrice or Kara who was hurt. However, Kara was at least able to move because she hurried to Beatrice and dragged her away from some of the barn roof that was creaking and ready to fall.

Holden pulled Nicky to her feet as well, and he ran to the back of the barn with her. "Watch behind us," he told her.

Nicky did that as best she could, and she saw the source of that engine. It was the SUV all right, and it was coming right toward them.

Holden pushed her behind him and fired. His bullets went right into the windshield. Kara shot at the tires, and the SUV finally came to a stop in the yard. Still, it was close. Too close. And those gunmen could start shooting or launch another grenade at them.

"We have to move," Holden said, and he turned, no doubt to get them started out the back door.

But it was too late.

The man came rushing in, and he was armed. It happened so fast, and while Holden was trying to get into position to fire, the man latched onto Beatrice. That's when Nicky got a better look at his face.

It was Lee Minton.

And he put a gun to his wife's head.

HOLDEN DEFINITELY DIDN'T need this. Whatever the *hell* this was.

"What are you doing?" Holden demanded.

"I'm getting her to confess," Minton said, his voice as shaky as his hand. Not a good combination to have a gun in the hands of a man who was clearly out of control. "She's the one who had me kidnapped." He jammed the gun even harder against Beatrice's head. "Admit it."

Beatrice didn't deny it, and she started sobbing again.

"Now isn't the time for this," Holden assured him. He kept watch on that SUV. On Minton, too.

But if Minton heard him, he didn't acknowledge it. The man had clearly worked himself up into a rage.

"I want to hear her admit it," Minton growled. "And don't lie, Beatrice, because I have the proof. The thug you hired confessed. You knew that, and that's why you had me kidnapped again."

"No!" Beatrice practically shouted. She winced when he dug the gun into her skin. "Yes, I did have you taken the first time. But not now. I had no part in this, I swear." She looked up at Holden and repeated that.

Maybe she was telling the truth, but Holden didn't care. She'd just admitted to kidnapping her husband, and it didn't matter if she'd done that once or twice. It meant she was capable of pretty much anything.

"There are two men with a grenade launcher in that SUV, and he can take down the rest of this barn with just one more blast," Holden reminded the senator.

Again, Minton didn't seem to hear Holden. "How could you have done that to me?" he shouted to his wife. "I always knew you were a gold digger, but I never expected you to have me kidnapped. And why? So you could get your hands on my money."

Holden was ready to throttle them both. "You can stay here and die," he finally told Minton. "Or you can try to get out of here with us."

Though Holden did have a problem with Beatrice tagging along. Since she was still wearing the plastic cuffs, she wasn't an immediate danger to them, but she could always call out to the thugs.

Holden looked out at the pasture just as his phone buzzed, and he saw the message from Grayson on the screen.

We're coming in. Watch your fire.

That was a reminder for Holden not to shoot unless he was certain of his target.

Behind them, the SUV started to move, and Holden knew he had to get moving as well. "Come on," Holden told Nicky, and he led them out the door.

He didn't get far, though.

Because the moment he stepped outside, someone put a gun in his face. And it wasn't one of the hired thugs.

It was Amanda.

"Move one inch," she warned him, "and I'll kill you."

Hell. How could he have let this happen? With the noise from the sirens and Minton's and Beatrice's chatter, he hadn't heard the woman approach. That could be the thing that got Nicky and the rest of them killed.

Amanda backed him into the barn and put the gun to his head. Holden still had his weapon. So did the others. But if he moved or did anything sudden, Amanda could shoot. And not necessarily shoot him, either. She could turn the gun on Nicky or Kara.

"I was beginning to wonder if you'd ever come out of there," Amanda complained. "I didn't want my men to have to fire off another grenade. Boys, you can come out now," she added, and it took Holden a moment to realize she was speaking into a small communicator clipped to her collar.

The *boys* were two armed thugs who got out of the SUV. And they weren't wearing ski masks. Definitely not good. Because it meant Amanda and the two guys intended to kill all of them.

"You want me to move the SUV to the back?" one of the thugs asked Amanda.

"No. I can't be sure the lawmen haven't made it back there."

That was a possibility, too, since Grayson would know the layout of the grounds. Plus, Grayson could have sent some deputies to one of the ranch trails that threaded all around the property.

"Guns on the ground *now*," the thug snarled, glancing at Holden, Nicky and Kara. He stayed near the front, and the other hurried to Amanda's side.

Without so much as a warning, the guy at the front took aim at Kara and fired, the shot slamming into her arm.

Damn. It took everything inside Holden to stop himself from charging the guy. But if he did, it would just get Kara killed. Kara groaned in pain and dropped to her knees.

"Weapons down now," the thug repeated. "Or the next shot goes right into her head."

They had no choice but to drop their weapons. Minton, however, kept his gun hidden on the side of his leg. Maybe Amanda and her goons hadn't seen it.

"This is how this will work," Amanda said, her voice so cold that he felt the chill all the way to his bones. "Beatrice and the senator will come with me. If they don't cooperate, I'll start putting bullets into them until they do."

"Because you need to set them up to take the blame for all of this," Holden said. It was just a theory, but he could tell from Amanda's slight smile that he was right.

Amanda was going to take Minton and Beatrice to a secondary location, where she could either force them to make a false confession or else plant something incriminating on them. The perfect way to end that would be to have their deaths look like a murder-suicide.

"How do you intend to get out of here?" Nicky snapped. "Backup has arrived."

"Yes." Amanda didn't show any emotion about that. "That's where you and Holden come in. I have some more men in place now, and they should be able to take care of any extra Silver Creek lawmen. But I need hostages, human shields, whatever you want to call it. Either way, we're leaving."

"But you'll have to take Nicky with you, too," Holden said. It was yet another theory. "Because you'll have to make sure she doesn't have copies of those files from Conceptions."

"I'm sure Nicky will tell me all about those to save you from dying a really painful death. Those files have other encrypted data in them," she added. "I will get them back."

Hell, that meant there could be other babies. Or at least plans to continue this sick surrogacy operation.

"You murdered a man," Nicky snapped. "You killed Paul."

Amanda didn't confirm that. Didn't have to. She'd ordered Paul's death when he wouldn't give her the files, and she would do the same to Nicky. Or at least she'd try. Holden only hoped Amanda didn't have one of her goons shoot him before he could put a stop to this.

Amanda motioned toward one of the thugs, and he went closer to Minton, taking aim at the senator. "What part of 'put down your gun' didn't you understand?"

Holden's stomach dropped. So, they'd seen Minton's gun after all.

The thug didn't add more to that order to Minton, probably because Amanda's threat had been enough. If Minton didn't cooperate, Amanda or one of the gunmen would shoot him.

Minton dropped the gun, and the moment it hit the ground, the thug came toward them. He latched onto Beatrice by her hair, yanking her to her feet. Beatrice yelled in pain, but he only whacked her upside the head with his weapon. When she collapsed, the guy threw her over his shoulder and started toward the SUV.

The sound of gunfire cracked through the air.

It was close, somewhere near the front of the house, and Holden prayed that none of the lawmen had been hurt. More shots came though. A flurry of gunfire.

"Wait just a few seconds," Amanda told the guy, and she added a profanity under her breath.

Maybe she'd expected that her lackeys could have finished off Grayson and the others by now. Or at least kept them at bay so they could start the process of getting the heck out of there.

The moments crawled by, and Holden glanced at Kara to see how she was holding up. She was bleeding and needed medical attention fast. That wasn't going to happen, though, until the danger had been neutralized. Since the gunfire was continuing, that might not be for a while.

"Just hang in there," Holden said to Kara.

Nicky looked at him. She didn't say anything, but he

could tell she was silently asking him what to do. Holden wasn't sure, not yet anyway. However, he knew if they got in that SUV, they'd be dead as soon as Amanda no longer needed them.

The shots outside finally stopped, and Amanda motioned for her man to get moving. The guy did, taking Minton and Beatrice toward the front of the barn and the SUV.

"Your turn," Amanda said to Nicky. "Go with Beatrice and the senator."

Nicky didn't jump to do that, but Holden nodded. She still hesitated but finally took several steps toward the thug who was in the process of tossing Beatrice into the vehicle.

Amanda put her mouth against Holden's ear. "Of course, you won't be going with them," she whispered. "Can't risk that since you and the deputy here would only try to kill us the first chance you get."

Holden had figured that out. Nicky was the only hostage Amanda needed, and the only reason the woman hadn't already tried to kill him was because she was using him to get Nicky to cooperate.

Nicky probably couldn't hear what the woman was saying, but she stopped, and stared at him.

"Keep moving!" the thug snarled, and after he stuffed the senator in the SUV, he started for Nicky.

Nothing about this was ideal, especially not with the armed goon right next to Amanda, but Holden figured it was now or never. He had to do something. He turned, slamming his body into Amanda's, hoping to knock the gun from her hand.

He didn't.

Amanda pulled the trigger.

EVERYTHING SEEMED TO FREEZE.

Nicky yelled for Holden to get down, but the shot

drowned out her voice. The sound was deafening, and it roared through the barn. Roared through her, too, and for some heart-stopping moments, Nicky thought Amanda had managed to shoot Holden.

And maybe she had.

It was hard to tell because Holden rammed into Amanda and her hired gun and sent all three of them crashing to the ground. Amanda screamed. Maybe because she was in pain. After all, she'd had a C-section just the week before. But judging from the profanity that followed, Amanda was also enraged at what Holden had done.

Kara scrambled across the floor toward the gun, causing the thug to take aim at her. Nicky couldn't just stand there and let him shoot the deputy again so she charged toward him. As Holden had done to Amanda, she plowed into him. She didn't hit him with her injured arm, but the jolt from the impact was painful enough. It was like ramming into a brick wall.

Unlike Amanda and the hired gun who'd been next to her, the brute didn't fall. However, he did stagger back just a little, and Nicky ducked out of the way to stop him from shooting or punching her. It was only a handful of seconds. But it was enough time for Kara to get the gun. She fired two shots at him.

That brought him down.

He dropped, clutching his chest, and that's when Nicky realized that Kara's shots had gone into the guy's Kevlar vest. He wasn't dead. He'd just had the breath knocked out of him. That meant she only had a couple of minutes to help Holden while the guy was out of commission.

Outside, there was the sound of more gunfire, closer than it had been before, and maybe that meant Grayson and the deputies were coming to help.

"Watch him," Nicky told Kara, and she hoped the

wounded deputy could shoot again if it came down to it. Kara was shaking, but she still managed to keep her gun aimed at the guy.

Nicky scooped up her gun and ran to Holden, but she still couldn't tell if he was injured. There was blood, but in the darkness it was impossible to see who was bleeding.

Impossible for Nicky to have a clean shot, either.

The thug was punching Holden, hard, and while Holden was fighting back, Amanda had latched onto his arm to prevent him from delivering a blow that would have stopped the gunman.

Amanda was also moaning in pain, and her moans turned to a shriek when her own man accidentally elbowed her. She rolled to the side, clutching her stomach, but she didn't move far enough away from Holden so that Nicky could shoot her. Worse, Amanda still had her gun.

A gun she pointed at Nicky.

Nicky jumped to the side just as Amanda pulled the trigger, and the bullet slammed into the SUV. Amanda howled out a feral sound, a mix of rage and pain, and she scrambled away from the fight. Before Nicky could take aim at her, Amanda limped out the back of the barn.

"No!" Nicky yelled. She couldn't get away.

But Nicky couldn't risk Holden being killed, either. She didn't run after the woman, and she still didn't have a clean shot so she kicked the thug in the head as hard as she could. The thug reached for her, trying to grab onto her leg.

Holden didn't let that happen, though.

"Move back," Holden shouted to her, and he snatched the guy's gun.

The thug didn't give up his weapon, though. He rammed his elbow into Holden's jaw. Holden's head flopped back, and Nicky saw something she didn't want to see. More blood.

And the man put his meaty grip around Holden's hand and gun.

The fight was on again. But it didn't last long. Because there was the sickening sound of a shot being fired. Nicky could have sworn her heart skipped some beats, and it took her several terrifying moments to realize who'd been shot.

Not Holden, thank God.

It was the hired gun.

Holden didn't waste any time pushing the guy off him. In the same motion, he got to his feet and started out the back of the barn.

Going after Amanda, no doubt.

However, Nicky didn't know if Amanda was out there alone or if there were other gunmen. There was still some shooting going on toward the front of the house, but it was possible one or more hired thugs had come near the barn to make sure their boss got out of this alive.

Even though Nicky knew Holden wouldn't approve, she followed him, watching to make sure he wasn't about to be ambushed. She didn't see any hired guns, nor did she see Amanda at first. That's because the woman was on the side of the barn, probably trying to get to the SUV.

Amanda hadn't made it far, mainly because she was staggering and practically doubled over. Nicky had no idea how long it took for a C-section incision to heal, but she suspected a week hadn't been nearly enough time. The pain didn't stop Amanda from turning and aiming her gun at Holden.

She fired.

Holden ducked behind the back of the barn, stepping in front of Nicky. "Watch behind us," he said.

Nicky did while Holden took aim at Amanda. There was no place for the woman to run for cover, and the SUV was still several yards away from her.

"Put down your gun," Holden ordered Amanda.

She laughed, but there was definitely no humor in it. "If you kill me, you'll never know if there are other babies from the Genesis Project."

Nicky's stomach twisted and turned at hearing that. Mercy, if there were more, they needed to find them.

"Put down your gun," Holden repeated.

Amanda didn't answer. Not with words anyway. She fired another shot, this one slamming into the barn. Holden cursed, leaned out and fired.

Even though Nicky couldn't actually see the woman, she knew Amanda had been hit. No mistaking the sound of the bullet hitting human flesh.

Holden tossed Nicky his phone, and he hurried toward Amanda. "Call Grayson and tell him to get an ambulance out here *fast*."

Chapter Eighteen

Holden paced across the break room of the sheriff's office because he didn't know how else to burn off some of this restless energy inside him. He felt ready to explode, but he had to keep it together. Not only for Nicky's sake, but also because they'd be seeing the twins soon, and he didn't want them picking up on the stress.

Nicky seemed past the point of having any restless energy. Or any energy at all for that matter. She was lying on the small sofa, staring up at the ceiling. Added to that, he could count on one hand how many sentences she'd said to him in the hour since they'd left Kayla's place.

She might be in shock, was almost certainly dealing with the adrenaline crash, but she'd still been vocal enough to insist on not going to the hospital to be checked.

Holden hadn't liked that, but at least she didn't have any visible injuries. Unlike Kara and Amanda. They had both been taken by ambulance to the hospital and were in surgery.

"It shouldn't be long now before we can leave," Holden said to Nicky.

She looked at him and nodded, and while she wasn't exactly jumping up and down, he figured she wanted to see the babies as much as he did. Especially now that it was safe to do that.

Amanda's thugs had been rounded up. At least the ones who were still alive. Grayson and the other deputies who'd responded to the scene had been forced to kill three men. Added to the one that Holden had shot in the barn, that left two, and last he'd heard, they were in holding cells awaiting interrogation.

Something that Holden wouldn't be doing.

He wanted answers—too much—and with all the emotions bubbling up inside of him, he might beat them senseless if they didn't tell him what he wanted to know. Besides, he didn't want to leave Nicky.

Holden went closer to the sofa, and Nicky scooted over so he could sit next to her. "If Amanda dies," she said, "how will we find out if there are other babies?"

He'd already thought about that a lot. "The files you took. Amanda said there was encrypted information in them."

"She could have been lying," Nicky pointed out.

He shook his head. "It was important for her to get those files." Heck, she'd been willing to kill to get them. So there had to be something she wanted concealed in them. "The FBI's going over them now, and they'll find whatever it is."

He hoped.

Nicky went back into silent mode for a moment, but then she reached out and touched the front of his shirt. "You should probably change that before we see the twins."

Holden glanced down and cursed when he saw the blood. It wasn't his blood or even Nicky's, thank God. It belonged to the thug he'd shot in the barn, but he definitely didn't want to hold his niece and nephew while wearing a bloody shirt.

There was a row of lockers on the wall, and Holden rummaged through them until he found one of Gage's shirts. Since they were about the same size, Holden knew it would fit and he stripped off his dirty clothes.

And Nicky gasped.

She got off the sofa as if something had scalded her, and she hurried to him. "You're hurt. You said you were all right."

By all right, he meant alive and not seriously injured. But yes, there were bruises, cuts and scrapes over most of his torso. His hands, too. It came with the territory of getting into a fistfight with a jerk who'd outsized him.

"Minor stuff," he assured her.

But Nicky didn't take his word for it. She ran her fingertips over one of the bruises. Which meant she ran those fingertips over his bare stomach. Holden would had to have been dead not to react to her touch. He reacted even more when she turned him around and explored the injuries to his back.

"This feels a little like foreplay," he joked.

She stepped around to face him, but that certainly wasn't a joking look in her eyes. It was tears. "You could have been killed," she said on a rise of breath.

Yeah, a couple of times over. It was the same for her, but Holden didn't want to remind either of them of that. Instead, he pulled her into his arms, and even though this was a hug of comfort, it felt like foreplay, too, since he was shirtless.

"It'll all be okay," he said, and he brushed a kiss on her forehead.

Holden also tried not to put pressure on any of her injuries. In addition to the stitches on her arm, he could see some bruises on her now. That certainly didn't help with all this extra energy inside him and was verification that he needed to stay far away from those captured gunmen. He wanted someone to pay for every injury on Nicky's body.

"Will it really be okay?" she asked, looking up at him.

"Yes." And Holden kissed her to prove it.

Of course, the kiss didn't prove anything except that he was attracted to her and that he cared for her, but maybe that would ease some of her worries. It didn't, though. When she pulled back from the kiss, the worry was still there.

So Holden kissed her again.

This time he deepened it, and he lingered a bit, easing her closer and closer until her body was right against his. Finally, he got a different look from her. Not nearly as much worry, and there was some heat mixed with it. But it wasn't nearly enough heat as far as Holden was concerned so he went back for a third kiss. He would have given a fourth, too, if he hadn't heard the footsteps.

"Interrupting anything?" Gage asked.

His cousin was already in the doorway of the break room before Nicky and Holden moved away from each other. It was too late, though, because Gage had already seen them. And it was a reminder to Holden that his family should see Nicky and him like this. He slipped his arm back around her, only to get another reminder.

That he was still shirtless.

Gage smiled again. "Why don't you go ahead and get dressed? It's time for us to leave for the safe house."

"Grayson gave the okay for that?" Holden quickly put on the shirt, trying not to wince when the movement caused his banged-up body to ache.

"He did. I can give you an update along the way."

Holden hoped those updates included lots and lots of good news because he wasn't sure Nicky could handle anything else tonight. Heck, Holden didn't want to handle any more bad news, either. He and Nicky had enough nightmares to last them a couple of lifetimes.

They made their way to the squad room, and Holden saw something that caused him to stop moving. Minton, and he was holding his son. Holden recognized the look on the senator's face. Love. Minton was already smitten with the newborn.

"Minton wanted his son here while he was giving his statement," Gage explained.

At the sound of his name, Minton turned and looked at Nicky and Holden. "Thank you," he said. "For everything."

Holden had been concerned as to the fate of the Minton baby, but he wasn't as concerned now. It was obvious the kid was in loving hands.

"What about Beatrice?" Nicky asked.

Minton's mouth tightened. "She's at the county jail where I hope she'll stay."

"She will," Gage assured him, and he turned to Holden and Nicky to finish his explanation. "The kidnapper Beatrice hired is testifying against her in exchange for a lesser sentence. Beatrice is being charged with kidnapping, forced imprisonment and some other charges."

"But Beatrice didn't have anything to do with the Genesis Project?" Holden added.

"No. There's no evidence she did anyway. That was all Amanda's doing."

Too bad. Because if Beatrice had been a co-conspirator, then she could have been offered her own deal if she helped them find out if there were any other babies.

Holden wished the senator good luck, and he and Nicky were about to leave when someone stepped out from one of the interview rooms.

Oscar.

Nicky groaned, which expressed Holden's sentiment. "I don't have time for another round of your threats," Nicky snapped. "You're not taking custody of Annie and Emmett's babies."

The muscles stirred in Oscar's jaw. "No. I'm not."

Nicky's shoulders came back. "Is this some kind of trick?"

"No. The sheriff is charging me with obstruction of justice for not reporting that I was with the kidnappers when they got the ransom from Beatrice. I don't think a judge will grant me custody after that. Do you?"

Holden hoped not.

Oscar didn't seem as bitter about that as Holden thought he would be. He looked defeated. "I'd like the see the babies," Oscar added.

Nicky glanced at Holden to see what his take was on this, but Holden didn't have one at the moment. "You're their grandfather," Holden finally said. "My advice is when you start acting like one—a good, decent one—then you'll get to see them."

Oscar didn't argue with that. He simply turned and went back into the interview room. Soon, Holden and Nicky would need to sit down with him and work out some ground rules for any future contact with the twins. For now, though, Holden just wanted to get out of there.

Nicky clearly felt the same, so they followed Gage to a cruiser. Even though they were certain they'd rounded up all of Amanda's thugs, they still hurried.

It might take a while before either one of them could step outside and not relive the memories of the attacks.

Holden got into the backseat with Nicky, and Gage took the wheel. It shouldn't take long for them to get to the safe house. Which was good. It was already late, and he didn't want to be in crash-and-burn mode when they got there. Not just because of the babies, either. Because he wanted to talk some things over with Nicky.

The problem was—Holden didn't know which things.

"First the good news," Gage said once he'd pulled away from the station. "Kara's going to be fine. The doc got her all stitched up, and she's already asking when she can come back to work."

That was a relief. The only reason Kara had been in that barn was because she'd been trying to help Nicky and him, and it would have been a hard blow if she'd lost her life because of it.

Still, as good as the news was, Holden couldn't celebrate because he figured if there was good news, then Gage was about to deliver some bad.

And he did.

"Amanda died in surgery," Gage said.

That felt like a punch right in the gut. Not only because Amanda couldn't tell them about those files, but also because Holden had been the one to kill her. Of course, she hadn't given him any choice but to shoot her. Still, it ate away at him to think he'd taken a life.

"Did Amanda happen to say anything before she died?" Nicky asked.

"No. She never regained consciousness after she was shot."

It wasn't much consolation, but Amanda probably wouldn't have said anything even if she had been awake. Not without a sweet plea deal on the table, and since she'd had a man murdered, that wouldn't have happened.

"So, what about you two?" Gage asked. "And yeah, I'm talking about that kissing you were doing in the break room."

"What about it?" Holden countered, mainly because he didn't know how to answer Gage's question.

What about Nicky and him?

And Holden looked at Nicky to see if she had the answer.

She didn't, not a verbal one anyway, but all in all it was a darn good way to respond. She kissed him. It wasn't one of those scorchers they'd shared in the break room, but it went a long way to soothing some of that acid inside him. In fact, it made him smile.

It was short-lived though because Holden's phone buzzed, and he saw Grayson's name on the screen. Holden put it on speaker so that Nicky and Gage could hear, but he hoped it wasn't another round of bad news.

"Did Gage tell you that Amanda died?" Grayson asked the moment Holden answered.

"Yeah. And that Kara was okay."

"She is. Something else is okay, too. One of Amanda's gunmen is cooperating. He's going to give the FBI info about the encryption."

"Thank God," Nicky said, her voice barely a whisper, and she repeated it several times.

"Are there other babies?" Holden asked.

"He says yes. There's one more. Not Emmett and Annie's baby, though," Grayson quickly added. "A surrogate is carrying a baby who belongs to a wealthy lawyer and his wife. The FBI will contact both the couple and the surrogate."

Good. It wasn't the ideal way for a couple to find out they were about to be parents, but since they'd gone to Conceptions Clinic that meant they'd been serious about having a child. And now they would get one. Holden made a mental note to check on them when things settled down a bit.

Whenever that would be.

"I'll keep you posted if we learn anything else from the files," Grayson went on. "But the gunman is convinced that's the last baby out there."

Four babies in total. And Amanda had two million of the four she'd planned to get. Heck, this could have just been phase one of her operation, too. All she had to do was find other embryos of wealthy parents and do the same thing to them that she'd done to the Mintons, the other couple and the Rylands.

"Where will you be taking the twins when you leave the safe house?" Grayson asked.

Good question, and Holden had to think about it for a couple of seconds. "For now, we'll go to my place near Silver Creek Ranch." His house wasn't on the main part of the ranch but rather on the land adjacent. He looked at Nicky to see if she was okay with that.

She nodded. "I wasn't exactly looking forward to going back to my house since the last time I was there, we were attacked."

Yeah, Holden remembered, and he was glad she'd agreed to go to the ranch. Except she hadn't, not really. That nod could have simply been to give her approval for the twins to go there.

"I'll call you if there are any updates," Grayson added, and he ended the call.

Holden put away his phone, but he wasn't finished with this conversation. "You're going to Silver Creek Ranch with me," Holden told Nicky.

Then he frowned.

That came out like an order, and judging from Nicky's expression she didn't approve of that any more than he did.

Gage chuckled. "Uh, you do know how to talk to a woman, don't you, cuz?"

Holden frowned even more, and he shut the Plexiglas slider between the seats, but it was hard to be angry with Gage since he was right. Apparently, Holden had lost the ability to speak to a woman.

Well, the only woman that mattered right now anyway.

"Kissing usually works," Nicky said, and the corner of her mouth came up a little.

She was right. So that's what Holden did. He kissed her again. It not only soothed his nerves, but it also reminded him of why this was easy. Easy because he knew now what he needed to say to her.

"I want you to come to my house," he amended. "Maybe not tonight because it's late, but first thing in the morning."

Nicky nodded.

It was the exact response Holden wanted so he kissed her again. The taste of her slid right through him, another reminder that he wanted a whole lot more from her. And not just kisses and sex, either. Now if he could only get the right words to come out of his mouth.

"I'll say it if you will," Nicky whispered.

Holden looked at her, to make sure they were on the same page. They were, but he kissed her to confirm it.

"I love you," Nicky said at the exact moment, Holden said, "I love you."

Yep, same page all right.

"Took you long enough to figure it out," Gage joked. Then he laughed.

Holden tuned him out because he wasn't done yet. Might never be done when it came to Nicky.

"I want it all," Holden said to her. "Raising the twins— together. Marriage. I'll even build a white picket fence. Just think about it and give me your answer."

Holden was willing to wait. However long it took, but Nicky didn't have to think on it for long. "Yes, to raising the twins together. Yes, to the marriage. The fence is optional."

Smiling, she caught onto the front of Holden's shirt and pulled him to her, and Nicky kissed him.

* * * * *

Look for USA TODAY *bestselling author
Delores Fossen's next book in*
THE LAWMEN OF SILVER
CREEK RANCH *series, DRURY,
when it goes on sale next month.*

*You'll find it wherever
Mills & Boon Intrigue books are sold!*

"Your battery is dead." Caveman glanced around. "You got another handy?"

She shook her head. "No. Fresh out."

"Got a helmet?"

She nodded. "Yeah, but I won't need it if I can't get my ATV started."

He spun and headed for the barn door. "You can ride on the back of mine," he called out over his shoulder.

Grace's heart fluttered at the thought of riding behind Caveman, holding him around the waist to keep from falling off. "No, thanks. Those trails are dangerous." She suspected the danger was more in how her pulse quickened around the man than the possibility of plunging over the edge of a drop-off.

"I grew up riding horses and four-wheelers on rugged mountain trails. I won't let you fall off a cliff." He held up a hand. "Promise."

She frowned. Knowing she only had a few minutes to get to the meeting location, Grace sighed. "Okay. I guess I'll put my life in your hands." She followed him out of the barn and closed the door behind her. "Although, I don't know why I should trust you. I don't even know you."

HOT TARGET

BY
ELLE JAMES

First Published in Great Britain 2017
By Mills & Boon, an imprint of HarperCollins*Publishers*
1 London Bridge Street, London, SE1 9GF

© 2017 Mary Jernigan

ISBN 978-0-263-92866-2

46-0317

Our policy is to use papers that are natural, renewable and recyclable products and made from wood grown in sustainable forests. The logging and manufacturing processes conform to the legal environmental regulations of the country of origin.

Printed and bound in Spain
by CPI, Barcelona

Elle James, a *New York Times* bestselling author, started writing when her sister challenged her to write a romance novel. She has managed a full-time job and raised three wonderful children, and she and her husband even tried ranching exotic birds (ostriches, emus and rheas). Ask her, and she'll tell you what it's like to go toe-to-toe with an angry three-hundred-and-fifty-pound bird! Elle loves to hear from fans at ellejames@earthlink.net or www.ellejames.com.

This book is dedicated to my mother and father, who taught me that the sky was the limit, and all I needed was to apply the hard work to reach for my dreams. I love you both to the moon and back.

Chapter One

Max "Caveman" Decker clung to the shadows of the mud-and-brick structures, the first SEAL into enemy territory. Reaching a forward position giving him sufficient range of fire, he dropped to one knee, scanned the street and buildings ahead through his night-vision goggles, searching for the telltale green heat signatures of warm enemy bodies. When he didn't detect any, he said softly into his mic, "Ready."

"Going in," Whiskey said. Armed with their M4A1 carbine rifles with the Special Forces Modification kit, he and Tank eased around the corner of a building in a small village in the troubled Helmand Province of Afghanistan.

Army Intelligence operatives had indicated the Pakistan-based Haqqani followers had set up a remote base of operations in the village located in the rugged hills north of Kandahar.

Caveman's job was to provide cover to his teammates as they moved ahead of him. Then they would cover for him until he reached a relatively secure location, thus leapfrogging through the village to their target, the biggest building at the center, where intel reported the Haqqani rebels had set up shop.

Caveman hunkered low, scanning the path ahead and the rooftops of the buildings for gun-toting enemy combatants. So far, so good. Through his night-vision goggles, he tracked the progress of the seven members of his squad working their way slowly toward the target.

An eighth green blip appeared ahead of his team and his arm swung wide.

"We've got incoming!" Caveman aimed his weapon at the eighth green heat signature and pulled the trigger. It was too late. A bright flash blinded him through the goggles, followed by the ear-rupturing concussion of a grenade. He jerked his goggles up over his helmet, cursing. When he blinked his eyes to regain his night vision, he stared at the scene in front of him.

All seven members of his squad lay on the ground, some moving, others not.

No! His job was to provide cover. They couldn't be dead. They had to be alive. He leaped to his feet.

Then, as if someone opened the door to a hive of bees, enemy combatants swarmed from around the corners into the street, carrying AK-47s.

With the majority of his squad down, maybe dead, maybe alive, Caveman didn't have any other choice.

He set his weapon on automatic, pulled his 9-millimeter pistol from the holster on his hip and stepped out of the cover of the building.

"What the hell are you doing?" Whiskey had shouted.

"Showing no mercy," he shouted through gritted teeth. He charged forward like John Wayne on the warpath, shooting from both hips, taking out one enemy rebel after the other.

Something hit him square in his armor-plated chest,

knocking him backward a step. It hurt like hell and made his breath lodge in his lungs, but it didn't stop him. He forged his way toward the enemy, firing until he ran out of ammo. Dropping to the ground, he slammed magazines into the rifle and the pistol and rolled to a prone position, aimed and fired, taking down as many of the enemy as he could. He'd be damned if even one of them survived.

When there were only two combatants left in the street, Caveman lurched to his feet and went after them. He wouldn't rest until the last one died.

He hadn't slowed as he rounded the corner. A bullet had hit him in the leg. Caveman grunted. He would have gone down, but the adrenaline in his veins surged, pushing him to his destination. He aimed his pistol at the shooter who'd plugged his leg and caught him between the eyes. Another bogey shot at him from above.

Caveman dove to the ground and rolled behind a stack of crates. Pain stabbed him in the shoulder and the leg, and warm wetness dripped down both. He leaned around the crates, pulled his night-vision goggles in place, located the shooter on the rooftop and took him out.

With the streets clear, he had a straight path to the original target. Holstering his handgun, he pulled a grenade out of his vest, pushed to his feet and staggered a few steps, pain slicing through him. He could barely feel his leg and really didn't give a damn.

Two steps, three... One after the other took him to the biggest structure in the neighborhood. As he rounded the corner, one of the two guards protecting the doorway fired at him.

The man's bullet hit the stucco beside him.

Caveman jerked back behind the corner, stuck his M4A1 around the corner and fired off a burst. Then he leaped out, threw himself to the ground, rolled and came up firing. Within moments, the two guards were dead.

The door was locked or barred from the inside. Pulling the pin on the grenade, Caveman dropped it in front of the barrier and then stepped back around the corner, covering his ears.

The blast shook the building and spewed dust and wooden splinters. Back at the front entrance, Caveman kicked the door the rest of the way in and entered the building.

Going from room to room, he fired his weapon, taking out every male occupant in his path. When he reached the last door, he kicked it open and stood back.

The expected gunfire riddled the wall opposite the door.

After the gunfire ceased, Caveman spun around and opened fire on the occupants of the room until no one stood or attempted escape.

His task complete, he radioed the platoon leader. "Eight down. Come get us." Only after each one of his enemies was dead did he allow himself to crumple to the ground. As if every bone in his body suddenly melted into goo, Caveman had no way left to hold himself up. Still armed with his M4A1, he sat in the big room and stared down at his leg. Blood flowed far too quickly. In the back of his mind, he knew he had to do something or he'd pass out and die. But every movement now took a monumental amount of effort, and gray fog gathered at the edges of his vision. He couldn't pass out now, his buddies needed him. They could be dead or dying.

No matter how hard he tried, he couldn't straighten, couldn't rise to his feet. The abyss claimed him, dragging him to the depths of despair.

"CAVEMAN," A VOICE SAID.

He dragged himself back from the edge of a very dark, extremely deep pool that was his past—a different time...a terrible place. He shook his head to clear the memories and glanced across the room at his new boss for the duration of this temporary assignment. "I'm sorry, sir. You were saying?"

The leader of Homeland Security's Special Task Force Safe Haven, Kevin Garner, narrowed his eyes. "How long did you say it's been since you were cleared for duty?"

"Two weeks," Caveman responded.

Kevin's frown deepened. "And when was the last time you met with a shrink?"

"All through the twelve weeks of physical therapy. She cleared me two weeks ago." His jaw tightened. "I'm fully capable of performing whatever assignment is given to me as a Delta Force soldier. I don't know why I've been assigned to this backcountry boondoggle."

Kevin's shrewd gaze studied Caveman so hard he could have been staring at him under a microscope. "Any TBI with your injury?"

"I was shot in the leg, not the head. No traumatic brain injury." Anger spiked with the need to get outside and breathe fresh air. Not that the air in the loft over the Blue Moose Tavern in Grizzly Pass, Wyoming, was stale. It was just that whenever Caveman was inside for extended periods, he got really twitchy. Claustrophobia, the therapist had called it. Probably brought on by PTSD.

A bunch of hooey, if you asked Caveman. Something the therapist could use against him to delay his return to the front. And by God, he'd get back to the front soon, if he had to stow away on a C-130 bound for Afghanistan. The enemy had to pay for the deaths of his friends; the members of his squad deserved retribution. Only one other man had survived, Whiskey, and he'd lost an eye in the firefight.

The slapping sound of a file folder hitting a tabletop made Caveman jump.

"That's your assignment," Kevin said. "RJ Khalig, pipeline inspector. He's had a few threats lately. I want you to touch bases with him and provide protection until we can figure out who's threatening him."

Caveman glared at the file. "I'm no bodyguard. I shoot people for a living."

"You know the stakes from our meeting a couple days ago in this same room, and you've seen what some of the people in this area are capable of. As I said then, we think terrorist cells are stirring up already volatile locals. Since we found evidence that someone is supplying semiautomatic weapons to what we suspect is a local group called Free America, we're afraid more violence is imminent."

"Just because you found some empty crates in that old mine doesn't mean whoever got the weapons plans to use them to start a war," Caveman argued.

"No, but we're concerned they might target individuals who could potentially stand in the way of their movements."

"Why not let local law enforcement handle it?" Caveman leaned forward, reluctant to open the file and commit to the assignment. He didn't want to be in Wyoming. "If this group picks off individuals, would that not be local jurisdiction?"

Kevin nodded. "As long as they aren't connected with terrorists. However, the activity on social media indicates something bigger is being planned and will take place soon."

"How soon?"

Kevin shook his head. "We don't know."

"Sounds pretty vague to me." Caveman stood and stretched.

"I set up this task force to stop a terrible thing from happening. If I had all of the answers, likely I wouldn't need you, Ghost, Hawkeye or T-Rex. I'm determined to stop something bad from happening, before it gets too big and a lot more lives are lost."

"I don't know if you have the right guy for this job. I'm no investigator, nor am I a bodyguard."

"I understand your concern, but we need trained combatants, familiar with tactics and subversive operations. As you've seen for yourself and know from experience, it's pretty rough country out here and the people can be stubborn and willing to take the law into their own hands. I'm afraid what happened at the mine two days ago could happen again."

Caveman snorted. "That was a bunch of disgruntled ranchers, mad about the confiscation of their herd."

"Agreed," Kevin said. "Granted, the Vanders family took it too far by kidnapping a busload of kids. But they knew about the weapons stored in that mine."

"Are any of them talking?"

"Not yet. We're waiting for one of them to throw the rest under the bus."

"You might be waiting a long time." Caveman crossed his arms over his chest. "People out here tend to be very stubborn."

"You're from this area," Kevin said. "You should know."

"I'm from a little farther north, in the Crazy Mountains of Montana. But we're all a tough bunch of cowboys who don't like it when the government interferes with our lives."

"Hold on to that stubbornness. You might need it around here. For today, you'll be an investigator and bodyguard. Mr. Khalig needs your help. He has an important job, inspecting the oil and gas pipelines running through this state. Contact his boss for his location, find him and get the skinny on what's going on. You might have to run him down in the backwoods."

Until he was cleared to return to his unit, Caveman would do the best he could for his temporary boss and the pipeline inspector. What choice did he have? As much as he hated to admit it, they needed help out in the hills and mountains of Wyoming. The three days he'd been there had proven that.

Caveman had met with Kevin's four-man special operations team members. One Navy SEAL, one Delta Force soldier, an Army ranger and a highly skilled Marine. Ghost, one of the Delta Force men, had been assigned to protect a woman who had been surfing the web for terrorist activity. Her daughter had been one of the children who had been kidnapped on the bus.

Caveman, Kevin and the other three members of the task force had mobilized to save the children and the three adults on board the bus. The bus driver didn't make it, but the children and the two women survived.

Kevin stood and held out his hand. "Thanks for helping out. We have such limited resources in this neck of the woods, and I feel there's a lot more to what's going on here than meets the eyes."

"I'll do what I can." Caveman shook Kevin's hand and left the loft, descending the stairs to the street below. When he'd entered the upstairs apartment, the sky had been clear and blue. In the twenty minutes he'd been inside, clouds had gathered. The superstitious would call it an omen, a sign or a portent of things to come. Caveman called them rain clouds. If he was going to get out to where Khalig was, he'd have to get moving.

GRACE SAUNDERS PULLED her horse to a halt and dismounted near the top of a ridge overlooking the mountain meadow where Molly's wolf pack had been spotted most recently. Based on the droppings she'd seen along the trail and the leftover bones of an elk carcass, they were still active in the area.

She tied her horse to a nearby tree and stretched her back and legs. Having been on horseback since early that morning, she was ready for a break. Moving to the highest point, she stared out at the brilliant view of the Wyoming Beartooth Mountain Range, with the snowcapped peaks and the tall lodgepole pines. The sky above had been blue when she'd started her trek that morning. Clouds had built to the west, a harbinger of rain to come soon. She'd have to head down soon or risk a cold drenching.

From where she stood, Grace could see clear across the small valley to the hilltop on the other side. She frowned, squinted her eyes and focused on something that didn't belong.

A four-wheeler stood at the top of the hill, halfway tucked into the shade of a lodgepole pine tree. She wondered what someone else was doing out in the woods. Most people stuck to the roads in and out of the national forest.

It wasn't unusual for the more adventurous souls to ride the trails surrounding Yellowstone National Park, since ATVs in the park itself were prohibited. Scanning the hilltop for the person belonging to the four-wheeler, Grace had to search hard. For a moment she worried the rider might be hurt. Then she spotted him, lying on his belly on the ground.

Grace's heartbeats ratcheted up several notches. The guy appeared to have a rifle of some sort with a scope. Since it was summer, the man with the gun had no reason to be aiming a rifle. It wasn't hunting season.

Grace followed the direction the barrel of the weapon was pointed, to the far side of the valley. She couldn't see any elk, white-tailed deer or moose. Was he aiming for wolves? Grace raised her binoculars to her eyes and looked closer.

A movement caught her attention. She almost missed it. But then she focused on the spot where she'd seen the movement and gasped.

A man squatted near the ground with a device in his hand. He stared at the device as he slowly stood.

Grace shifted the lenses of her binoculars to the man on the ridge. He tensed, his eye lining up with the scope. Surely he wasn't aiming at the man on the ground.

Her pulse hammering, Grace lowered her binoculars and shouted to the man below. "Get down!"

At the same time as she shouted, the sound of rifle fire reached her.

The man on the floor of the valley jerked, pressed a hand to his chest and looked down at blood spreading across his shirt. He dropped to his knees and then fell forward.

Grace pressed a hand to her chest, her heart hammering against her ribs. What had just happened? In her heart she knew. She'd just witnessed a murder. Raising her binoculars to the man on the hilltop, she stared at him, trying to get a good look at him so that she could pick him out in a lineup of criminals.

He had brown hair. And that was all she could get before she noticed the gun he'd used to kill the man on the valley floor was pointing in her direction, and he was aiming at her.

Instinctively, Grace dropped to the ground and rolled to the side. Dust kicked up at the point she'd been standing a moment before. The rifle's report sounded half a second later.

Grace rolled again until she was below the top of the ridge. Afraid to stand and risk being shot, she crawled on all fours down to where she'd left her horse tied to a tree.

An engine revved on the other side of the ridge, the sound echoing off the rocky bluffs.

Her pulse slamming through her body, Grace staggered to her feet, her knees shaking. She ran toward the horse. The animal backed away, sensing her distress, pulling the knot tighter on the tree branch.

Her hands trembling, Grace struggled to untie the knot.

Tears stung her eyes. She wanted to go back to the

man on the ground and see if he was still alive, but the shooter would take her out before she could get there. Her best bet was to get back down the mountain and notify the sheriff. If she rode hard, she could be down in thirty minutes.

Finally jerking the reins free of the branch, Grace swung up onto the horse.

The gelding leaped forward as soon as her butt hit the saddle, galloping down the trail they'd climbed moments before.

Grace slowed as she approached a point at which the trail narrowed and dropped off on one side. With the gelding straining at the bit to speed up, Grace held him in check as they eased down the trail. She glanced back at the ridge where she'd been. A four-wheeler stood on top, the rider holding a rifle to his shoulder.

Something hit the bluff beside her. Dust and rocks splintered off, blinding her briefly. Throwing caution to the wind, she gave the horse his head and held on, praying they didn't fall off the side of the trail. She didn't have a choice. If she didn't get around the corner soon, she'd be shot.

Her gelding pushed forward, more sure of his footing than Grace. She ducked low in the saddle and held on, praying they made it soon. The bluff jutted out of the hillside and would provide sufficient cover for a few minutes. Long enough for her to make it to the trees. The shooter could still catch up, but the trail twisting through the thick trunks of the evergreens would give her more cover and concealment than being in the open. If she made it down to the paved road, she could wave someone down.

Riding like her hair was on fire, Grace erupted from

the trees at the base of the mountain trail. A truck with a trailer on the back was parked on the dirt road. She slowed to read the sign on the door, indicating Rocky Mountain Pipeline Inc. No sooner had she stopped than a shot rang out, plinking into the side of the truck.

Grace leaned low over her horse and yelled, "Go, go, go!" The horse took off across a field, galloping hard.

Then, as if he tripped, he stumbled and pitched forward.

Grace sailed through the air, every move appearing in slow motion. She made a complete somersault before she landed on her feet. Momentum carried her forward and she landed hard on her belly in the tall grass, her forehead bumping the ground hard. For a moment, she couldn't breathe and her vision blurred. She knew she couldn't stay there. The guy on the four-wheeler would catch up to her and finish the job.

An engine roared somewhere nearby.

Grace low-crawled through the grass, blinking hard to clear the darkness slowing her down. When she could go no farther, she collapsed in the grass, no longer able to fight against the fog closing in around her. She closed her eyes.

It wouldn't take the gunman long to find her and end it.

Then she felt a hand on her shoulder and heard a man calling to her as if from the far end of a long tunnel.

"Hey, are you all right?" a deep, resonant voice called out.

Grace gave the last bit of her strength to pushing herself over onto her back. She made it halfway and groaned.

The hand on her shoulder eased her the rest of the

way, until she lay facing her attacker. "Are you going to kill me?"

"What?" he said. "Why would I want to kill you?"

"You killed the man in the valley. And you tried to kill me," she said, her voice fading into a whisper.

"I'm not here to kill anyone."

"If you do. Just make it quick." She tried to blink her eyes open, but they wouldn't move. "Just shoot me. But don't hurt my horse." And she passed out.

Chapter Two

Caveman shook his head as he stared down at the strange woman. "Shoot you? I don't even know you," he muttered. He glanced around, searching for others in the area. She had to have a reason to think he was there to kill her.

He ran his gaze over her body, searching for wounds. Other than the bump on her forehead, she appeared to be okay, despite being tossed by her horse.

The animal had recovered his footing and taken off toward the highway.

Caveman would have the sheriff come out and retrieve the horse. For now, the woman needed to be taken to the hospital. He ran back to his truck for his cell phone, knowing the chances it would work out there were slim to none. But he had to try. He checked. No service.

How the heck was he supposed to call for an airlift? Then he remembered where he was. The foothills of the Beartooth Mountains. He didn't have the radio communications he was used to, or the helicopter support to bring injured teammates out of a bad situation.

With no other choice, he threw open the truck's rear door, returned to the woman, scooped her up in his arms and carried her to his truck. Carefully laying her on the backseat, he buckled a seat belt around her hips and stared down at her. Just to make certain she was still alive, he checked for a pulse.

Still beating. *Good.*

She had straight, sandy-blond hair, clear, makeup-free skin and appeared to be somewhere between twenty-five and thirty years old. The spill she'd taken from her horse could have caused a head, neck or back injury. If they weren't in the mountains, where bears, wolves and other animals could find her, he would have left her lying still until a medic could bring a backboard, to avoid further injury. But out in the open, with wolves and grizzlies a real threat, Caveman couldn't leave the woman.

He shut the door and climbed into the driver's seat. The man he was supposed to meet out there would have to wait. This woman needed immediate medical attention.

As soon as he got closer to the little town of Grizzly Pass, he checked his phone for service. He had enough to get a call through to Kevin Garner. "Caveman here. I have an injured woman in the backseat of my truck. I'm taking her to the local clinic. You'll have to send someone else out to meet with Mr. Khalig. I don't know when I'll get back out there."

"Who've you got?" Kevin asked.

"I don't know. She was thrown from the horse she was riding. She hasn't been conscious long enough to tell me her life history, much less her name."

"Grace," a gravelly voice said from the backseat.

Caveman glanced over his shoulder.

"My name's Grace Saunders." The woman he'd settled on the backseat pushed to a sitting position and pressed a hand to the back of her head. "Who are you? Where am I?"

"I take it she's awake?" Kevin said into Caveman's ear.

"Roger." He shot a glance at the rearview mirror, into the soft gray eyes of the woman he'd rescued. "Gotta go, Kevin. Will update you as soon as I know anything."

"I'll see if I can find someone I can send out to check on Mr. Khalig," Kevin said.

His gaze moving from the road ahead to the reflection of the woman behind him, Caveman focused on Kevin's words. "I found a truck and trailer where his office staff said it would be, but the man himself wasn't anywhere nearby."

"I suspect that truck and trailer either belong to the dead man or the man who was doing the shooting," the woman in the backseat said.

"Dead man?" Caveman removed his foot from the accelerator. "What dead man? What shooting?"

"I'll tell you when we get to town. Right now my head hurts." She touched the lump on her forehead and winced. "Where are we going?"

He didn't demand to know what she was talking about, knowing the woman needed medical attention after her fall. "To the clinic in Grizzly Pass." He'd get the full story once she had been checked out.

"I don't need to go to the clinic." She leaned over the back of the seat and touched his shoulder. "Take me to the sheriff's office."

Caveman frowned. "Lady, you need to see a doctor. You were out cold."

"My name is Grace, and I know what I need. And that's to see the sheriff. *Now.*"

He glanced at her face in the mirror. "Okay, but if you pass out, I'm taking you to the clinic. No argument."

"Deal." She nodded toward the road ahead. "You'd better slow down or you'll miss the turn."

Caveman slammed on his brakes in time to pull into the parking lot.

Grace braced her hands on the backs of the seats and swayed with the vehicle as it made the sharp turn. "I was okay, until you nearly gave me whiplash." She didn't wait for him to come to a complete stop before she pushed open her door and dropped down from the truck, crumpling to the ground.

Out of the truck and around the front, Caveman bent to help, sliding his hands beneath her thighs. "We're going to the clinic."

She pushed him away. "I don't need to be carried. I can stand on my own."

"As you have so clearly demonstrated." He drew in a breath and let it out slowly. "Fine. At least let me help you stand upright." He slipped an arm around her waist and lifted her to her feet.

When she was standing on her own, she nodded. "I've got it now."

"Uh-huh. Prove it." He let go of her for a brief moment.

Grace swayed and would have fallen if he'd let her. But he didn't. Instead he wrapped his arm around her waist again and led her into the sheriff's office.

With his help, she made it inside to the front desk.

The deputy on the other side glanced up with a slight frown, his gaze on Caveman. "May I help you?" His

frown deepened as he looked toward the woman leaning on Caveman. "Grace?" He popped up from his desk.
"Are you all right?"

"I'm fine, Johnny. Is Sheriff Scott in? I need to talk
to him ASAP."

"Yeah. I'll get him." He glanced from her to Caveman and back. "As long as you're okay."

Anger simmered beneath the surface. Caveman
glanced at the man's name tag. "Deputy Pierce, just
get the damn sheriff. I'm not going to hurt her. If I was,
I would have left her lying where her horse threw her."

The deputy's lips twitched. "Going." He spun on his
heels and hurried through a door and down a hallway.
A moment later, he returned with an older man, dressed
in a similar tan shirt and brown slacks. "Grace, Johnny
said you were thrown by your horse." He held out his
hand. "Shouldn't you be at the clinic?"

Grace took the proffered hand and shook her head.
"I don't need to see a doctor. I need you and your men
to follow me back out to the trail I was on. Now."

"Why? What's wrong?" Sheriff Scott squeezed her
hand between both of his. "The wolves in trouble?"

"It's not the wolves I'm worried about right now."
She drew in a deep breath. "There was a man. Actually there were two men." She stiffened in the curve
of Caveman's arm. "Hell, Sheriff, I witnessed a murder." She let her hand drop to her side as she sagged
against Caveman. "I saw it all happen…and I was too
far away…to do anything to stop it." She sniffed. "You
have to get out there. Just in case he isn't dead. It'll get
dark soon. The wolves will find him."

"Is that why you were riding your horse like you
were?" Caveman asked.

She nodded. "That, and someone was shooting at me. That's why Bear threw me." Her head came up and she stared at the sheriff. "I need to find Bear. He's running around out there, probably scared out of his mind."

Sheriff Scott touched her arm. "I'll send someone out to look for him and bring him back to your place." He glanced at Caveman. "And you are?"

"Max Decker. But my friends call me Caveman."

The sheriff's eyes narrowed. "And what do you have to do with all of this?"

Grace leaned back and stared up at the man she'd been leaning on. "Yeah, why were you out in the middle of nowhere?"

"I was sent to check on a Mr. Khalig, a pipeline inspector for Rocky Mountain Pipeline Inc. I was told he'd been receiving threats."

"RJ Khalig?" the sheriff asked.

Caveman nodded. "That's the one."

"He's been a regular at the Blue Moose Tavern since he arrived in town a couple weeks ago. He's staying at Mama Jo's Bed-and-Breakfast," Sheriff Scott added.

Grace shook her head. "I'll bet he's the man I saw get shot. He appeared to be checking some device in a valley when the shooter took him down."

"What exactly did you see?" Sheriff Scott asked.

"Yeah," Caveman said. "I'd like to know, as well."

GRACE'S INSIDES CLENCHED and her pulse sped up. "I was searching for one of the wolves we'd collared last spring. His transponder still works, but hasn't moved in the past two days. Either he's lost his collar, or he's dead. I needed to know." Grace took a breath and let it out, the horror of the scene she'd witnessed threatening to overwhelm her.

"I was coming up to the top of a hill, hoping to see the wolf pack in the valley below, so I tied my horse to a tree short of the crown of the ridge. When I climbed to the crest, I saw a vehicle on a hilltop on the other side of the valley. It was an all-terrain vehicle, a four-wheeler. I thought maybe the rider had fallen off or was hurt, so I looked for him and spotted him in the shade of a tree, lying in the prone position on the ground, and he was aiming a rifle at something in the valley." She twisted her fingers. "My first thought was of the wolves. But when I glanced down into the valley, the wolf pack wasn't there. A man was squatting near the ground, looking at a handheld device.

"When I realized what was about to happen, I yelled. But not soon enough. The shooter fired his shot at the same time. The man in the valley didn't have a chance." She met the sheriff's gaze. "I couldn't even go check on him because the shooter must have heard my shout. The next thing I knew, he was aiming his rifle at me." She shivered. "I got on my horse and raced to the bottom of the mountain."

"And he followed?"

She nodded. "He shot at me a couple of times. I thought I might have outrun him, but he caught up about the time I reached the truck and trailer Mr. Decker mentioned. He shot at me, hit the truck, my horse threw me and I woke up in the backseat of Mr. Decker's truck." She inhaled deeply and let it all out. "We have to go back to that valley. If there's even a chance Mr. Khalig is alive, he won't be by morning."

"I'll take my men and check it out."

Grace touched his arm. "I'm going with you. It'll take less time for you to find him if I show you the exact location."

"You need to see a doctor," the sheriff said. "As you said, I don't have time to wait for that." He glanced at Caveman. "Do you want me to have one of my deputies take you to the clinic?"

Grace's lips firmed into a straight line. "I'm not going to a clinic. I'm going back to check on that man. I won't rest until I know what happened to him. If you won't take me, I'll get on my own four-wheeler and go up there. You're going to need all-terrain vehicles, anyway. Your truck won't make it up those trails."

The sheriff nodded toward his deputy. "Load up the trailer with the two four-wheelers. We're going into the mountains." He faced Grace. "And we're taking her with us."

"I'll meet you out at Khalig's truck in fifteen minutes. It'll take me that long to get to my place, grab my four-wheeler and get back to the location." She faced Caveman. "Do you mind dropping me off at my house? It's at the end of Main Street."

"I'm going with you," Caveman said.

"You're under no obligation to," she pointed out.

"No, but when you find an unconscious woman in the wilderness, you tend to invest in her well-being." His eyes narrowed. He could be as stubborn as she was. "I'm going."

"Do you have a four-wheeler?"

"No, but I know someone who probably does." Given the mission of Task Force Safe Haven, Kevin Garner had to have the equipment he needed to navigate the rocky hills and trails. If not horses, he had to have four-wheelers.

"I'm not waiting for you," Grace warned.

"You're not leaving without me," he countered.

"Is that a command?" She raised her brows. "I'll have you know, I'll do whatever the hell I please."

Caveman sighed. "It's a suggestion. Face it, if your shooter is still out there, you'll need protection."

"The sheriff and deputy will provide any protection I might need."

"They will be busy processing a crime scene."

"Then, I can take care of myself," Grace said. "I've been going out in these mountains alone for nearly a decade. I don't need a man to follow me, or protect me."

The sheriff laid a hand on her arm. "Grace, he's right. We'll be busy processing a crime scene. Once you get us there, we won't have time to keep an eye on you."

"I can keep an eye on myself," she said. "I'm the one person most interested in my own well-being."

Caveman pressed a finger to her lips. "You're an independent woman. I get that. But before now, you probably have never had someone shooting at you. I have." He took her hand. "Even in the worst battlefield scenarios, I rely on my battle buddies to have my back. Let me get your back."

For a moment, she stared at his hand holding hers. Then she glanced up into his gaze. "Fine. But if you can't keep up, I'll leave you behind."

He nodded. "Deal."

SHE GAVE THE truck and trailer's location to the sheriff and the deputy. Because she didn't want to slow them down from getting out to the site, she was forced to accept a ride from the man who'd picked her up off the ground and carried her around like she was little more than a child.

A shiver slipped through her at the thought of Caveman touching her body in places that hadn't been touched by a man in too long. And he'd found her unconscious. Had she been in the city, anything could have happened to her. In the mountains, with a shooter after her, she hated to think what would have happened had Caveman not come along when he had.

If the killer hadn't finished her off, the wolves, a bear, a mountain lion could have done it for him. Much as she hated to admit it, she was glad the stranger had come along and tucked her into the backseat of his truck.

"We'll meet you in fifteen minutes," Grace said to the sheriff.

He tipped his cowboy hat. "Roger." Then he was all business back on the telephone before Grace made it to the door.

Once outside, Grace strode toward Caveman's truck, now fully in control of the muscles in her legs. She didn't need to lean on anyone. Nor did she need help getting up into the truck.

Caveman beat her to the truck and opened the passenger door.

She frowned at the gesture, seeing it as a challenge to her ability to take care of herself.

"Just so you don't think I'm being chauvinistic, I always open doors for women. My mother drilled that into my head at a very young age. It's a hard habit to break, and I have no intention of doing that now. It's just being polite."

Grace slid into the seat and gave a low-key grunt. "You don't have to make a big deal out of it," she said through clenched teeth.

Caveman rounded the front of the truck, his broad shoulders and trim waist evidence of a man who took pride in fitness. She'd bet there wasn't an ounce of fat on his body, yet he didn't strut to show off his physique. The man had purpose in his stride, and it wasn't the purpose of looking good, though he'd accomplished that in spades. And he was polite, which made Grace feel churlish and unappreciative of all he'd done for her.

When he slid into the driver's seat beside her, she stared straight ahead, her lips twisting into a wry smile. "Thank you for helping me when I was unconscious. And thank you for giving me a ride to my house." She glanced across at him. "And thank you for opening my door for me. It's nice to know chivalry isn't dead."

His lips twitched. "You're welcome." Twisting the key in the ignition, he shot a glance toward her. "Where to?"

She gave him the directions to her little cottage sitting on an acre of land on the edge of town. She hoped Bear had found his way home after his earlier scare. The town of Grizzly Pass was situated in a valley between hills that led up into the mountains. Grace had ridden out that morning from the little barn behind her house.

As she neared the white clapboard cottage with the wide front porch and antique blue shutters, she leaned forward, trying to see around the house to the barn. Was that a tail swishing near the back gate?

Caveman pulled into the driveway.

Before he could shift into Park, she was out of the truck and hurrying around to the back of the house.

Her protector switched off the engine and hurried after her. "Hey, wait up," he called out.

Grace ignored him, bent and slipped through the fence rails and ran toward the back gate next to the barn, her heart soaring.

Bear stood at the gate, tossing his head and dancing back on his hooves.

She opened the gate and held it wide.

Bear slipped through and turned to nuzzle her hand.

Grace reached into her jeans pocket and pulled out the piece of carrot she'd planned on giving Bear as a treat at the end of the day. She held it out in the palm of her hand.

Bear's big, velvety lips took the carrot and he crunched it between his teeth, nodding his head in approval.

Wrapping her arms around his neck, Grace hugged the horse, relieved he wasn't hurt by the bullet or by wandering around the countryside and crossing highways. "Hey, big boy. Glad you made it home without me." She held on to his bridle and leaned her forehead against his. "I bet you're hungry and thirsty."

Bear tossed his head and whinnied.

With a laugh, Grace straightened and walked toward the barn. Bear followed.

Inside, she opened the stall door. Bear trotted in.

She removed Bear's bridle and was surprised to find Caveman beside her loosening the leather strap holding the girth around the horse's middle. "I can take care of that," she assured him.

"I know my way around horses," he said, and pulled the saddle from Bear's back. "Tack room?"

"At the back of the barn. I can handle the rest. I just want to get him situated before we leave."

"No problem." He took the saddle and carried it to the tack room. Caveman reappeared outside the stall. "I'll be right back."

"I'm leaving as soon as I'm done here."

"Understood." He took off at a jog out of the barn.

With her self-appointed protector gone, Grace suddenly had a feeling of being exposed. Shrugging off the insecurity, she went to work, giving the horse food and water, and then closed the stall.

From another stall, she rolled her four-wheeler out into the open. She hadn't ridden it in a month and the last time she had, it had been slow to start. She'd had to charge the battery and probably needed to buy a new one, but she didn't have time now. She'd promised to meet the sheriff in fifteen minutes. Already five had passed.

The next five minutes, she did everything she knew to start the vehicle and it refused.

Just when she was about to give up and call the sheriff, a small engine's roar sounded outside the barn.

She walked out and shook her head.

Caveman sat on a newer-model ATV. "Ready?"

"Where did you get that?"

"My boss dropped it off." He checked the instruments, revved the throttle and looked up. "I thought you'd be gone by now."

"I can't get mine to start, and we're supposed to be there in five minutes."

"Let me take a look." He killed the engine and entered the barn.

Okay, so she wasn't that knowledgeable about

mechanics. She knew Wally, who had a small-engine repair shop in his barn. He fixed anything she had issues with. That didn't mean she couldn't take care of herself.

"Your battery is dead." Caveman glanced around. "You got another handy?"

She shook her head. "No. Fresh out."

"Got a helmet?"

She nodded. "Yeah, but I won't need it if I can't get my ATV started."

He spun and headed for the barn door. "You can ride on the back of mine," he called out over his shoulder.

Grace's heart fluttered at the thought riding behind Caveman, holding him around the waist to keep from falling off. "No, thanks. Those trails are dangerous." She suspected the danger was more in how her pulse quickened around the man than the possibility of plunging over the edge of a drop-off.

"I grew up riding horses and four-wheelers on rugged mountain trails. I won't let you fall off a cliff." He held up a hand. "Promise."

She frowned. But she knew she only had a few minutes to get to the meeting location and relented, sighing. "Okay. I guess I'll put my life in your hands." She followed him out of the barn and closed the door behind her. "Although I don't know why I should trust you. I don't even know you."

Chapter Three

Caveman settled on the seat of the ATV and tipped his head toward the rear. "Hop on."

Grace fitted her helmet on her head and buckled the strap beneath her chin. "Wouldn't it make more sense for me to drive, since I know the way?"

"Actually, it does." He grinned, scooted to the back of the seat and glanced toward her, raising his brows in challenge.

Still, Grace hesitated for a moment, gnawing on her bottom lip.

God, when she did that, Caveman's groin clenched and he fought the urge to kiss that worried lip and suck it into his mouth. The woman probably had no clue how crazy she could make a man. And he was no exception.

Finally, she slid onto the seat in front of Caveman. "Hold on." She thumbed the throttle and the four-wheeler leaped forward.

Caveman wrapped his arms around her waist and pressed his chest to her back. Oh, yeah, this was much better than driving.

Grace aimed for the back gate to the pasture, blew through and followed a dirt road up into the hills, zig-zagging through fields and gullies until she crossed a highway and ended up on the road leading to Khalig's truck and trailer. Another truck and trailer stood beside the original, this one marked with the county sheriff logo. Sheriff Scott and Deputy Pierce were mounted on four-wheelers.

Grace nodded as she passed them, leading the way up the side of a mountain, the trail narrowing significantly. There was no way a full-size truck or even an SUV could navigate the trajectories. Barely wide enough for the four-wheeler, the path clung to the side of a bluff. The downhill side was so steep it might as well be considered a drop-off. Anyone who fell over the edge wouldn't stop until they hit the bottom a hundred or more feet below.

Now not so sure he'd chosen the right position, Caveman wished he had control of steering the ATV. He tightened his arms around Grace's slim waist, wondering if she had the strength to keep them both on the vehicle if they hit a really big bump.

Caveman vowed to be the driver on the way back down the mountain. In the meantime, he concentrated on leaning into the curves and staying on the ATV.

As they neared the top of a steep hill, Grace slowed and rolled to a stop. "This is where I tied off my horse."

The sheriff and deputy pulled up beside them. Everyone dismounted.

Fighting the urge to drop to a prone position on the ground and kiss the earth, Caveman stood and pretended the ride up the treacherous trail hadn't been a big deal at all. "You rode your horse down that trail?"

She nodded. "Normally, I take it slowly. But I had a gunman taking shots at me. I let Bear have his head. I have to admit, I wanted to close my eyes several times on the way down."

The sheriff nodded toward the ridgeline. "Was that your vantage point?"

She nodded, but didn't move toward the top. "The shooter was on the ridge to the north."

Sheriff Scott and the deputy drew their weapons and climbed. As they neared the top, they dropped to their bellies and low-crawled the rest of the way. The sheriff lifted binoculars to his eyes.

Caveman stayed with Grace in case the shooter was watching for her.

A couple minutes later, Sheriff Scott waved. "All clear. Grace, I need you to show me what you were talking about."

Grace frowned, scrambled up to the top and squatted beside the sheriff.

Caveman followed, his gaze taking in the valley below and the ridge to the north. Nothing moved and nothing stood out as not belonging.

Grace pointed to the opposite hilltop. "The shooter was over there." Then she glanced down at the valley, her frown deepening. "The man he shot was in the valley just to the right of that pine."

The sheriff raised his binoculars to his eyes again. "He's not there."

"What?" She held out her hand. "Let me see."

Sheriff Scott handed her the binoculars. Grace adjusted them and stared down at the valley below. "I don't understand. He was in that valley. Hell, his truck and trailer are still parked back at the road. Where could he have gone?" She handed the binoculars back to the sheriff. "Do you think he was only wounded and crawled beneath a bush or something?" She was on her feet and headed back to the ATV. "We need to get down there. If that man is still alive, he could be in a bad way."

The sheriff hurried to catch up to her. "Grace, I want you to stay up here with Mr. Decker."

She'd reached the ATV and had thrown her leg over the seat before she turned to stare at the sheriff. "Are you kidding? I left him once, when I could have saved him."

The sheriff shook his head. "You don't know that. You could have ended up a second victim, and nobody would have known where to find either one of you." He touched her arm. "You did the right thing by coming straight to my office."

When the lawman turned away, Grace captured his hand. "Sheriff, I need to know. I feel like I could have done something to stop that man from shooting the other guy. I know it's irrational, but somehow I feel responsible."

The way she stared at the sheriff with her soft gray eyes made Caveman want the sheriff to let her accompany him to the valley floor.

"You promise to stay back enough not to disturb what could potentially be a crime scene?" Sheriff Scott asked.

She held up her hand like she was swearing in front of a judge. "I promise."

The sheriff shot a glance at Caveman. "Mr. Decker, will you keep an eye on her to make sure she's safe?"

"I will," Caveman said. He wanted to know what was in that valley as well, but if it meant leaving Grace alone on the ridge, he would have stayed with her.

"Fine. Come along, but stay back." Sheriff Scott and

the deputy climbed onto their four-wheelers and eased their way down a narrow path to the valley floor.

Caveman let Grace drive again, knowing she was better protected with his body wrapped around her than if she'd ridden on the back.

At the bottom of the hill, Grace parked the four-wheeler twenty yards from the pine tree she'd indicated. "We'll see a lot more on foot than on an ATV."

"True." Caveman studied the surrounding area, careful to stay out of the way of the sheriff and his deputy.

"Grace," the sheriff called out.

She and Caveman hurried over to where the sheriff squatted on his haunches, staring at the dirt. He pointed. "Is this the spot where he fell?"

Grace glanced around at the nearby tree and nodded. "I think so."

The sheriff's lips pressed together and he pointed at the ground. "This looks like dried blood."

Caveman stared at the dark blotches, his belly tightening. He'd seen similar dark stains in the dust of an Afghanistan village where his brothers in arms had bled out.

"Got tire tracks here." Deputy Pierce stared at the ground a few yards away.

The sheriff straightened and walked slowly toward the deputy. "And there's a trail of blood leading toward the tracks."

Caveman circled wide, studying the ground until he saw what he thought he might find. "More tracks over here." The tracks led toward a hill. Without waiting for permission, Caveman climbed the hill, parallel to the tracks. As the ground grew rockier, the tracks became harder to follow. At that point, Caveman looked for disturbed pebbles, scraped rocks and anything that would indicate a heavy four-wheeler had passed that direction.

At the top of the hill, the slope leveled off briefly and then fell in a sheer two-hundred-foot drop-off to a boulder-strewn creek bed below. Caveman's stomach tightened as he spotted what appeared to be the wreckage of an ATV. "I found the ATV." He squinted. What was that next to the big boulder shaped like an anvil? He leaned over the edge a little farther and noticed what appeared to be a shoe…attached to a foot. "I'm sorry to say, but I think I found Mr. Khalig."

Grace scrambled to the top of the hill and nearly pitched over the edge.

Caveman shot out his hand, stopping her short of following the pipeline inspector to a horrible death. "Oh, dear Lord."

Wrapping his arm around her shoulders, Caveman pulled her against him.

She burrowed her face into his chest. "I should have stayed."

"You couldn't," Caveman said. "You would have been shot."

"I could have circled back," she said, her voice quivering.

"On that trail?" Caveman shook his head. "No way. You did the right thing."

Sheriff Scott appeared beside Caveman. "Mr. Decker's right. You wouldn't be alive if you'd stopped to help a man who could have been dead before he went over the edge."

Grace lifted her head and stared at the sheriff through watery eyes. "What do you mean?"

"We noticed footprints and drag marks in the dirt back there," Deputy Pierce said.

The sheriff nodded. "I suspect the killer came back, dragged the body onto the ATV and rode it up to the hill. Then he pushed it over the edge with Mr. Khalig still on it." He glanced over at the deputy. "We'll get the state rescue team in to recover the body. The coroner will conduct an autopsy. He'll know whether the bullet killed him or the fall."

"Is there anything we can do to help?" Grace asked.

Sheriff Scott nodded. "I'd like you to come in and sign a statement detailing what you saw and at what time."

"Anything you need. I'll be there." Grace shivered. "I wish I'd seen the killer's face."

"I do, too." The sheriff stared down at the creek bed. "Murder cases are seldom solved so easily." He glanced across at Grace. "You might want to watch your back. If he thinks you could pick him out in a lineup, he might come after you."

Grace shivered again. "We live in a small town." Her gaze captured the sheriff's. "There's a good chance I might know him."

"If the law isn't knocking on his door within twenty-four hours," Caveman said, "he might figure out that you didn't see enough of him to turn him in."

"In which case, he'd be smart to keep a low profile and leave you alone," the sheriff added.

"Or not." Grace sighed. "I can't stay holed up in my house. I have work to do. I still haven't found my wolf."

"It might not be safe for you to be roaming the woods right now," the sheriff said. "By yourself, you present an easy target with no witnesses."

Grace's shoulders squared. "I won't let fear run my life. I ran today, and Mr. Khalig is dead because I did."

Caveman shook his head. "No, Mr. Khalig is dead because someone shot him. Not because you didn't stop that someone from shooting him. You are not responsible for that man's death. You didn't pull the trigger." The words were an echo from his psychologist's arsenal of phrases she'd used to help him through survivor's guilt. Using them now with Grace helped him see the truth of them.

He hadn't detonated the bomb that had killed his teammates, nor had he pulled the trigger on the AK-47s that had taken out more of his battle buddies. He couldn't have done anything differently other than die in his teammates' place by being the forward element at that exact moment. He couldn't have known. It didn't make it easier. Only time would help him accept the truth.

"THERE IS SOMETHING you could do for me," the sheriff said.

Grace perked up. "Anything." After all that had happened, she refused to be a victim. She wanted to help.

"Go back down, get in my service vehicle and let dispatch know to call in the mountain rescue crew. Johnny and I will stay and make sure the wolves don't clean up before they get here."

"Will do," Grace said. "Do you need me to come back?"

"No. We can handle it from here. You should head home. And please consider lying low for a while until we're sure the killer isn't still gunning for you."

"Okay," Grace said. Though she had work to do,

she now knew she wasn't keen on being the target of a gunman. She'd give it at least a day for the man to realize she hadn't seen him and couldn't identify his face. "You'll let me know what they find out about the man down there?"

"You bet," Sherriff Scott said. "Thank you, Grace, for letting us know as soon as possible."

But not soon enough to help Mr. Khalig. She turned and started back down the hill. Her feet slipped in the gravel and she would have fallen, but Caveman was right beside her and helped her get steady on her feet. He hooked her elbow and assisted her the rest of the way down the steep incline.

At the bottom, he turned her to face him. "Are you okay?"

She nodded. "I'm fine, just a little shaken. It's not every day I witness a murder."

His lips twisted. "How many murders have you witnessed?"

"Counting today?" She snorted. "One." With a nod toward the ATV, she said, "You can drive. I'm not sure I can hold it steady." She held up a hand, demonstrating how much it trembled.

"Thanks. I would rather navigate the downhill trail. Coming up was bad enough." He climbed onto the ATV and scooted forward, allowing room for her to mount behind him.

At this point, Grace didn't care that he was a stranger. The man had found her unconscious, sought help for her and then gone with her to show the sheriff where a murder had taken place. If he'd been the shooter, he'd have killed her by now and avoided the sheriff altogether.

She slipped onto the seat and held on to the metal

rack bolted to the back of the machine, thinking it would be enough to keep her seated.

"You need to hold on around my waist," Caveman advised. "It's a lot different being on the back than holding on to the handlebars."

"I'll be okay," she assured him.

Caveman shrugged, started the engine and eased his thumb onto the throttle.

The ATV leapt forward, nearly leaving Grace behind.

She swallowed a yelp, wrapped her arms around his waist and didn't argue anymore as they traversed the downhill trail to the bottom.

When she'd been the target of the shooter, she hadn't had time to worry about falling off her sure-footed horse. Now that she wasn't in control of the ATV and was completely reliant on Caveman, she felt every bump and worried the next would be the one that would throw her over the edge. She tightened her hold around his middle, slightly reassured by the solid muscles beneath his shirt.

For a moment, she closed her eyes and inhaled the scent of pure male—a mix of aftershave and raw, outdoor sensuality. It calmed her.

Although she'd always valued her independence, she could appreciate having someone to lean on in this new and dangerous world she lived in. Before, she'd only had to worry about bears and wolves killing her. Now she had to worry about a man diabolical enough to hunt another man down like an animal.

By the time they finally reached the bottom and made their way back to the parked trucks, Grace's body had adjusted to Caveman's movements, making them seem like one person—riding the trails, absorbing every bump and leaning into every turn.

When the vehicles came into view, she pulled herself back to the task at hand.

Caveman stopped next to the sheriff's truck and switched off the ATV's engine.

Grace climbed off the back, the cool mountain air hitting her front where the heat generated by Caveman still clung to her. Shaking off the feeling of loss, she opened the passenger door of the sheriff's vehicle, slid onto the front seat, grabbed the radio mic and pressed the button. "Hello."

"This is dispatch, who am I talking to?"

"Grace Saunders. Sheriff Scott wanted me to relay a request for a mountain rescue team to be deployed to his location as soon as possible."

"Could you provide a little detail to pass on to the team?" the dispatcher asked.

Grace inhaled and let out a long slow breath before responding. "There's a man at the bottom of a deep drop-off."

"Is he unconscious?"

The hollow feeling in her chest intensified. "We believe he's dead. He's not moving and he could be the victim of a gunshot wound."

"Got it. I'll relay the GPS coordinate and have the team sent out as soon as they can mobilize."

"Thank you." Grace hung the mic on the radio and climbed out of the sheriff's SUV.

"Now what?" Caveman asked. He'd dismounted from the four-wheeler and stepped up beside the sheriff's vehicle while she'd been talking on the radio.

She shrugged. "If you could take me back to my place, I have work to do."

Caveman frowned. "When we get there, will you let me take you to the clinic to see a doctor?"

"I don't need one." Her head hurt and she was a little nauseated, but she wouldn't admit it to him. "I'd rather stay home."

"I'll make a deal with you. I'll take you home if you promise to let me take you from there to see a doctor."

She sighed. "You're not going to let it go, are you?"

He crossed his arms over his chest and shook his head. "Nope."

"And if I don't agree, either I walk home—which I don't mind, but I'm not in the mood—or I wait until the sheriff is done retrieving Mr. Khalig's body."

His lips twitched. "That about sums it up. See a doctor, walk home alone or wait for a very long time." He raised his hands, palms up. "It's a no-brainer to me."

Her eyes narrowed. "I'll walk." She brushed past him and lengthened her stride, knowing she was too emotionally exhausted to make the long trek all the way back to her house, but too stubborn to let Caveman win the argument.

The ATV roared to life behind her and the crunch of gravel heralded its approach.

"You might also consider that by walking home, you put yourself up as an easy target for a man who has proven he can take a man down from a significant distance. Are you willing to be his next target?"

His words socked her in the gut. She stopped in her tracks and her lips pressed together in a hard line.

Damn. The man had a good point. "Fine." She spun and slipped her leg over the back of the four-wheeler.

"You can take me to my house. From there, I'll take myself to the clinic."

Caveman shook his head, refusing to engage the engine and send the ATV toward Grace's house. "That's not the deal. I take you home. Then I will take you to the clinic. When the doctor clears you to drive, you can take yourself anywhere you want to go."

"Okay. We'll do it your way." She wrapped her arms loosely around his waist, unwilling to be caught up in the pheromones the man put off. "Can we go, already?"

"Now we can go." He goosed the throttle. The ATV jumped, nearly unseating Grace.

She tightened her hold around Caveman's waist and pressed her body against his as they bumped along the dirt road with more potholes than she remembered on the way out. Perhaps because she noticed them more this time because she wasn't the one in control of the steering. Either way, she held on, her thighs tightly clamped around his hips and the seat.

By the time they arrived at her cottage, she could barely breathe—the fact having nothing to do with the actual ride so much as it did with the feel of the man's body pressed against hers. She was almost disappointed when he brought the vehicle to a standstill next to her gate.

Grace climbed off and opened the gate. The distance between them helped her to get her head on straight and for her pulse to slow down to normal.

He followed her to her house. "We'll take my truck. Grab your purse and whatever else you'll need."

When she opened her mouth to protest, he held up his hand.

"You promised." He frowned and crossed his arms

over his chest again. "Where I come from, a promise is sacred."

Her brows met in the middle. "Where *do* you come from?"

His frown disappeared and he grinned. "Montana."

Caveman started toward the house, Grace fell in step beside him. "Is that where you were before you arrived in Grizzly Pass?"

His grin slipped. "No."

She shot a glance his direction. A shadow had descended on his face and he appeared to be ten years older.

"Where *did* you come from?"

He stared out at the mountains. "Bethesda, Maryland."

There was so much she didn't know about this man. "That's a long way from Montana."

"Yes, it is." He stopped short of her porch. "I'll be in my truck when you're ready." Before she could say more, he turned and strode toward the corner of her house.

For a moment, Grace allowed herself the pleasure of watching the way his butt twitched in his blue jeans. The man was pure male and so ruggedly handsome he took her breath away. What was he doing hanging around her? Since she was being forced to ride with him to the clinic, she'd drill him with questions until she was satisfied with the answers. For starters, why did he call himself Caveman? And what was the importance of Bethesda, Maryland, that had made him go from being relaxed and helpful to stiff and unapproachable?

Caveman disappeared around the corner.

Grace faced her house, fished her key from her pocket and climbed the stairs. She opened the screen door and held out the key, ready to fit it into the lock when she noticed something hanging on the handle. It rocked back and forth and then fell at her feet.

She jumped back, emitting a short, sharp scream, her heart thundering against her ribs. With her hand pressed to her chest, she squatted and stared at the item, a lead weight settling in the pit of her belly as she recognized the circular band with the rectangular plastic box affixed to it.

It was the radio collar for the wolf she'd been looking for earlier that day, and it was covered in blood.

Chapter Four

Caveman had been about to climb into his truck when he heard Grace's scream. All thoughts of Bethesda, physical therapy and war wounds disappeared in a split second. He pulled his pistol from beneath the seat and raced back around the house to find Grace sitting on the porch, her back leaning against the screen door, her hand pressed to her chest.

"What's wrong?" His heart thundered against his ribs and his breathing was erratic as he stared around the back porch, searching for the threat.

"This." She pointed toward something on the porch in front of her. It appeared to be some kind of collar. Her gaze rose to his, her eyes wide, filling with tears. "This is the collar for the wolf I was looking for when I ran across the murder scene."

"What the hell's it doing here?"

"It was hanging on the handle of the door. Someone put it there."

"Do you have any coworkers who would have brought it to you?" Caveman reached out a hand to her.

She laid her slim fingers into his palm and allowed him to pull her to her feet and into his arms. "It has blood on it and it's been cut."

"Why would someone put it on your doorknob?" he asked.

She drew in a deep breath and let it out. "I was out in the mountains where I was because I was following the signal for this collar. It had stopped moving as of two days ago. The only other people aware of the wolf's movement, or lack thereof, were my coworkers on the Wolf Project out of Yellowstone National Park. This collar belonged to Loki, a black male wolf out of Molly's pack. I rescued him as a cub when his mother had been killed by a local rancher." Her jaw tightened, she drew herself up and gave him a level stare through moist eyes. "We suspected he was dead, but had hoped of natural causes. That someone brought me the collar without a note of why it was covered in blood leaves me to think all kinds of bad things."

"You think the shooter who killed Khalig might have killed the wolf?"

"If he didn't kill the wolf, I think he wants me to believe he did."

"And he left the collar as a warning or a trophy?"

Grace stared down at the offensive object and nodded. "What else am I supposed to think? Unless someone else owns up to leaving the collar on my back porch doorknob, I can only imagine why it was left." She bent, reaching for the collar.

Caveman grabbed her arm to keep her from retrieving it. "Leave it there for the sheriff. They might be able to pull fingerprints from the plastic box."

Grace straightened. "Why do people have to be so destructive and heartless with nature?"

"I don't know, but let's get you inside, just in case the shooter is lurking nearby."

Grace shot a glance over her shoulder. "Do you think he might be out there watching?" A shiver shook her body.

"He could be." Caveman held out his hand. "Let me have your key."

She pointed at the porch near the collar. "I dropped it."

Caveman retrieved it from the porch and straightened. "Let's go through the front door." Slipping his arm around her, he shielded her body with his as much as possible as he led her around the house to the front door. There he opened the screen door. Before he fit the key into the lock, he tried the knob. It was locked. He fit the key in the knob, twisted and pushed the door open. "Let me go first."

She nodded and allowed him to enter first, following right behind him.

Closing the door behind her, he stared down into her eyes. "I want to check the house. Stay here."

Again, she nodded.

Caveman moved from room to room, holding his 9-millimeter pistol in front of him, checking around the corners of each wall before moving into a room. When he reached the back door, he checked the handle. The door was locked. As far as he could tell, the house hadn't been entered. "All clear," he called out.

"The sheriff will be busy up in the hills until they retrieve the body," Grace said, walking into the kitchen, her arms wrapped around her body. "I don't like the idea of leaving the collar on the porch."

"Do you have a paper bag we can use and maybe some rubber gloves?"

"I do." She hurried into a pantry off the kitchen and

emerged with a box of rubber gloves and what appeared to be a paper lunch bag. Setting the box of gloves on the counter, she pulled on a pair. "These won't fit your big hands. I'll take care of the collar."

He opened the back door and looked before stepping over the collar and standing on the porch. He used his body as a shield to protect Grace in case the shooter had her in his sights. Given the killer had good aim with a rifle and scope, he could be hiding in the nearby woods, his sights trained on her back door.

Grace scooped up the collar by the nylon band and dropped it into the paper bag, touching as little as possible.

Once she had the collar in the bag, she nodded. "I'll grab my purse. We can drop this off at the sheriff's office."

"On the way to the clinic," Caveman added.

Her lush lips pulled into a twisted frown. "On the way to the clinic." The frown turned up on the corners. "You are a stubborn man, aren't you?"

He grinned and followed her back into the house, locking the door behind him. "I prefer to call it being persistent."

She walked back through the house. "If you give me just a minute, I'd like to wash my hands and face."

"Take your time. I'll wait by the front door."

Grace turned down the hallway and ducked into the bathroom, closing the door behind her.

Caveman waited in the front entrance, staring at the pictures hanging on the walls. Many were of wolves. Some were of people. One had a group of men and women standing in front of a cabin, all grinning, wearing outdoor clothing. Another photo was of Grace, maybe a few years younger, with a man. They were kissing with the sun setting over snowcapped peaks in the background. She looked young, happy and in love.

Something tugged at Caveman's chest. He'd assumed Grace was single.

The door opened to the bathroom and Grace appeared, her face freshly scrubbed, still makeup-free. She'd brushed her hair and left it falling around her shoulders the way it was in the picture.

"You have some interesting pictures on your wall." Caveman nodded toward the wolves.

She nodded. "I'm living my dream job as a biologist working on the Wolf Project, among others. The pictures are of some of the wolves I've been tracking for the past five years."

Caveman pointed toward the group picture.

Grace smiled. "Those are the crew of biologists working in Yellowstone National Park. We keep in touch by phone, internet and through in-person meetings once a month."

"Do you live alone?" Caveman asked, his gaze on the picture of her kissing the man. "Should I be concerned about a jealous husband walking through the door at any moment?"

The smile left Grace's eyes. "Yes, I live alone. No, you don't have to worry." She grabbed a brown leather purse from a hallway table and opened the front door. "I'm ready."

"I take it I hit a sore spot," he said, passing her to exit the house first.

"I'm not married, anymore."

But she was once. Caveman vowed not to pry. Apparently, she wasn't over her ex-husband. Not if she still had his picture hanging in her front entrance.

Grace paused to lock the front door and then turned to follow him toward the truck. "For the record, I'm a widow. My husband died in a parasailing accident six years ago."

GRACE CLIMBED INTO the passenger seat of Caveman's truck. "You really don't have to take me to the clinic. I've been getting around fine for the past couple of hours without blacking out. I could drive myself there, for that matter."

"Humor me. I feel—"

"Responsible," she finished for him. "Well, you're not. You've done more than you had to. You could have dropped me off at the sheriff's office earlier today and been done with me."

"That's not the kind of guy I am."

She tilted her head and stared across the console at him. "No, I got that impression." She settled back in her seat, closed her eyes and let him take control, something she wasn't quite used to. "Well, thank you for coming to my rescue. If you hadn't been there…" She shivered. What would have happened? Would the shooter have caught up to her and finished her off like he'd done Mr. Khalig?

A hand touched hers.

She opened her eyes, her gaze going to where his hand held hers and warmth spread from that point throughout her body. She hadn't had that kind of re-action to a man's touch since Jack had died, and she wasn't sure she wanted it.

"I'm glad I was there." Caveman squeezed her fingers gently, briefly and let go. "I'm sorry about your husband."

"Yeah. Me, too. We were supposed to be doing this together." She shrugged and let go of the breath she hadn't known she was holding the whole time Caveman's hand had been on hers. "But that was six years ago. Life goes on. Turn left at the next street. The clinic is three blocks on the right."

They arrived in front of the Grizzly Pass Clinic a few minutes before it was due to close. "I doubt they can get me in."

"If they can't, where's the nearest emergency room?" Caveman shifted into Park and stepped down from the truck. Rounding the front of the vehicle, he arrived in time to help her down.

"The nearest would be in Bozeman, an hour and a half away."

"Guess we better get inside quickly." He cupped her elbow and guided her through the door.

Fortunately, the doctor had enough time left to check her over while her self-appointed bodyguard waited in the lobby.

"You appear to be all right. If you get any dizzy spells or feel nauseated, you might want to call the EMTs and have them transport you to the nearest hospital for further evaluation. But so far, I don't see anything that makes me too concerned." He offered her a prescription for painkillers, which she refused. "Then take some over-the-counter pain relievers if you get a headache."

She smiled. "Thank you for seeing me on such short notice."

"I'm glad I was here for you." He walked her to the

door. "Have you considered wearing a helmet when you go horseback riding?"

"I have considered it. And I might resort to it, if I continue to fall off my horse." She might also consider a bulletproof vest and making the helmet a bulletproof one if she continued to be the target of a sniper. She didn't say it out loud, nor had she told the doctor why she'd fallen off her horse. The medical professional had been ready to go home before she'd shown up and he wasn't the one being shot at.

When she stepped out of the examination room into the lobby, she found Caveman laughing at something the cute receptionist had said. The smile on his face transformed him from the serious, rugged cowboy to someone more lighthearted and approachable. The sparkle in his eyes made him even more handsome than before.

A territorial feeling washed over Grace. Suddenly she had a better understanding of the urge the alpha wolf had to guard his mate and keep her to himself. Not that Caveman was Grace's mate. Hell, they'd just met!

But that didn't stop her fingers from curling into her palms or her gut from clenching when the receptionist smiled up at the man.

"Are you ready to take me home?" Grace asked, her voice a little sharper than usual.

Caveman straightened and turned his smile toward her, brightening the entire room with its full force. Then it faded and his brows pulled together. "What did the doctor say?"

"I'm fine. Can we go now?" She started for the door, ready to leave the office and the cute, young receptionist as soon as possible.

Grace was outside on the sidewalk by the time Caveman caught up with her and gripped her arm. "Slow down. It might not be safe for you to be out in the open. Care to elaborate on the doctor's prognosis?"

"He said I'm fine and can carry on, business as usual." She shook off his hand.

"No concussion?"

"No concussion. Which means you can drop me off at my house, and your responsibility toward me is complete."

He nodded and opened the truck door for her. "If you don't mind, I'd like to stop by my boss's office for a few minutes. I need to brief him on what happened. He might want to hear what you have to say."

"Now that we're not being shot at, and I'm not dying of a concussion, maybe you can answer a few questions for me."

"Shoot." He winced. "Sorry. I didn't mean the pun."

She inhaled and thought of all the questions she had for this man. "Okay. Who's your boss?"

"The US Army, but I'm on temporary loan to a special task force with the Department of Homeland Security. I'm reporting to a man named Kevin Garner."

"I've seen Kevin around. I didn't know he was heading a special task force."

"It's new. I'm new. I got in a couple days ago, and I'm still trying to figure out what it is I'm supposed to be doing."

"Army?" That would explain the short hair, the military bearing and the scars. "For how long?"

"Eleven years."

"Deployed?"

He nodded, his gaze on the road ahead. "What is this? An interrogation?"

"I've been all over the mountains with you and I don't know who you are."

"I told you, I'm Max Decker, but my friends call me—"

"Caveman." She crossed her arms over her chest. "Why?"

"Why what?"

"Why do they call you Caveman?"

"I don't know. I guess because I look like a caveman? I got tagged with it in Delta Force training, and it's stuck ever since."

"Army Delta Force?" She looked at him anew. "Isn't that like the elite of the elite?"

He shrugged. "I like to think of it as highly skilled. I'm not an elitist."

"And you're assigned to the Department of Homeland Security?" She shook her head. "Who'd you make mad?"

His fingers tightened on the steering wheel until his knuckles turned white. "I'd like to know that myself."

"Wait." Her eyes narrowed. "You said you came from Bethesda. Isn't that where Walter Reed Army Hospital is located?"

A muscle ticked in his jaw. "Yeah. I was injured in battle. I just completed physical therapy and was waiting for orders to return to my unit."

"And you got pulled to help out here." It was a statement, not a question. "Any you carried me to your truck." She raked his body with her gaze. "I don't see you limping or anything."

"I told you. I finished my physical therapy. I've been working out since. I'm back to normal. Well, almost."

"What did you injure?"

He dropped his left hand to his thigh. "My leg."

"Gunshot?"

"Yeah."

"I'm sorry." She dragged her gaze away from him. "I didn't mean to get too personal."

"It's okay. When you're in the hospital, everyone gets pretty damned personal. I'm used to it by now."

"It had to be hard."

"What?"

"The hospital."

His replaced his hand on the steering wheel, as he pulled into the parking lot of the Blue Moose Tavern. "At least I made it to the hospital," he muttered.

Grace heard his words but didn't dig deeper to learn their meaning. She could guess. He'd made it to the hospital. Apparently, some of his teammates hadn't.

Sometimes recovering from an injury was easier than recovering from a loss. She knew. Having lost her husband in a parasailing accident, she understood what it felt like to lose someone you loved.

From what she knew about the Delta Force soldiers, they were a tightly knit organization. A brotherhood. Those guys fought for their country and for each other.

Grace realized she and Caveman had more in common than she'd originally thought.

Chapter Five

Caveman got out of the truck in front of the Blue Moose Tavern, his thoughts on the men who'd lost their lives in that last battle. For a moment, he forgot where he was. He looked up at the sign on the front of the tavern and shook his head.

Like Grace had said, life moves on. He couldn't live in the past. Squaring his shoulders, he focused on the present and the woman who'd witnessed a murder. Kevin would want to hear what she had to say. Since the man who'd been shot was most likely RJ Khalig, it had to have something to do with the threats the man had reported, the reason Garner had sent Caveman out to find the pipeline inspector.

A pang of guilt tugged at his insides. If he hadn't delayed his departure, arguing over his assigned duties, would he have found Khalig before the sniper?

He shook his head. When he'd arrived at the base of the trail, he wouldn't have been able to find the man without GPS tracking and an all-terrain vehicle. *No.* He couldn't have gotten to Khalig before the shooter.

Grace was out of the truck before Caveman could reach her door. She sniffed the air. "I didn't realize how hungry I was until now."

Caveman inhaled the scent of grilled hamburgers and his mouth watered. "Let's make it quick with Garner. If you're like me, you haven't eaten since breakfast this morning."

"And that was a granola bar." She glanced toward the tavern door. "They make good burgers here."

"Then we'll eat as soon as we're done upstairs." Caveman waved a hand toward the outside staircase leading up to the apartment above the tavern.

Grace rested her hand on the railing and climbed to the top.

Caveman followed closely, once again shielding Grace's body from a sniper's sights.

Before they reached the top landing, the door swung open. Kevin Garner greeted them. "Caveman, I'm glad you stopped by." He stepped back, allowing them to enter the upstairs apartment. Once they were inside, he closed the door, turned to Grace and held out his hand. "I've seen you in passing, but let me introduce myself. Kevin Garner, Department of Homeland Security."

"Grace Saunders. I'm a biologist assigned to the Wolf Project, working remotely with the National Park Service out of Yellowstone."

"Interesting work." Garner shook her hand. "I'm glad you stopped by. I wanted to hear what happened today. The last thing I knew, you were recovering from being thrown by your horse, and Caveman needed a four-wheeler to go back into the mountains. Care to fill me in on what's happened since you got up this morning?"

Grace spent the next five minutes detailing what she'd seen on that ridge in the mountains and what had followed, taking him all the way to her back porch and the present she'd received.

She held out the paper bag with the dog collar inside. "Can I assume you have some of the same capabilities or access to the same support facilities as the sheriff's office?"

Garner took the bag, opened it and stared inside, his brows furrowing. "What do you have here?"

"The collar for number 755. Loki, the wolf I was tracking when I went up in the mountains this morning."

"I don't understand." His glance shot from Grace to Caveman and back to Grace. "Where's the wolf?"

Her lips firmed into a tight line. "Most likely dead. But I haven't seen the body to confirm." Grace nodded toward the bag. "That was left on my back porch as a gift."

"We suspect that whoever killed Khalig might have killed the wolf and decided to leave this on Grace's back porch," Caveman said.

Kevin's brows twisted. "Why?"

His jaw tightening, Caveman glanced toward Grace. "Possibly as a warning to keep her mouth shut about the murder she witnessed."

Kevin stared at the collar. "Or he might be a sadistic bastard, trying to scare her. Otherwise, why would he kill the wolf?"

"Target practice?" Grace suggested, her face pale, her jaw tight.

"Could he be one of the local ranchers who has lost livestock because of the reintroduction of wolves to the Yellowstone ecosystem?" Garner asked.

Grace nodded. "He could be."

"Or he could be a game hunter wanting a trophy for

his collection," Caveman said. "Why else would he re-move the collar?"

Grace frowned. "You think he killed the wolf before he took out Mr. Khalig?"

Caveman caught Grace's gaze and held it. "You said, yourself, the collar had been stalled in the same loca-tion for two days. He had to have killed the wolf two days ago."

"And he retraced his steps to where he'd killed him just to retrieve the collar?" Grace shook her head. "Doesn't make sense. I saw him kill Mr. Khalig. You'd think he'd get the hell off the mountain and come up with an alibi for where he was when I witnessed the murder."

"Unless he's cocky and wants to play games with you," Caveman said.

Grace shivered and wrapped her arms around her middle. "That's a lot of assumption."

"Still, if this guy thinks he can get away with the murder, and he's flaunting that fact by gifting you with this collar, you need to be careful," Garner said. "If he thinks you can identify him, he might take it a step further."

Grace turned and paced away from Garner and Cave-man. Then she spun and marched back. "I don't have time to play games with a killer. I have work to do."

Caveman closed the distance between them and gripped her arms. "And who will do that work if you're dead?"

She stared up at him, her gray eyes widening. "You really think he'll come after me?"

"He already has once, right after the murder. If he left that collar, that makes two times."

"Three's a charm," Grace muttered, raising her hands to rest on Caveman's chest. Instead of pushing him away, she curled her fingers into his shirt. "What am I supposed to do?"

Garner tapped an ink pen on a tabletop where he had a map of the area spread out. "Khalig had received threats. I hadn't been able to pinpoint from whom. I have to assume whoever was threatening him had to have a gripe with the pipeline industry."

"What kind of threats?" Caveman asked.

"Someone painted 'Go Home' on his company truck's windshield two days ago. Yesterday, he had all four tires slashed. I tried to talk him out of going out into the field until we got to the bottom of it, but he insisted he had work to do."

Caveman raised his brows and stared down at the woman in his arms. "Sound familiar?"

"Okay." Grace rolled her eyes. "I get the point." She stepped back, out of Caveman's grip. "I don't know anything about the pipeline. Except that it goes through this area. Supposedly it's buried deep and not in an active volcanic location."

"There's been quite a bit of controversy about the pipelines and whether or not we should even have them. Activists love a cause," Garner said. "With oil prices going down, a lot of pipeline employees are out of work. That makes for some unhappy people who depended on the pipeline companies for their jobs. Then there are the ranchers who are angry at the pipeline companies having free access to cross their lands."

"And there are the ranchers who are mad at the government interfering with grazing rights on government property," Caveman added. "Like Old Man Vanders, whose herd was confiscated because he refused to pay the required fees for grazing on federally owned land."

Garner nodded. "That's what stirred up a lot of folks around here. There's a local group calling itself Free America. We found empty crates in the Lucky Lou Mine with indication they'd once been full of AR-15 rifles. We think the Free America folks have them and might be preparing to stage an attack on a government facility." Garner raised a hand. "I know. It's a lot to take in. Thus the need for me to borrow some of the best from the military."

Grace shook her head. "I had no idea things were getting so bad around here." She snorted. "With all that, don't forget the ranchers angry with the government for reintroducing wolves to the area. I know I get a lot of nastiness from cattlemen when they find one of their prize heifers downed by a wolf pack."

Caveman crossed his arms over his chest. "Since Khalig is a pipeline inspector, is it safe to assume the shooter targeted him because of something to do with the pipeline?"

"That would be my bet. But that doesn't negate the possibility that Khalig might have stumbled across something secret the Free America militia were plotting."

"He was checking some kind of instrument," Grace reiterated. "From what I could tell, he didn't appear to be afraid or nervous about anything. He straightened, still glancing down at his equipment, when the shooter took him down."

"For whatever reason he was murdered," Garner said, "we don't want anything to happen to you, just because you witnessed it."

Grace stiffened. "Don't worry about me. I can take care of myself."

"Do you own a gun?" Kevin asked.

Her chin tilted upward. "I do. A .40-caliber pistol."

"Do you know how to use it?" Caveman asked.

Her gaze shifted to the wall behind him. "Enough to protect myself."

"Are you sure about that?"

"I know how to load it, to turn off the safety and point it at the target."

"When was the last time you fired the weapon?" Caveman asked.

Her cheeks reddened. "Last year I took it to the range and familiarized with it."

Caveman's eyes widened. "A year?" He drew in a deep breath and let it out slowly. "Lady, you're no expert."

Her lips firmed and she pushed back her shoulders. "I didn't say I was. I said I knew how to use my gun."

"It's not enough," Garner said.

Grace turned her frown toward the DHS man. "What do you mean?"

Garner's gaze connected with Caveman's.

Caveman's gut tightened. He knew where Garner was going with what he'd just stated, and he knew he was getting the task.

"You need protection," Garner turned toward Grace.

She flung her hands in the air. "Why won't anyone believe me when I say I don't need someone following me around?" Those same hands fisted and planted on her hips. "I can take care of myself. I don't need some stranger intruding in my life."

"I wasn't going to suggest a stranger," Kevin said.

"Well, the sheriff's department has their hands full policing this area and finding a murderer," Grace shook her head. "I wouldn't ask them to babysit me, when I have my own gun."

"You need someone to watch your back." Garner held up a hand to stop Grace's next flow of words. "I wasn't going to suggest a stranger." He shifted his glance toward Caveman.

His lips twitching on the corners, Caveman couldn't help the grin pulling at his mouth when he stared at the horrified expression on Grace's face. Suddenly, being in Wyoming on temporary duty didn't seem so bad. Not if he could get under the skin of a beautiful biologist. As long as when it was all said and done, he could return to his unit and the career he'd committed his life to.

"YOU WANT *HIM* to follow me around?" Grace waved her hand toward Caveman. "He doesn't even want to be in Wyoming." She narrowed her eyes as she glared at Garner. "And you said you wouldn't suggest a stranger. I didn't know this man until sometime around noon today when I found myself loaded in the backseat of his truck like a kidnap victim." She shook her head. "No offense, but no thanks."

Garner's brows dipped. "Am I missing something? I thought you two were getting along fine."

Oh, they had gotten along fine, but she couldn't ignore the sensual pull the man had on her. "You are missing something," Grace said. "You're missing the point. I don't need a babysitter. I'm a grown woman, perfectly capable of taking care of myself." Perhaps the more she reiterated the argument, the more she would begin to believe it. Today had shaken her more than she cared to admit.

"Agreed," Garner said. "In most cases. But based on the evidence you've presented, you have a sniper after you. Who better than another sniper to protect you? Caveman is one of the most highly trained soldiers you'll ever have the privilege to meet. He understands how a sniper works, having been one himself."

Grace glanced at Caveman. Was it true? Was he a sniper as well as a trained Delta Force soldier?

He nodded without responding in words.

Her belly tightening, Grace continued to stare at this man who was basically a war hero stuck in Grizzly Pass, Wyoming.

"He's the most qualified person around to make sure you're not the next victim," the Homeland Security man said.

"But I—" Grace started.

"Let me finish." Garner laced his fingers together. "I'll speak with the sheriff's department and ask them if they have someone who could provide twenty-four/seven protection for you."

Grace shook her head. "They don't have the manpower."

"Then I'll query the state police," Garner countered.

"They're stretched thin." Grace wasn't helping herself by shooting down every contingency plan Garner had.

"Look, Grace." Garner lifted her hand. "Let Caveman protect you until I can come up with an alternative." He squeezed her hand. "What's it going to hurt? So you have to put him up for a few nights. You have enough room in your house."

Caveman chuckled. "I promise to clean up after myself. And I can cook—if you like steaks on the grill or carryout."

She chewed on her bottom lip, worry chiseling away at her resistance. "You really think I'm at risk?"

Garner held up the paper bag and nodded. "Yes."

"And you can't always be looking over your shoulder," Caveman added. "I respect your independence, but even the most independent of us need help sometimes. I'll do my best not to disturb your work and stay out of your way as much as I can. The fact is, a killer has taken one life and he's left his calling card on your door. If I was you, I'd want a second pair of eyes watching out for me."

"What do you say?" Garner pressed.

Grace's lips twisted and her eyes narrowed as she stared at Caveman. She didn't want to be around him that much. He stirred up physical responses she hadn't felt since her husband died. It confused her and made her feel off balance. But they were right. She couldn't keep looking over her shoulder. She needed help. "I still want to get out and check on the other wolves."

"We'll talk about it," Caveman said.

"We'll do it," she insisted. "And I won't be confined to my house."

"We'll talk about going out in the woods. And I promise not to confine you to your house." He waved his hand out to the side. "We're having dinner at the tavern today. See? I can be flexible."

Another moment passed and Grace finally conceded. "Okay, but only for the short term. I'm used to living by myself. Having another person in my house will only irritate me."

"Fair enough." Garner grinned. "I'll see what I can do to resolve the situation so that you don't need to have a bodyguard."

"Thank you." Grace's stomach rumbled loudly, her cheeks heated and she gave a weak smile. "As for eating, *clearly* you know that I'm ready."

Again, Caveman chuckled. "Let's feed the beast. We can talk about where to go from here, over a greasy burger and fries."

Her belly growled again at the mention of food. "Now you're talking."

Garner walked them to the door and held it open. "Be careful and stick close to Caveman. He'll protect you."

"What about the collar?" Grace asked.

"I'll get it to the state crime lab. If they can lift prints, they'll be able to run them through the nationwide AFIS database to see if they have a match. I'll let you know as soon as I hear anything."

"Thanks, Kevin." Grace held out her hand.

He took it, his lips lifting on one corner. "You're welcome. I'm glad you'll be with Caveman."

Caveman was first out the door of the upstairs loft apartment, his gaze scanning the area, searching for anything, or anyone, out of the ordinary or carrying a rifle with a scope. Apparently satisfied the coast was clear, he held out his hand to Grace. "Stay behind me."

"Why behind you?" she asked.

"The best probability of getting a good shot comes from the west." He pointed toward the building on the south. "The buildings provide cover from the north to the south. And I'm your shield from the west. The staircase blocks the shooter's ability to get off a clear shot."

His explanation made sense. "But I don't want you

to be a shield. That means if the killer takes a shot, he'll hit you first."

"That's the idea. If that happens, duck as soon as you hear the shot fired. If I'm hit and go down, he'll continue to fire rounds until he gets you."

"Seriously. You can't be that dense." She touched his shoulder, a blast of electricity shooting through her fingers, up her arms and into her chest. "I don't want you to take a bullet for me."

"Most likely the shooter won't be aiming for me. If I'm in the way, he'll wait for me to move out of the way so that he can get to you."

"That makes me feel *so* much better," she said, her voice strained. "We don't know that he'll come gunning for me, anyway."

"No, we don't. But are you willing to take the risk?"

Grace sighed. "No." What use was it to argue? The longer they were out in the open, the longer Caveman was exposed to Grace's shooter. "Hurry up then, before I pass out from hunger."

A chuckle drifted up to her. "Bossy much?"

"I get cranky when my blood sugar drops."

"I'll try to remember that and bring along snacks to keep that from happening." Caveman paused at the bottom of the stairs, hooked her arm with one of his hands and slipped the other around her shoulders.

Her pulse rocketed and she frowned up at him. "Is that necessary?"

"Absolutely. My arm around you makes it hard for anyone to distinguish one body from the other. Especially at a distance." His lips quirked on the edges. "I'll consider your reaction more of the low blood sugar crankiness."

Again, shut up by a valid argument, Grace suffered in silence. Although suffer was a harsh word when in fact she was far from suffering, unless she considered unfulfilled lust as something to struggle with.

Caveman opened the door to the tavern and waved her inside.

"Grace, it's been a while since you were in." A young woman with bright blond hair and blue eyes greeted them. "Would you like a table or to sit at the bar?"

"Hi, Melissa. We'd like a table," Grace responded.

"Hold on, just a minute. Let me see if there's one available." She disappeared into the crowded room.

"Is it always this busy?" Caveman stared around the room, his brows rising.

"As one of two restaurants in town, yes. The other one doesn't serve alcohol."

"I understand." He glanced around the room. "Do you know most of the people here?"

"Most," she said. "Not all. It's a small town, but we have people drift in who work on the pipeline or cowboys who come in town looking for work."

Caveman nodded. "It was like that in Montana, where I'm from. Everyone knew everyone else."

Melissa appeared in front of them. "I have a seat ready, if you'll follow me. Is this a date?" she asked, her gaze shooting to Grace.

"No," Grace replied quickly. She wasn't interested in Caveman as anything other than a bodyguard to keep her safe until they caught the killer.

"Oh? Business?" She turned her smile on Caveman.

"You could say that," Grace said.

"Yes, strictly business," Caveman agreed.

"That's nice." Melissa's eyelids dropped low. "In town for long?"

"I don't know," Caveman said.

Grace wasn't sure she liked the smile Melissa gave to Caveman, or that she was openly flirting with him when Grace was on the other side of the man. She wanted to call the girl out on her rude behavior, but was afraid she'd look like a jealous shrew. So she kept her mouth shut and seethed inwardly.

Not that she cared. Caveman could date any woman he wanted. Grace had no hold on him and would never have one. She'd sworn off men years ago, afraid to date one or form a bond. The men she'd been attracted to in the past had all died of one cause or another. The common denominator was their relationship with her.

Though she was a biologist and didn't believe in ghosts or fairy tales, she couldn't refute the evidence. Men who professed an affection for her died. What did that say about her? That she was a jinx.

The first had been her high school sweetheart, Billy Mays, who'd died in a head-on collision with a drunk man. The second had been when her husband, Jack, who'd died in a freak parasailing accident on their honeymoon in the US Virgin Islands. The third had been Patrick Jones, a man she'd only dated a few times. He'd died when he'd fallen off the big combine he'd been driving, and had been chopped into a hundred pieces before anyone could stop the combine.

Since then, she'd steered clear of relationships, hoping to spare any more deaths in the male population of Grizzly Pass, Wyoming. Which meant staying away from any entanglements with Caveman, the handsome Delta Force soldier who was only there on a temporary duty assignment. When he'd completed his assignment, he'd head back to his unit. Wherever that was. Even if she wasn't cursed, a connection with Caveman wasn't possible.

This meant she had no right to be jealous of Melissa's flirting with Caveman. The waitress was welcome to him.

Yeah, maybe not. The woman could have the decency to wait until Grace wasn't around.

In the meantime, Grace would have his full attention. She might as well find out more about the man, to better understand the person who would be providing her personal protection until a murderer was caught and incarcerated.

She hoped that was sooner rather than later. It was hard to take a seat across the table from the soldier who made her pulse thunder. It reminded her of everything she'd been missing since she'd given up on men.

Chapter Six

Caveman leaned across the table and captured Grace's hand in his. He'd been watching her glancing right and left as if searching for an escape route from the booth. "Hey. I really don't bite."

She gave him a poor attempt at a smile. "Sorry. I guess I've been alone so much lately that being in a crowded room makes me antsy."

"Concentrate on the menu." He picked up one and opened it. "What are you going to have?"

"A bacon cheeseburger," she said without even looking. "They make the best."

"Sounds good." He closed the menu without having looked. "I'll have the same."

A harried waitress arrived and plunked two cups of ice water on the table. "What can I get you to drink?"

"A draft beer for me."

"Me, too," Grace said. "And we're ready to order."

The waitress took their order and left, returning a few minutes later with two mugs filled with beer.

Caveman lifted his. "To finding a killer."

"Hear, hear." Grace touched her mug to his and drank a long swallow.

"I don't know too many women who like beer," Caveman said.

"And you say you're from Montana?" Grace snorted. "Lots of women drink beer around here."

He nodded. "It has been a while since I've been back in this area of the country. Hell, the world."

Grace set her mug on the table, leaned back and stared around the tavern. "Is it hard coming back?"

He nodded. "I feel like I have so much more to accomplish before I retire from the military."

"More battles to be fought and won?" Grace asked.

"Something like that." More like retribution for his brothers who'd lost their lives. He wanted to take out the enemy who'd lured them into an ambush and then slaughtered his teammates. Caveman shook his head and focused on Grace. "What about you? Are you from this area?"

She nodded. "Born and raised."

"Why don't you go live with your folks while the police search for the murderer?"

She laughed. "My work is here. My parents left Wyoming behind when my father retired from ranching. They live in a retirement community in Florida. They're even taking lessons on golfing."

"Are you an only child?"

A shadow crossed her face. "I am now."

"Sorry. I didn't mean to bring up bad memories."

"That's okay. It's been a long time. My little brother died of cancer when he was three. Leukemia."

"I'm so sorry."

"We all were. William was a ray of sunshine up to the very end. I believe he was stronger than all of us."

The waitress reappeared carrying two heaping plates.

She set them on the table in front of them, along with a caddy of condiments. "If you need a refill, just wave me down. Enjoy."

She was off again, leaving Caveman and Grace to their meals.

Caveman gave himself over to the enjoyment of the best burger he'd ever tasted. "You weren't kidding," he said as he polished off the last bite. "I've never had a burger taste that good. What's their secret?"

"They grill them out back on a real charcoal grill. Even in the dead of winter, they have the grill going." Grace finished her burger and wiped the mustard off her fingers.

Caveman waved for the waitress and ordered two more draft beers and sat back to digest. "Do you mind my asking what happened to your husband?"

A shadow crossed her face and she pushed her fries around on her plate. "I told you, he died in a parasailing accident."

"You couldn't have been barely out of college six years ago."

"That's where we met. We were both studying biology. He went to work with Game and Fish, I landed a job with Yellowstone National Park. A match made in heaven," she whispered, her gaze going to the far corner of the room.

"That must have been hard. Was it on a lake around here?"

Her lips stretched in a sad kind of smile. "No, it was on our honeymoon in the Virgin Islands," she said, her voice matter-of-fact and emotionless.

Her words hit him square in the gut. "Wow. What a

horrible ending to a new beginning." He covered her hand with his. "I'm sorry for your loss."

She stared at the top of his hand. "Like I said. It was a long time ago."

"You never remarried?"

She shook her head. "No."

"Didn't you say life goes on?"

"Yes, but that doesn't mean I had to go out and find another man to share my life. I'm content being alone."

Caveman wasn't dense. He could hear the finality of her statement. She wasn't looking for love from him or any other man. Which was a shame. She was beautiful in a natural, girl-next-door way. Not only was she pretty, she was intelligent and passionate about her work. A woman who was passionate about what she did had to be passionate in bed. At least that was Caveman's theory.

He found himself wondering just how passionate she could be beneath the sheets. His groin tightened and his pulse leaped at the thought. "You sound pretty adamant about staying alone. Don't you want to fall in love again?"

"No." She said that one word with emphasis. "Could we talk about something else?"

"Sure." He lifted his mug. "How about a toast to the next few days of togetherness."

"Okay. Let me." She raised her mug and tapped it against his, her gaze meeting his in an intense stare. "To keeping our relationship professional."

Caveman frowned. He didn't share her toast and didn't drink after she'd said the words. Though he knew he'd only be there until he got orders to return to his unit, he didn't discount the possibility of getting to know Grace better. And the more he was with her, the more he focused on the lushness of her lips and the gentle swell of her hips. This was a woman he could see himself in bed with, bringing out the same intensity of passion she displayed for her wolves.

Hell, he could see her as a challenge, one he'd meet head-on. Maybe she only *thought* she liked being alone. After a week with him, she might change her mind.

The thought of staying with her for the night evoked a myriad of images, none of which were professional or platonic. He had to remind himself that he was there to work, not to get too close to the woman he was tasked with protecting. She obviously had loved her husband. Six years after the man's death, she had yet to get over him.

He could swear he'd felt something when he touched her. An electric surge charging his blood, sending it pulsing through his body on a path south to pool low in his belly. Riding behind her on the ATV, his arms wrapped around her slim waist, he'd leaned in to sniff the fresh scent of her hair, the mountain-clean aroma reminding him of his home in Montana.

He'd take her to her house, make sure she got inside all right and then he'd sleep on the porch or on the couch. The woman was hands-off. He didn't need the complication a woman could become. Especially one with sandy-blond hair and eyes the gray of a stormy Montana sky.

They didn't talk much through the remainder of their dinner. Before long, they were on their way to her house, silence stretching between them. The thought of being with this desirable woman had Caveman tied in knots.

His fingers wrapped tightly around the steering wheel all the way to her house. When he pulled up in her drive, he wondered if he should just drop her off and leave. She had temptation written all over her, and he was a man who'd gone a long time without a woman. Grace was not the woman with whom to break that dry spell.

Chapter Seven

Caveman pulled up the driveway in front of Grace's house, shoved the gear into Park and climbed down from the truck.

Grace pushed her door open and was halfway out when he made it around the front of the truck to help her down. With his hand on her arm, he eased her to the ground. "How are you feeling?"

The color was high in her cheeks, but she answered, "Fine. Really. No dizziness or nausea. I don't see any reason for you to stay the night here. I'll lock the doors and sleep with my gun under my pillow."

He shook his head, the decision already made. "No use shooting your ear off. I'm staying."

She frowned, pulled the keys from her pocket and opened the door. "I can take—"

"I know. I know. You can take care of yourself." Hell, she'd given him the out he needed. Why was he arguing?

She unlocked the door and entered.

Caveman stopped her before she got too far ahead of him. "Do you mind if I have a look around before you get comfortable?" he asked.

"Are you going to do this every time we enter my house?" she asked.

He nodded. "Until the killer is caught."

"Be my guest." She stepped into the hallway and made room for him to pass.

He slipped by, pulled his gun from beneath his jacket and made a sweep of the house, checking all the rooms. By the time he'd returned from the back bedrooms, Grace had left the front hallway.

He followed sounds of cabinet doors opening and closing in the kitchen where he found Grace, nuking a couple of mugs in the microwave.

"I hope you like instant coffee or hot tea."

"Coffee. Instant is fine."

The microwave beeped and she pulled the mugs out, set them on the counter and plunked a tea bag in one of them. "I'd drink coffee, but I don't want to be up all night. How do you do it?"

"Do what?"

"Sleep after drinking coffee?" she asked.

"You learn to sleep through almost anything when you're tired enough. Including a shot of caffeine."

She scooped a couple of spoonfuls of instant coffee into the hot water, dropped the spoon into the mug and set it on the kitchen table. Then she fished in the cupboard pulling out a bag of store-bought cookies. Carrying the cookies and her tea, she took the seat across from Caveman.

"So what's your story?" Grace dropped a teabag into her mug of hot water and dipped it several times.

The aroma of coffee and Earl Grey tea filled Caveman's nostrils and it calmed him without him actually having taken a sip. He inhaled deeply, took that sip and thought about her question.

Sitting in the comfort of her kitchen, the warm glow

of the overhead light made the setting intimate somehow. Her gray-eyed gaze was soft and inviting, making
him want to tell her everything there was to know about
Max Decker. But he wouldn't be around long enough
to make it worth the effort. She was part of the job. He
was going back to his unit soon. No use wasting time
getting to know each other. "I don't have a story."

"We've already established that you're from Montana." She raised her tea to her lips and blew a stream
of air at the liquid's surface.

The motion drew his attention to the sexiest part of
her face—her lips. Or was it her eyes?

"It's not a secret." He lifted his mug and sipped on
the scalding hot coffee, more for something to do. He
really hadn't wanted the drink.

She tipped her head to the side. "What did you do
before the military?"

Grace wasn't going to let him get away with short
answers. He might as well get the interview over with.
"Worked odd jobs after high school. But I left for the
military as soon as I graduated college."

Her gaze dropped to the tea in her cup. "Married?"

Cavemen felt his lips tug upward at the corners.
"No."

"Ever?" Grace met his gaze.

"Never."

"Never have?" Her eyes narrowed. "Or never will?"

"Both."

Grace lifted her mug to her lips and took a tentative
sip of the piping hot liquid and winced. "How long have
you been away from your unit?" she continued with
the inquisition.

Caveman sighed. "Fourteen weeks, five days and thirteen hours."

"But who's counting?" Grace smiled, the gesture lighting her eyes and her face.

Wow. He hadn't realized just how pretty she was until that moment. Her understated beauty was that of an outdoorsy woman with confidence and intelligence.

"Some say you either love the military or hate it? Which side of the fence are you on?" she asked.

His chest swelled. "Yeah, there have been some really bad times, but being a part of the military has been like being a part of a really big family. It's a part of me."

"I'll take that as a 'Love it.'"

Turnabout was fair play. She didn't have the corner on the questions market. Caveman told himself, he wanted to learn more about her because the information might help him keep her safe. But that wouldn't be totally true. He really was interested in her answers. He leaned back in his seat. "What about you?"

GRACE STIFFENED. "NOPE. This interrogation is all about you. If I'm to trust you, I need to know more about you."

Caveman's lips quirked upward on the corners. "That's an unfair advantage."

"I never said I was fair. I am, however, nosy." She grinned and eased her mug onto the table to let the tea cool a little before she attempted another sip. "How are you with horses?"

He frowned. "Why?"

She pushed to her feet. "I need to feed and water my gelding. He's probably a little skittish after being shot at today." Grace started for the back door.

Caveman reached it before her. "You know, you

put yourself in danger every time you step out into the open."

"I know, but I put my livestock in danger by not feeding or watering them. I'm going out to take care of my horse. You can come or finish your coffee. Your choice."

"Coming." He opened the door and stepped out on the porch. After a cursory glance in both directions, he waved her out onto the porch and slipped his arm around her. "Just stay close to me. Don't give a shooter an easy target."

As much as she hated to admit it, she liked the feel of Caveman's arm around her. Though she knew a shooter could kill them both, if he really wanted to, she felt safer with the man's body next to hers.

Inside the barn, Bear whinnied and pawed the stall door.

"I'm coming," Grace said. She scooped a bucket of grain from the feed bin, opened the stall door and stepped inside.

Caveman grabbed a brush and entered with her.

Bear's nostrils flared. He pawed the ground and tossed his head, as if telling Grace he wasn't pleased with the other human entering his domain.

"Bear doesn't like strangers."

Caveman didn't get the hint. Instead he stood in the stall with the brush in his hand, not moving or getting any closer to the horse.

Grace opened her mouth to ask Caveman to leave, but he started speaking soft, nonsensical words in a deep, calming tone.

Bear tossed his head several times, not easily won over, but he didn't paw the ground or snort his dissent.

Soon the animal lowered his head and let Caveman reach out to scratch behind his ears.

"I'll be damned," Grace whispered.

Caveman covered Bear's ears. "Shh. Don't let that foulmouthed biologist scare you," he whispered.

The horse nuzzled the man's chest and leaned into the hand scratching his ear.

"So, not only are you a Delta Force soldier, you're a horse whisperer?" Grace snorted.

"I told you. I'm from Montana."

"And one of those odd jobs just happened to be on a ranch?"

He grinned. "Yes and no. I grew up on a ranch. I worked there during the summers for spending money."

"A cowboy. My mother warned me about getting involved with a cowboy."

"From what you said, your father was one."

"Exactly why she warned me." Though her mother was still crazy in love with her father, even after over thirty years of marriage.

"Why cowboys?" Caveman asked.

She met his gaze head-on. "They tend to like their horses better than their wives."

"Horses don't talk back as much, or make you fold laundry."

Grace chuckled. "I've had my share of sassy horses."

"Okay, so they don't make you clean the house."

"And I've cleaned my share of stalls." She crossed her arms over her chest and raised her eyebrows. "Care to try again?"

"I can sell a horse that's giving me a hard time, thus getting money for my trouble. Getting rid of a woman costs a heck of a lot more than ditching a horse."

"Okay, you got me on that one," Grace said. "But a horse won't be warming your bed and giving you children."

"Most of my married friends don't have sex more now that they're married. In fact, the kids suck the life out of their wives' sex drive."

"But your buddies have someone to come home to. People who care about them."

"Sometimes. Then there are the Dear John letters they get when in a hellhole fighting the enemy with their hands tied behind their backs by politicians. Meanwhile the wife back home has been having an affair with the banker next door."

Grace's brows rose. "Cynical much?"

Caveman shrugged. "I've seen some of the toughest soldiers commit suicide because they can't go home to salvage the relationship."

Caveman had worked himself up a rung on Grace's perception ladder with his horse trick. But she wasn't ready to fall for the big guy, yet. And despite her mother's warning not to fall for a cowboy, she had a soft spot in her heart for them, since her father had been one.

Hell, a man who had a way with animals, who'd been raised a cowboy, was a war hero and looked as good as Caveman could easily find his way beneath her defenses. If she wasn't careful, he might be the next victim of her curse.

Grace held out her hand. "I can take care of Bear."

He handed her the brush. "I'll haul the water."

"Not necessary. As soon as he's done eating, I'll let him out in the pasture. There's a trough in the paddock." She rounded the horse to the other side and went to work brushing his coat.

Caveman's presence raised the temperature of every blood cell in Grace's body. Fully aware of his every move, she knew when he left the stall. She let out a sigh and relaxed a little as she worked her way toward the horse's hindquarters.

The stall door squealed softly, announcing Caveman's return. He'd retrieved a currycomb and went to work on Bear's tangled mane and tail. Soon the horse was fully groomed, full of grain and ready to be turned loose in the pasture.

Yeah, the soldier had gone up another rung. Not every man would take the time to groom a horse. Not every man knew how to do it right.

She'd have to talk to Caveman's boss and ask him to send someone else. How would she approach the request? *Please send someone who isn't quite as drool-worthy. Maybe someone who is happily married, has a beer belly, belches in public and is not at all interesting.*

Grace hooked Bear's halter and led him through the barn and out to the gate.

Caveman moved ahead of her and had the gate open before she got there.

She let go of Bear's halter and the horse ran into the pasture, straight for the water trough.

Grace backed up, trying to get out of the way of the gate. Her foot caught on the uneven ground and she tipped backward.

Caveman caught her in his arms and hauled her up against his chest. "Are you all right?"

No, she wasn't. Cinched tightly to the man's chest, she could barely breathe, much less think. She tried to tell herself that the malfunctioning of her involuntary reflexes had nothing to do with how close Caveman was to her. Neither were his arms, which were hooked beneath her breasts, causing all kinds of problems with her pulse and blood pressure. "I'm fine. Seriously, you can let go of me."

For a long moment, he stared down at her, his arms unmoving. "Anyone ever tell you that your eyes sparkle in the moonlight?"

And there went any measure of resistance. "No." Whether her one-word answer was in response to his question or in response to her rising desire, she refused to pick it apart.

"They do," he said. "And your lips clearly were made to be kissed."

Her heart hammering against her ribs, Grace watched as Caveman lowered his head, his mouth coming so close to hers she could feel the warmth of his breath on her skin. She tipped her head upward, her eyelids, sweeping low, her pulse racing. Dear Lord, he was going to kiss her. And she was going to let him!

A BREATH AWAY from touching his mouth to hers, Caveman came to his senses. What was he thinking? This woman had nearly died that day. He was responsible for her safety, not for making a pass at her. As much as he wanted to kiss her, he shouldn't. It would compromise his ability to remain objective. Then why had he mentioned how her eyes sparkled and how her lips were meant to be kissed?

Because, man! He wanted to kiss her. With a deep sigh, he untangled his arms from around her.

Grace opened her eyes and blinked. Even in the moonlight, Caveman could see the color rise in her cheeks. She stepped out of his reach, careful not to trip again, straightened her blouse and nodded. "Thanks for catching me. In the future, I'll do my best not to fall."

As she headed back to the house, he followed closely behind her, using his body as a shield. Should the shooter decide to follow her to her home, he wouldn't have a clear target. He'd have to go through Caveman first.

Once inside the house, Grace gathered a blanket and pillow, handed them to him and pointed to the couch. "You can stay on the couch."

The couch beat his truck and the front porch, but it might still be too close.

Grace disappeared into the only bathroom in the house.

Caveman could hear the sound of the shower and his imagination went wild, picturing the beautiful biologist stripping out of her clothes, stepping into the shower and water running in rivulets down her naked body.

He left the blanket on the couch and slipped out onto the front porch. Yeah, sleeping on the hard, wood planks with a solid wood door locked between them would be the right thing to do. Knowing she'd be in the bed down the hall made his groin tight and guaranteed he wouldn't sleep any better than the night before when he'd caught a few hours cramped in the front seat of his truck.

Tomorrow, he'd speak with Kevin about assigning another one of the team members to watch over Grace. Apparently, he'd been too long without a woman. What else would make him so attracted to Grace when he'd only known her a few hours?

The door behind him opened and Grace stuck her head through the screen door. "The shower's all yours."

She wore a baggy T-shirt that hung halfway down

her thighs. If she had on shorts, the shirt covered them. And when she turned to the side, her shirt stretched over her chest.

Caveman sucked in a breath and his jeans got even tighter.

She wasn't wearing a bra beneath the shirt. The beaded tips of her nipples made tiny tents against the fabric.

What had she said? Oh, yes. The shower was all his. He really should have told her he didn't need one and that he would sleep outside. But no, that might require more explanation than he was prepared to give. And it might scare her to think the man who was supposed to protect her wanted to jump her bones. "I'll be there in a minute."

"Okay." She started to turn, paused and then faced him. "Thank you for rescuing me today."

"You're welcome." *Now, go straight to your bedroom and lock your door.* Caveman clenched his fists to keep from reaching out and dragging her into his arms. "Have a good night," he said, his voice huskier than usual.

Again, she started to turn, changed her mind and stepped through the door, closed the distance between them. When she stood in front of him, she raised up on her toes and brushed her lips across his cheek. Before Caveman could react, Grace turned and ran back into the house.

He groaned and adjusted the tightness of his jeans. Yeah, he wouldn't get much sleep. When he could move comfortably again, he walked out to his truck, grabbed his duffel bag from the backseat and returned to the house, locking the front door behind him. He made another pass through the house, checking all of the doors and windows with the exception of Grace's bedroom.

When he was certain the house was locked down, he entered the bathroom, shucked his clothes and turned on the cold water. After several minutes beneath the icy spray, he was back in control, his head on straight and his resolve strengthened.

Grace Saunders was off-limits. Period. End of subject.

He lay on the couch, his gun close by, and stared at the ceiling for the next few hours. Finally, in the wee hours of the morning he fell asleep and dreamed of making love to a beautiful, sandy-blond-haired biologist who loved wolves. Even in his dream, he knew he was treading the fine line of professionalism, but he couldn't resist. The crow of a rooster jolted him away as the gray light of predawn edged through the window.

He had breakfast on the table by the time Grace emerged from her bedroom.

"You're kind of handy to have around." She yawned and stretched. "Not only do you rescue damsels in distress, you can scramble eggs? You'll make someone a great wife."

"Don't get used to it. I cooked out of self-defense." He handed her one of the two places of fluffy yellow eggs. "I was starving."

She smiled and padded barefoot to the table. "What's the plan for today?"

"I thought we'd stop by the tavern and see if Kevin and his computer guy have come up with any potential murder suspects."

"You think they might have more than the sheriff and his deputies have come up with?"

"Hack, Kevin's computer guy, is a pretty talented techie. He's been following up on the Vanders family and their connections in the community. He might have found someone who was as trigger-happy as the Vanders."

Grace chewed on a bite of toast and swallowed. "What's wrong with people? In the past, all we had to complain about was the weather and taxes. Now people are shooting at each other. Last night all I could think about was Mr. Khalig's family. Did he leave a wife and children behind? People who loved him and looked forward to his return?"

Her face was sad, making Caveman want to wrap his arms around her and make everything okay. But he couldn't. No amount of hugging would bring back a dead man. Hugging was a bad idea, anyway. He'd promised himself that he'd steer clear of temptation.

Caveman looked down to keep from staring at Grace's sad eyes. He poked his fork at his eggs. "Not everyone is bad or crazy."

"You're right." She chuckled. "I was lucky enough one of the good guys was there when I needed someone." She ate the rest of her eggs and toast with a gusto most women didn't demonstrate.

Caveman finished his breakfast, as well. When he reached for her plate, she held up her hand. "I'll take care of the dishes since you cooked." She took his plate to the sink, and filled it with water and soapsuds.

Having grown up on a ranch where his mother worked outside as much as his father did, Caveman couldn't stand by and not help. He grabbed a dry dish towel and stepped up beside Grace. "You wash, I'll dry. We'll get it done in no time."

She smiled, and it seemed like the sun chose that moment to shine through the window.

Caveman forced himself to focus on the dish in his hand, not the sun in Grace's hair.

When they were done, and the dishes were stacked neatly in the cabinet, Grace disappeared into her bedroom and came out wearing boots and a jacket, her hair brushed neatly and pulled back into a ponytail.

Caveman liked her hair hanging down around her shoulders, the long straight strands like silver-gold silk swaying back and forth with each step. Lord help him, he was waxing poetic in his head. His buddies back in his unit would have a field day if they knew. "Come on. We need to stop by the sheriff's office and give him your official statement and see what else they can tell us about the shootings."

"I hope they were able to retrieve Mr. Khalig's body."

Caveman stepped out on the porch and searched the tree line and shadows for movement before he allowed Grace out of the house. "I spoke briefly with Kevin on the phone. They did. He's with the coroner in Jackson. They'll provide a report as soon as they can."

Grace locked the front door and followed Caveman to the truck.

Within ten minutes, they were inside the sheriff's office.

Grace gave her statement. The sheriff recorded the session and made notes. When she was done, he stared across the table at her. "I'd like to think you'll be okay. Since you didn't see who it was, you can't identify the shooter. For your sake, I hope he lays low and leaves you alone."

"I wish I *had* seen him. I'd rather know and be

hunted than not know. As it is, it could have been anyone." She pushed to her feet.

The sheriff did too and held out his hand.

She ignored the hand and hugged the older man.
"Thank you, for all you do. Give your wife my love."

Caveman felt a stab of envy for the hug the sheriff
was getting from the pretty biologist.

Sheriff Scott hugged her back and patted her back.
"You be careful out there. Can't have our favorite wolf
lady getting hurt."

Caveman gave his brief statement of how he'd found
Grace and thanked the sheriff.

"Where to?"

"Operations Center," Caveman said, a little more
brusquely than he intended. That jolt of envy for a
friendly hug Grace had given the sheriff had set Caveman off balance. He barely knew Grace. Perhaps the
hit he'd taken to his leg and all the morphine he'd had
during the operation and recovery had scrambled his
wits. He needed to get his head on straight. Soon. He
wasn't going to be around long enough to get to know
the woman, nor was he in the market for a long-term
relationship. He had a unit to get back to.

But the sway of Grace's hips, and the way she smiled
with her lips and her eyes, seemed to replay in his head
like a movie track stuck in replay mode.

By the time they had debriefed Kevin and Hack, the
computer guru, they'd missed lunch and the evening
crowd had begun to gather at the tavern below.

"Want to grab something to eat before we head back
to my house?" Grace's lips twisted into a wry grin. "I
don't cook often, and I'm certain it was a fluke you actually found something in the refrigerator for breakfast."

"Sure," Caveman said. "Then we can stop at the store for some groceries, if it's still open when we're done."

"I'm game."

For the second time in the past two days, Caveman and Grace entered the tavern and asked for a seat in the dining area.

"If you ever want to find out what's going on, you need to people-watch in the tavern or go to the grocery store. Mrs. Penders knows all of the gossip."

"Then we're definitely going to the store next."

"Hi, Grace, good to see you again. Who's this?"

Grace smiled at a pretty, young waitress with bleach-blond hair. "Lisa Lambert, this is Max Decker. You can call him Caveman. He's a…friend of mine."

Lisa grinned. "Caveman? Is that a statement on how you are with the ladies?" She winked. "Nice to meet you." She held out a hand.

Caveman shook it, and gave Lisa a smile. "Nice to meet you, Lisa."

"You know, if it's all the same to you," Grace said. "I'd like to get the food to go and eat it at home."

"We can do that," Lisa said. She took their order and hurried to the back. She returned a few minutes later with two glasses of water and a smile. "The cook said it will take him ten minutes."

"Great." After Lisa left, Caveman leaned toward Grace. "See anyone here that might be your killer?"

She glanced around the room. "I see a bunch of people I've known all my life. I find it hard to believe any of them could be a killer. I grew up with some of them, went to church on Sunday with others and say hello to others at community functions."

"Anyone who might have a beef with the pipeline inspector?"

Grace studied the people. "Some of the men worked on the pipeline. Maybe the ones who were laid off are angry because Mr. Khalig still had his job? I don't know. I work with wolves, not pipeline workers."

"What about the property owners the pipelines cross?" Caveman asked.

"Maybe. I'm not sure who they are, though. The pipelines cross the entire state. Mr. Khalig was on federal land when he was shot."

A few minutes later, Lisa returned with a bag filled with two covered plates.

Handing her several bills, Caveman told her to keep the tip. He had turned to leave when he heard a commotion behind him.

"I don't care what you say!" a slurred male voice yelled over the sound of other patrons talking.

Caveman spun toward the bar to see a man leaning with his back to the bar. "The BLM isn't a law unto themselves. You have no right to confiscate a man's herd or have him arrested for trespassing on the land his cattle have grazed on since his great-great-grandfather settled this area."

"If the man doesn't pay the grazing fees for his animals, and he doesn't remove them from federal property, he forfeits them to the government," another man said, his voice lower. "It's in the contract he signed."

A pause in general conversation allowed Caveman to hear the man's quiet response. "Who are the two arguing?"

"The man at the bar is Ernie Martin," Grace said. "He poured all his money into raising Angora goats, counting on the subsidies the government gave ranchers for raising them. The subsidies were cut from the federal budget, and now he's facing bankruptcy."

"And the other guy?" Caveman prompted.

"Daryl Bradley. He's a local Bureau of Land Management representative. They sent him in to feed information to the agency on how it's going out here. They had a man who wouldn't pay his grazing fees try to shoot the sheriff. It's been pretty volatile out here. *You* should know. I heard you had a hand in rescuing the school bus full of kids just the other day."

He nodded. "Vanders was the man who tried to shoot the sheriff. And it was his sons who kidnapped the kids. That could have turned out a whole lot worse than it did."

Grace nodded. "It was bad enough old Mr. Green died. He was a good man."

Caveman nodded. "Thankfully, all of the kids survived."

Grace shook her head. "I never would have thought members of our little community could be that desperate they could kill a kind old man and kidnap a bunch of innocent kids."

"It ain't right," Ernie shouted. "How's a man supposed to make a living when the government is out to squeeze every ounce of blood from his livelihood? The land doesn't cost the government anything to maintain. *We* fix the fences. *We* provide the water and feed for the cattle. And the BLM collects the money. For what? To fund some pork belly program nobody wants or needs."

"The BLM hasn't raised the fees in years," Daryl said. "We haven't even kept up with inflation. It was time."

"That's taxation without representation. Our forefathers dumped tea in a harbor to protest the government raising taxes without them having a say in it." Ernie slammed his mug on the bar, sloshing beer over the top. "It's time we take back our country, the land our grandfathers fought to protect, and boot the likes of you out."

Daryl stood, pushing back his chair so hard it tipped over and crashed to the floor. "Is that a threat?"

"Call it whatever you want," Ernie shouted. "It's time we took matters into our own hands and set things straight in the US."

A tall, slender man rose from his chair and ambled over to the fray. "Oh, pipe down, Ernie. You're just mad because they cut the government subsidies for Angora goats."

Grace leaned close to Caveman. "That's Ryan Parker. Owns the Circle C Ranch."

"Yeah, you're right, I'm mad." Ernie poked a finger toward Ryan. "I sold my cattle to invest in those damned goats. It's like they timed it perfectly to close me down. I've already had to sell half of my land. It won't be long before I sell the other half, just to pay my mortgage and taxes." He puffed out his chest. "The government has to understand the decisions they make affect real people."

"That's why we go to the voting booths and elect the representatives who will take our message to Washington." Ryan waved toward the door. "Go home, Ernie."

"And what good will voting do?" Ernie shouted. "You're not in much better shape. What has our government done for you? You had to sell most of your breeding stock to make ends meet. How are you going to recover from that? Not only that, you didn't have a choice on that pipeline cutting through your property.

What if it breaks? What if it leaks? Your remaining live-stock could be poisoned, the land ruined for grazing."

"Or we could all die in the next volcanic eruption. We can't predict the future." Ryan crossed his arms over his chest. "No one made you sell all of your livestock to invest the money in goats. Any ranch owner worth his salt knows not to put all his eggs in one basket."

"So now you're saying I'm not worth my salt?" Ernie marched across the floor and stood toe-to-toe with Ryan.

Caveman tensed and extended a hand to Grace. "Might be getting bad in here. Are you ready to go?"

Her gaze was riveted on the two men shouting at each other. "Think we should do anything to stop them?"

"My job is to protect *you*, not break up a barroom fight."

"I didn't go to war to fight for your right to collect subsidies from our government." Ryan glared down at Ernie. "You made a bad financial decision. Live with it."

"Why, you—" Ernie swung his fist.

Ryan Parker caught it in his palm and shoved it back at him. "Don't ever take a swing at me again. I won't let it go next time."

Ernie spat on Ryan's cowboy boots. "You're one of them."

"And if you mean I'm a patriot who loves my country and fought to keep it free for dumbasses like you, then yes. I'm one of them. What have you done for your country lately, Ernie?"

Ernie rubbed his fist. If his glare was a knife it would have skewered Ryan through the heart. "I might not have joined the military, but I'm willing to fight for my rights."

"And what rights are those? The right to raise goats at the taxpayer's expense?" Ryan shook his head. "Get a real life, Ernie. One that you've earned, not one that you've gambled on and lost."

Ernie's face turned a mottled shade of red. He reached into his pocket, his eyes narrowing into slits.

Grace started toward the man before Caveman realized what she was doing.

He leaped forward and grabbed her arm, pulling her back behind him.

"But Ernie's going to do something stupid," Grace said. "Ryan's one of the good guys."

"I'll handle it," Caveman said between clenched teeth. "Stay out of it," he ordered and strode toward the angry man.

"You'll see." Ernie eased his hand out of his pocket, something metal and shiny cupped in his palm. Based on the size and shape, it had to be a knife. "You and every other governmental tyrant will see. Just you wait, Parker." Ernie's brows drew together and he took a step toward Ryan. "You'll see. We'll have a free America again. And it won't be because you went to fight in a foreign country. We'll bring the fight back home where it belongs."

"What do you mean?" Ryan stood his ground.

Caveman also wanted to know what the belligerent Ernie meant by bringing the fight home, but he wasn't willing to wait for the angry drunk to explain.

Ernie started forward, cocked his arm, preparing to thrust his hand at Ryan.

Caveman popped Ernie's wrist with his fist in a short, fast impact that caused the man to drop the knife.

"Sorry. Didn't mean to bump into you," he said and kicked the knife beneath a table, out of Ernie's reach.

Clenching his empty hand into a fist, Ernie glared at Caveman and then turned his attention back to Ryan. "It won't be long. And you'll see."

Two other men stepped between Ernie and Ryan. "You've said enough," one of the men muttered.

"That's fine." Ernie snorted. "I'm done here." He turned toward the door and pushed his way through the crowd that had gathered around him and Ryan. "Move. Get out of my way."

As the tavern returned to its normal dull roar of voices, Caveman made his way back to where he'd left Grace. "What was Ernie talking about, *bringing the fight back home?*"

Grace's brow formed a V over her nose. "I'm not sure. We've heard rumblings about a militia group forming in the area. But that's the first I've heard anyone actually talk about bringing the fight here." She glanced around as if looking at the crowd with fresh eyes.

"Who were the guys who stopped Ernie?" Caveman looked for the men, but didn't see them. They'd disappeared into the crowd and Ryan had stepped up to the bar to pay his bill.

"That was Quincy Kemp and Wayne Batson. Quincy was the one who spoke to Ernie. He's not the nicest or most reputable individual in Grizzly Pass. But he does make good sausage. All of the hunters go to him to have their antlers mounted and the meat turned into steaks, sausage or jerky."

"He's a butcher *and* a taxidermist?" Caveman asked.

"Yes. He has a shop in town, but he lives off the

grid. His home is up in the hills. He uses wind and solar power and hunts for his food."

"Pretty good shot?"

"I'd say he'd have to be to feed himself and his family." Her lips pulled up on the corner. "As for Wayne Batson, he nearly went bankrupt when ranching got too expensive. He sank a lot of money into making his place a sportsman's paradise, building high fences around his ten-thousand-acre ranch and stocking it with exotic deer, elk, wolves and wildcats. He also has one of the most sophisticated outdoor rifle ranges in the state. Men come to train on his range and hunt on his land."

"Maybe we should ask the sheriff to check their alibis."

"Wayne and Quincy are highly skilled hunters." Grace smiled. "But, if we were looking for the best hunters in the area as our potential shooter, you'd have to question half the people in this county alone. You know how it is. Most men in these parts grew up with a guns in their hands. They're all avid hunters and are good with a rifle and scope. We even have a man from here who became the state champion rifle marksman."

"You're right. It was the same in Montana. I guess I've been in other parts of this country too long, where most people wouldn't know how to load a gun, much less shoot one."

"Most of them don't need one to survive." She gathered her purse. "We should go. I need to log my notes into the project database and notify my boss of the loss of Loki."

Normally, Caveman would have held the door for Grace, but he wanted to go out first and scan the parking lot for danger before he allowed her to leave the relative security of the tavern.

He stopped in the doorway and looked around.

Three men stood near a truck talking in hushed voices, their faces intense. One of them was Ernie Martin. The other men had their backs to Caveman, but based on the one's greasy brown hair and slouchy blue jeans, he appeared to be Quincy Kemp, the local meat processor and taxidermist. The other had the swaggering stance of the man Grace had called Wayne Batson.

"What's going on," Grace asked, her breath warming Caveman's shoulder, sending a thrill of awareness through him.

"Ernie, Wayne and Quincy are having a conversation."

"I'm not afraid of them," she said.

He looked around for any other threats. The sun had set and the gray of dusk provided enough light to make their way to their truck, but not enough to see into the shadows. "Stay close to me. When we get to the truck, get in and stay down. Don't provide any kind of silhouette."

"I'm still not quite convinced the shooter is actually after me anymore. He has to know by now that I couldn't identify him. Otherwise someone would have been knocking at his door."

"That doesn't mean he won't take pleasure in keeping you guessing. A man who'd hang a dead wolf's collar on your door might go to the trouble of continuing to scare you." Caveman handed her up into the passenger seat. "Even if you're not scared of him, I might be. For you, of course." He winked, his hand on the door. "Again, stay down until we're back at your house."

She rolled her eyes, but complied, doubling over in her seat, bringing her head below the dash, out of sight of any passerby, or shooter aiming at the truck.

Caveman climbed into the truck, started the engine and pulled out of the Blue Moose parking lot onto the road headed toward Grace's house.

Chapter Eight

"I feel silly bending over this long." Grace lay over, her face near the sack of food, the smells making her mouth water. "Are we there yet? My stomach is rumbling."

"Rather silly than sorry," he said.

"Easy for you to say. You're not the one scrunched over your seat." She straightened for a moment and worked the kink out of her neck. "Seriously, this is nuts. I went all day without anyone making a move. Nobody is going to shoot at me at night."

A sharp tink sounded and a hole appeared in the passenger seat window a few inches away from Grace's head. "What the hell?" She reached out her hand to touch the round hole. Splinters of glass flaked off at her touch.

"Get down!" Caveman yelled and swerved into the middle of the road.

Someone was shooting at them! Caveman jerked, his hand, twisting the steering wheel to the right. He cursed and held on, straightening the truck before he plowed into a ditch and flipped the vehicle.

Caveman steadied the vehicle, slammed his foot on the accelerator and sped forward. When he glanced at the matching holes in the window, his heart stopped for a second. Those were bullet holes. Had Grace been leaning a few inches forward in her seat, those bullets would have hit her in the head.

His gut clenched.

Grace lay doubled over, her head between her knees to keep from being seen by the enemy. "Should we go straight to the sheriff's office?" she asked from her bent position.

"Probably, but I'm not sure what that will accomplish since the sheriff will have gone home by now," Caveman said.

"Should we go to my house? We could call the sheriff from there." The shooter already knew where she lived and had been there the day before.

"Is there anywhere else we could go?" Caveman asked.

Grace shook her head. "We could drive up to the park at Yellowstone and see if they can fit us into one of the cabins."

"And if they can't?" Caveman glanced across the console at her.

"We could drive on into Jackson Hole. There's bound to be a hotel there."

"That's a lot of driving late at night."

"Then we go to my place," she decided. "I don't like leaving my horse for too long, anyway. If this guy shoots wolves, he doesn't have a sense of compassion in dealing with animals. He could decide to hurt my horse."

"Almost there," Caveman pulled into her driveway and shone the headlights at her small cottage. Nothing seemed amiss. Then he drove around the side of the house and shone the headlights at the small barn. The lights reflected off the horse's eyes, but everything appeared normal.

He parked at the rear of the house.

"I know," Grace said. "I'm to stay put while you check it out." She sighed. "I'm sorry about your window."

"Don't worry about it. I'm glad you weren't hit." He pushed open the door to his truck. The overhead light illuminated Grace's pale face and worried eyes.

He reached over and touched a hand to her cheek, wanting to take her into his arms, as if by doing so he could protect her from whoever was shooting at her. "If you had any doubts the shooter is after you, I hope you're convinced now."

"I am," she said, quietly. "Completely." She covered his hand with hers and leaned into his palm. "But why? I still don't have a clue who it is. It's not like I'm a threat to him."

"Doesn't matter at this point. What does matter is that we get you inside that house safely before the gunman has the chance to get here from his previous location."

"Caveman?"

"Yeah."

"Thanks for being here for me."

Caveman pressed his lips together. "Don't thank me until the gunman is caught." She was still in danger and he could be the best bodyguard around, but a skilled sniper could take someone out from up to four hundred yards away.

He wasn't sure what they'd do next. He didn't see any other option but to stay inside the house, avoid all the windows and pray whoever was shooting wouldn't get lucky and hit Grace. Though he'd only known her a very short time, he wouldn't want anything to happen to the dedicated biologist.

Chapter Nine

Grace felt strange running for the door of her house. This was Grizzly Pass, Wyoming, not some village in a war-torn nation. People didn't shoot at you for no reason.

Unless you witnessed a murder, and the killer was crazier than a rabid skunk, and fired on you when you were driving home from town.

Ducking low, Grace ran up the porch steps.

Caveman was right behind her, using his body as a shield to protect hers, again. Was he insane?

When her hand shook too much to insert the key in the lock, Caveman took the key from her and opened the door. With his palm on the small of her back, he hurried her through and closed the door behind them.

She rounded on him, realizing too late that she hadn't given him much room to get in the door and close it. She stood toe-to-toe with the man, feeling the heat radiating off his body. "Why do you keep doing that?"

He raised his hands to cup her elbows. "Doing what?"

"Using your body to shield mine? You don't have to take a bullet for me." She touched his arm. "You hardly know me."

He gave her a half smile. "Let's just say, what I know,

I like and admire." His lips twitched and his eyes twin-kled. "You're the first woman I've met who likes beer. What's not to love about you?"

Her heart warmed at his playful words. If she wasn't such a deadly jinx, she'd be tempted to flirt with the man. "Well, don't do it, again. I don't think I could live with myself if something happened to you because of me." She set her purse on the hall table and would have walked away, but Caveman took her hand and laced his fingers with hers.

"Sweetheart, I'm here to protect you. I'm not going to leave you exposed to a sniper's sights."

"I'm not your sweetheart, and you should wear a bulletproof vest if you're going to be around me." She stared up into his eyes, her own stinging. Her chest ached with an overwhelming fear for his life. "I don't want to be the cause of another death."

"You have to stop beating yourself up." He raised her hand to his lips, pressed a kiss to her knuckles and sent sparks shooting through her veins. "Khalig didn't die because of you."

"I know." She stared at where his lips had been. She wished he would claim her mouth instead of wasting kisses on her fingers. But, no, that wouldn't work. Grace shook her head. "I can't do this to you."

"Do what?"

"Nothing." She pulled her hand free and turned away.

Caveman caught her arm and pulled her around to face him. "Do what to me?" He cupped her cheek in his palm. "Drive me crazy? Too late. For some reason, I'm insanely attracted to you. But every time I think I'm about to kiss you, you pull away, or my head gets screwed on straight. Well, I'm tired of doing the right thing. I swear your eyes are saying yes, but the next thing I know, you're running. Is it something I said? Is it my cologne? I'll change it."

Grace rested her hand on his chest as tears welled in her eyes. "Don't say nice things. Don't try to kiss me."

"Why not?" He brushed his thumb across her lips. "You're beautiful. And I might be reading too much into your body language, but I think you want to kiss me, too."

Yes, she did. But now, she couldn't. "I can't do this to you."

He stepped closer, bringing his body nearer to hers, the warmth crushing her ability to resist. "Can't do what to me? Talk to me, Grace. You're not making sense."

"I can't curse you."

He leaned his head back, his brows forming a V in the center of his forehead. "Curse me? I don't understand."

"I'm cursed. If you kiss me, I'll jinx you. I don't want something terrible to happen to you." She curled her fingers into his shirt, knowing she should push him away, but she couldn't. Now that they were so close, her brain stopped thinking and her body took over. She wanted, more than anything, for him to kiss her.

"Let me get this straight. You think that by kissing me, you'll jinx me?" He stared down at her for a long moment. Finally, he said, "What in the Sam-dog-hell are you talking about?"

Her brows lifted and her lips twitched. "Sam-dog-hell?" She gave a shaky laugh.

"Don't change the subject." He brushed his thumb across her lips again, his glance shifting to his thumb's path. "I was just about to kiss you."

"I didn't change the subject. And you can't kiss me." She was saying one thing while she allowed him to tip her chin up, her lips coming to within a breath of his. "Kissing me is a really bad idea," she whispered.

"Damn it, Grace, if kissing you is a bad idea, then color me bad. I have to do it." He bent to claim her lips. "Curses be damned," he muttered into her mouth, sliding his tongue between her teeth, claiming her tongue with a warm, wet caress that curled Grace's toes.

She pressed her body against his, longing to be closer, their clothes just one more barrier to overcome so that she could be skin-to-skin with this big soldier who'd take a bullet for a relative stranger. What had she done to deserve him?

Nothing. So how could she stand there kissing him, knowing it would put him in mortal danger? Grace pushed against his chest, though the effort was only halfhearted and less than convincing.

His arms tightened and then loosened. "If you really want me to let go, just say the word." He stared down into her eyes. "Otherwise, I'm going to continue kissing you."

She fell into his gaze, her heart hammering against her ribs. Slowly, her hands slid up his chest to lock behind his head, pulling him down for that promised kiss. "If you die, I'll never forgive myself."

He chuckled. "I'll take my chances." Then he kissed her until her insides tingled and she forgot the need to breathe. When he raised his head, she lowered her hands to the buttons on his shirt, working them loose as fast as her fingers could push them through the holes. Her goal was to get to the skin beneath, before her brain kicked in and reminded her why she shouldn't be kissing him and whatever else might come next.

As she reached for the rivet on his blue jeans, he captured her hands in his. "Are you sure about this? You know I want it, but I don't want you to do something you'll regret later."

She caught her lower lip between her teeth and stared down at the button on his jeans, wishing he hadn't stopped her, praying her brain wouldn't kick in. "You're a soldier, right?" she said.

"Yes. So?"

"You've lived through some pretty serious battles, I assume?"

"Again, yes."

"You can take care of yourself, right?"

"I can."

"Then kiss me and tell me you'll be all right."

"Grace, no one is guaranteed to live to old age." He threaded his hands through her hair. "We have to live every day like it could be our last."

"Yeah, but I don't want your life to be cut short because of me."

"Let *me* make that choice. The only decision you need to make is whether you want to make love here, against the wall or take it to the bedroom?"

Her pulse raced, and her breathing grew ragged. "Here. Now." She ripped open the button on his jeans and dragged the zipper down.

Caveman grabbed the hem of her shirt, pulled it up over her head and dropped it on the hall table. Then he bent to kiss her neck, just below her ear. He nibbled at her earlobe and trailed his lips down the length of her neck. Continuing lower, he tongued the swell of her right breast, while pushing the strap over her shoulder and down her arm.

Past anything resembling patience, Grace reached

behind her and unclipped her bra. Her breasts freed, she shrugged out of the garment and it fell to the floor.

Caveman cupped both orbs in his hands and plumped them, thumbing the nipples until they hardened into tight little beads. He bent to take one into his mouth, sucking it deep, then flicking it with the tip of tongue.

Grace moaned and arched her back, wanting so much more. They still had too many clothes on. She shoved her hands into the back of his jeans, cupped his bottom and pulled him close. His shaft sprang free of his open fly and pushed into her belly.

"I want to feel your skin against mine," he said, his words warm on her wet breast.

"What's holding you back?" she managed to get out between ragged gasps.

"These." He flipped the button of her jeans through the hole and dragged the denim down her legs. Dropping to his haunches, he pulled off her cowboy boots and helped her step free. As he rose, he skimmed his knuckles along her inner thigh, all the way up to the triangle of silk covering her sex.

His gaze met hers as he hooked the elastic waistband of her panties and he dragged them over her hips and down her thighs.

Her body on fire, Grace couldn't take it anymore. She pushed his jeans down his legs and waited for him to toe off his boots, kicking them to the side. He shucked his pants, pulling his wallet from the back pocket before he slung them against the wall. Then they were both naked in the hallway of her home.

A cool waft of air almost brought her back to her senses.

Before it could, Caveman retrieved a condom from

his wallet, tossed the wallet on the hallway table and handed her the packet. "We might need that."

"I'm glad *someone* is thinking," she said. She sure wasn't. Grace tore open the foil, rolled the condom over his engorged shaft all the way to the base. Sweet heaven, he was hard, long and so big, her breath caught and held.

Caveman tipped her chin and brushed a light kiss over her lips, then scooped her up by the backs of her thighs and wrapped her legs around his waist. Pinning her wrists to the wall above her head, he pressed his shaft to her damp entrance. "Slow and easy, or hard and fast?"

Her eyes widened. No man had ever asked her how she liked it. Not even her husband. She assumed it was up to the guy to establish the pace.

She only took a moment to decide. With her body on fire, her channel slick and ready, there was only one choice. "Hard and fast."

He eased into her, let her adjust to his thickness and then pulled out. Dropping his grip on her wrists, Caveman held her hips, his fingers digging into the flesh. Soon, he was pumping in and out of her, moving faster and faster, their movements making thumping sounds against the wall.

Grace held on to his shoulders, her head tipped back, her breath lodged in her chest as wave after wave of sensations ebbed through her, consuming her in a massive firestorm of desire. When she thought it couldn't get any better, he hit the sweet spot and sent her catapulting over the edge. She held on, riding him to the end.

One last thrust and he drove deep inside, pressing her firmly against the wall, his staff throbbing inside her. He leaned his forehead against hers, his breaths short and fast, like a marathon runner's.

A minute passed, and then two.

Grace didn't care, she teetered on the brink of a euphoric high. He could do it all again, and she'd be perfectly happy.

Caveman tightened his hold around her and carried her into the master bedroom, where he laid her on the bed. In the process, he lost their connection.

Grace ached inside, the emptiness leaving her cold. But not for long.

He slipped onto the mattress behind her and pulled her back to his front. His still-hard shaft nudged her between her legs and pressed against her entrance, sliding easily inside. Slipping his arms around her, he held her close, driving the chill from the air and her body.

She could be content to lie with him forever. After making love against the wall and being completely pleased, she could imagine how much more satisfying making love in the comfort of a bed might be.

If he stayed with her through the night, she vowed to find out before morning.

Pushing all the niggling thoughts of her curse to the back of her mind, she snuggled closer, giving him time to recuperate before she tested his ability to perform more than once in a night.

A CURSE. CAVEMAN had wanted to laugh off Grace's mention of it, but she'd been very adamant to the point she'd held him at arm's length. Until she couldn't fight the attraction another minute. He felt a twinge of guilt for teasing her into abandoning her cause and making love to him.

"So why is it you think I will be cursed?" he said, nuzzling the back of her ear.

She stiffened in his arms.

Caveman could have kicked himself for bringing it up after the most amazing sex he'd had in a very long time. "Never mind. I'm not very superstitious, anyway."

For a long time, she lay silent in his arms.

He began to think she'd gone to sleep.

"My high school sweetheart died in a head-on collision the night after I lost my virginity to him," she said. "He was eighteen."

Caveman kissed the curve of her shoulder. "Could have happened to anyone."

"That's what I thought." She inhaled deeply and let it out. "My husband died on our honeymoon. The day after we got there. We went parasailing. The cable holding his chute to the boat broke. He had no way to control the parachute. It slammed him into a cliff and he crashed to the rocks below. He was only twenty-four."

"Just because two of the guys you cared about died doesn't mean you are cursed."

She snorted softly. "A couple years ago, I decided to get back into the dating scene. I met a nice man. We dated three times. After our third date, I didn't hear from him for a few days. I called his cell phone number. A woman answered. I asked where he was. She broke down and cried, saying he'd died in a farming accident."

"Grace, you can't blame yourself for their deaths. Sometimes your number is just up. Those cases were all unrelated and coincidental."

"No, they were related. I cared about all three of them. The common denominator was me." She eased away from him, turned and faced him, her head lying on the pillow, her hand falling to his chest. "I haven't had a date since. I keep on friendly but distant terms with the men in my life." Her gaze shifted from his eyes to where her hand lay on his chest. "Until you." She looked up again. "Now…dear Lord, I've cursed you."

He kissed her forehead and pulled her into his arms. "You aren't cursed and nothing's going to happen to me just because we made love tonight."

Grace rested her cheek against his chest, her head moving back and forth. "I shouldn't have risked it. You've been good to me, rescuing me when I was thrown from my horse. This is no way to repay you."

"I didn't ask for payment. I made love to you because I find you intelligent, sexy and brave."

"Not brave," she said, burying her face against his chest. "I ran when Mr. Khalig was killed."

"You had no choice."

"I did. I chose to run."

"You chose to live." He pressed a kiss to her forehead. "Sleep. Tomorrow is another day."

"Tomorrow's another day," she echoed. Her hand slid down his chest to touch him there. "But there's still tonight."

And just like that, he was ready. He jumped out of the bed, ran to where he'd left his wallet in the hallway and returned with protection for round two.

Later, while Grace slept, he slipped from the bed and used the phone in the hallway to call Kevin before midnight. He filled him in on the bullets fired at Grace in his truck. "We will make a full report to the sheriff in the morning. Did the coroner get a positive ID on the body?"

"Yes. It was RJ Khalig."

Caveman's chest tightened. "I should have gotten there sooner."

"How could you have?" Kevin asked. "You didn't know where 'there' was."

His head told him the same, but the man was his assignment and he'd let him down. "Anything on his cause of death?"

"He definitely had a gunshot wound to the chest. The coroner is still trying to determine whether or not it was enough to kill him, and whether he was alive or dead when he fell over the cliff."

Caveman walked into Grace's living room and nudged the curtain aside to look out at the street in front of her house. "My bet is that he was dead. Whoever shot him went back to finish the job." Moonlight shone down on the grass, the driveway and the street. Nothing moved. No vehicles passed.

"We'll know when the coroner's report is complete. In the meantime, how's Ms. Saunders?"

His pulse leaped and his groin tightened. Ms. Saunders was amazing. "Holding her own, but scared."

"She has every right to be." Kevin said something, but the sound was muffled. "I need to go. My wife is getting jealous of my job."

"Sorry to call so late."

"Don't be. I'm here for you. It's like I told you in the beginning, there's a lot more going on than meets the eye. I have a feeling this area is a powder keg waiting for someone to light the fuse."

As much as he would like to disagree with his new boss, he couldn't. In his gut, he knew the man was right.

"Stop by the loft in the morning," Kevin said.

"Maybe Hack will have something on the men who were arguing in the tavern earlier."

"Will do." Caveman ended the call.

A sound drew his attention from the scene through the front window to the woman standing in the doorway to the living room. She stood in the meager light from the moon edging its way around the curtains. Her sandy-blond hair tumbled around her shoulders, her lips were swollen from his kisses and she'd loosely wrapped the sheet from the bed around her naked body.

"For someone who wasn't sure she wanted to make love, you're sending all the wrong signals." He chuckled and stalked toward her, his eyes narrowing as he got closer.

"I woke up, and you were gone."

"Not far. I couldn't leave, knowing there was a beautiful woman keeping the sheets warm."

"The sheets are cold." She lifted her arms to wrap around his neck. As she did, the sheet drifted down past her hips and floated to pool at her ankles.

"Mmm. Perhaps I need to warm them again." He bent, scooped her up into his arms and carried her back to the bedroom. "I'm out of condoms," he said, as he laid her out on the bed and climbed in beside her.

"We'll make do." She touched his cheek. "I just hope that since you're not going to be around for longer than this assignment lasts, you will be immune to the curse."

He turned his face into her hand and kissed her palm. "You're not cursed. And what if I stick around longer?" Now that he was in Wyoming, and the trouble Kevin had mentioned was turning out to be very real and imminent, he didn't see a pressing need for him to return to his unit, just to be sidelined until his leg was 100 percent and he could pass a fitness test. He could stay in Grizzly Pass and get to know Grace a little better, make love to her again…and again.

"Seriously." She brushed her lips across his. "Promise me that you won't fall in love with me. Not that you are or anything. But just to be safe, please…promise me."

His heart twisted. Promise not to love her? Hell, he'd only just met her. How could he fall in love with her so quickly? He kissed her palm again. "Don't you think it's a little early to think about love?" He pressed his lips to the tip of her nose. "Lust, I can understand—"

She touched a finger to his lips. "Please. Just promise."

Caveman opened his mouth to comply, but the words lodged in his throat. "I—" The words she wanted to hear refused to leave his lips. He couldn't even think them. Not love Grace? His twisting heart seemed to open into a gaping void at the thought of leaving Grizzly Pass and never talking to her again. He looked around the room, searching for the right words, knowing there weren't any. His gaze paused at the window. Light shone around the edges of the curtain, a bright white light getting lighter by the moment. He shot a glance at the clock on the nightstand. Was it already morning?

The green numbers on the digital clock read 12:36.

His pulse leaped, he grabbed Grace and rolled to the far side of the bed and off, taking her with him. Just as they landed hard on the floor, a loud crashing sound filled the air, the bed slid toward them, and the mattress upended and slammed them against the wall. Drywall crumbled, sending the ceiling and loose insulation cascading down around them, filling the air with dust so thick Caveman wouldn't have been able to see his hand in front of his face. If he could get his hand free to raise to his face. He and Grace were trapped between the mattress and the wall, unable to move.

Chapter Ten

Grace struggled to turn her head to the side, pulled her face out of a pillow and gasped for air. Something heavy lay on top of her and the mattress held her tightly against the wall. "Caveman?"

He coughed, making his body wiggle against hers, explaining the weight lying across her. "Grace? Are you all right?"

"I think so," she said. "But it's hard to breathe."

An engine sounded really close and the smell of exhaust warred with the dust filling her lungs. "What happened?" she whispered, barely able to draw in enough air to activate her vocal cords.

"I think someone crashed into your house."

"Dear God. How?" She tried to draw in a deep breath, but with everything smashing her to the floor and wall, she couldn't. The darkness surrounding her was nothing compared to the dizzying fog of losing consciousness. If they didn't get out of there soon, she'd suffocate.

"I...can't...get up." Caveman twisted his shoulders, his hands pressing down on her, searching for something else to brace against and finding nothing.

"Just push against me," she said.

"I'm sorry." He braced a hand on her chest and shoved himself backward, sliding down her body, inch by inch. As he moved past her chest, she was able to get a little more air to her lungs. She dragged it in, uncaring that it was filled with dust. The oxygen cleared her brain.

"I'm out," Caveman said.

She heard the sound of boards being kicked to the side. Then she heard the engine revving and the metal clank of gears shifting; the pressure eased off the mattress and her.

She lay for a moment, letting air fill her lungs. Then she struggled to push the heavy mattress off her.

Suddenly the bed shifted and fell away from her.

Caveman leaned down, extending a hand.

Grace took it and let him draw her to her feet and into his arms.

He held her for a long time, smoothing his hand over her hair. Finally, he pushed her to arm's length and swept his gaze over the length of her. "Are you all right? No broken bones, concussion, abrasions?"

She shook her head and stared around at the disaster that was her bedroom. "Maybe a bruised tailbone, but nothing compared to what it could have been if you hadn't thought so quickly." The front wall was caved in, the ceiling joists lay on the floor, electrical wires sparked dangerously close.

"Where's your breaker box?" Caveman asked.

"In the kitchen."

He scooped her up into his arms and waded through the splintered two-by-fours and broken sheets of drywall until he reached the intact hallway. There, he set her on her feet, grabbed her hand and led the way to the kitchen.

Grace took him to the breaker box in the pantry.

He flipped the master switch, shutting off all electricity to the house. "Gas?"

"Propane tank out back."

Caveman hurried to the front hallway and returned a minute later wearing his jeans. He handed her the clothes she'd shed earlier, her boots and her purse. "Put these on and stand out on the porch while I shut off the gas to the house."

Grace dressed on the back porch, shivering in the cold.

Caveman returned and put his arm around her.

"What happened?" she asked, trembling uncontrollably.

"Someone drove my truck into the house."

"Oh, no. Did it ruin your truck?"

Caveman chuckled. "You were almost killed and you're worried about my truck? Sweetheart, you have to get your priorities straight."

"You were in the same place I was. Which means you were almost killed, as well." She leaned into him, slipping her arm around his waist. "If you hadn't noticed the lights headed our way…"

"Sorry about the rough landing, but at least we're alive."

"The driver?" she asked.

"Took off. I'm sure he's long gone by now." With his arm still around her, he led her down the back porch stairs and away from the damaged house. "We can't stay here tonight."

"We could go to my folks' place. I have a key." Grace

laughed, the sound more like a sob. "If you want to dig it out. It's somewhere in my jewelry box on my dresser…"

"Beneath all the rubble." Caveman shook his head. "Hopefully Kevin can help us out."

"I can't believe someone drove your truck into my house." She turned back. "I can't leave it like this. What if it rains?"

Caveman stared up at the clear night sky. "It's not supposed to rain for a couple days. We can come back in the morning and see what we can salvage." He steered her toward the front of the house where his truck stood, the front end smashed in, one of the tires flat. "We'll have to take your vehicle, unless you want to wait while I attempt to change that flat."

"We'll take my SUV." Grace fished in her purse, pulling out her keys. She handed them to Caveman. "I'd drive, but I'm not feeling very steady right now."

"Don't worry. I'll get us there."

Sitting in the passenger seat of her SUV didn't make her feel any better. Nothing about what had happened in the last thirty-six hours felt right.

Except making love to Caveman. And he wasn't much more than a stranger. A stranger who'd saved her life three times now. That had to make up for the fact that they'd known each other such a short amount of time.

"I think it's time to wake the sheriff." Caveman turned the key in the ignition.

It clicked once, but the engine didn't turn over.

Caveman's hand froze on the key, his brows descending. "Grace, get out."

"But we can't take your truck. It's damaged."

"Just get out. Now!" He reached across the seat,

pulled the handle on her door and shoved her through. "Run!"

The pure desperation in his tone shook Grace out of the stunned state she'd been in since her world had come crashing down around her. Her feet grew wings and she ran faster than she had since the high school track team. She didn't know where she was going, as long as it was away from the vehicle.

Twenty feet from her old but trusted SUV, the world exploded around her for the second time that night. She flew forward, landing hard on the ground, the air forced from her lungs, her ears ringing.

She lay for a moment, trying to remember how to breathe.

"Caveman," she said and pushed up to her knees. "Caveman!" she shouted, but couldn't hear an answering response due to the loud ringing in her ears. She ran back to the burning hulk that had been her SUV. He'd been so adamant about getting her out of the vehicle he hadn't had time to get himself out.

Grace reached for the door handle of the burning vehicle. She couldn't leave him in there, she had to get him out. The heat made her skin hurt. Right before her hand touched the metal handle, a voice shouted.

"Grace!"

The sound came to her through her throbbing ears and over the roar of the fire. She turned toward it.

Caveman rounded the edge of the blaze and ran toward her. He pulled her away from the flames and held her close.

Several minutes passed, neither one of them in a hurry to move away.

A siren sounded in the distance and then another.

Soon the yard was filled with emergency vehicles. The sheriff's deputy was first on the scene, followed by all of the vehicles belonging to the Grizzly Pass Volunteer Fire Department.

The Emergency Medical Technicians checked Grace and Caveman. Other than a few scrapes and bruises they'd live to see another day.

Soon the blaze was out.

Grace checked on her horse in the pasture on the other side of the barn. The fire had been in the front yard. The barn had sustained no damage, but her horse galloped around the paddock, frightened by the sirens and the smoke.

Caveman helped her catch the horse and soothe him. When she finally released him, he ran to the farthest point away from the smoke.

Grace made certain he had sufficient water before she returned to the front of the house. She and Caveman gave a detailed description of the bullets fired on their way home, and what had happened to her house and finally her vehicle. Caveman borrowed a cell phone from the deputy and placed a call to Kevin. The DHS agent offered to let them sleep in the loft above the tavern until they could come up with another arrangement.

The sheriff appeared shortly after they'd finished their account. He wore jeans and a denim jacket and looked like he'd just gotten out of bed.

Grace and Caveman recounted their story again for the sheriff's benefit.

"Grace, the man who killed Mr. Khalig is definitely after you. Do you know where you're going from here?"

"The Blue Moose Tavern."

The sheriff frowned. "They're closed."

"We'll be staying in the apartment above the tavern tonight," Caveman said.

"Come. You can ride with me," the sheriff said.

"Please." Grace didn't care who she rode with as long as there was a shower and a clean bed wherever they landed. Grace climbed into the back of the sheriff's vehicle. Caveman slid in next to her and pulled her into the crook of his arm. He was covered in dust and soot, but she didn't care. She was equally dirty, but alive. She nestled against him, but when she closed her eyes, images of the fire burned through her eyelids. Her pulse quickened and her heart thudded against her ribs.

"It's okay. We're going to be okay," Caveman said in that same tone he'd used on her horse. It worked on humans just as well.

Grace felt the tension ease. "I thought you were still in my SUV."

"I got out right after you." He smoothed his hand over her hair. "What's important is that we're both okay."

"I have my men watching the roads leading into and out of town," the sheriff said. "If someone is still out and about, they'll bring him in for questioning."

"Whoever did this will be long gone, if he's smart," Caveman said.

The sheriff glanced at them in his rearview mirror. "Whoever it was is getting more serious about these attacks."

"The question is why?" Grace said. "I couldn't see him from the distance when he killed Mr. Khalig. He should know by now."

"No search warrants have been issued," the sheriff said. "I haven't called anyone in for questioning. He's in the clear. As far as we know, it could have been anyone."

"What good does it do to kill me?" Grace shivered. "I'm nobody. Just a biologist."

Caveman tightened his arm around her. "Who happened to be in the wrong place at the wrong time and witnessed a murder."

"And escaped before the shooter could kill you, too." Sheriff Scott glanced back at her in the rearview mirror. "You're the one who got away."

Another tremor shook Grace's body. "I can't keep running."

"You can't get out in the open and give him something to shoot at." Caveman held her close. "I won't let you."

"I won't stand by and let him get away with destroying my home, my car and my life."

Caveman frowned. "What do you propose to do?"

She shook her head. "I don't know, but I'll think of something." Snuggling closer, she laid her cheek on his chest. "After a shower and some sleep."

THE LOFT ABOVE the Blue Moose Tavern was a fully furnished apartment with a single bedroom, bathroom and a living room with a foldout couch. The living area had been transformed into an operations center with a bay of computers and a large folding table covered with contour maps.

Kevin and Hack, his computer guru, waited in front of the tavern when the sheriff dropped off Caveman and Grace. The two DHS employees led the tired pair up the stairs. After a quick debriefing, Kevin offered Grace clothes his wife had sent and sweats and a T-shirt for Caveman. "We'll help you sift through the debris at your house tomorrow. For tonight, we hope this will do." Kevin's wife had also sent along a toiletries kit with a tube of toothpaste, shampoo, soap and toothbrushes still in their packages.

Grace gathered the kit, the clothes and a fresh towel. "This is one of those times when I'll gladly claim the 'ladies first' clause." She disappeared into the bathroom leaving the men to discuss the events of the day.

"I don't like it," Caveman said as soon as Grace was out of earshot.

"I don't blame you," Kevin agreed.

"There have been too many near misses today and we have yet to identify who's doing it."

"Do you think maybe there's more than one person involved?" Kevin asked.

"I don't know. But what I do know is that whoever it is knows something about weapons and explosives. He wired Grace's ignition with a damn detonator." Anger bubbled up inside him, spilling over. Caveman stalked away from Hack and Kevin, his fists clenched. He needed to fight back, but he didn't have a clue who he was fighting against. He spun and strode back to where Kevin stood. "If I hadn't gone with my gut when the vehicle didn't start, Grace wouldn't be in this apartment now. If I hadn't been there when she came barreling out of the mountains and was thrown by her horse, she'd be dead."

Kevin nodded. "We're still trying to trace the crates we found in the abandoned mine. Someone did a good job transporting them so that no one could identify their origin. We did a count, though, and based on the empty boxes, there were one hundred AR-15s in those crates. You don't hide one hundred AR-15s just any-

where. Someone has an armory around here and they're
stockpiling weapons and ammunition."

"And the infrared satellite images we had from a
week ago indicated fifteen individuals who helped un-
load those weapons. The Vanders family would account
for at least four of those heat signatures, which leaves
eleven."

"Hell, that's half the people in this county," Caveman said.

"I know this town is small, but there are a lot of out-
lying homes and ranches comprising the entire community of Grizzly Pass." Kevin scrubbed his hand down
his face. The shadows under his eyes made him appear
much older. "People are preparing for something. It's
our jobs to stop them before they hurt others."

Caveman paced the room again, thinking. "This Free
America group. Who are the members?"

"We don't know for certain," Hack said. "LeRoy
Vanders and his sons admit to being members. They're
talking about who else."

"What about the loudmouth last night in the tavern?
Ernie Martin," Caveman shot out.

Kevin nodded. "He's one we're watching."

"I've tapped into his home internet account and his
cell phone." Hack pulled out his chair and sat at the bank
of computers, bringing up a screen. "His computer is
clean, and I'm not finding any significant connections
on the cell numbers he calls. If he's communicating
with the group, he's doing it in person or on a burner
phone I can't trace." He tapped several keys, booting
the computer to life.

"You don't have to stay and work through the night,"

Caveman said. "I'm with Grace. All I want right now is a shower and some sleep."

"Do you want one of us to stand guard while you get some rest?" Kevin asked.

"No." Caveman wanted to be alone. With Grace. "The sheriff will have a deputy swing by every half hour until daylight. We should be all right."

Kevin straightened. "Then we'll leave you to get some rest. The sofa folds out into a queen-size bed. You can find sheets and blankets in the chest at the end of the bed. Help yourselves to anything in the refrigerator. I had it stocked with drinks and snacks."

"Thanks." Caveman could hear the shower going in the other room.

Hack powered the computer off and followed Kevin to the door.

"If you need me, give me a call. I can be here in five minutes." Kevin held out his hand. "Bet you weren't counting on so much activity in Wyoming. Were you?"

Caveman shook the man's hand. "No, I thought this would be a mini vacation and I'd be on my way back to my unit."

"And now?"

"I'm beginning to understand your concerns." And he couldn't leave, knowing Grace was in trouble.

"So you'll stay a little longer?"

"As long as you need me and my unit doesn't."

Kevin nodded. "Glad to hear it. We need good soldiers like you."

"I'll do what I can."

"I'm only five minutes away, as well," Hack said. He held up his cell phone. "Call, if you need me."

"Roger." Caveman closed the door behind the two

men and twisted the dead bolt lock. Not that a dead bolt would have stopped a truck from crashing through Grace's bedroom wall. He hurried to the back of the apartment, stripping off his dirty clothes and kicking off his boots. The shower was still going when he stepped through the bathroom door.

He pushed the curtain aside and slipped into the tub.

"I wondered how long it would take you to get rid of those two." Grace turned around, her body clean and glistening beneath the spray. "I was beginning to prune." She slid a handful of suds over his chest, making mud out of the dirt, soot and dust.

Caveman didn't care. She could smear mud all over his body if she wanted as long as her hands were doing the smearing. She poured shampoo into her palm and lathered his hair.

With his hands free to explore, he lathered up and smoothed his fingers over her shoulders and down to her breasts, where he tweaked the nipples into tight buds. Moving lower, he cupped her sex and parted her folds, strumming the nubbin of flesh between.

She moaned and widened her stance. "No protection," she said, her voice catching in her throat as he flicked her there again.

"This isn't about me."

Grace moaned again, her hand sliding over his shoulders, washing away all of the grime, dirty bubbles carrying it down the drain. "Not all about me." She wrapped her hands around his shaft and stroked the length of him.

It was his turn to groan.

Touching and testing the sweet spots, they felt their way to an orgasm that left Caveman satisfied and frustrated at the same time. First thing in the morning, he'd hit the local drug store for reinforcements. This woman's appetite rivaled his own, and he didn't want to be caught unprepared.

By the time they'd explored every inch of each other's body, the water had cooled to the point of discomfort.

Caveman turned off the shower, grabbed a towel and gently dried Grace. She returned the favor and sighed, her face sad.

"Why so sad?" he asked. "Didn't you like that?"

"Too much." She took his hand and led him to the bed. "I'm going to miss it when you're gone."

"Who said I'm going anywhere?"

"You know what I mean." She lay down on the bed and scooted over, making room for him. "You said it yourself. You're only going to be here for a short time."

"What if I decide to stay?" He might not have a job to go back to in the army. If the Medical Review Board didn't clear him, he'd be discharged, or given a desk job. He'd rather move back to Montana or Wyoming than take a desk job.

Grace's brows descended. "You can't stay. Look what nearly happened tonight. You were almost killed."

"But I wasn't. And neither were you."

She snuggled closer, her eyes drooping. "I'm too tired to argue about it. Just keep your promise, and don't do something stupid like fall in love with me." Her voice trailed off and her breathing grew steadier.

Caveman brushed a strand of hair away from her cheek and bent to kiss her. "I never made that promise. And it might be too late." Never in a million years, would Max "Caveman" Decker have guessed he would fall in love with a woman after knowing her for less than a week. But the thought of leaving and going back to his unit didn't hold the same appeal. In fact, even the mention of leaving made him feel like someone had a hand on his heart, squeezing the life out of him.

Maybe it was too soon for love, but only time would tell. Caveman wasn't so sure he'd have the time to find out, if Khalig's killer had his way with Grace. Tonight would have been the end of her had Caveman left when he'd originally wanted. Now, he couldn't leave. Not as long as Grace was in danger.

Chapter Eleven

Grace slept until after ten the following morning. When she woke, she stretched her arm across the bed, expecting to feel a naked body next to hers. When she didn't, she opened her eyes.

Caveman was gone.

For a moment, panic ripped through her. After all that had happened, she'd begun to rely on him to rescue her. Then she reminded herself he wouldn't have left without saying goodbye. Not after last night.

They'd shared more than a near-death experience, they'd connected on a level even more intimate.

Male voices sounded through the paneling of the bedroom door.

Grace bolted to a sitting position, dragging the sheet up over her bare breasts. She'd forgotten that the living area was being used as the command center for the DHS representatives. They'd probably been there for at least an hour, while she'd slept in.

Her cheeks heated. She wondered if Caveman had risen before they arrived to spare her the embarrassment of the team finding them in bed together.

She rose, grabbed the clothes Kevin's wife had provided and slipped into the bathroom. Five minutes later, she was dressed, had her hair pulled back into a neat ponytail and had brushed her teeth. She was ready to face the world. Or at least Kevin's team. She opened the door to the bedroom and stepped out.

The group of men standing around the array of computer monitors turned as one.

Heat rose into Grace's cheeks. Did they know she and Caveman had slept naked in the next room? Did she care? She squared her shoulders and forced a smile to her face.

In addition to Kevin, Caveman and Hack, three more men were in attendance. All there to witness Grace emerging from the back bedroom. Yeah, not what a woman wanted that early in the morning. "Good morning."

"Grace." Kevin stepped forward. "I trust you slept well?"

She nodded, her gaze going to the three men she didn't recognize.

Kevin turned to them. "Grace, have you met the other members of my task force?"

"No, I have not."

He turned to a big man with red hair and blue eyes. "This is Jon Caspar, US Navy SEAL. They call him Ghost."

Ghost shook her hand. "I've seen you around. Nice to meet you."

Kevin moved to the next man, who was not quite as tall as Ghost, but had black hair and ice-blue eyes. "Trace Walsh, aka Hawkeye, is an Army Ranger."

Grace shook hands with Hawkeye. "Pleasure to meet you."

He grinned. "The pleasure's all mine."

Caveman grunted behind her. If she wasn't mistaken, it was a grunt of anger, maybe jealousy? Her heart swelled.

The last man Kevin introduced had really short auburn hair and hazel eyes. Almost as tall as Ghost, he looked like he could chew nails and spit them out. "This is Rex Trainor."

"My friends call me T-Rex." The man stuck out a hand. "I'm with the US Marine Corps."

When T-Rex shook her hand, he nearly crushed the bones.

Introductions complete, Grace glanced at the computer monitors. "Am I missing something?"

Kevin shook his head. "Not at all. We were just going through some of the most likely suspects who live in the area."

"Like?" She stepped up beside Caveman and looked over Hack's shoulder at pictures of people on the different monitors. Some of them were mug shots, others were driver's license pictures or photos from yearbooks. She recognized most of them, having lived in the area for the majority of her life. Small-town life was like that.

"Quincy Kemp and Ernie Martin," Caveman said.

"Mathis Herrington, Wayne Batson," Kevin added.

"And, of course, Tim Cramer and the Vanders family, who have already been detained." Hack tapped the keys on the computer keyboard. "We've been trying to find the connection between all of them."

Grace yawned and stretched, her muscles sore from everything that had happened over the past couple of days. "Has anyone thought to ask Mrs. Penders at the grocery store?"

Four of the five men frowned.

Ghost grinned. "That's where my girl, Charlie McClain, goes when she wants to know what's going on. Mrs. Penders seems to have her finger on the pulse of everything going on in town."

"I'll go question her." Caveman turned toward the door. "Mrs. Penders is her name?"

Grace held up her hand. "You can't just barge in and interrogate the woman. She likes to gossip, not answer a barrage of very pointed questions. Since my house was destroyed last night, she'll be eager to hear all of the details straight from the horse's mouth. Give a little, get a lot." She glanced down at the clothes Kevin's wife had loaned her. "Kevin, tell your wife thank you for the loaner. I'll get them back as soon as I dig my wardrobe out from under the rubble."

"She said to keep them as long as you need them," Kevin said. "And we plan to help with the cleanup."

"Thanks, but I'd rather you found the killer." She drew in a deep breath and let it out. "I don't know how much longer I can play this game with him, before he scores." *With my death.* "Now, if you will excuse me, I'm going across the street to talk to Mrs. Penders and buy a few supplies I might need in the cleanup process."

"I'm going with you," Caveman said.

Grace shook her head. "You can't. Mrs. Penders will be more likely to talk if I'm alone."

"You can't waltz around town like anyone else." Caveman gripped her arms. "You have a killer after you. One who is a crack shot with a rifle and scope."

Placing a hand on his chest, Grace smiled up at him. "Then I'll zigzag, or whatever it is you trained combatants do to run through enemy territory."

The other men chuckled. Not Caveman.

His face hardened. "It's not a joke."

Her smile fading, Grace nodded. "I know. It's not every day you have someone drive a truck into your bedroom, or have someone shooting at you. I'll be careful and look for trouble before I cross the street."

"I'm walking you across the street."

Her first instinct was to argue, but one glance at Caveman's face and she knew she would lose that argument. And frankly, she liked having him around. "Okay." She walked to the door and followed Caveman down the steps to the street.

He looped his arm around her shoulders, pulling her close to his body. They probably appeared to be lovers who couldn't get enough of each other. After last night, the look fit Grace. She wondered if Caveman felt the same, or if he truly only thought of her as a temporary distraction until he returned to his unit.

At the corner of the grocery store, Grace stopped and placed a hand on Caveman's chest. "This is where I get off. I'll see you as soon as I get all of the information I can out of Mrs. Penders."

"I'll be right here. All you have to do is yell if you need me."

"Thank you." Then, before she could talk herself out of it, she leaned up on her toes and pressed her lips to his. It was meant to be a quick show of appreciation. However, she was more than gratified when Caveman took the kiss to the next level.

He cinched his arm around her waist, crushing her to his body, his lips claiming hers in a kiss that stole her breath away and made her knees turn to gelatin. Had Caveman not been holding her, she would have melted to the ground. When he set her away from him, she swayed.

She raised a hand to her lips. "Wow."

He chuckled, the warm, deep resonance of the sound heating her from the inside out. "I don't like you standing out in the open for long." He turned her toward the grocery store entrance, gave her bottom a pat and sent her on her way. "Hurry back. I have more where that came from."

She ran her tongue across her bottom lip, tasting him.

"On second thought, forget going inside. We can drive out to the local lake and make out in the backseat of my pickup."

She laughed. "You're not making this easy."

He held up his hands. "What am I supposed to make easy?"

"Letting go of you when you leave Grizzly Pass."

"Maybe that's my plan."

Her smile faded. "You have to, eventually."

"Let's not talk about that now. In fact, take your time inside. Don't come out until you see me walk by the windows. I want to look around town."

She snorted. "That won't take long."

"Exactly. So take all the time you need. Just don't come outside until I'm here to protect you."

She nodded. Grace wanted to run for the door, zip in, suck information out of Mrs. Pender's brain in record time and return for another of those soul-defining kisses.

She'd warned him not to fall in love with her, but maybe she'd been warning the wrong person. Grace needed to take her own advice. Perhaps the curse was on anyone *she* fell in love with, not who fell in love with her.

With no time to contemplate her thoughts, she stepped into the store and greeted the female store owner with a smile. "Good morning, Mrs. Penders."

"Grace, honey, I was shocked to hear someone bull-dozed your house last night. What can I do to help?"

OUTSIDE, LEANING ON a light post, Caveman studied the people who entered and exited the small store. The only one of its kind in town, it had the corner on the market. If people wanted more than what the Penderses offered, they had to drive thirty minutes to an hour to the nearest big town. Too far for a loaf of bread or a gallon of milk.

After a few minutes, he pushed away from the light post and walked to the end of the block—still within a reasonable distance to listen for a scream or see some-one entering the store who might appear to be there for nefarious reasons rather than to buy a can of soup or a loaf of bread.

From his vantage point at the street corner, he could see to the end of Main Street. A storefront on the op-posite side had a stuffed bear outside on the sidewalk. Not the teddy bear of the fake fur, cotton-filled vari-ety. No, this was an eleven-foot tall grizzly, profession-ally mounted by a skillful taxidermist. He stood on his hind legs, his front legs outstretched, the wicked claws appearing to be ready to swipe at passersby. And the mouth was open, every razor-sharp tooth on display. Yes, Quincy Kemp was very good at making the car-casses appear alive.

With a quick glance toward the grocery store to make certain Grace hadn't ended her information-gathering mission early, he turned toward the meat processing and taxidermist shop.

The door stood open; the scents of cedar, pepper and the musk of animal hides filled his senses, bringing back memories of a similar place in Caveman's hometown. In states where hunting was the major pastime of residents and tourists, every town seemed to have one of these kinds of stores.

A man emerged from a back room, wiping his hands on a towel. "What can I do for you?"

Caveman recognized him as Quincy Kemp. "I heard you made jerky."

"You heard right," Quincy said with one of the best poker faces Caveman had encountered.

"Do you happen to have buffalo or venison jerky?"

The man nodded and pulled a plastic butter tub from beneath the counter, opened it and selected a strip of jerky. "Try before you buy. I don't do refunds. This is buffalo."

Caveman popped the piece of jerky in his mouth and then chewed and chewed. The explosion of flavors made his mouth water.

Quincy crossed his arms over his chest, lifted his chin and looked down his nose at Caveman. "Well?"

"Good. I'd like to purchase a pound of the buffalo jerky."

While Quincy weighed several strips of the flavored, dried meat, Caveman wandered around the store. Besides a glass case of jerky and a refrigerated case of raw meat labeled Beef, Venison, Buffalo, Elk and Red Deer, there were numerous animals mounted on the wall.

"Did you do all of these?" Caveman waved at the

lifelike animals staring down at him from shelves and nooks along the wall.

Quincy slipped the strips of jerky into a plastic bag and sealed it before answering. "Yeah. That'll be fifteen bucks."

Caveman fished his wallet out of his pocket, which reminded him he needed to hit the store for a refill of condoms. He placed a twenty on the counter. "What kinds of animals have you done?"

"What you see."

Caveman had noticed the bear, bobcat, rattle snake, elk, moose and coyote. "What about mountain lion?"

"I've done a couple."

"Bobcat?"

He shrugged. "Four."

"Is there an open season on bobcat and mountain lion?"

The man's eyes narrowed. "Do you have a point?"

"Just wondering. I might like to buy a hunting license while I'm here."

Quincy slapped the change on the counter and pushed the plastic bag of jerky toward Caveman. "Hunting season isn't open until the fall. If that's all you want, I don't have time to talk. I have work to do."

Caveman lifted the bag of jerky and grinned. "Thanks."

Quincy didn't wait for Caveman to leave the store before he returned to the back room.

Caveman would like to have followed the man to the back to see what job he was all fired up about. The man looked like someone who could chew nails. Not that he scared Caveman, but he wouldn't take kindly to being followed.

But then, Caveman could claim he wanted to see Quincy's work in case he wanted the man to stuff his next trophy kill. Not that Caveman ever killed just for the trophy. He hunted back in Montana, but always ate what he bagged.

Easing behind the counter, Caveman worked his way to the door leading to the back of the building. Quincy had left it open, presumably to hear for customers entering the shop.

Through the door was a workroom filled with hides and tools of the taxidermist trade. A short corridor led to a workshop in the back. The meat packaging plant was probably at the end of the hallway.

Quincy was nowhere to be seen.

Caveman studied the hides, curious about what the taxidermist did.

"Hey!" Quincy emerged from a door in the back. "What are you doing back here?"

Startled by the man's abrupt appearance, Caveman snapped around, his legs bent in a ready stance, his fists clenched in a defensive reflex. "I had a question for you."

"Well, take it out to the front. Nobody comes back here, but me."

"Sorry." Caveman held up his hands in surrender. "I didn't touch anything."

"Doesn't matter. You don't belong back here." Quincy marched toward him.

Caveman backed through the door, pretending to be afraid, but ready to take on the man if he pushed him too far. "I wanted to know if you could stuff a wolf I hit on my way into town. I threw him in the back of my truck, hating to waste a good-looking hide. I think he'd look really great in my man cave back home in North Carolina."

"Man, you need to get rid of the carcass. It's illegal to keep a wolf, dead or alive, in the state of Wyoming."

"So you wouldn't stuff him? What if I sneak him in here at night? Could you?"

"Hell, no. I don't plan on spending the next five years in jail. Been there, done that. I'm never going back. I'd die before I let them take me back."

"Okay. I totally understand. No worries. I'll find someone else to do it."

"You won't."

"Won't what?"

"Find another taxidermist. No one will touch a wolf, unless the government commissions it."

"Well, there goes my idea for a centerpiece in my living room." Caveman raised a hand in a half wave. "I guess that's all I needed to know. I must say, I'm disappointed."

Quincy's mouth formed into a tightly pressed line and his eyes narrowed.

Caveman waved the bag of jerky again. "Thanks again for the jerky and all the information on taxidermist rules in Wyoming." He left the shop and strolled down the street toward the tavern, his gaze on the grocery store where he'd left Grace.

When he was far enough away from Quincy's shop, Caveman crossed the street and waited outside the grocery store, chewing on the buffalo jerky he'd purchased from Quincy, wondering what the man might be hiding in the back of his building. Perhaps he'd bring it up to Kevin and let the boss decide who he could send in to check. At this point, from what Caveman could tell of his role with Task Force Safe Haven, his primary purpose was to protect Grace from a killer. Kevin and the others could do the sleuthing to find out if what was happening in Grizzly Pass was a terrorist plot to take over the government.

"MARK RUTHERFORD SHOULD be available to help you fix the damage to your house. He's a good handyman and carpenter. And Lord knows he could use the work," Mrs. Penders said. "What with his daddy having to pay the additional grazing fees when he just forked out a wad of cash to install a new pump in his well. I'm sure Mark would appreciate the extra income."

"I'll check with him as soon as I assess the damage. I just can't understand why someone would deliberately crash into my house."

"Are you sure it wasn't an accident?"

"No, it was deliberate. He broke into the truck and drove it into my bedroom wall as if he knew I was in bed." Grace glanced around the store. "I'll need some trash bags and cleaning supplies."

"Sweetie, let me help you."

"Oh, I can't take you away from the register."

"There's no one in the store right now. I want to help." Mrs. Penders locked the register and led the way down the aisle of cleaning supplies, plucking off a couple bottles of disinfectant spray and cleaner. "I don't know what's going on in town, what with the Vanderses going crazy and kidnapping a busload of little ones. And now someone's murdered Mr. Khalig. He came into the store the other day for a bag of butterscotch candies." She smiled sadly. "Such a nice man. I imagine his wife will be devastated."

"Who would want to kill Mr. Khalig?"

Mrs. Penders rounded the end of the cleaning supplies aisle and started up the one with paper products and boxes of trash bags. She grabbed one of the boxes, read the front and put it back, selecting one with a larger number of bags. "Mr. Khalig worked as an inspector for the pipeline. If he doesn't approve what's going on, the pipeline shuts down. He could have reported some safety issues. Some people think he's the reason they got laid off."

"Did he ever say anything about any safety issues?" Grace asked, taking some of the cleaning supplies from Mrs. Penders. They walked back to front of the store and set the items on the counter.

"I could use some paper plates and disposable cutlery. I have a feeling my electricity will be off and on as they work on my house."

Mrs. Penders turned and led the way to the plastic forks and spoons. "Mr. Khalig wasn't allowed to discuss his work on account of confidentiality. But I could tell he wasn't happy with what he was finding. He started out warm and friendly. The longer he was here, the quieter and more secretive he became. And he kept looking over his shoulder, like someone was watching him." Mrs. Penders sighed. "And somebody had to have been, in order to shoot him from a distance. Poor, poor man. How awful."

"How do you know all of this?"

Mrs. Penders carried the boxes of spoons and forks to the counter and gave Grace a smile. "I just do. As for who, there are quite a few people I can think of. All of them worked for the pipeline and lost their jobs. The sheriff should start there. I mean look at what happened with Tim Cramer. He lost his job with the pipeline, his wife filed for divorce and now he's in jail. He was so desperate he helped with that kidnapping."

"He couldn't have been the one to kill Mr. Khalig. He was in jail when it happened."

"True. But there are others on the verge of bankruptcy, losing their homes and destroying their families." Mrs. Penders clucked her tongue. "Such a shame. I wish that pipeline had never crossed this state."

"Most of those who worked for the pipeline would have moved out of state to find jobs by now."

"Yes, but they wouldn't be as desperate." Mrs. Penders unlocked the register. "It's as if someone is sabotaging this area and the people in it."

"Who would do that, and why?" As Mrs. Penders rang up Grace's purchases, Grace put them into a bag. "We don't have anything here anyone would want."

"Maybe they want the pipeline to fail, but then maybe not, if they shot the inspector who could have shut down the whole thing." Mrs. Penders took Grace's money and handed her the change. "Then there are the folks who are tired of everything to do with the government. They would prefer to have the entire state of Wyoming secede from the United States. Bunch of crazies, if you ask me. Even scarier, they're a bunch of armed nut jobs."

"Do you know any of them?"

"Nobody comes out and says they're part of the group Free America. But I have my suspicions."

"Who?"

The older woman glanced around to make sure no one else was in the store. "I think Ernie Martin, Quincy Kemp, Don Sweeney and Mathis Herrington belong to that group. I'm sure there are a lot more who aren't as vocal. Some not from this county, but a county over."

"If they aren't telling you, how do you know?"

The older woman lifted her chin. "I have ears. Sometimes they run into each other in the store while I'm stocking shelves. I can hear them talking. In fact, I'm pretty sure they're having some meeting tomorrow night."

Butterflies erupted in Grace's belly. "Where?"

Mrs. Penders shrugged. "I don't know. Ernie and Quincy were in here buying lighter fluid and briquettes earlier today for a barbeque. They said something about getting together at the range."

"Range?" Grace's mind exploded with possibilities. "As in front range? Good Lord, that could be almost anywhere." Or maybe… "Or do they mean like a gun range?"

A mother carrying a baby in a car seat walked into the store.

The store owner smiled at the woman. "Good morning, Bayleigh, how's Lucas?"

The young mother smiled. "He's finally sleeping through the night."

"That's wonderful. Are you here for that formula you ordered?"

"I am," Bayleigh answered.

Mrs. Penders raised her finger. "One minute. I'll get it from the back."

"Please, take your time," Bayleigh said. "I have other shopping to do."

Grace gathered her bags. She couldn't take up any more of Mrs. Penders's time. "Thank you for everything, Mrs. P."

"Let me know if you need anything. Remember to check with Mark Rutherford. He's got time on his hands and probably can start right away on the repairs."

"I'll do that." Grace paused at the entrance, a frown pulling at her brows. A meeting at the range. When she spotted Caveman waiting outside, she pushed through the door and hurried toward the man who made her heart beat faster. "We need to talk to the team."

Chapter Twelve

Caveman paced the length of the operations center.

"How do you propose we get an invite to that meeting tomorrow evening?" Kevin asked. "We're not even sure what Mrs. Penders meant by 'the range.'"

"I'd bet my last dollar it's Wayne Batson's gun range," Ghost said.

Hack nodded. "He has the fences and security system in place to hold off an initial attack. And his computer system has a helluva firewall. I've yet to hack into it."

"Sounds like someone with something to hide," Caveman said.

"Why don't we just walk in?" Grace asked.

All five men turned toward her.

"Walk in?" Kevin asked. "What do you mean?"

"By now, everyone in town will know I've been the target of a shooter and someone who likes crashing trucks into my house. What if I ask Wayne to give me some time on his range, maybe even shooting lessons?"

"No way," Caveman said. "Putting you on a rifle range with a bunch of loaded weapons is a recipe for getting shot. What if the shooter is Wayne or one of his buddies?"

"So, I take my bodyguard and announce it to the

world I'm going to the range. The sheriff knows, everyone in town knows. If someone shoots me at the range, they'll have to shoot Caveman, too. They might get away with an accident killing one person, but they won't get away with killing two."

Anger tinged with a healthy dose of fear bubbled up inside Caveman. "So who shall we offer up as the one?" He shook his head. "It's too dangerous."

Grace turned toward Kevin. "At the very least, we go in, find the weaknesses of Batson's security system, leave and come back at night when we can slip in under the cover of darkness."

Caveman couldn't believe what she was saying. If one of Batson's friends was the shooter, he'd have no trouble lining up his sights and taking her down. "There is no 'we' in slipping back into Batson's property." He poked a finger at her. "*You're* not going anywhere."

"But I'm the one with the big target on my back."

Crossing his arms over his chest, he refused to back down. "Exactly. Now you're beginning to understand."

Her frown deepened and her cheeks reddened. "Don't patronize me, Max Decker. I'm the one who has to keep looking over her shoulder. I'm the one whose house is now a wreck. I have the biggest stake in finding the killer. I deserve to go."

"But you don't deserve to die." His face firmed and his eyes narrowed. "You're not going."

Her chin lifted. "Then I'll go without you. I need practice with my .40-caliber pistol, and I don't need your permission." She started for the door. "Gentlemen, I have a house to sift through and arrangements to make to get me onto Batson's rifle range." She sailed past Caveman and almost made it to the door when he grabbed her arm and yanked her back.

"We need to talk," he said. He couldn't let her walk out the door unprotected and waltz into the enemy's camp. If Batson was truly the enemy. "Let's at least talk this through before we go off half-cocked."

"I'm done talking." She glared at the hand on her arm. "Let go of me."

"Grace." Kevin stepped over to where they stood by the door. "We need to make a plan. We also need to understand who we're dealing with. What motivation does Wayne Batson have to host a Free America meeting on his range?"

"Maybe he's training recruits for the takeover of the government," Ghost offered. "The message Charlie picked up off that social media site was clear. They're planning a takeover of something."

"Why would Batson lead the charge?" Kevin asked. "He has to have a reason."

Grace pressed her fingers to the bridge of her nose. "I don't know. Wayne Batson seems to be the only person in the county who has pulled himself up out of hard times. When he was faced with bankruptcy, he found investors and turned his ranch into a sportsman's paradise. Why destroy a good thing by plotting against the government?"

"Having been in a bad situation, maybe he harbors animosity toward the government for some reason," Hawkeye said. "You never know what will push a man over the edge and make him think he has to take control of the world."

"Are you saying we might be barking up the wrong tree?" Grace asked. "That Batson might not be our guy?

His ranch with the rifle range might not be the meeting place?"

Kevin shook his head. "No. I think you're on to something."

"Then what's your plan?" She planted her fists on her hips. "If I take Caveman with me to practice my shooting skills, we can at least get inside and look around."

Caveman turned toward Kevin. "What do you have in the way of communications equipment? We had the radio headsets we used when we stormed the Lucky Lou Mine in the rescue attempt to save the kidnapped kids. Could we have something like that? And do you have any kind of webcam we can hide in a pen?"

Kevin grinned. "You must have me mistaken with the CIA."

Hack spun in his chair and opened his mouth to say something.

Before he could, Kevin held up his hand. "As a matter of fact, I invested some of the project funding in just what you're talking about. We have a webcam button we can attach to your shirt. Hack will get you two wired up."

Grace smiled. "Thank you."

Caveman wasn't happy about the situation, but he could either shut up and go, or send someone else with Grace. The woman was going whether or not he wanted her to. And because he found himself just a little bit protective of her, he didn't trust anyone else to take care of her as well as he would. Not that the others weren't fully capable. They just didn't have the connection he had with her.

Hack went to a footlocker in the corner, unlocked the combination lock and pulled out radio headsets and a small case with a little white button. "Doesn't look like much, but it sends a pretty clear picture to our computer." He handed it to Grace. "The idea is to replace a button on a shirt, so it will take a little bit of sewing skills." He handed her a small sewing kit like the ones found in hotel rooms.

"I can handle that." She glanced at Caveman. "Since your shirt has the buttons and you'll know better what to look for, you should have the camera on you. I can sew this onto your shirt."

"I'm pretty handy with a needle and thread, if you'd rather I did it," he offered.

"No use taking off your shirt. Let me call Batson and see if we can even get onto the range this afternoon."

Hack looked up the Lonesome Pine Ranch and passed her the contact number.

Grace pulled her cell phone from her purse, entered the number and waited.

Part of Caveman wished no one would answer or, if they did, they wouldn't allow her to book time on the gun range.

"This is Grace Saunders. I've had some troubles lately with someone following me."

Caveman snorted softly. Grace had conveniently left off the fact that someone was not only following her, but trying to kill her.

"Thank you. Yes, I'm okay," Grace said. "The sheriff suggested I call and see if I could get some time on the range to practice with my pistol. The sooner the better. I was hoping to get out there this afternoon. It will be two of us. Me and my…boyfriend." She paused, nodding at whatever the person on the other end of the call was telling her. "That would be great. Four o'clock works perfectly. Yes, we'll bring our own guns. I'll see you at four. Thank you." She clicked the end call button and looked across at Caveman. "We're on for four o'clock. I might have to dig my pistol out from under the rubble of my bedroom."

"I have one you could use," Kevin offered.

"If I can't find mine, I'll take you up on the offer," Grace said. "In the meantime, I'd like to get something going on the cleanup effort at my house. I don't want to wait until it rains and ruins even more of my belongings."

For the next few hours, Grace was on the phone with an insurance adjuster and a handyman.

Caveman took her out to her house to meet with the adjuster. Once the man left with a page full of notes, Caveman started sorting through broken boards and crumbled drywall to get to Grace's nightstand where she kept her pistol. He helped her locate the boxes of bullets she'd need at the range.

They cleared enough debris to allow her to get into her drawers and closets to pack several suitcases. Without a way to lock her home, she couldn't stay in the house until the wall was back up.

Grace called Mark Rutherford, the handyman Mrs. Penders had recommended. He showed up, surveyed the damage and gave her an estimate on how much it would cost to fix it. He'd only take a week to clear the debris and rebuild the wall. He'd need the better part of the next week to do the finishing work on the inside and outside.

Throughout the day, he watched Grace handle the disaster of her house with calm and patience, talking to the handyman and the adjuster with a smile and a handshake. The sheriff came out to survey the damage in the daylight and take pictures of the house and the truck. When she told him she'd be going out to Wayne Batson's range for target practice, he nodded.

"It's a good idea to be proficient and have confidence in the handling of your own weapon."

She didn't tell him why she'd chosen Batson's range or that there might be a meeting of the Free America group there the next night.

Caveman was tempted, but he figured she didn't want the sheriff to try to talk her out of it.

His gut clenched all day. He was torn between calling the whole thing off and going through with the plan. If they could get in and out without being shot and killed, they could bring back enough information for the task force team to enter the secure ranch compound. The team could find out what the rebel group was planning and maybe determine who might have killed Mr. Khalig.

After the sheriff left, Caveman brought a mug of hot cocoa out to the porch for Grace and insisted she sit for a few minutes. She chose the porch swing and sat far enough over for Caveman to join her. "How did you make hot cocoa?"

Caveman grinned. "I found a camp stove in a closet."

For a few minutes, they shared the silence, sipping cocoa and staring at the caved-in portion of her home.

"Why would a rebel group like Free America want to kill a pipeline inspector? They don't work for the government. They contract out to the big oil companies." Grace sighed. "I hope we're not wasting our time going out to the Lonesome Pine Ranch, chasing a wild goose."

"If you're concerned, why don't you stay in town

and let me go alone? The activities of the Free America group are a concern of Task Force Safe Haven. Kevin's responsibility as an agent with the Department of Homeland Security is to keep our homeland safe. If this group is planning to take a government facility that would be considered an act of terror. We have to investigate. This is the first real information we've received on when and where they will meet. We have to check it out. But you don't."

"If they have anything to do with Mr. Khalig's death and the subsequent threats to my life, I sure as hell have to go. I refuse to continue playing the victim. It's time I fought back."

Caveman took her empty cup and set it on the end table beside the swing and put his next to it. Then he took Grace's hands in his. "I want you to promise you won't do anything that will make Batson or his employees think we're spying on him. If he is part of this rebel group, he might want to keep it under wraps. In which case, he might go to all lengths to keep that secret."

"I promise I will do my best not to draw unnecessary attention. We'll get in there, and get out with the data your team needs to do what they have to do to protect our nation."

"Then we'd better get going. Your appointment is for four o'clock." He stood, pulled her to her feet and into his arms.

She rested her hands on his chest. "Are you going to kiss me?"

He chuckled. "I'm thinking about it."

Her hands slipped up around his neck. "Stop thinking, and start kissing."

"Do you still think your curse will be the death of me?"

"Not if we don't fall in love."

If her curse was real, he was doomed. In the short amount of time he'd been with Grace, she'd found her way into his mind, body and soul. He knew there would be no going back. Convincing her that she wouldn't kill him with a crazy curse would be the first challenge. Figuring out where they'd go from Grizzly Pass would be the second.

She laced her fingers at the back of his head and pulled his head down to hers. "Now, are you going to kiss me?"

"Damn right, I am." His lips crashed down on hers, his tongue pushing past her teeth to caress hers. This was what he'd wanted all day.

Grace didn't hold back. Her tongue twisted and thrust, her body pressing tightly to his.

When he had to breathe again, Caveman rested his cheek against her temple. "I worry about you," he whispered.

"You don't have to. I can make my own decisions and live with the consequences of my actions."

His chest tightened as if someone was squeezing him really hard. "If you're fortunate enough to live."

GRACE CLENCHED HER hands in her lap, as she stared at the road ahead, with every intention of staying alive. As far as she was concerned, she was going to get in some target practice with her handgun. Then she'd leave. If they just happened to find out more about a certain antigovernment organization, so be it. She'd keep those little gems of information to herself until she was off the Lonesome Pine Ranch and back where it was safe.

She had no problem letting the trained soldiers handle the major spying mission, although she would love to be a fly on the wall and listen in on the Free America meeting. After all, it was her country, too. She didn't appreciate terrorists trying to take over the land of the free and the home of the brave.

But she wasn't trained in combat tactics and would slow them down. She'd help them more by gathering information that would help them infiltrate after dark.

She'd sewn the webcam button onto Caveman's shirt and watched as he tucked the radio communication device in his ear. She put one in hers as well, but she wasn't as confident using it. She turned her head away from Caveman. "Can you hear me?"

"Loud and clear," he said.

"We can hear you, too," Hack said from his desk in the operations center.

Grace grinned. "I feel like I fell into a spy movie."

"Yeah, well, this isn't make-believe. Stick to the script and keep a low profile."

"Got it." Grace's heartbeat sped as Caveman pulled up to the gate of the Lonesome Pine Ranch and punched the button on the control panel.

"Grace Saunders and Max Decker here for range practice," he said into the speaker.

"Welcome. Please drive through." The giant wrought-iron gate swung open.

Caveman pulled through the gate.

Grace glanced over her shoulder as the big gate closed. Her breath caught in her throat. For a moment, she felt like an animal caught in a trap. Forcing a calm she didn't feel, she smiled over at Caveman. "Ready for some target practice?"

"You bet." He laid his hand over the console.

Grace placed hers in his for a brief squeeze before he returned his grip to the steering wheel.

Signs for the gun range directed them to turn before they reached the big house perched on top of a hill. The road ended in a small parking area. Wayne Batson waited for them, a holster buckled around his hips. In his cowboy boots, jeans and leather vest, he looked like a man straight out of the Old West.

A shiver rippled across Grace's skin. What if this man was the one who'd been shooting at her? Would he take the opportunity now to kill her? Maybe she'd been a little too naive to think a killer wouldn't shoot her in broad daylight even when the sheriff knew where she was going.

Instead of an old-fashioned revolver in the holster, Wayne had a sleek, dark-gray pistol, probably a 9-millimeter by the size and shape.

Grace pasted a smile on her face and climbed out of the truck. "Good afternoon, Mr. Batson. Thank you for letting me come out for some target practice on such short notice."

"My pleasure," he said. "I hear you're having a little trouble and want to make sure you can defend yourself."

She nodded. "I've had this gun since I graduated from college, but I don't get nearly enough practice with it."

"No use having one if you don't know how to use it properly," Batson said.

"I told her the same." Caveman stepped up to Batson and held out his hand. "Max Decker. You must be Wayne Batson, the owner of Lonesome Pine Ranch?"

Batson nodded and shook his hand. "It's been in the family for over a century. I hope to keep it in the family for another century." He glanced from Caveman to Grace. "Show me what you have in the way of firepower."

Grace pulled out the case with her .40-caliber H&K pistol. It was small, light and fit her hand perfectly.

Caveman brought out a 9-millimeter Glock.

Batson assigned them lanes on the range and handed them paper targets. Once the targets were stapled in place, they stood back at the firing position.

Batson joined Grace in her lane. "How often do you fire this weapon?"

"At least once a year."

"That's not nearly enough to feel comfortable holding and aiming." He demonstrated the proper technique for holding a pistol and then had her show him the same.

"How's it been here at the Lonesome Pine since you turned it into a big game hunting ranch?" Grace asked.

"Business is good," he answered, his tone clipped.

Grace lined up her sites with the target. "Lot of people from out of state?" She squeezed the trigger, remembering not to anticipate the sound and slight movement of the gun. The pungent scent of gunpowder reminded her of her father and the first time he'd taken her out to shoot. As his only daughter, he wanted her to be safe and know how to defend herself should she have to. Her heart squeezed hard in her chest. Her father would be horrified to know she'd been the target of a killer. He'd be on the first plane back to Wyoming from their retirement home in Florida.

Grace refused to call them and tell them she was in trouble. They'd fly back in an instant and place themselves in the line of fire. She'd be damned if she let some low-life killer touch her family. Now if only she could stay alive so they didn't come back to a funeral.

She studied Wayne Batson out of the corner of her eye.

He was tall, muscular and lean. The man would have been incredibly handsome, but for the slight sneer on his lip that pushed him past handsome to annoyingly arrogant.

She fired several rounds, adjusting her aim, working for a tighter grouping.

Batson holstered his gun and turned toward Caveman. "Do you have any questions?"

Caveman gave him a friendly smile. "I have one. Do you have many locals come out to fire on your range, or is it mainly the out-of-towners?"

Grace ejected her magazine and made slow work of loading bullets, wanting to hear every word of the conversation between Batson and Caveman.

"I get locals who need a place to practice with real targets at specific distances. They come to improve their skills for hunting season, just like my out-of-towners. The only difference is that the locals can come more often."

"How do you keep the game contained inside the perimeter?" Caveman asked, while reloading his magazine.

"You might have noticed on your drive in, we have high fences surrounding all ten thousand acres. It's one of the largest fully contained game ranches in the state. We offer guided hunts of all kinds."

"A client could select the preferred prey?"

Batson nodded. "My clients can be very specific."

"You've stocked the ranch with animals, and they can choose what they want to hunt?" Caveman asked.

"Yes."

Caveman smacked the magazine into the grip of his pistol and stared across at Batson. "The fences keep all of them in?"

"Only the best materials were used," Batson said. "We have high-tech monitoring to detect breeches so that we can get to the exact location and fix them quickly."

"That had to cost," Grace said.

"My clients pay."

"Then why bother with a range like this if your big game hunts are paying the bills?"

"I've learned diversification is important. When all we had were cattle and horses, we had some hard times. I almost lost the ranch to the government for back taxes. I promised myself I'd never get in that situation again. I will not let the government take my family home, like they're trying to take the Vanderses'."

"You sound pretty adamant," Grace said.

Batson's jaw tightened. "I am."

Grace fit her magazine in the grip of her handgun and slammed it home. She stared down the barrel at the target and squeezed the trigger. Five rounds fired made five little holes on the silhouette target where the heart would be on a man. All her father's lessons came back with a little practice.

"Nice," Caveman commented. He brought his weapon up, aiming it downrange. "One other question for you, Mr. Batson."

"Shoot."

Caveman fired five rounds, hitting the silhouette

target in the head, the holes the bullets made in such a tight grouping they appeared to be one big hole. He turned toward Batson with a friendly smile. "What do you prefer, handgun or rifle?"

Grace had been ejecting her magazine from her pistol. When she heard Caveman's unexpected question, she fumbled the magazine and it fell to the dirt.

Batson's eyes narrowed. For a moment, Grace didn't think the game ranch owner would answer the question.

"It depends on several things—how close I plan to get to the target, how accurate I want to be and how intelligent my quarry is." He touched a hand to his ear where he had a very small Bluetooth earpiece. "What is it, Laura?" He listened for a moment and then spoke. "Fine, let them in." His gaze returned to Grace. "Pardon me. It seems the sheriff wants to see me."

"The timing couldn't be better," Caveman said. "It's starting to get dark and we need to head back to town."

"Good." Batson nodded. "I don't usually leave guests on the range without supervision."

"Then we'll head out." Grace left the magazine out of her pistol, pulled back the bolt and inspected the chamber to make sure it was empty. Then she laid the weapon in its case. "Thank you for allowing us to come out on such short notice."

They shook hands with Batson and stowed the gun cases in the backseat of Caveman's truck.

The sheriff's vehicle was pulling up as they drove away. Grace slowed and started to lower her window.

"Just wave and keep driving," Caveman advised.

"Won't the sheriff think that strange?"

"I'm not concerned about what the sheriff thinks." Caveman waved her forward. "I want to use the time he keeps Batson occupied to leave slowly and capture as much information as I can about the security system used around the perimeter."

Grace slowed, nodded and pulled past the sheriff as she headed down the road toward the gate.

Caveman studied the fences and the gate, making comments aloud about the cameras located at the top of the gate pillar, aimed at the road.

Once they were through the gate, Grace crept along the highway, moving slowly enough Caveman could study the fencing. "I didn't notice it before, but stop for a minute."

Grace glanced in the rearview mirror. Nobody was behind her so she pulled to the side of the road and stopped. "Why are we stopping?"

"I want to test a theory." He opened his door, reached toward the ground and came up with a rock the size of a golf ball. Then he tossed it toward the fence wire. When the rock hit the fence, a shower of sparks shot out.

Grace gasped. "It's electric."

"Pretty expensive fencing for a game ranch."

"That'll keep the game in," Grace said.

Caveman's eyes narrowed to slits. "And uninvited guests out."

Wayne Batson had more than a game ranch on his huge spread: he had a locked-down compound capable of keeping out nosy people. As Grace drove back to town, a chill spread over her body. Her friendly community of Grizzly Pass had a darker side she never knew existed.

Chapter Thirteen

It was late by the time Caveman finished debriefing the team. He learned Kevin had sent the sheriff out to the Lonesome Pine Ranch to run interference for them so that they could leave unimpeded.

"While you two were on the inside, we had a drone flying over," Kevin said. "Between the information you two collected and the footage from the drone, we'll have our hands full tonight, determining the best way we can get in before the meeting tomorrow."

"Could we grab a bite to eat before we start?" Caveman asked.

"We can do better than that," Kevin said. He held out a key. "I got you two a suite at Mama Jo's Bed-and-Breakfast a couple blocks away. You can eat, catch some sleep and come back in the morning to see what we found."

"You don't need us?" Grace asked.

"With four of us looking at the monitors, it will be crowded enough. And you two have already done enough. Get some food and rest. Tomorrow will be another day. We'll brief you on the plan then."

Hack chuckled. "We hope to *have* one by then. I anticipate pulling an all-nighter."

Caveman would have liked to have stayed and looked over the drone images, but he was hungry, and he bet Grace was, too.

They called down to the tavern and ordered carryout. A few minutes later they left the team, collected their food and drove to the quaint Victorian house just off Main Street. They had all of the second floor, which consisted of two bedrooms, a shared bathroom and a sitting room, complete with a television and a small dining table.

"I'm going to hit the shower before I eat," Grace said. "I feel dusty from being out on the range this afternoon."

"Want company?" Caveman asked.

"What do you think?" She smiled, dragged her shirt up over her head and dropped it on the floor. Turning, she walked into the bathroom, half closed the door and then dangled her bra through the opening.

Caveman was already halfway out of his clothes, tripping over his boots as he kicked them off.

The next minute, he was in the shower with Grace, lathering her body, rinsing, kissing and repeating the process until they had the bathroom steaming. They made love under the warm spray and stayed until the water chilled. By the time they'd dried, the night had settled in on Grizzly Pass. Traffic slowed on Main Street and folks went home to their families.

Caveman and Grace ate their dinner and then moved to the king-size bed where they made love again. Nearing midnight, they lay in each other's arms, sated, but not sleepy.

"We should go back to the operations center and see if they've discovered anything new," Grace said.

Caveman sighed and brushed his lips across hers. "I know you're right. But I can't help it. I don't want our time together to end."

"Me, either." She sighed, too, and kissed him hard.

He would have stayed right where he was, with Grace's warm body pressed against his, but they weren't done for the night. Caveman rolled out of the bed and extended his hand. "Ready?"

She shook her head, laid her hand in his and let him pull her to her feet. "I'll only be a minute." Grace grabbed her clothes and hurried into the bathroom.

"I'll call and let Kevin know we're coming," Caveman said. He made the call to learn Kevin, Hack, Ghost, T-Rex and Hawkeye were still up and poring over the videos. They'd noted a few items of interest they wanted to show Caveman. "Good," he said. "We'll be there soon."

He dressed quickly, pulled on his boots and waited by the window. From their room, he had a good view of Main Street and the front of Quincy Kemp's meat packing shop. It was dark, like most of the businesses in town at that hour. He wondered what was in the back of Quincy's shop that the man hadn't wanted Caveman to see. Could he have the wolf carcass, preparing it to be stuffed? And, if he did, he would know who killed it. Or was he hiding the AR-15s in one of his freezers behind big slabs of meat?

Dressed in a black turtleneck shirt and black jeans, Grace stepped up beside him and looked through the window. "What are you looking at?"

"Quincy's place. I went there while you were with Mrs. Penders. He didn't want me in the back of his building. He was pretty adamant about it. Which makes me think he has something to hide."

"What are you thinking?" She pulled on her boots and straightened. "Want to go there first?"

"I can send another member of the team to investigate."

"Why? They have enough on their plates. Obviously, Kemp isn't in his shop now. Not with all of the lights out, and no one moving around. We could get in, do a little spying and leave with no one the wiser."

His lips quirked on the corners. "You realize you're talking about breaking and entering."

"We're not stealing anything," Grace argued.

"It's still illegal."

"You're right." She chewed on her bottom lip. "You can't afford to be caught. It might get you in trouble with the military."

He didn't like the calculating look in her eyes. "What are you thinking?"

"That I'm brilliant, and you don't have to commit a crime. You could keep watch outside while I go in and poke around. That way you aren't in on the crime. If I'm caught, I'll be the only one charged."

"Have you heard of aiding and abetting?" Caveman countered.

She shrugged. "You just have to deny everything. I'll tell them I snuck off, leaving you wondering where I'd gone. It will all be on me."

"I'm surprised you would even consider it." He reached for her hand. "I took you for a by-the-books kind of woman."

Her lips thinned into a tight line. "I was, until someone started shooting at me. Desperate times call for... you know."

"Desperate measures." Caveman didn't like Grace's plan at all, but his gut told him Quincy was hiding something in the back of his shop. "Look, you're not going anywhere without me."

She smiled up at him, her brows rising in challenge. "Then I guess you'll be breaking the law with me, because I'm going into Quincy's place to see what he was hiding from you."

He slipped his arm around her waist and kissed her. "You're a stubborn woman, Grace Saunders."

"I have to be in my line of business."

"I'll bet you do." He kissed her again and then turned to scan what he could see of the street and buildings around Quincy's shop. Other than the tavern, the town of Grizzly Pass had more or less rolled up its sidewalks.

Grace headed for the door. "If we're going to do this, we should get moving."

Caveman shrugged into his jacket and followed. "Stay close."

"I told you, I don't like you playing the role of my bullet shield." She pulled on a dark coat and swept her hair up into a ponytail.

"Humor me, will you?" He grabbed her hand and led her out of the bed-and-breakfast, hugging the shadows of the building to the corner where it connected to Main Street. The road was clear of people and vehicles as far as Caveman could tell, but he didn't know who might be watching from any of the buildings.

"Come on." He looped his arm over her shoulder and pulled her close. "We're just lovers on a late-night stroll."

"I like the sound of that," Grace whispered. "It would be even better if we weren't on someone's hot target list."

They crossed the street and walked past Quincy's place, turned down the next street and slipped into the back alley behind the meat packaging store.

Fortunately, the light over the back entrance was burned out, leaving the area completely in shadows.

Caveman slipped a knife from his pocket and pushed the blade in between the door and the jamb. With a few jiggles, he disengaged the lock, opened the door and hurried both of them inside.

Grace lifted her cell phone and shone the built-in flashlight around the room. The very back of the building was the meat packaging area with stainless-steel tables, sinks and refrigerators. The scents of blood, raw meat and disinfectants warred with each other.

Caveman checked the big walk-in freezers first. Finding nothing inside other than slabs of meat and big carcasses, he closed the doors. A quick survey of the rest of the room revealed nothing unusual or suspicious.

Quickly moving on, he led the way to a long corridor with a door on either side. This area separated the meat processing operations from the taxidermy workroom. He tried the handles. One was locked, the other wasn't. He pushed it open, only to find a variety of cleaning supplies: mops, aprons, bottles of disinfectant and various packaging supplies. The room was nothing more than a closet with shelves. Caveman checked the walls and floors for hidden doors.

"Anything?" Grace asked from the hall.

"Nothing." He left the supplies closet, locking it behind him.

Moving to the door across the way, Caveman used his knife to disengage the lock. Inside, he found an office with a desk, file cabinet and shelves. This room wasn't much bigger than the janitor's closet. Neither room was as wide as the shop front or the meat processing rear.

Caveman exited the office for a moment and walked into the taxidermy work area. It was as wide as the meat processing area, but square.

Grace gasped.

"What's wrong?"

She pointed to the hide of what appeared to be a black wolf. Tears welled in her eyes. "Loki." She shook her head, her fists bunching. "The bastard killed Loki."

Caveman pulled her against him and held her for a brief moment. "I'm sorry. But we have to keep moving."

"I know." She wiped a tear from her cheek and pushed away, turning her back to the wolf she'd raised from a pup.

Caveman's heart pinched at her sadness, but they had bigger, more immediate problems. "The office and supply room aren't as deep as the two work rooms. Where's the rest of the space?"

He hurried back into the office and checked the walls. In the back corner, on the far side of a large filing cabinet, was a wall with a pegboard attached. On the board, different tools hung neatly. Everywhere else in the office boxes were stacked on the floor, blocking access to the walls, except in front of the pegboard lined with tools.

Caveman pushed the pegboard and the entire wall moved just a little. He tapped on the wall, creating a hollow sound. Running his fingers along the outer edge of the pegboard he traced one end and then the other. Halfway down the right side, his finger encountered a hidden latch. He released it and the pegboard and wall swung toward him.

"I'll be damned," Grace muttered behind him.

He glanced back at the woman standing in the doorway of the office. "Could you keep an eye on the hallway while I go in to check it out?"

Grace nodded. "Okay, but don't be too long." She shot a nervous glance over her shoulder. "I have a bad feeling about this."

"I'll hurry." He ducked into the room, shining his cell phone flashlight at the far walls, looking for windows to the outside. When he didn't locate any, he flipped the light switch on the wall and studied the contents of the room, his stomach clenching into a vicious knot.

Racks filled with guns stood in short, neat rows. Shelves lined the walls loaded with boxes of ammunition.

"I think I found at least half of the AR-15s here in this room."

"Uh, Max…" Grace's voice sounded strained behind him, closer than if she'd been in the hallway. "We have a problem."

Caveman turned to face her.

She stood with her head tilted backward, a darkly clothed arm wrapped around her neck, her eyes wide and frightened.

In the split second it took Caveman to realize what had happened, he was already too late.

Two probes hit him in the chest and a charge of electricity ripped through his body. He clenched his teeth to keep from crying out. Then he fell, his muscles refusing to hold up his frame.

"Caveman!" Grace screamed.

Unable to control his fall, he hit his head against the corner of a low cabinet and blackness engulfed him in a shroud of darkness and pain.

GRACE FOUGHT AGAINST the hands holding her, desperate to get to Caveman.

The man with the Taser moved forward, his head and face concealed in a ski mask, his hands in leather gloves. He yanked Caveman's wrists together behind his back and slipped a zip tie around them, cinching it tightly. Then he rolled Caveman onto his side, pulled the probes out of his chest and nodded. "He's down."

A jagged cut on Caveman's temple oozed blood onto the floor.

Grace wanted to go to him, but the man holding her was so much stronger than she was, and his arm around her throat squeezed just hard enough to limit her air intake. Gray fog crept in on the corners of her vision. *No.* She couldn't pass out. She had to find a way to extricate herself and Caveman from this dangerous situation.

"What do we do with them?" one of the men asked.

"Boss wants them." Even with the mask, the man was easy to recognize just by his low, gravelly voice.

"Quincy," Grace said. "Don't do this. You won't get away with it."

"Shut up." Quincy backhanded her, his knuckles slamming into her cheekbone.

Grace's head whipped back with the blow and pain knifed through her. She fought the dizzying spinning in her head that threatened to take her down. "What are you going to do with us?"

"That's not for me to decide," he said.

"So you do the dirty work of capturing us, committing a crime to do it, and your boss sits back and lets you take the rap?"

He backhanded her again, this time hitting her in the mouth, splitting her lip. "You should have stayed out of this. Now, you'll pay the price for meddling."

Her jaw ached and the coppery taste of blood invaded her mouth. Anger roiled inside, pushing aside the wobbly feeling of an oncoming faint.

Caveman lay on the floor, his body still, and Grace could do nothing. The man holding her was a lot bigger and stronger. And there were two of them to one of her. Outnumbered and overpowered, she didn't have a choice. But she had to do something.

"You know you won't get away with this. There's probably a sheriff's deputy driving by as we speak."

Quincy's lip curled back in a snarl. "No one knows you're back here, and no one can see inside this part of the building. Even if the police came in, I'd be legally in the right. You two trespassed on private property. Last I checked, breaking and entering was illegal. I could shoot you and claim self-defense. Now, enough talk." He shoved a rag in her mouth, then threw a pillowcase over her head and down her arms. "Take her out to the van."

The big man holding her scooped her off her feet, slung her over his shoulder where she landed hard on her belly, the breath knocked out of her lungs. She couldn't see anything through the fabric of the pillowcase, but she could tell the man was carrying her back the way they'd entered the shop. When they stepped out of the building, cool night air wrapped around her legs. The sound of a metal door sliding sideways gave her renewed determination to break free. She kicked and struggled, bucking in the man's grip.

Finally, she was flung away from him, landing on what she was sure was the floorboard of a commercial van. She hit the surface hard, her head bouncing off the metal.

Then something was stuck up against her arm and a jolt of electricity sliced through her. Her body went limp and her struggles ceased. But she could still tell a little of what was going on. Someone tied her wrists behind her back with a zip tie. Another body was dumped onto the floor beside her.

It had to be Caveman.

With her wrists bound and a pillowcase wrapped loosely around her head, her body in a catatonic state, she could do little to free herself or her head so that she could see. She vowed that as soon as she regained control of her muscles, she'd work her way out of the case and zip tie.

Meanwhile, she was conscious. She listened, trying to gauge which direction they were headed and how far they were going. She could tell when they left the back alley and emerged on paved highway. She guessed they were headed south on Main Street. If only she could get up, throw open the door and scream. Alas, she could barely wiggle her toes by the time she was certain they'd driven out of the little town.

Would they take them out to a remote location, shoot them and leave their bodies to rot?

Grace's chest tightened. She couldn't let that happen. All of this was her fault. If she hadn't witnessed the killer shooting at Mr. Khalig, none of this would be happening to her and Caveman.

Caveman.

He was the innocent bystander in all of this. And because she'd allowed him to get past the walls she'd erected around her heart, he would die.

She squeezed her fist, anger fueling her. When her toes tingled, she wiggled them. Slowly, the feeling came back to her legs and arms. She was able to roll onto her side, but she couldn't lift her arms to pull off the pillowcase. Instead, she scooted along the floor, trying to maneuver her way out of the fabric covering her head.

They had been traveling ten minutes when she finally made it out of the pillowcase.

Lifting her head, she looked around the interior of an empty utility van with metal sides and floors. The two men who'd captured them sat in the front seat, staring out the window as they slowed for a stop.

Grace tried to see what they were seeing. It appeared to be a gate of some sort.

The van lurched forward and the tires crunched on what sounded like gravel.

With little light to see by, Grace searched the interior of the van for something sharp to break the zip tie holding her wrists tightly together behind her. No sharp edges stuck out, no tools lay on the metal floor.

And Caveman lay as still as death.

She inched her way over to him and laid her face close to his. For a long moment she held her breath, praying he was still alive. Then she felt the warmth of his breath against her cheek. Her heart swelled with joy. He was still alive.

Somehow, she had to get them both out of the van and away from their captors.

The gravel road ended, but the van continued to move forward on a much bumpier, hard-packed road.

Several times, Grace tried to sit up, only to be flung across the van floor. She was better off lying on her side, praying they'd stop before she was bounced to death.

Caveman groaned softly and his legs moved. "Grace?" he whispered.

"I'm here," she replied softly, so as not to draw attention from the men in the front seats.

"Where are we?"

"We're in the back of a van and have been on the road for over twenty minutes as far as I can guess. Other than that, I'm not sure where we are. Based on the road conditions, I'd bet we're way out in the boondocks."

"Have they said what they're going to do with us?"

"No." She glanced at the back of the driver's head. "Quincy said something about it wasn't up to them. The boss would decide."

"So he's not in charge."

The van came to a jerky stop.

Grace waited for them to start up again, but they didn't. The engine switched off and the two men climbed out. A moment later, the side door slid open and moonlight shone into the interior.

Grace blinked up at the men.

Quincy had taken off his ski mask, but the other man hadn't. They grabbed Grace by her upper arms and dragged her out of the van and onto her feet.

"Hurt her, and I'll kill you," Caveman said, his voice little more than a feral growl.

Quincy snorted. "That would be really hard to do when you're all tied up, now wouldn't it?"

They grabbed Caveman by the arms and slid him out of the van, dumping him on the ground at their feet.

He rolled to his side, bunched his legs and pushed to his feet. "What now?"

"Now, the fun begins," another voice said from behind Quincy and his accomplice. A big man wearing a combat helmet, camouflage clothing and carrying a military-grade rifle stepped between their two captors. His face was blackened with paint and he sported a pair of what appeared to be night-vision goggles pushed up onto his helmet.

"What do you mean, 'now the fun begins'?"

"I told you. I provide all kinds of prey for my clients—elk, lion, moose, bear and…human."

Grace gasped, a heavy, sick feeling filling her belly. "You can't be serious."

"Oh, I'm serious, all right."

Grace squinted, trying to see past the paint. "Wayne?"

The man sneered. "Surprised?"

"Actually, I am." She shook her head. "Why would you risk losing everything you have by killing people? You won't get away with it for long?"

"I've been getting away with it for the past five years. I'll continue to get away with it as long as no one finds the bodies. *Your* bodies."

"You're insane."

"No, I'm tired of the government stealing what's mine. I'm tired of working my butt off for the pittance you make off cattle, only for the government to steal every cent I make by charging an insane amount of taxes."

"You've been selling human hunts for the past five years?" Grace shook her head. "How did no one know this?"

"The people who work for me know not to say anything. And the people we hunt don't live long enough to tell."

"Was Mr. Khalig one of your *hunts*?" Grace's stomach churned so hard she fought to keep from losing her dinner.

Wayne snorted. "Hell no. He was a paid gig. And an easy target."

"Paid gig?" What was wrong with the man? He acted like killing a man was no worse than being paid to perform on stage.

"*Highly* paid gig." Wayne shifted his rifle to his other hand. "But that's not why we're here tonight."

"Why are we here?" Caveman asked, his gaze direct, the shadows cast by the bright moon making him appear dangerous.

"You two are going to be a little training opportunity for my men. A little night ops search-and-destroy. You get a chance to run. They get to practice and test their night hunting skills with live animals."

"That's like shooting lions in a zoo. Where's the sport in that?"

"Oh, there will be sport. We're going to let you loose, give you a little bit of a head start, and then we're coming after you."

"Unarmed?" Caveman goaded. "How is that a training exercise?"

"I can't turn over a loaded weapon to a trained soldier. How would we explain so many people with gun-shot wounds?" Wayne nodded to Quincy. "Release them."

Quincy frowned. "Now?"

"Now." Wayne fixed his stare on Caveman. "If you make a move toward me or my men, I'll put a bullet in Ms. Saunders." He nodded. "Take her and leave. You'll only have five minutes to get as far as you can, before we come after you." He glanced down at his watch.

"Three minutes on foot won't get us far," Caveman pointed out.

"You're lucky I'm giving you that." He looked again at his watch. "Four minutes thirty-five seconds."

"Aren't you going to cut the zip ties?" Grace's pulse hammered so loudly in her ears she could barely hear herself think.

"Not my problem." Wayne Batson raised his brows. "Four minutes fifteen seconds."

"Grace, come on." Caveman pushed her with his elbow and herded her away from Batson.

She hurried with Caveman toward the tree line. Her last glimpse of the three hunters was the image of Quincy and the other man dressed in the combat helmet, multi-pocketed vests and camouflage clothing. They were in the process of loading ammunition magazines into their vests.

And she thought getting away from the men would be hard enough. *Staying* away from Wayne Batson and his thugs, while their hands were tied behind their backs, would be a lot more of a challenge than she could imagine.

Chapter Fourteen

They jogged into the tree line. Caveman's leg hurt like hell, but he refused to slow them down. "We have to get as far away from them as possible and find a rock hill or cliff to put between us and them. Are you able to run for long?"

"I can hold my own," Grace said. "I'm used to hiking in the hills. When I'm not working, I train to run half marathons."

Caveman snorted. "I'll have a hard time keeping up with you. Why don't you lead the way?"

"Do you think we're on Batson's ranch?" she asked, jogging alongside Caveman while they were on a fairly wide path between trees.

"That's my bet. Not only do those fences keep people out, they keep his pets in."

"Any chance we can get out of these zip ties?" she asked.

"As soon as we reach that outcropping of rocks. We have to put something solid and impenetrable between us and them for cover as well as concealment against their night-vision goggles." He glanced across at her face in the moonlight. "Can you run faster?"

"I'm game," she said, though her breathing had become more labored.

Caveman increased his speed, glancing back often enough to make certain Grace kept up. He was aiming for the base of the mountain he'd glimpsed through gaps in the trees. It appeared to be right in front of them, but looks could be deceiving, especially at night.

The full moon helped them find their way, but it also made it all too easy for Batson and his gang to see them. The sooner they made it into the hills, the better.

He figured the five-minute head start had long since expired and still they hadn't reached the relative safety of the mountain.

A crash behind him brought Caveman to a halt.

Grace lay on the ground, struggling to get to her feet. "Don't wait on me. I'll catch up," she insisted.

"Like hell you will." He squatted next to her. "Grab a sturdy tree branch or a jagged rock."

She did, rolled over to hand it to him and then worked herself to a sitting position. "What are you going to do with it?"

"I'm going to try and use it as a saw." He nodded. "But we have to keep moving. Lean on me to get up."

She leaned her shoulder against him and pushed herself to stand.

"Ready?" he said.

"Go." Grace followed him, keeping closer this time.

While he ran, Caveman rubbed the small tree branch against the plastic of the zip tie. It wasn't much, but he hoped with enough friction, it would eventually cut through.

They emerged in a small opening in the forest, finding themselves at the base of a bluff.

Caveman glanced each direction, then turned north toward a large outcropping of boulders. If they could get behind them, they could stop long enough to break the zip ties. But they couldn't stay long. They had to go deep into the mountains and stay alive long enough for Kevin and the team to figure out they were in trouble.

A sinking feeling settled low in his belly. Though he'd given Kevin a heads-up that they'd be over to review drone footage, he hadn't given him a definitive time. All they could hope for was that Kevin would get worried when they didn't show up within thirty minutes of the call. Still, the team wouldn't know where they'd gone, or where to start looking.

Their best bet was to avoid the hunters long enough to make it back to one of the perimeter fences. Then they'd have to figure out how to get through it and fast enough they could make it to a road and catch a ride to town. Timing would be crucial since Batson had the fence wired to tell him exactly where the breech occurred.

Caveman kept his thoughts to himself. Grace had enough to worry about just staying a step ahead of Batson and his gang.

In order for them to reach the giant boulders for cover, they would have to cross a wide-open expanse, flooded by bright moonlight.

"I don't know how close they are. When we start out across the open area, run as fast as you can and zigzag to make it harder for someone to sight in on you." He gripped Grace's arms. "Are you okay?"

She nodded, breathing hard. "I'll be fine. Let's go." With a deep breath, she took off running across the rocky terrain, dodging back and forth, leaping over brush and smaller boulders.

Caveman was right behind her, hoping the hunters hadn't yet caught up to them.

A shot rang out, kicking up the dirt near Caveman's feet. He ran faster, changing directions erratically, hoping the gunmen couldn't get a bead on him and take him out.

Grace had just made it to the boulder when another shot rang out. She stumbled and fell against the huge rock, righted herself and slipped out of sight.

Caveman dodged once more to the right, then sprinted the remaining ten steps and dove behind the boulder.

Grace was on her knees, breathing hard, but rubbing the zip tie against a jagged stone jutting out of the hillside.

"We don't have time to break these. We have to keep moving," Caveman warned.

The zip tie snapped. "I'm ready." She grabbed a sharp rock and pointed to a flat one. "Put your hands here." She quickly positioned him, then put all of her weight behind the sharp rock and cut through his zip tie.

Caveman took her hand and ran for a ravine thirty feet from where they were standing. Together, they climbed the side of the hill, working their way over the rocks upward to a ridge. If they could drop over the other side, they'd have a chance of staying out of range of the rifles. He wasn't sure how much longer Grace would last. His sore leg ached and he worried it slowed him down too much. They didn't have weapons and they couldn't fight back. He had to keep them moving.

Grace slipped beside him and slid several feet down

the hillside and stopped abruptly when her foot hit a tree root. "Damn." She doubled over, clutching at her leg. She pushed to her feet, but fell back as soon as she put weight on her foot.

Caveman slid down next to her, his gaze scanning the bottom of the ravine. "What's wrong?"

"I think I've sprained my ankle." She looked up at him. "Don't stop. You have to keep going. Get help."

He pressed his lips together. "Grace, I'm not leaving without you." He bent, draped her arm over his shoulder and lifted her. "Come on. We're not stopping here."

Together, they limped up the side of the steep hill, slipping and sliding on the loose gravel. When they reached the top of the ridge, Caveman studied the other side. There was a steep drop-off close to where they stood and a trail leading down the other side. If they were careful, they might make it down to the bottom before the others caught up to them. From there, he could see the fence in the distance. And, if he wasn't mistaken, the cutaway between a stand of trees had to be the highway. "See that?"

"The fence," Grace said through gritted teeth. "Think we can make it?"

"I don't think it, I know it." With his arm around her waist, he hurried down the trail toward the bottom of the hill, knowing this trail was the path of least resistance and it would make it far too easy for the hunters to spot them from a distance and catch up to them all too quickly. They only had to get close enough to sight in on them.

A good sniper would be able to pick them off at two-hundred meters. A great sniper would be able to take them out at four-hundred. If they could get down to the trees before the hunters topped the ridge, they might have a little more of a chance to make it to the fence. At that point, they'd have to figure out how to keep from getting electrocuted.

HOPPING ON ONE foot all the way down the side of a hill wasn't getting them where they needed to be fast enough. And every time she bumped her right foot, pain shot through her, bringing her close to tears. She refused to cry. Not when they needed every bit of their wits about them to escape the insanity that was Wayne Batson. "Leave me," she begged. "I don't want you to die because of me."

"Not up for discussion," he said, grunting as he took the brunt of her weight and hurried her along. "Save your breath and mine."

She knew any further argument would be ignored and took his advice to save him further aggravation. They rounded several hip-high boulders as they neared the bottom of the hill. A shot rang out and pinged off one of the boulders.

A sharp stinging sensation bit Grace's shoulder. "Ow!"

"Get down!" Caveman pulled her down behind the boulder. He looked ahead to the next big rock. "Can you crawl to the next one?"

"Probably faster than I could walk it by myself."

"Then go, while I distract them."

"What do you mean 'distract them'?" she asked, hesitant to leave him, even for a moment.

He shed his jacket and hung it on a stick. "Ready? Go!" He ran the stick up over the top of the rock.

Grace crawled as fast as she could over rocks, gravel

and brush, bruising her knees, but not caring. When she made it to the next rock, she rolled behind it and called out, "Made it!" She sneaked a peek around the edge in time to see Caveman make his dash to join her.

He hunkered low and ran, diving behind the rock as two more shots echoed off the canyon walls. "Are you all right?" he asked, his attention on the hill above them.

"A little worse for the wear, but alive." She pressed a hand to the stinging spot on her shoulder and winced. When she brought her hand back in front of her, she grimaced. It was covered in dark warm liquid she suspected was her blood. She hid her hand from Caveman. If she was badly wounded, she wouldn't have been able to move her arm. Now wasn't the time to faint at the sight of blood.

"Right now, they have the advantage with their night-vision goggles. They can see us, but we can't see them."

She snorted. "They have all the advantages. They have the guns. We're unarmed."

He glanced behind them. "We could try for the tree line, but it's a long way."

"And I move too slowly." She shook her head. "Leave me here. Go for help. It's the only way."

"I'm not leaving you."

"Then what do you suggest?"

He glanced around the moonlit area. "The fence is two football fields away. Even if we could make it there, we don't have a way to cut through."

"Then that's out," she said.

"We've run out of places to hide. This is the last large boulder between us and them."

"True."

"We only have one choice." He drew in a deep breath and let it out. "We wait until they come to us."

Grace nodded, knowing the odds were stacked against them, but unwilling to admit defeat. She wouldn't go down without a helluva fight. "Then we have to be prepared."

"You're willing to stick it out?"

She chuckled. Her ankle hurt like hell, she was bleeding and she didn't know if she'd live to see another sunrise. "Seems like our only recourse. So, Army Special Forces dude, what can we do to get ready to rumble?"

"Stay here."

She laughed out loud. "Like I could get up and dance a jig?"

"You know what I mean. Don't poke your head out. Stay behind the rock so that I don't have to worry about what's happening while I'm not here."

She frowned. "Not here? Where are you going?" Grace reached out and touched his arm. "You can't leave the safety of the boulder. They'll shoot you."

He took her hand in his and looked down into her eyes. "I'm not dying today. I'm going to debunk your curse."

"Sweetheart, I hope and pray you do." She wrapped her other arm around his neck and pulled him close. "I'd really like to spend a little more time with you. Two days is not nearly enough."

"I'm thinking a life time won't be enough." He kissed her hard, his tongue sweeping across hers. Then he pulled away. "Now, I have to see what I can come up with. I'll be back."

"I'm counting on it," Grace whispered.

The night stood still. Not even the crickets or coyotes sang in the dark.

Caveman got up on his haunches, breathed in and out, then dove toward a stand of trees nearby.

The crack of gunfire rang out.

Grace flinched and strained her eyes, searching for movement in the shadows. She could hear the crunch of leaves and the snapping of sticks. Caveman was moving.

Another shot pierced the silence. This one seemed closer, though it was hard to tell when the sound bounced off the hillsides.

With her breath lodged in her throat, Grace waited for Caveman's return. She gathered stones, rocks and anything she could use as a weapon, no matter how puny they seemed compared to a high-powered rifle. She even scraped up a pile of sand next to her.

Then Caveman came running toward her. Just as he was about to make it behind the boulder, gunfire sounded so close, Grace yelped.

Caveman fell behind the boulder, his arms loaded with sticks and what looked like half a tree. He lay still for a moment, his breathing ragged.

"Are you okay?" Grace crawled toward him, pushing aside the sticks and brush.

"I'm fine, just winded." He drew himself up to a sitting position. "They're getting closer." He handed her several long sticks. "They aren't much, but you can use them like spears. The hunters have to come around the boulder to get to us. That's when we surprise them with these."

"What if they swing wide?"

"Hey, I'm trying to be positive. Help me out." He kissed her cheek. "Seriously, we could do with the power of positive thinking. It's just about all we have left."

"Okay, I'm positive they can swing wide and stay out of spear range, but I'm willing to try anything. I'm not ready to leave this world."

"Good, because we're going to play dead," Caveman said.

"What?"

"You heard me. We're going to play dead. It's risky, but we don't have any other way to lure them in." He grabbed some of the bigger rocks and stones, placing them in circle around them where the boulder would not provide protection. "We'll lie as flat as we can against the ground, thus we won't present much of a target. They will have to come closer to finish us off. That's when we hit them. Got it?"

"Got it."

"Now, before they get any closer, we need to assume the dead cockroach position with our spears at our side." He waited while she lay on her back, her hand on her the spear.

Grace's pulse thumped hard in her veins, her breath came in shaky gasps. In her mind, she told herself she was not ready to die. She wanted to live. To kiss Caveman and make love to him again in the comfort of a bed.

"Shh." Caveman pressed a finger to his lips and laid down beside her. "They're coming."

Grace lay as still as death, her breath caught in her throat, trying not to make even the sound of her breathing.

As she remained there counting what could possibly be the last beats of her heart, she heard another sound.

A *thump, thump, thumping* sound that started out soft, but grew louder with each passing minute.

"What the hell?" Caveman started to sit up. The crack of a gunshot sounded so close, it could have been right beside them.

Caveman dropped back down on his back and groaned loudly.

"Are you okay?" Grace whispered.

"I'm fine. That was for effect."

The thumping grew louder. "What's that sound?"

"I hope it's what I think it is."

"What?"

"The cavalry arriving to save the day."

Another shot rang out, and another, each getting closer. One kicked up rocks near Grace's hand. Another pinged against the boulder, ricocheted off the surface and hit the ground so near to her head she swore she could feel the whoosh of air.

Grace finally recognized the thumping sound as that of helicopter rotors churning the air. A bright light pierced the night, shining down to the ground.

"Stay down," Caveman said. "That light will make their night-vision goggles useless. I'm going after them."

"But you're unarmed," she cried out. She rolled onto her stomach and watched as Caveman disappeared into the darkness surround the ray of light.

A burst of gunfire ripped through the air, followed by an answering burst from the helicopter above.

Grace rose to her knees, her heart in her throat. Where was Caveman?

Chapter Fifteen

The helicopter was taking on fire. Caveman didn't want to get in the way as they fired back. He watched as the beam of light played over the ground.

There. One of the men stood near a tree, aiming his weapon toward the chopper.

Caveman was torn between going after him and staying close to Grace. If he let the man shoot at the helicopter, he could kill the men inside and possibly bring the helicopter down. A burst of semiautomatic gunfire erupted from the aircraft. The man caught in the beam of light dropped to the ground and lay still.

More shots rang out.

Caveman wanted to go after the hunters, but the light from the helicopter was blinding him, as well. Then a shot hit the bulb on the light and it blinked out. The chopper swung around and lowered to the ground.

Giving his eyes a few moments to adjust to the moonlight, Caveman hunkered low to the ground near a tree a couple yards from where Grace lay. A movement alerted him to someone moving nearby. He recognized the man as Quincy Kemp.

When the meat packer walked within three feet of Caveman's position, he raised his rifle, aiming at Grace.

Caveman swung the limb he'd been holding as hard as he could. The limb caught the man's arm, tipping the rifle upward as it went off.

Caveman struck again, catching Quincy in the chin, knocking him backward so forcefully he fell, hitting his head against a rock. The man didn't move.

Grabbing the rifle from the ground, Caveman searched the darkness for the last man standing. His gut told him it was Wayne Batson.

Shouts sounded off in the field near the helicopter. The silhouettes of men disengaged from that of the aircraft, all running toward Caveman's position. Still, he couldn't see Wayne. Where had he gone? Had he run as soon as the helicopter showed up?

Then a movement near the giant boulder caught his attention. Wayne Batson stepped out of the shadows and pointed his rifle at Grace where she lay on the ground. "Come any closer and I kill the girl!"

Caveman froze, his heart slammed to a stop. *No. Not Grace!* He wanted to shout. But he was afraid any movement would push Batson over the edge and he'd pull the trigger. The man was crazy. You couldn't reason with crazy.

Batson reached down, bending over Grace's inert form. Then the ground beneath him erupted.

Grace jerked the spear she'd been holding up into the man's belly. She rolled to the side at the same time, sweeping her good leg out to catch Batson's.

Batson pitched forward, falling onto the makeshift spear. He screamed out loud, and pulled the trigger on his rifle. The shots hit the dirt. He toppled to the ground beside Grace, losing his hold on the weapon. Grace tried to get away, but the man grabbed a handful of her hair.

Caveman lunged forward, kicked the rifle out of Batson's reach and slammed his foot into the man's face.

Batson flew backward, letting go of Grace's hair, and lay motionless.

Caveman scooped Grace up off the ground and held her in his arms, crushing her against him. "Sweet Jesus, woman. I thought I'd lost you!"

She wrapped her arms around his neck and pulled him close for a kiss. "I wasn't going anywhere without you. I told myself, I had to get out of this so that I could kiss you."

"Please. Kiss me all you want, because that's what I want, too."

"Caveman? Grace?" Kevin Garner's voice called out. "Are you two okay?"

Caveman broke off the kiss long enough to say, "We're alive." And he went back to kissing her.

"Are there anymore bogies? We counted three."

Grace broke their kiss this time. "Three were all there was. By the way. Thanks. Your timing was impeccable." She grinned at Kevin as the DHS man stepped out of the tree line and approached them.

"The sheriff's on his way," Hack said, emerging from the tree line, dressed in a bulletproof vest and helmet. He was carrying a satellite phone and an AR-15. "Thank goodness we decided to run the drone tonight, or we might not have found you."

Grace laughed. "Thank God for drones and Hack." She turned to Caveman. "As much as I love when you hold me close, you can set me on my own feet. Or foot."

Caveman shook his head. "If it's all the same to you, I'd rather get you back to town and have a doctor look at your ankle and that shoulder. You're bleeding all over me."

"Take the chopper," Kevin said. "We'll stay here and wait for the sheriff."

Caveman glanced across at Kevin. "Thanks."

Kevin smiled. "If you still want to go back to your unit at the end of the week, I'll make it happen."

Grace shot a look up at him.

Caveman shook his head. "If it's all the same to you, I'd like to stay and see this operation through to the end." His gaze dropped to Grace. "I'm just getting to know the locals. I'd like to get to know them a little better. Maybe something will come of it."

Kevin clapped a hand on his shoulder. "Yeah. They have a way of growing on you. As you can see, we can use all the help we can get."

"Count me in," he said. "In the meantime, I'll see that Miss Saunders gets to a doctor."

"You do that. When you're both rested up, stop by the loft for a debriefing."

"You got it." Caveman carried Grace to the helicopter.

"Isn't your leg bothering you?" Grace asked.

"What leg? I don't feel a thing except the beat of my heart."

She snorted. "The Delta Force soldier is a closet poet?"

"Hey, don't knock it." He set her in the seat and buckled the seat belt around her, his fingers grazing her breasts. Then he handed her a headset, helping her to fit them over her ears.

He climbed in next to her, buckled his belt and positioned a headset over his ears.

"Where did Kevin get a helicopter?" Grace asked into her mic.

"I think it's the one they used in the hostage rescue." He leaned over the back of the seat toward the pilot. "How did you get here so quickly?"

"I was still in town, waiting for some replacement parts I got in today," the pilot said into the headset. "I was due to fly out tomorrow, but I think I'll be delayed yet again."

As the chopper rose from the ground, the gray light of predawn crept up to the edge of the peaks.

Caveman stared down at the men on the ground, standing guard over the hunters who'd gambled their lives on an evil sport and lost.

"Think they'll live to testify?" Grace asked, her voice crackling over the radio headset.

"I hope so. I'd like to know who paid Batson to shoot Khalig."

"Me, too."

"Somehow, I don't think we'll get that answer from Batson."

"No, he wasn't looking so good," Grace said, her face pale, her brow furrowed. "If he dies, that will be the first man I've ever killed."

"And hopefully the last."

Her lips firmed. "I refuse to feel bad about it. The man was pure evil."

"Agreed." He squeezed her hand. "In the meantime, I have more work to do. We still don't know why Mr. Khalig had been killed and who had paid Wayne Batson to do the job."

Grace nodded. "True."

Caveman tipped her chin up and stared down into her eyes. "Do you still believe you're cursed?"

Grace shrugged. "I have to admit, you dodged death enough in the past couple of hours it makes me think you're the only man who could possibly break the curse."

"You're not cursed."

"Okay. Maybe I'm not." She laid her hand in his, silence stretching between them. "Caveman?"

"Yes, sweetheart?" Despite talking into a radio, he'd never felt closer to her.

"Do you believe in love at first sight?" she asked.

"I didn't." He squeezed her hand and raised it to his lips. "Not until I met you."

"Excuse me," another voice sounded in Caveman's ear.

He shot a glance toward the pilot and grimaced.

"I hate to break up your little lovefest, Caveman, but we're about to land. I suggest you save the rest of it until you get her alone."

"Thanks, I will."

The chopper landed, Caveman climbed out and lifted Grace out, but refused to set her on her feet until they were clear of the rotors.

Grace insisted they watch until the helicopter lifted off. Then she turned to Caveman. "Let's get to the doctor and back to the room. I think there's a shower calling my name."

"I hear my name in there, too."

"Darn right, you do."

He lifted her into his arms and kissed her, glad he'd been stuck with this strange assignment out in the wilds of Wyoming. This woman seemed to be his perfect match with the potential to be the love of his life. He planned on exploring that theory. One kiss at a time.

* * * * *

MILLS & BOON®

INTRIGUE
Romantic Suspense

A SEDUCTIVE COMBINATION OF DANGER AND DESIRE

A sneak peek at next month's titles...

In stores from 9th March 2017:

0317/46